Evil Lurks In The Darkness

Even When Strong Men Stand Watch

Earl Snort

Barlow Adams Series Book IV

TotalRecall Publications, Inc.
1103 Middlecreek
Friendswood, Texas 77546
281-992-3131 Tel
www.totalrecallpress.com

Copyright © 2022 by Earl Snort

ISBN: 978-1-64883-1782
UPC: 6-43977-41782-4

Library of Congress Control Number: 2022942828

FIRST EDITION
1   2   3   4   5   6   7   8   9   10

Not a speck of this is true. It's all a pack of lies.

To My Loving Wife

This is dedicated to my wife of more than 50 years, and to everyone of those kind souls who encourage me to keep on writing. You know who you are. You are the air under my wings. Additional thanks go to JFW, grammarian, Mexican linguist, and decades-long friend.

"Wrapped around each other, trying hard to stay warm, that first cold winter together, lying in each other's arms, watching those old movies, falling in love so desperately. Honey, I was your hero and you were my leading lady. We had it all, just like Bogie and Bacall, staring in our own, late, late show, sailing away to Key Largo."
- Key Largo - Recorded by Bertie Higgins -

"Can you hear me running? Can you hear me calling you? . . . . Don't believe the church and state and everything they tell you. . . . . Better you should pray to God, the Father, and the Spirit. Will guide you and protect from up here . . . . Teach the children quietly. For someday sons and daughters will rise up and fight while we stood still."
- Silent Running - Recorded by Mike & the Mechanics -

Earl Snort - 2022

LIST OF MAJOR CHARACTERS

Barlow Adams - protagonist- deputy
Sarah Adams - Barlow's wife
Ernest "Ernie" Atwater - deputy
Arthur Baker - rancher - Sarah's father
Clarice Baker - Sarah's mother
Cordell Barker - rancher - Sarah's brother
Darla Baker - Sarah's sister-in-law
Casper T. Brooks - victim
Noble "Chunk" Bustamante - deputy
Dewey Carruthers - deputy
Eduardo Castillo - Mexican attorney
Samuel "Sam" Davis - public defender
Able DeWitt - district attorney
LaRue Dinkins - banker - county supervisor
Ella Mae Gillespie - deputy
Randall "Randy" Meacham – deputy
Oswaldo Nighthawk- private investigator
Clarence "Slick" Oldman - deputy
Pedro Padilla - ranch hand
Carlita Pasquale - waitress – informant
Solomon "Sol" Pratt - sheriff
Kirk Shoemaker - deputy
Wirsolaw Josef Snihirowicz - psychiatrist
Alexander "Chief Alex" Snodgrass - chief deputy
Maxwell Sweeney - county judge
Archibald "Archie" Willis - retired deputy
Arnold S. Wrigley- rancher

Augusto "La Serpiente" Afilado-Rojo - criminal kingpin
Jesús Alvarado - criminal
Emil T. "Polecat" Cadigan - criminal
Oscar "Jaybird" Cadigan - criminal
Enrique Calderon - criminal
Espantapájaros - criminal
Antonio Fuentes - criminal
Humberto - criminal
Rafael "El Gordo" Larosa - criminal
Ignacio Pastor - criminal
Roberto "Doodlebug" Peña - criminal
Ernesto Robles - criminal
José "Pinky" Salazar - criminal
Taco - criminal
Leonardo Trujillo - criminal
Julio "El Toro" Valdez - criminal
Xavier - criminal
Filipe Zapata- criminal

Times are tough for us!
Be safe friends!

ABOUT THE BOOK

The year is 1972. Quayle County, located in the Trans-Pecos region of Texas, has seen an uptick of illegal alien smuggling from across the Rio Grande. The alien smugglers are determined and violent. The Border Patrol is overwhelmed with greater numbers of human trafficking cases in other areas, and therefore is unable to assist. Illegal aliens and Americans are dying alike. The small sheriff's office and the local population are left to their own devices to resolve this crisis.

Once again, Sheriff Solomon Pratt, Deputy Barlow Adams, Deputy Slick Oldman, retired Deputy Archie Willis, plus the new rookie, Deputy E.M. Gillespie, and the rest of the staff on the Quayle County Sheriff's Office rise to the occasion to vanquish the threat.

PROLOGUE

Pursuit of a Fool's Errand

Friday, November 5, 1971

He drove all night to get there. He didn't call ahead. He didn't even know if she still worked there. It had been five months. He didn't keep his word. She probably wouldn't speak to him, assuming she even recognized him. Thing is, he couldn't get her out of his mind. He had to know. No doubt he was on a fool's errand. "There's no fool like an old fool." Ain't that what they all say?

It was 0530. It was still dark. She had told him she got off work at 0600. He pulled into the parking lot of Joe Bob's All Night Phillips 66 Truck Stop, at the intersection of TX 44 and US 77 in Robstown, Texas, which was only 10 miles west of Corpus Christi. He turned off the ignition. He adjusted his hat, checking it in the rear view mirror. He took a deep breath. Then he stepped out of his truck, locked up, and stepped inside the diner.

Glory be! She was busing a place setting at the counter where a customer had just gotten up to leave. He sat on the stool next to it. When she picked up the dishes, she looked up and saw him. He smiled.

"Well, mercy me! What's it been - four, five months? I wondered if you'd ever come back. How come you never called?"

"I shoulda called. It took me some time to get up the nerve to come back. No doubt you made me out for a liar. In a way, I guess I am. I never told you what I do, nor exactly the reason I was here."

"What do you mean?"

"I was a lawman. Now I'm retired. I was on an assignment to

find another lawman who was on his honeymoon. An escaped convict he and I arrested a couple of years back was on a vendetta, looking for this lawman to kill him and his new bride. They were unaware. We all collided in New Orleans and then again by happenstance in Sonora, Texas. Maybe you know where that is. Maybe not. The lawman and his bride and I got in a shootout at a rest stop on I-10. We killed all four of the outlaw bikers who were hunting for them. One of them shot me. You might have heard about it in the news. I'm better now, but I still have a slight limp.

"I shoulda called but I didn't. I apologize. Maybe you will forgive me. Maybe you won't. Maybe you don't like cops. Either way, I felt a connection with you that I haven't felt in years. I had to come tell you in person."

"I think I did hear about it. In fact, I think probably everyone in Texas heard about it. Was one of the outlaws an escapee from Huntsville?"

"That's the guy. They called him Joe Shit the Ragman."

"Did you come here at this specific time because you remembered that my end of shift is at 6 o'clock?"

"Yep."

"Now I work 'til 7. I'm glad you're okay. Let me get you some breakfast. Tell me what you want. I'll decide if I forgive you when I get off from work."

"Fair enough. I'll take biscuits and sausage gravy with two sausage patties on the side and a small orange juice and a black coffee."

"Coming up."

She punched out right on the money at 7 o'clock. They walked outside. She told him, "That sweet, green, '71 Chevy Nova is mine. I take it that white GMC with the set of long horns is yours."

"Correctamundo."

"I live 1-1/2 miles east from here. Follow me home. We can

talk. I'm still deciding."

"Gotcha."

"Before we go, tell me my name."

"Your name is Twyla. You're the only Twyla I ever met. Do you want to know mine?"

"I know your name."

"I don't remember telling you."

"You didn't. I saw your photograph in the newspaper when they reported the shootout. Your name is Archibald X. Willis from Quayle County, Texas. That's how I know you aren't a liar."

Archie smiled for the first time in many days. He knew now for certain that he was forgiven. Glory be! He followed her home.

Twyla Jo (née Davis) Armstrong lived alone in Robstown in a charming, small, white, clapboard, circa 1940, single-story dwelling with powder blue trim and a grey hip roof. It had an unattached carport with a chain link fence around the backyard, and neatly trimmed bushes and two tall, gnarly cedar trees in the front yard. It was located at 509 Perkins Street, which parallels TX 44 one block to the south, approximately eight miles west of Corpus Christi. She parked in the carport. Archie parked right behind her.

They entered through the side door into the kitchen. She lead him to the living room, which faced the street. He took a seat in a wooden rocker. She offered him something to drink.

He asked, "What are you having?"

She replied, "Sweetie, I work the midnight shift. This is my afternoon. I generally like something to relax me before I call it a day. My preference is Old Fitzgerald on the rocks. It helps me fall asleep."

"A woman after my own heart. Make it two."

"Why did you retire?"

"It was time, although my preference would have been to go at the end of the year. There were some politics involved but it had nothing to do with the sheriff. I been a lawman nearly all my life. I got a small ranch and I break and train horses on the side. Now I do that full time."

"What's small?"

"Let's put it this way. Compared to the King Ranch, what I own would be considered their employee parking lot. I got 115 acres, and I have water."

"How many horses do you have?"

"I have 12 I expect to sell and three I would never sell. I also have one burro, who thinks he's a full-fledged jackass."

"How long have you been a widower?"

"I didn't know it showed. Nearly 13 years now. What about you?"

"Oh, it shows. I can tell you loved her very much. My husband, Amos, and I were married for 21 years. He died of a heart attack hoeing our garden in the back yard at age 41. That was 15 years ago. We have two kids. Amos Junior is 35. He's career Army - a platoon sergeant in the 3rd Ranger Battalion stationed at Fort Bragg, North Carolina. He's divorced but no kids, thank goodness. It seems like he's deployed all the time. Two tours in Vietnam. Elise is 32. She has two kids, Eva, who's 12, going on 16, and Chester, who's 11. She works part-time as a checker at the Piggly Wiggly. Her husband, Maynard, is a Trailways bus driver. Been there 11 years now. Before that he was in the Army, too, in the Transportation Corps. That's how he got the job at Trailways. The Army taught him how to drive big rigs and buses.

"What kind of work did Amos do?"

"He was a brakeman for the Santa Fe Railway. It used to be called the Atchison, Topeka, and Santa Fe. It was a good job and he loved it. Me too, because I get a little pension from it."

"Would you like to get to know me better?"

"I would. How about you?"

"That's why I'm here. I couldn't get you out of my mind."

"That's because when I met you, I suggested that we go rodeo.

Truth is, I was attracted to you like a moth is to fire. It's been a long time since I've been with a man. You probably think I'm a slut."

"Not at all. It's been a long time for me too. In fact, I thought that aspect of my life was over. I'm 71 years old, and before you know it, I'll be 72, God willing. You roused Roscoe, and I thought he was no longer interested in women. Now I know different. Thing is, I'm not sure if Roscoe is capable of pleasuring a woman even though he swears he is."

"Maybe Roscoe would surprise you. I'm 55 and more forgiving than I might have been when I was 25."

"How would this work out?"

"My preference is you follow me back to the bedroom and we shuck our clothes and get under the covers, but first I want to see your scar. You said you still have a slight limp. I'd be happy to rub it for you to see if I can work out the kinks. We'll see where that takes us."

"Well my scar is a might close to Roscoe. You could say that except for the grace of God, Roscoe could have got hisself shot off."

"That's all the more reason for you to show me. Maybe Roscoe could use some TLC. You never know. Maybe Roscoe has more spunk than you give him credit for."

"Oh, goodness gracious. I think you captured Roscoe's undivided attention."

"Well, get the lead out, and I don't mean from your pencil. Let's go to the bedroom. Help me get undressed and I'll help you."

"You might have woke up a sleeping giant."

"I pray to God I did. No more talk."

· · · · · · ·

Archie awoke with a start. It was almost dark. He looked at his watch. It was 5:15! Twyla was still fast asleep curled up next to him. They were both in their birthday suits. What a body! What a woman! What a day! She rocked his world. What happens now?

He slipped out of bed as quietly as possible to use the bathroom. When he returned, she was awake. She asked, "Happy?"

"More than you'll ever know."

"Me, too. Let's get cleaned up. I have to go to work tonight. I'll fix you some supper first. What would you think about country ham and mashed potatoes with red eye gravy, a tossed salad, homemade applesauce, and biscuits? You can wash it down with ice tea or coffee."

"All of the above. I gotta get back home anyway. Are you up for a rematch?"

"How about same time, same place next Friday, except this time you stay over? I'll introduce you to Elise and the grandkids. Maybe we can catch a movie or something over in Corpus.

"I can't wait. One night or two?"

"Two, if you can."

"What will Elise think about me staying over?"

"She'll think her mother is one lucky dog, especially after her eyes feast on you. She's always pestering me to get back out there. Up until now I didn't have the interest. I walled myself in. Amos was a good man. I never really let go. Now I realize that I still have a lot of life to live."

"Maybe I'm too old for you. It's highly unlikely that I will last as long as you."

"I'll take whatever I can get and thank God for it every single day."

"Me, too. Maybe in December or January you can come visit at my house.

"You're on. I've never been to Quayle County."

"Not many folks have, not even native Texans. We're way off the beaten path, but if you like the desert and small towns, it's a good place to be. My family's been there for nearly a century, although both of my kids moved off. One lives in Oklahoma City and the other lives in Omaha."

"Home is where the heart is. Your heart is on your ranch. Mine is here. Even so, who knows what the future holds for either of us?"

"Will you drive to Mosby?"

"No. Trailways goes right through there en route to El Paso. I get a family discount. I can nap on the bus so I can be frisky when I arrive."

"Now I'm sorry I gotta get back tonight."

"You couldn't stay one more night?"

"Not this time. Sorry. Next week."

"You better not leave me hanging like you did last summer, you old hound dog."

"Never again. An Act of Congress couldn't keep me away. Promise."

"Okay. I'm holding you to it."

CHAPTER 1

Looking Back on 1971

Saturday, January 1, 1972

Sarah and Barlow were out on a horseback ride at the Bar B ranch. Happy, their pooch, came along, too. They were working off a fabulous meal consumed at the Baker homestead with Sarah's parents, Arthur and Clarice, her brother, Cordell, and his wife, Darla.

Sarah's other brother, Hank, couldn't attend, but promised to be there next year upon completion of his two-year commitment in the Army. This year, Second Lieutenant Henry G. Baker was celebrating New Years with the rest of his mechanized infantry platoon in the Republic of Vietnam. So far, so good. He had already completed nine months of his year-long tour, and he was doing well, or so he reported in his letters. He said his platoon was staffed with some of the best men he had ever known. They'd had some casualties, but no one had been killed. (He neglected to mention his own Purple Heart for a shrapnel wound from an enemy grenade.) He asked for prayers that they all would return home safe and sound. He received his request just before the meal began, and again every night at bedtime from everyone in the family.

Sarah's mother had prepared a prime rib for dinner. The meat was tender and medium rare. Side dishes included cabbage and black-eyed peas (with a dash of Tabasco) in keeping with the New Year tradition, so they would be blessed with folding money and coins. Dessert was your choice of German chocolate cake or pecan pie. Sarah's father contributed to the festivities by tending to the fire in the family room, and by keeping everyone's glasses filled with a lightly-chilled burgundy wine.

Today, in the Trans-Pecos region of Texas, the weather was a comfortable 75 degrees with a slight breeze. Sarah was mounted on her favorite Baker family horse, Festus, and Barlow was riding his only horse, Boyo, who had been a wedding gift from Arthur and Clarice. It was a glorious day for a ride. They rode all the way down to the Rio Grande. It was beautiful. They took turns shooting Barlow's pre-'64, .30-30, lever-action Winchester at soft drink cans they threw in the river, which was fairly shallow here, and moving in a slow, indolent, pace. When they demolished all the cans they brought with, they kicked back and lay on a blanket and watched the clouds float by. Conversation lapsed after a little while, and they both drifted into mostly pleasant and peaceful memories.

New Year's Day had always been a day of reflection in Barlow's family. This year was no exception. Now Sarah was Barlow's immediate family, and had been since they married six months ago. The other immediate family member was Happy, a border collie rescued by Judge Sweeney, who handed him down to Barlow. By the same token, Barlow was the newest official member of the Baker clan. He was blessed by this inclusion since his own clan was so small. This caused him to shift his thoughts to days gone by before his parents and grandmother passed away, and before his sister married and moved away to Bisbee, Arizona. Bittersweet memories all. He put those thoughts behind him and evaluated the year just passed.

By all accounts, 1971 had been a good year for them. Barlow had graduated from junior college; he became a certified Texas law enforcement officer; Sarah and he had married; the threat from dangerous stalkers no longer existed; and, they both had jobs they loved.

There were iffy things, too, including being stalked by murdering outlaw bikers; killing all four of them; Archie getting shot and retiring; Sheriff Sol bringing on a controversial new hire to replace Archie; still being assigned to the midnight shift; and, the decision Sarah and he just made to enroll in senior college with classes beginning in only 10 days.

When he thought about the iffy things, his head started spinning. The transition in their lives in 1971 was a lot to wrap his arms around. The upcoming transition in 1972 was beginning to look like it would be even greater. Would Sarah and he be up to the challenges? The answer was, they had to be!

Barlow decided to concentrate his thoughts on the new developments from the point Archie decided to retire in June. Archie had wanted to retire yesterday, on December 31st. After all, he had nearly 47 years on the job and it should have been his choice. It didn't work out that way. Instead, he retired on September 30th.

Sheriff Sol was sorry to see Archie retire but he understood. It was time. Sol had known this day would come, so he already had a person in mind as a potential replacement, someone who, like Barlow (at the time he was hired) was not a certified law enforcement officer. Due to the new state law, the newbie would have to complete the 400 hours of Police Officers Standard Training (POST) before getting sworn in.

Sheriff Sol interviewed his candidate, who was appreciative and eager to join, so Sheriff Sol decided to move forward. He checked on the dates for the next POST course at West Texas Junior College (WTJC), learning that it ran from October 4th through December 18th. He went to the Quayle County Board of Supervisors meeting in August, requesting permission to temporarily be one position over strength by adding a 10th deputy to his staff for the 3-month period October through December while the new hire was in training.

The board has three supervisors who are elected for 3-year terms, which are staggered so that one position comes up for election each year. That way the board always has at least two tenured supervisors, avoiding a situation wherein the entire board could be comprised of newly-elected supervisors with no experience. The senior board member assumes the position of President of the Board.

The president in 1971 was Mr. LaRue Dinkins, who had served on the board for 8-1/2 consecutive years. He was also the President of the Pecos Bank & Trust, which was the only bank in Quayle County. Nearly everyone in the county banked there, so he was a powerful personage. He was also mean-spirited and a notorious skinflint. He was able to control the other two board members because he held the mortgages on their businesses. Ergo, most proposals were approved or disapproved by a 3-to-0 vote.

Mr. Dinkins was incensed that Sheriff Sol would even contemplate such a proposal. The county couldn't afford such an extravagance! This was preposterous! The other two board members, Hiram Templeton, a rancher on the north side of the county, and Fritz Krauthammer, an independent insurance agent, looked down at their hands while Mr. Dinkins was railing, spittle landing on anyone within a four-feet dispersal area. Neither asked any questions, nor did either comment. Mr. Dinkins called for a vote, and Sheriff Sol's proposal went down in flames, 3-to-0.

Sheriff Sol said, "Sorry you gentlemen feel this way. The cost to the county would have been less than $3,000, which includes salary, benefits, uniforms, tuition, and dormitory fees. The county has no shortage of funds, but nevertheless, the sheriff's department operates on a very lean budget because this board is so tight-fisted. This means Deputy Willis will have to retire the end of September or I won't have a replacement I can put to work before April at the very earliest. This could have grave consequences. Mark my words. You all will come to rue the day you turned down my request. Good day!"

Mr. Dinkins responded, "Sheriff Pratt, is your little temper tantrum today indicative of a threat?"

Sheriff Sol replied, "Not a threat, Mr. Dinkins. A prediction. Wait and see." With that, he turned and strode out of the room.

It didn't take long for Sheriff Sol's prediction to begin to materialize. When Archie learned about the vote, he went to see Judge Maxwell B. Sweeney, the preeminent citizen in all of Quayle County. Judge Sweeney said he had heard that the board turned down Sheriff Sol's request. He also said LaRue Dinkins was the most despicable man in Quayle County. Then he said he would miss Archie after he retired. He commended Archie for all his years of faithful service. Finally, he asked Arch why he came to see him.

Archie said, "Judge, I'll retire the end of September so Sheriff Sol can hire my replacement in time for the October POST class. Our notorious president of the board comes up for re-election on June 27, 1972. I've decided to run against that sidewinder. Sheriff Sol is endorsing me. I was wondering if you would consider doing the same. It's about time we got someone on the board who cares about the people in this county, rather than just wanting to lord his power and influence over everyone."

Judge Sweeney responded, "Deputy Willis, I think you would make a splendid supervisor! However, aren't you afraid to take on Mr. Dinkins? If you have a note at his bank, or if you ever need to borrow money, he will do everything in his power to bankrupt you."

"Judge, they got banks in Brewster and Val Verde Counties, too. Any merchant here in town will cash one of my checks no matter which bank it's drawn from. I plan to start banking with one of them. Also, as it turns out, I don't owe anyone a red cent. My ranch is small - only 115 acres, but it's all I need to break and train saddle stock. My needs are not great. I have enough money set aside to carry me through hard times. So no Sir, I am not afraid that Mr. Dinkins will bankrupt me. What I am, is ashamed that I didn't withdraw my money from the Pecos Bank & Trust a long time ago and put it in a bank which cares more about people than Mr. LaRue Dinkins."

"Well stated. I may start shopping around for another bank myself. You have my full support. In fact, as soon as you retire, get out and start knocking on doors, shaking hands, and kissing babies. I'll have a fundraising barbecue for you at the Triple S the first week in October. I think Mr. LaRue Dinkins is long overdue for a comeuppance and a defeat at the polls. Folks are fed up with his bombastic attitude. It's definitely time for a change around here. Now please excuse me and go back to whatever else you need to do. I must go to court."

"Thank you, Judge."

Potential candidates for the office couldn't officially declare until January 3rd, but the word had been out since August that Archie was running. His ties to the community were significantly deeper than Mr. Dinkins'. Not only that, nearly everyone loved and respected Archie, in contrast with Mr. Dinkins, who could count his true friends on one hand. However, what he did have was the bank. A lot of folks owed him money. He had intimidation on his side, but no one knows how a person votes once he steps inside the voting booth. Things were slipping out of Mr. Dinkins' grasp and he knew it. If one could kill a person by evil thoughts alone, Archie would have perished months ago.

Thinking about Archie's retirement brought the new hire to mind. Sheriff Sol threw everyone for a loop with his selection. He met the prospective candidate a year ago when they were working the rustling case in Brewster County and on up into New Mexico. The individual was employed by Brewster County Sheriff Leland Waters and was even related to him. Normally it would have been considered poaching for Sheriff Sol to approach an employee of another law enforcement agency with an offer of employment, but it wasn't so in this case. In fact, Sheriff Waters considered this a tremendous favor, "doing him a solid" as they say. It had nothing to do with allegations of nepotism within

Sheriff Waters' own department, either.

The newbie was a property clerk, not a deputy. Sheriff Waters was "between a rock and a hard place." The clerk was pushing hard for a sworn position as a deputy and had rightfully earned it after nearly two years as the best property clerk Brewster SO ever had. Being a close relation even made things stickier.

The problem was that Gillespie was a girl! Ella Mae (née Bowman) Gillespie was Sheriff Waters' niece, his sister's only child! She was an attractive, athletic, 5-feet, 8-inch, 140-pound, 29-year-old, divorcée (from a U.S. Marine captain who couldn't keep his trousers zippered), gymnast, and former girls physical education teacher with a bachelors degree, who was born and reared in Bakersfield, California, a state which has radical ideas such as it being perfectly normal to have female law enforcement officers. To make things even worse, everyone who knew Gillespie thought the world of her. She was loved and highly respected by everyone on Brewster County SO and in Alpine at large.

There were no girls on any sheriff's department anywhere in West Texas, nor anywhere else in the state, so far as Sheriff Waters could ascertain. He had checked. He didn't call all 254 counties, but he did call every sheriff within 300 miles of Alpine and a few as far away as Dallas, and the answer was a resounding no. Of course the answer was no. It's true that the bigger SOs, like El Paso, had female deputies working in the jail, but they were matrons in the female section, correction officers, not law enforcement officers per se. They weren't even required to go to POST as per the new state law. Also, it was rumored that a few big city police departments had started hiring female officers, but working in a rural county as a deputy was entirely a horse of a different color.

Anyone who hired a female to be a deputy, a job wherein most officers patrol alone in rural areas without backup and need to be savvy enough to enforce the law without getting stomped or killed, was just asking for trouble. Besides that, there's a reason that the Navy doesn't put female sailors on ships and the Army doesn't put them in the combat branches. It would absolutely kill esprit de corps. All the men would be fighting each other over the few females assigned to their units. What? Are the proponents of such nonsense oblivious to the raging hormones in young men and women? What makes them believe law enforcement is immune from the Laws of Nature?

Sheriff Waters was at war with his sister and his niece over this issue, and was at risk of a lifelong parting of the ways with them and other members of his family. Everyone loved his niece. He did, too. Very much so. He just couldn't do it. He did not want to put her in harm's way. It was against common sense and everything he believed to be true and right. So when Sheriff Sol said he would like to hire Gillespie as a deputy, Sheriff Waters thanked the Good Lord for His grace in resolving this impasse.

Sheriff Sol was not oblivious to conventional thinking on this issue. At the same time, he was a good judge of character. He thought Gillespie would make a great deputy, and that she would blend well with his staff and be accepted by them all. He also knew that Barlow was the key, so he brought him into his plan before he told anyone else on his staff.

There had been no women enrolled at POST at WTJC. This would require some adjustments by the staff. Also, the male trainees would be fighting for their own survival in this course, so they would have to be extremely careful regarding any overt harassment of Gillespie at the risk of being expelled from the program. It would be Barlow's job to monitor this from behind the scenes and to resolve as many issues as he could informally. At the same time, Gillespie would have to handle most issues on her own. She said she understood and that she was capable of taking care of herself. Sheriff Sol believed that she could or he never would have offered her the job.

Gillespie (she told everyone to call her by her last name)

graduated on December 18th, 6th in her class of 40. Between her personality and competence, there had been very few problems. The staff and her classmates all thought highly of her. Sheriff Sol's intuition was correct. Now she was assigned to the midnight shift with Barlow.

Gillespie was good people. She was also smart, and she was willing to take on all the crap jobs nobody wanted to do. If she could handle the truly vicious bad boys, she would be fine. Nobody ever knows if he's up to that until the time comes. Barlow didn't. Joseph Schitt and Maynard Creech were Barlow's "baptism under fire" in this regard. Archie was on "overwatch" that night, and stepped in at the right time to douse the last flames of hooliganism. Barlow had acquitted himself well, but it had been a dicey situation that might well have gone the other way. Now training and overwatch were Barlow's responsibility to Gillespie.

Moving on to the final iffy (and related) topics, Barlow would prefer to work on days or afternoons instead of midnights. Sheriff Sol knew that and had promised to plug Barlow in on the other shifts as often as he could. However, now that he and Sarah had decided to go back to college, working midnights was the best option for him.

Barlow and Sarah had checked it out. The only four-year college within commuting distance was Sul Ross State University (SRSU) in Alpine, which was about a 100 miles away. Sarah's preference was to pursue a bachelors degree in agriculture, following up on her associates degree. Barlow felt the same way about criminal justice. What they learned was that the university did not offer agriculture classes during night school, nor did it have a criminal justice program. Sarah and Barlow examined the traditional liberal arts program courses which were available in night school, and each decided to pursue a major in history. They both enjoyed learning as much as they could about history, especially U.S. history.

Their goal was to earn a bachelors degree while they were still young and had no children. They knew that having a degree from a fully-accredited college was more important than the major itself. Sheriff Sol's degree from UTEP was in English; Deputy Kirk Shoemaker's degree from SRSU was in social studies; Deputy Randall Meacham's degree from Texas A&M was in biology; and Ella Mae Gillespie's degree from the University of California-Riverside was in physical education. Nobody else on Quayle County SO had a college degree. Sarah's boss at the Quayle County Rodeo Grounds did not have a degree either. Problem resolved.

Barlow still had 18 months of Veterans Administration (G.I. Bill) benefits remaining. They would expire in 1979, 10 years after he was honorably discharged from the Army. Use it or lose it. The 18 months would cover two 9-month academic school years, which was enough time to complete their degrees, assuming they took the standard load of 15 hours per semester. Barlow received $288 per month from VA during the 18 months he took classes at WTJC as a full-time student. He was single then. As a married vet, he would receive $342 per month as a full-time student. Tuition at SRSU was $140 a semester full-time. One month's benefits would more than cover a semester's tuition for both of them.

The problem was, they couldn't possibly handle 15 hours a semester. They both had full-time jobs. Evening classes were available on Monday through Friday. The classes ran from 6 p.m. to 10 p.m. One was considered a full-time student if he took 12 hours a semester. They decided to do that, taking the same classes together, hoping to get their classes on Monday through Thursday with Fridays free. If they had to take a Friday class, so be it. They would have a free day some other weekday.

This schedule meant they would need five semesters to graduate, or maybe six if they needed more than 60 hours. The VA benefits would run out after four semesters, but they should have a fair amount of money left over to cover all their college expenses. Besides, they felt fortunate to receive anything. The G.I. Bill was a godsend.

Sarah worked 8-to-4. Barlow's schedule was 12-to-8. When Sarah got home from work, Barlow would be out of bed and ready to leave for school. When they returned home, he would get ready for work and she would go to bed. The trip each way was about 1-1/2 hours. It worked out to about 800 miles per week. That's nearly 30,000 miles a year just commuting back and forth to school.

Sarah assumed they would drive Barlow's Dodge truck. It was a '65 and in great shape because he loved it like a second wife. He even named it Jade because of its color. Jade got about 15 miles-per-gallon. On the other hand, Sarah's car was a '61 Chevy II Nova with 275,000 miles. It had a 4-cylinder engine which got about 20 miles-per-gallon; however, it was completely worn out. Arthur didn't pull maintenance on a vehicle until it nearly stopped running. He gave Sarah this car when she 16. He never expected her to drive it anywhere except in Mosby. She knew her car wouldn't last a week without breaking down, running back and forth to Alpine.

Barlow knew that as well. Sarah didn't know it yet, but that's why he was taking her to Del Rio on Monday just as soon as she got off from work. They would drive her beater. Del Rio had a Volkswagen dealership. They would trade in her jalopy for a new bug. He figured it would cost him about $2,000 after tax and title. The trade-in wasn't worth a $100, if that. Sarah could pick out the new car and the color. He was glad he banked all of his G.I. Bill money when he was going to WTJC. It would pinch a little bit but they could still pay cash.

By getting the car tomorrow, she could learn how to drive a four-on-the-floor stick shift (even if it only had a 34 horsepower engine and a one-barrel carburetor) before classes began the following week. The Beetles only had a 10-gallon tank. That meant they'd be filling up about five days a week. Gas was 32 cents per gallon. That was another reason it was time to get her another car.

Also, the Volkswagen was a simple automobile. Top speed was 70 miles-per-hour unless you were going downhill with a strong tailwind. That might let you eke out a couple more miles per hour. The heater worked by turning a valve on the floorboard. It recycled heat from the engine. The windshield washer operated by bleeding air from the spare tire, which was stored next to the windshield under the hood in the front. The battery was stored under the backseat cushion. The VW had 15-inch wheels instead of 14-inch like most compact automobiles. The '72 model had a vent behind the rear windows (which don't open), to enable fresh air to cycle through the car (assuming the front windows were open) without creating a whirlwind in the backseat. The engine (mounted in the rear) only weighed 35 pounds and was held in place by four bolts. It was easy to remove for major repairs. Besides that, Barlow could pull the maintenance on it himself. He sincerely hoped she would go for it.

Barlow checked his watch. It was 4:30. Time to head back to the Bar B. He'd tell Sarah about the car on the ride back.

Chapter 2

The First Workweek of the Year Begins

Monday, January 3, 1972

Barlow arrived at work at 2330 hours military time on Sunday, January 2nd. He pushed off (relieved) Deputy Ernest Atwater 15 minutes early. Deputy Gillespie had not arrived. Barlow thought it was strange calling Gillespie by her surname instead of Ella Mae, but that's what she wanted.

Sheriff Sol had given Gillespie December 20th-24th off, the week after graduation, so she could move out of the dormitory at WTJC and find a place to live in Mosby. She had been living with her mother, Doris (née Waters) Bowman, and her Grandmother Waters in Alpine. Gillespie still had a fair amount of stuff to move to Mosby, not to mention tying up other loose ends, such as changing the address on her drivers and automobile licenses, changing her address at the post office, closing and opening bank accounts, etc.

Chief Alex had mentioned a widow woman by the name Mrs. Jasmine Beanblossom (everyone called her Biddy Beanblossom) who resided at 87 North Sul Ross Street near the intersection of Washington Avenue. She owned a big, two-story house (her deceased husband had been a railroad superintendent) with a room to let. Ella Mae (Biddy refused to call Gillespie by her last name) checked it out and was pleasantly surprised to find a sweet, charming landlady who would give her the run of the house, to include use of the kitchen and the laundry, for only $60 a month!

During Gillespie's first week in the office, Barlow had explained office procedures, the filing systems, operation of the jail when they had prisoners, rules of the property/evidence vault, radio procedures, protocol regarding the official cars, radio call signs, county geography, secure storage, cleaning of the long guns (to include the four Thompson submachine guns), and everything else he could think of that she needed to know. It was a lot to learn but she was catching on fast.

Now that she was on board, the radio call signs had changed for half of the staff. Sheriff Solomon Pratt and Chief Alexander Snodgrass were still Quayle County 1 and 2, and the part-time deputies, Dewey Carruthers, Randall Meacham, and Clarence "Slick" Oldman were still Quayle County 8, 9, and 10, respectfully. The rest of the deputies moved up a notch according to their seniority. Ernest Atwater was now QC 3, Noble "Chunk" Bustamante was now QC 4, Kirk Shoemaker became QC 5, Barlow was QC 6, and Gillespie was QC 7.

Barlow brewed a fresh pot of coffee and got himself situated for the shift. He had no idea what they would do this week. He guessed he would have Gillespie read all the incident reports and the criminal case files for 1971. As it turned out, at this time they had very few open investigations, and most of those were awaiting further judicial status, such as a court appearance on a ticket, locating and serving arrest warrants on defendants who failed to appear in court, serving civil process papers, and so forth.

Gillespie arrived precisely at the prescribed time of 11:45. She was effervescent. Nothing new there. She was always effervescent, but somehow even more so this evening if that were even possible.

"What's up, Deputy? You look like the "cat who ate the canary"."

"See anything different about me today?" She pirouetted for him to identify the difference.

"Let me see. Hmmm. Your teeth look exceptionally bright. Did you brush them tonight?"

"Nice try, Doctor Watson. Sherlock Holmes would fire you. Your powers of observation are seriously impaired. Looky here. I have a brand new gun! I returned Uncle Leland's Colt, Police Positive .38 that he loaned me until the gun I ordered came in.

"This is the newest police service revolver on the market. It's a Ruger Security Six, blue-steel, six-shot, .38 Special revolver with a four-inch barrel. It weighs more than the Smith & Wesson Model 19 and the Colt Trooper, because the frame and barrel are a little heavier, but they all fit in the same-size holster. They all have target sights. One substantive difference is that the cylinder release on the Smith has to be pushed forward, and the Colt's has to be pulled to the rear. The Ruger has a button you push in, making it easier, if not faster to operate. Take a look."

Gillespie unloaded her weapon and handed it to Barlow to inspect. He gave it a thorough examination and handed it back to her. He asked, "Did you buy this at Jake's Pawn Shop?"

"Nope. I got it at Savvy Steve Mason's Firearms in Alpine. They call him Savvy Steve because he has a talent for spotting a bargain before anyone else, and cashing in early while everyone else pays full price. He's a close friend of my Uncle Leland's. Most of the officers in Alpine get their guns from him. This gun just hit the retail market. It's $18 cheaper than the Smith and $23 cheaper than the Colt."

"Well I'll be. Guess I'll have to start calling you Savvy Gillespie. Have you had a chance to shoot it yet?"

"Nope. I'll take it out after work this morning. I also bought two boxes of the Winchester .38 Special, copper-jacketed, 130-grain military ball cartridges with brass casings, and two boxes of the Remington 200-grain, lead, round-nose bullets in the nickel casings. I'm using the military ammo for on-duty because it's shinier and looks better in my cartridge loops."

"You sound just like Kirk Shoemaker. He likes the shiny cartridges, too. I didn't know anyone made a 200-grain, .38 Special bullet. You might want to tell Kirk. He also carries a .38.

His is nickel-plated. I believe he's carrying the standard 158-grain, lead, round-nose ammo. That's the load I carry in my off-duty gun. Kirk might want to try out the 200-grain ammo. Anyway, your Ruger looks like a mighty fine gun to me. I think you made a good selection."

"Thank you. I can't wait to shoot it."

Once Gillespie poured herself a cup of joe and got settled, Barlow had her pull the 1971 incident reports and start reading them, beginning with the oldest and finishing with the most recent. While she was doing that, Barlow cleaned his own service revolver, a Smith & Wesson, Military & Police Model 58, .41 Magnum, using the automotive section of Sunday's El Paso *Bugle* as a mat, which he selected so he could look for articles and advertisements on Volkswagens.

At 2:35, the telephone, which seldom rang during the midnight shift, began to make its presence known. Barlow answered it.

"Quayle County Sheriff's Office. Deputy Adams speaking. How may I help you?"

He was answered by a soft whisper. "Deputy, this is Mrs. Harriett Enright. I live at 21 North Lubbock Street. It's near Jackson Avenue. Someone is prowling around in my garage. I don't know who it is. I'm all alone. I've got my husband's shotgun. It's loaded with birdshot. I'm scared. Can you come right away?"

"Miss Harriett, I know exactly where you live. Stay inside. We'll be over there right away."

"Oh, praise the Lord! Thank you. I'll keep an eye out. Hurry!"

Gillespie was all ears. "What's up?"

Barlow forwarded the phone to the answering service.

"We got a prowler run. Get out your pocket notebook and write this down. "0235 hours. Mrs. Harriett Enright, 21 North Lubbock Street, called to report a prowler in her garage." Got it?"

"Yes."

"Do you have a flashlight?"

"Yes."

"Bring it. You're driving. Check out Unit 81. Remember which car that is?"

"That's the '66 Chevy Bel Air."

"Roger that. It's the oldest car in the fleet. We're taking that because the last time I went on a call like this, the burglar shot our cruiser all to Hell. I'll grab a shotgun."

Barlow checked out one of the Remington 12-gauge, pump shotguns. He loaded it with four rounds of double-aught buckshot in the magazine, plus one in the chamber, and set the safety. He locked the courthouse door on their way out to the parking lot. They were rolling within six minutes of the squeal.

"Do you know where 21 North Lubbock Street is?"

"Well, I know Francis Lubbock Street is one block west of Texas Street, but I'm not sure what the nearest cross avenue is to number 21."

"Not bad. It's just south of Jackson Avenue on the left side. Less than two blocks north of America Avenue. Normally, we would roll with the red light flashing but no siren. Tonight we won't even do that because traffic is non-existent and 21 North Lubbock is only three blocks away. We don't want to alert the prowler to our presence. We want to be on top of him (or them) before they spot us. You can break traffic laws but don't be reckless."

"Got it."

"Okay. We'll park just shy of the address. I'll show you where. Be as quiet as you can. Okay. Slow down to a crawl. Park on the street here. Put the car keys in your pocket. Ease the door shut. Don't lock it. We may have to leave in a hurry. Take your flashlight, but don't turn it on until you have to. Get on my left. Walk slowly. Be alert."

The house was on the west side of the street, three doors down from the end of the block at Jackson Avenue. It was small - maybe

1,200 square feet. The unattached, single-car garage was on the left side and to the rear of the house. The house was completely dark. The front porch light wasn't even on. The only ambient light was coming from the half moon and from a street light two doors down. Both were partially obscured by a large tree and the houses on either side. The only sounds they heard were from chirping crickets.

The driveway consisted of two, 12-inch-wide concrete strips with a hardy blend of grass growing in between. It was about 30 feet long. As expected, the garage door for the automobile was all the way down. The "people" door, which had six small windowpanes, was on the right side of the garage about six feet from the front. The inside of the garage was dark.

Barlow tested the doorknob. It was unlocked. He motioned for Gillespie to move closer. Then he put his hand over his mouth and whispered in her ear. "This garage is like mine. The door opens inward left to right. The light switch is on the wall to the left about a foot from the door frame. I'll open the door slowly. I hope it doesn't squeak. You reach in and turn on the light. Then move inside to the left and wait for me. I'll come in fast and sweep the building with the shotgun. If anyone's inside and he surrenders peacefully, I'll keep my gun on him while you cuff him. If he shoots or tries to flee, just do what you were trained to do. Nod your head twice if you savvy."

Gillespie nodded twice. She had her brand new Ruger revolver in her right hand down by her side. Her flashlight was in her left. Barlow slowly pushed the door wide open. Thankfully, it didn't squeak. Gillespie stepped inside and flicked the light switch on. She stepped to the left just as Barlow came crashing in, sweeping the shotgun left to right. The only thing they saw was Miss Harriett's two-tone, dark-blue-over-medium-blue, 1952, Studebaker Champion Custom, two-door sedan. Barlow was in lust. The automobile was showroom quality pristine.

They stood in place and scanned the room more carefully for just a few seconds. Everything was deathly quiet. Barlow shouted, "Police! Hands in the air!"

A burley white guy in blue jeans and a white tee shirt exploded upward on the driver's side of the car near the front fender, and started running towards the open garage door splitting the difference between Barlow and Gillespie. The perp didn't have anything in his hands, but he did have black, shaggy hair, and a wild, crazy look in his eyes. He managed to slip past Gillespie just momentarily before Barlow butt-stroked him hard in the gut with the shotgun. As he was going down, Gillespie smashed him on the back of his skull with her heavy-duty, cast aluminum, five-D-cell, Kel-Lite brand, police flashlight. The combination of blows felled him like a mighty oak at the hands of energetic lumberjacks. Gillespie squatted down and handcuffed him behind his back. He didn't resist. Any fight he had in him had been knocked into the next county.

Barlow said, "Tell him what his legal status is and then check him for ID."

Gillespie said, "You're under arrest, knot-head!" Then she searched his rear pockets and retrieved his wallet. She handed it to Barlow.

Barlow pulled out the drivers license and read aloud, "Emil T. Cadigan, DOB May 12, 1946, of Rural Route 4, Box 74, Mosby, Texas." Then he asked, "What are you doing here, Mr. Cadigan?"

"I'm bleeding, God damn you! That's what I'm doing! I need a fucking doctor!"

"You'll get one. I asked you a question. What are you doing here?"

"Kiss my ass! I know my rights. I have nothing else to say."

"As you wish. You're being charged with outhouse burglary. I'm sure we'll add some other charges before you appear in court this morning.

"Deputy Gillespie, help me lift Mr. Cadigan up off the floor. Then I want you to search him so thoroughly that if he has a BB hidden up his ass, you'll shove it all the way through and make him spit it out his mouth.

"Take everything out of his pockets and remove his belt and shoelaces. When you're done, get the bellyband and the leg irons out of the trunk and truss him up so he can't escape. Cinch him up good and tight. Real tight, like he's wearing a corset. Then we'll put him in the back seat of the cruiser. If he resists, put another knot on his head with that flashlight of yours. (I need to buy one of those!) Savvy?"

"Savvy."

Gillespie searched Cadigan like he was a child molester and she was the child's mother. He didn't have any family secrets left at all after she was done. What a tiny package for such a burley guy! Definitely not a stud muffin. Then she retrieved the bellyband and leg irons. Barlow showed her how to truss him up like an octopus in a fish net. Then they perp-walked him back to the unit and placed him in the back seat (with windows up, no window cranks, door handles, or door locks he could access) behind the mesh shield. Then they locked the doors.

Normally, Barlow would not have used the maximum security transport chains on a prisoner just to drive three blocks, but besides turning this into a training lesson for Gillespie, he was using it for the "shock and awe" effect. Barlow wanted to demonstrate to Cadigan that his situation was dire, in an effort "to lead him to Jesus." Help him to have an epiphany. Hopefully, Cadigan would see the error of his ways and uninvoke his Miranda Warning rights. No telling how many other people were involved or how many other victims there were.

Barlow and Gillespie returned to the garage to look for evidence. They found a toolbox chock full of Craftsman tools, a small generator, a box of sockets and wrenches, an electric drill and wooden box of bits, a half-full, 18-inch in diameter spool of copper wire, a Stihl chainsaw, and a battery charging unit all placed together in a tight, tidy collection on the floor on the driver's side of the car. They didn't touch anything.

Barlow said, "Bring the camera out of the trunk. We need to take a few photographs. If you're uncertain how this one operates, I'll show you. Chief Alex will take his own photos but he may not get out here for awhile. We want to document everything in the garage the way it was when we arrived. Take pictures of everything, even this blood spot on the floor where he resisted arrest and we prevented him from escaping. It will prove we didn't just beat the daylights out of him (like he deserved). I know Cadigan's type. He's a coward. He'll be crying "police brutality" to anyone (except for us) who will listen. In the meantime, I'll talk to Miss Harriett, assuming she will answer the door."

"You got it."

Gillespie left. Barlow knocked on Miss Harriett's back door. She was waiting inside the kitchen, standing in the dark, peering through the window curtain. She opened the door right away.

"Miss Harriett, I'm Deputy Adams."

"I know who you are. I'm glad I finally got a chance to meet you. Who's the other deputy?"

"That's Deputy Ella Mae Gillespie. She used to work for the Brewster County Sheriff's Office. She's been with us since October, but she just graduated from the training academy a couple of weeks ago. Here she is now. Miss Harriett, meet Deputy Gillespie."

"Glad to make your acquaintance, Ma'am."

"Glad to meet you too, I'm sure. I didn't know they let girls join the sheriff's office."

"I'm the first. I hope you won't think any the less of me."

"Oh heavens no! If Sheriff Sol hired you, you must be first rate. Sheriff Sol doesn't hire sorry people."

Barlow interjected, "Thank you, Miss Harriett, on behalf of all the Quayle County staff. Deputy Gillespie had to put a lump on the burglar's head when he tried to resist arrest. She knows what she's doing."

"Well all righty, then. Who is this hooligan and what was he doing in my garage?"

"His drivers license says he's Emil Cadigan the Hooligan, I suppose, from up on the north side of the county. I don't know him. Do you?"

"No, but there used to be some Cadigans living up off Rural Route 4 on County Road 10. After the Great War, when my Eugene returned from the Army, he became a postman here, and years later the postmaster with over forty years of dedicated service altogether. He knew where everyone in this county lived. He died five years ago come this April 30th. You didn't know him did you?"

"No, Ma'am. I moved here in July of '69."

"You would've loved him. Everybody did. If he was still alive today, he would've taken care of that white trash all by hisself. He never would have called you all until after he'd ventilated Mr. Emil Cadigan, or scared him so bad he soiled his trousers. Take my word on it! What was that yardbird doing in my garage, anyway?"

"He was gathering up tools and the like which I suspect he was planning to steal. Had 'em all separated in a neat little pile."

"Just as I figured! What are you all going to do with him?"

"Oh, he's going to the calaboose. Take him before Judge Sweeney this morning. Before that though, we're going to try to locate his car. Also, Chief Alex will probably want to come out and take some pictures and dust for fingerprints. Don't go out there until after he's done. Okay?"

"Okay. I'll call you all if anything else should happen before Chief Alex gets here."

"All righty. Understand that no one's in the courthouse while we're out here, but we'll be back there soon, I hope."

"Of course. Goodbye, and thanks for coming. Nice to meet you both."

Gillespie responded for them both. "You, too. Bye."

As they were walking back to the cruiser, Barlow whispered, "Cadigan the Hooligan didn't walk here. He's got a car or a truck parked someplace nearby. For all we know, it may have evidence in it of other burglaries he's pulled tonight. Also, it's possible that he has an accomplice waiting in it, ready to "sky up" if he thinks we're on to him.

"We'll cruise very slowly north a little ways on Lubbock, past Jackson. Then turn left on Monroe, and then south on Houston. Look for a vehicle parked on the street, especially one with the engine running or somebody in it. Nobody parks on the street here unless they have company. It shouldn't be too hard to locate. If we don't find it by Taylor, turn east there and go to Texas and turn north. We have to find it. Also, do not talk to the prisoner. Do not answer any of his questions. He doesn't want to cooperate and I don't plan to make life easy for him. Also, don't say anything in front of him that will let him know what we're thinking or doing. Savvy?"

"Savvy."

When they returned to the cruiser, Cadigan the Hooligan began running his mouth, whining that his stomach hurt and his head was pounding. He was full of complaints, threats, and bluster. Finally, Barlow got fed up. He turned around and shouted, "Shut up, you stinky, grubby weasel, or I'll come back there and give you something to really cry about! Savvy? This is your last warning!"

Cadigan was smarter than he looked. He shut up.

They got lucky. They spotted a beat-up, white, '60 Ford pickup truck parked at the end of Jackson Avenue facing west towards the open field. In fact, it was exactly one block north of Barlow's house on Zachary Taylor Avenue. This was just a little too close to home for Barlow. Sarah was home asleep with no idea the creepy crawlers were this close to invading her tranquility.

Sure enough, as soon as they made the turn west on Jackson Avenue and their headlights shone on the truck, they saw a head on the driver's side above the back of the seat drop out of sight. Barlow exclaimed, "Goose it!" Gillespie goosed it, then parked it to the left and rear of the truck. She turned on the oscillating, overhead red light. She fixed the spotlight on the left side of the rear window. It would blind anyone who looked in their direction. (These were all smart moves for a rookie cop. She had learned patrol procedures very well in the academy.)

Gillespie and Barlow both exited the cruiser. They left it unlocked. Gillespie remembered to take the car keys with her. With sidearms drawn, they slowly approached the cab of the truck. Both doors were unlocked. Gillespie looked at Barlow. He nodded his head. They both yanked open a door, ready to shoot anyone who pointed a gun at them. What they saw was a heavier, younger version of Emil Cadigan, also wearing jeans and a dirty white tee shirt, lying face down across the seat. He raised his hands above his head and said, "Don't shoot! I'm not armed!"

Barlow ordered him out of the truck on the passenger side and shoved him face down across the hood of the truck. Barlow holstered his revolver and handcuffed the suspect behind the back. Then he pulled him around so they stood facing each other. By then, Gillespie was standing by Barlow's side. Barlow asked, "What's your name, Bud?"

"Name's not Bud. It's Oscar Cadigan. They calls me Jaybird. Why are you rousting me? I ain't done nothin' wrong."

"Jaybird, you must be confused. I ask the questions and you answer 'em. Savvy?"

"Yes, Sir. Sorry. It's just that you all scared the shit outta me. I was tired and decided to take a nap. Didn't think nobody would mind. Is that okay? Can I go now?"

"Jaybird, what did I tell you? Are you allowed to ask questions?"

"No, Sir. Sorry."

"Good. I was starting to think you were a slow learner. Are you a slow learner, Jaybird?"

"No, Sir."

"Who's truck is this, Jaybird?"

"My brother's."

"What's his name?"

"Emil Cadigan. They calls him Polecat."

"How come?"

"Hate to say in front of a lady."

"Say it anyway."

"He usually has gas."

"Polecat let you drive his truck?"

"Yes, Sir."

"Where's he at?"

"Back home."

"Where's home?"

"Up on County Road 10 by where the Cactus Cantina used to be before it closed down."

"What are you doing here? Folks are scared you might be a burglar or a rapist. Are you a burglar or a rapist, Jaybird? Tell the truth, now!"

"Oh, no Sir! I got a job! I wouldn't rape nobody! Serious."

"What kinda job?"

"I picks up stuff people throws away, like used washing machines, junk cars, anything metal, and I sells it at the scrapyard in Alpine. I also picks up empty soda and beer bottles and cash 'em in for the deposit money."

"You know Jasper Elrod? I think he lives out your way."

"Yes, Sir. I works for him."

"What are you doing here, Jaybird?"

"Just trying to take a nap, Sir. I didn't mean nobody no harm."

"Deputy Gillespie, search the bed of the truck."

"10-4." She shined her flashlight in the bed. It was empty

except for a worn-out spare tire, a canvas tarp, two dozen empty beer bottles, and a half-dozen different lengths of hemp rope. "Nothin' here but a tarp and some rope."

"Thanks. Jaybird, why are you here? You're about 40 miles from home. You better not lie to me or it'll go real bad for you. Your momma will cry for weeks. Savvy?"

"Yes, Sir. I ain't got no excuse. I knows I don't belong here."

"Are you waiting for someone - maybe a woman to leave her house unlocked so you can rape her, or maybe some married woman who lives nearby and is running around on her husband and she's gonna get in the truck and commit adultery with you? Is that it? I'll bet that's it! You're plannin' to have sex with another man's wife! You low-down, dirty dog!"

"Oh, no Sir. Honest. It ain't nothin' like that. I'm just waiting for my brother."

"Where's your brother? You said he was at home."

"I ain't for sure. He said he wanted to go see a man in this neighborhood about some junk he had for sale. He told me to wait right here. That's all I know."

"Now I know you're lying.

"Deputy Gillespie, search Jaybird v-e-r-y thoroughly, just like before. Then check the cab and the glovebox for weapons. See if the registration is in there. Then check Jaybird's wallet for his drivers license."

"You got it."

"Sir, I ain't got no license. I never got one on account of I ain't got no truck. This'n here belongs to my brother, like I said. I wasn't drivin' it. I was just sittin' in it. Honest!"

"What's your date of birth?"

"December 27, 1950."

"So you're 21."

"Yes, Sir."

"Did you finish high school."

"No, Sir."

"How far did you get?"

"I quit at the end of the 9th grade."

"How come?"

"I was 20 years old. Just didn't seem like I was gettin' nowhere. Everyone else was younger than me."

"Hmmm."

Gillespie searched Jaybird. Except for a nearly empty wallet and a house key, his pockets were as empty as Al Capone's secret vault. Then she checked the cab of the truck. No weapons. A lot of trash. Empty beer bottles, overflowing ashtray, crowbar, discarded cigarette packs, candy wrappers, filthy gloves, dirt and mud everywhere. She found the vehicle registration in the glovebox (which was nearly empty) and read out loud, "Belongs to Emil T. Cadigan. License plate expired two months ago."

"Told ya so."

"Where's your brother? This is the last time I'm gonna ask you!"

"He's on the street behind me, third house from the end of the block that away (nodding his head north) on the lefthand side. I was supposed to go get him a few minutes ago about the time you all stopped me. He was meeting a man about some junk. That's all I know."

"Did you drop him off there?"

"Yes."

"Why didn't you wait for him?"

"He told me not to. He said to give him an hour and then come pick him up. Honest. That's all I know."

"Deputy Gillespie, read this fellow his rights."

"Oh, please don't read me my rights. I ain't done nothin' wrong."

"You have the right to remain silent. Anything you say can, and will be used against you in a court of law. You have the right to speak to an attorney, and to have an attorney present during questioning. If you cannot afford a lawyer, one will be appointed for you at government expense. Do you understand and waive your rights?"

"Yes, Ma'am."

"Yes, you understand, or yes you waive your rights?"

"Both."

Barlow interrupted. "Jaybird, your brother didn't go to see a man about buying any junk did he?"

"That's what he said."

"Maybe so, but that's not what he went to go do, was it?"

"No, Sir."

"What did he go to do, Jaybird?"

"Break into a woman's garage and steal some stuff."

"What stuff?"

"I don't know. Some tools and a generator, I think."

"Okay. How did he find out about this garage?"

"He overheard some guy talking about a antique car this old lady had, and how it was worth a lot of money. The guy said you couldn't get away with stealing the car 'cause it was so rare, but he said the garage had a lot of other neat stuff in it that could be sold. That's all I know."

"Where did he hear this conversation?"

"The Dry Gulch Saloon."

"How long ago?"

"The day before Christmas."

"Was the guy in it with your brother?"

"No, Sir. He wasn't even talking to my brother. He was talking to some other dude."

"Who did he hear it from?"

"I don't know. My brother said he didn't know. Just some old man."

"Did he know the other man that was listening?"

"I don't know. He didn't say. I doubt it."

"Did you drive your brother over to the house where the garage is that he was planning to break into?"

"Yes, Sir."

"And you knew that was what he was gonna do?"

"Yes, Sir."

"And you were supposed to pick him up in an hour, but we stopped you first so you couldn't?"

"Yes, Sir."

"And you don't have a drivers license, do you?"

"No, Sir."

"Now that wasn't so hard, was it?"

"No, Sir."

"Deputy Gillespie, put Jaybird in the backseat next to his brother. I'll get the key out of the ignition and lock the truck. Then take us back to the jail. It's 4:30 and our night has only just begun."

"Oh my God! You had my brother all this time? We're fucked, ain't we, Deputy? Oh my God! Say it ain't so! Please, officer! I didn't mean no harm. Honest!"

"Jaybird, calm down. You'll get through this unless you die first. Now pipe down so I don't have to clock ya. Savvy?"

"Savvy."

CHAPTER 3

A Busy Night Becomes a Busier Day

Monday, January 3, 1972

When Gillespie and Barlow returned to the cruiser, they were almost overcome by toxic fumes. Barlow asked, "Emil, did you drop a load in your britches? This smells worse than a pig sty!"

Jaybird chimed in, "Told ya. He does this all the time. Welcome to my world. That's why everyone calls him Polecat."

Polecat responded, "Fuck you! Fuck all of you! Jaybird, I'll beat your ass soon as I get these cuffs off!"

Barlow replied, "That's enough, both of you! Pipe down! Come on, Deputy Gillespie. Let's get out of here," as he rolled down his window.

Gillespie drove them back to the sheriff's office, usually referred to as the jail by the courthouse staff. They housed Polecat in Cell #1 and Jaybird in Cell #2, leaving them temporarily unattended in violation of departmental protocol. Then they went back to the office to begin the various tasks that were supposed to be initiated immediately. Barlow switched the phones back to the jail and checked for messages. There were none. He unloaded and checked in the shotgun. He made sure Gillespie logged in Unit 81 according to procedure. Then he asked, "What do you think? Any questions or comments?"

She replied, "Oh my gosh! What an adrenaline rush! This is the most exciting thing I've ever done! It was scary but I loved it. This is why I wanted to become a cop. Thank you for teaching me."

"You did well. This is why most of us went into law

enforcement. What you just experienced was the fun part of the job. Thirty minutes of exhilaration, which morphs into hours of paperwork, court appearances, and sometimes getting grilled like we're the bad guys. Mark my word. One day you will get accused of police misconduct or brutality or even worse. It's happened to all of us. Unfortunately, that's the way the system works. When the defendant doesn't have a leg to stand on, invariably his strategy becomes to blame the cops. It's all their fault. Nevertheless, very few officers change career fields. Law enforcement is an avocation, just like being a clergyman, or a doctor, or a nurse.

"Listen up. Tonight your shift just went from 8 hours to 12 or more. No overtime pay. This is why the sheriff gives us uncharged time off whenever he can (assuming we earned it). That's how he makes up for days like today.

"Between the paperwork and court appearances, you'll have to shift gears from cop to jailer, starting right now. Being a jailer is a facet of this job that we all dread, but it comes with the territory. Usually, it's the rookie's job, but the jail has to be covered on all three shifts whenever we have a prisoner. Even the senior deputies get rope-a-doped into being jailers.

"It's boring, but dangerous. The jailer is held accountable if a prisoner hangs himself or otherwise does himself or another person harm. The cells are small. It's hot in there and they have nothing to do except for read the Bible. No other reading material allowed except for court documents. No TV. No radio. No library. No dessert with supper. No exercise time outside of the cell. One shower a week. No visitors except for their lawyer or clergyman. Not even a window to look out of. They do very hard time here. The prisoners are hating life every single minute of the day while they're in our custody. It's designed that way on purpose. Jail is supposed to suck. The inmates take their misery out on the jailer because he's the only person they ever see.

It's a tough way to earn your money, but we've all done it,

and we'll all do it again and again. You'll feel like complaining, but you absolutely must not. No one wants to hear it. Never. No bitching. You just have to suck it up and pray for the day you get released from purgatory. At least here in Quayle County, Judge Sweeney does all he can to process convicted felons quickly and send them on their way. Savvy?"

"Savvy."

"Good. This is what we have to do. First, I have to call Sheriff Sol and fill him in. He'll come down here because this is your first arrest - arrests. You are the primary arresting officer. I'm secondary."

"But you're senior. You told me what I needed to do. I did it. I didn't think about looking for Polecat's truck. I would never have gotten a confession from Jaybird. You did it all."

"I did what I was supposed to do as a training officer. The first time I arrested someone who wasn't already wanted on a warrant, Archie did for me what I just did for you. That's the way we do things here. You learn by doing. On-the-job training, otherwise called OJT. A senior deputy is on overwatch. Capeesh?"

"Capeesh. Thank you."

"No problem. Okay. The sheriff will probably tell me to call Chief Alex so he can process the crime scene and begin the follow-up investigation. He will also probably tell me to call Dewey because he's on day shift today. He'll probably be assigned to help Chief to do the crime scene investigation. Maybe take a formal statement from Miss Harriett or anything else Chief needs. Then Dewey will be relegated to jail duty. I also need to call Doc Boykin to come in and check out Polecat before court, just to make sure his injuries aren't serious. He might need a few stitches."

"What do I do?"

"You have a lot to do. First, you need to write up the incident report. Good thing you've been reading incident reports so you have an idea of what is expected. This is the first one of the year, so it's 72-1. Begin with the call from Mrs. Enright. Finish up with the two arrests. Show it to me when you're done. We want to get it right before you turn it in to Chief or Sheriff Sol. "You are also responsible for the booking slips, personal property reports, and fingerprinting and photographing the prisoners. Also, the evidence report, which Chief will probably do for you, and the criminal complaint, which I will also help you to do. Not for nothing, but you're primarily responsible for outfitting our jailbirds in black-and-white stripes, but since you have so much on your plate, someone else will probably do that for you."

"Thanks."

Gillespie got busy. Barlow made his calls. When he finished, he said, "Sheriff Sol, Chief Alex, Dewey, and Doc Boykin are all en route. I'm going to check on the prisoners. Come get me if you need some help."

"10-4."

Barlow locked his revolver in one of the small gun safes, stuck his billy club in his belt ring, and then went into the jail. He decided to check on Emil first. Emil's cut on the back of his head had quit bleeding, but he was definitely going to need some stitches. Barlow told him to strip naked. It didn't take long. Emil didn't even whine.

Barlow took Emil's garments (including underwear), shoes, and belt, plus the few contents of his pockets, and locked the cell door behind him. Then he went into the cabinet in the jailer's room, stuffed Emil's property into a personal property bag (which he marked for identification) and secured it in a locker. Then from the clothing cabinet, he selected a set of jail garments for each brother. A set includes one pair of baggy trousers with elastic waistbands, one pullover, long-sleeve shirt, and a pair of shower clogs. The shirt and trousers have 2-inch wide, horizontal, black-and-white stripes. A set does not include underwear. Each inmate goes "commando." Barlow passed Emil's new outfit to him through the bars. Then he repeated the process with Oscar. By the time he was done, both Sheriff Sol and Doc Boykin had joined the party.

"Sheriff Sol asked, "Emil, what on Earth were you thinking? Don't you know Judge Sweeney will probably send both you and Jaybird "up the river?" You barely stayed out of jail the last time we nabbed you."

Emil never looked up. He slumped on the bed and studied his toes.

Then Sheriff Sol turned around in looked in Cell #2. Jaybird was cringing in a corner, bawling his eyes out. "Jaybird, I'm ashamed of you. I thought you were better than this. Are you bucking for prison, too?"

"Sheriff, I'm so sorry. I didn't mean nuthin'. All I did was the drivin'. Please don't put me in prison. I promise I'll never do nuthin' like this again."

"That will be up to the judge. Since you've never been arrested before, he might be lenient on you, but I wouldn't count on it. If he does give you a break, you better do everything he says, and be in church bright and early each Sunday morning to show him you're sincere. He belongs to the Baptist Church. I suggest you make it a habit going there each Sunday so he can see you making amends. Understand?"

"I do. I really do. I promise, Sheriff. I'll never fuck up again."

"We'll see. You say this now, but you'll probably backslide and wind up in the prison cell next to your brother making license plates in Huntsville."

"God forbid, Sheriff! I seen the light. Truly."

"You'll have your opportunity to convince the judge in court. You better be telling the truth. Judge Sweeney can sniff out a liar a mile away, and he hates liars. So do I. Savvy?"

"Savvy."

Emil shouted, "You better clam up, Jaybird, or I'll fuck you up good the first chance I get!"

Sheriff Sol responded, "Shut up, Polecat! You just bought

yourself a charge of terroristic threatening."

Sheriff Sol went back to the office to check on Gillespie.

Doc Boykin checked the bruise on Emil's stomach. It looked bad but it wasn't a serious injury. He cleaned Emil's head wound and shaved all around it so he could suture the cut. It took five stitches. When he was done, Barlow let Doc out of the cell.

Doc said, "He'll be just fine. I don't think he has a concussion. I'm sure he has a splitting headache, no pun intended, and he'll have pain each time he flatulates but otherwise he's okay." Then he left just as quickly as Barlow could unlock and open the jail doors.

Polecat was living up to his nickname by "peeling the paint off the walls." Doc's parting words were, "Barlow, you ought to get hazardous duty pay just for breathing the toxic air in here. It's overwhelming! It smells worse than a broken sewer line. It would gag a maggot!"

Barlow was stuck in the jail, doing his best not to breathe the noxious fumes emanating from Polecat, waiting stoically for someone to relieve him. He figured he would be there until Chief Alex and Dewey completed the crime scene investigation and took Miss Harriett's statement. He also figured Sheriff Sol would help Gillespie with the complaint and prep her for court this morning. Ergo, as long as he was cooling his heels, he might as well make himself useful. He completed the personal property inventory reports. He also fingerprinted and took mugshots of both jailbirds. Then he stood next to the only window in the jail, and pressed his face into the bars so he could smell the fresh air. If only there were just a slight breeze!

It was almost 8 o'clock before Barlow got a push from Dewey. Gillespie showed Barlow the incident report and complaints which had been approved by Sheriff Sol. He had instructed her to charge Emil with outhouse burglary, resisting arrest (for trying to flee), terroristic threats against Oscar, and ownership of a motor vehicle on a public road with an expired vehicle registration (license plates). They charged Oscar with accessory before the fact to outhouse burglary. That was a felony charge, too, punishable just like outhouse burglary by up to five years in prison.

Chief Alex had completed the crime scene and inventoried the evidence, which he left in Miss Harriett's custody. He had photographs, plus he knew this case was never going to trial. Even Polecat had better sense than that. If he decided to go to trial and lost, which he would, Judge Sweeney would max out each sentence and "stack 'em like cordwood." Polecat would wind up serving seven or eight years - all at hard labor!

Dewey had completed the NCIC and NLETS wanted and computerized criminal record checks, as well as the DMV checks. Emil had one prior misdemeanor conviction for trespassing and another for disorderly conduct. Oscar's record was clean. He did not have a drivers license, but he wasn't charged with driving without a license because that's a misdemeanor charge and the deputies did not see him do it. (Different from felonies, misdemeanors must be witnessed.)

Emil's truck had been impounded and was locked in Buck's Phillips 66 storage lot. Someone would have to renew the vehicle registration and pay towing and storage fees before the truck would be released. Otherwise, when the fees began to exceed the value of the vehicle, it would be sold at a sheriff's auction to recover the costs. In that this truck probably wasn't worth $150, he had about a month to get it out of hock before it would be auctioned off.

Everything was done except for taking the brothers upstairs for their initial appearances and bond hearings, which were scheduled for 10 o'clock before Judge Sweeney. Also, at 1 o'clock, Gillespie was slated to testify before the Grand Jury to present the felony charges. Assuming that both men were indicted, they would have an arraignment Tuesday morning. Gillespie would be called as the witness to present the allocution. She was pinging.

Sheriff Sol thanked Barlow and told him to go home. He said this was Gillespie's rodeo. Barlow smiled. He remembered his first arrest with Archie. Baptism by fire. Barlow came out of it just fine. So would Gillespie.

CHAPTER 4

Shopping for a Car

Monday, January 3, 1972

Sarah and Barlow were cruising down the highway to Del Rio as soon as she got off from work. He told her all about the arrests while they were en route. When he expounded upon the essence of Polecat in close quarters, she said, "Oh, that's disgusting! Poor Ella Mae! She has to guard him all night tonight. I feel so sorry for her!"

"What about me or Dewey? Slick's guarding him now. We all had to endure it!"

"Yeah, but you're all men. You're used to it. She doesn't understand what she signed up for. She may decide she'd rather be a property clerk. I'd never want to be a deputy. You have to endure so many awful things."

"Sarah, nobody ever gets used to a malodorous subhuman like Polecat. Nevertheless, Gillespie will be fine. She knew what she was getting into. She's tough. Besides that, since she's decided to be a pioneer for women in law enforcement, if she wimps out, she's done. Simple as that. What about nurses? They have to clean up people who are sick and can't take themselves to the bathroom. Being a deputy is a cushy job compared to that."

"Touché, Mr. Adams, but you need to push her off every now and then. Don't be a hard case. Everyone appreciates a helping hand."

"Don't worry. I'll treat her right. You should know that by now. I bet she wears a strong perfume after her first night in the dungeon with Polecat."

"I do know you're a considerate man. You might consider

calling her tonight and mention the perfume."

The miles ticked away. They found Reasonable Rick Rohde's Volkswagen Dealership on US Highway 90 on the east side of town. The dealership was quite a bit larger than either of them remembered from the last time they drove through here. There must have been 50 new cars on the lot, plus some clean used ones.

As soon as they parked, they were greeted by an attractive blonde woman about 30 years of age. She had on a long sleeve white blouse, red scarf, black, white, and red plaid miniskirt, and white go-go boots. She smiled fetchingly and asked, "What can I do for you folks today?"

Barlow responded, "We're looking for a salesman. We want to take a look at your new Volkswagens."

"Well, you've come to the right place. My name is Larissa. I'll be glad to help you all out."

Sarah asked, "You mean you're a sales lady?"

"Darlin', I'm a sales lady, service rep, receptionist, parts clerk, auto loan officer, auto insurance agent, clean-up girl, and the manager whenever my daddy's not here. He owns this joint. Opened it in 1956. I grew up on this little patch of heaven. I can do 'most anything you need here except for body work, valve jobs, and electrical repairs. Whenever my daddy decides to retire, I'll be the next owner. Now, aren't you glad you met me? I'd love to sell you all a Volkswagen if you see one that suits your fancy."

Sarah blushed. "Oh, I hope I didn't offend you, Miss Larissa. I just never imagined meeting someone as beautiful as you working in a car dealership. I've never purchased a car before. I apologize. I am so glad we have you to take care of us. My name is Sarah and this is my husband, Barlow. We're looking for a car for me. This old Chevy is my car. It's pretty worn out. It will be our trade-in if we find something we like and can afford."

"Sarah, don't think another thing about it. A lot of folks are surprised when they see a woman selling cars. Barlow, I'm glad to meet you both. Where you all from?"

"We're from Mosby. We noticed your dealership about six months ago when we went to the hospital to see a friend. Sarah has family here - her grandmother and aunt. Anyway, we need to find Sarah an inexpensive, reliable ride that gets good gas mileage. I thought maybe a VW would be just the thing."

"Well, my gosh! Sarah, What are their names. Maybe I know them."

"My grandma is Helena Parker. She lives on Live Oak Street. My aunt is Lacy Lynch. She's married to a proctologist. His first name is Dennis. He's a department head at the hospital. They live on Lunar Eclipse Way. Do you know them?"

"Well, I know of Dr. Lynch. He's fishing buddies with my dentist, Dr. Szego, and my uncle, Jolly John Carroll. He owns Jolly John's Liquors. My, my. It's a small world.

"Well, we're so happy you remembered us. Are you all looking for new or used?"

"New."

"Beetle or Karmann Ghia?"

"Beetle."

"Excellent. Right now we have 39 new Beetles and six new Ghias. The Beetles come in 13 different colors. Right now we have nine of them - the the most popular colors, anyway. Why don't we walk over there and see if any of these cars strike your fancy?

"Just so you know, most of the cars have the same standard features - AM radio, black wall tires, leatherette seats, cigar lighter, and so forth. We can install an AM/FM radio, aluminum wheel rings, whitewall tires, aluminum rain guards, upgraded floor mats, luggage rack, custom chrome accents, things such as that, right here at the shop if you want it. A few of the cars have air conditioning but I'll tell you right up front, the Germans don't need A/C and it's not as good as it is on a full size American automobile. We just don't sell many Beetles with A/C, but I do have three or four on the lot. I'm letting you know just in case air conditioning is important to you. If it is, you may want to look for a different make of automobile. We both know it gets sizzling hot down here in the Trans-Pecos."

They browsed through the aisles. Sarah was amazed at all the bright colors - red, orange, two different blues, metallic turquoise, yellow, green, and so forth. She sat in six of them. Finally she said, "I like this yellow one and that red one. Can we take a test drive?"

"Sure you can. Can you drive a stick?"

"Yes, but the ones I'm used to are on the column."

"Okey dokey. Doesn't matter. The clutch works just the same. Which one would you like to drive first - the Texas yellow or the Kansas red?"

"Oh! The Texas yellow, of course!"

"Let me check the inventory board and get the keys. I'll be right back."

Sarah drove the yellow car several miles through town, pointing out where her grandmother and aunt live. She fell in love with the car. Barlow drove it back to the lot. It ran like a Swiss watch. German engineering. (Ha!) They decided to take it. Barlow had them add the wheel rings, floor mats, and rain guards. Then it was time to negotiate a deal.

Larissa said Volkswagen didn't discount cars like dealers for American cars do. The sticker price is the price. At the same time, Volkswagen doesn't pad the sticker price and then reduce it to make the customer think he got a deal. Call any VW dealer. They'll tell you the same thing.

In the end, Barlow wrote a check for $2,044.37. He got $100 for the Nova, which was about what he expected. Sarah drove them home. Happy campers both. Sarah was thrilled to finally have reliable transportation. Barlow had just enough time for Sarah to demonstrate her appreciation before he had to shower, get dressed, and drive to work. She was so appreciative that he was almost late, not to mention nearly worn out.

CHAPTER 5

Gillespie's Debut in Corrections

Tuesday, January 4, 1972

Gillespie beat Barlow to work. She was still euphoric, buzzed, from making her first arrests, court appearance, and Grand Jury appearance. At the same time, she knew tonight would probably be a grueling shift as the jailer for a troglodyte and a simpleton. She was dreading it, but determined not to show it under any circumstances. No one would ever be able to accuse her of not being able to pull her own weight. She was thankful that nobody at the sheriff's office here had been condescending to her or tried to make her feel uncomfortable. In fact, it was just the opposite. She would strive hard to earn her keep without being a toady or a screaming feminist.

She relieved Ernie Atwater early. He thanked her and suggested she wear some nose plugs if she had some. If not that, put Vicks Vaporub on the bottom of her nostrils or bum a cigar from Barlow. She said she was prepared. She brought some incense to burn.

She locked her gun in one of the gun safes and put on a fresh pot of coffee. She filled her thermos and trudged to the jail. There were three locked doors: the wooden door from the office bullpen; the traditional, arched, heavy steel door into the jail itself with iron bars floor to ceiling; and, the heavy metal mesh door to the cellblock area, and to the rear jail storage and break area (with the only window in the dungeon serving as its single source for fresh air and circulation).

Her olfactory senses came under siege as soon as she opened the wooden door. She lit an incense stick before she even considered checking the well-being of her two jailbirds. Then she walked past the cellblock into the rear storage area to insure that the solitary window, which had iron bars on the outside of the glass, was wide open. It was. She adjusted the oscillating pole fan to make sure it blew fresh air all the way to the front where the jailer's desk was located.

It really sucked not having air conditioning in this portion of the courthouse which housed the jail. Heck, the rest of the courthouse only got air conditioning in 1968! The Quayle County Board of Supervisors was notoriously tight-fisted and had no intention of mollycoddling prisoners. They weren't the least bit concerned about the deputies either, as evidenced by the fact that they still refused to purchase marked patrol cars with air conditioning.

Gillespie looked in on her charges. Polecat and Jaybird were still alive. Jaybird was asleep. Polecat was feigning sleep. When she turned to walk back to the desk, he ripped a raucous, five-second fart before convulsing into laughter. So that was how it as going to be, huh?

She opened her canvas ditty bag and pulled out her secret weapon. She bought it at Jake's Pawn Shop after she got off work. It was a half-ounce bottle of skunk oil. Hunters use it to mask their scent. They usually only put one drop on each boot heel. She put four drops on a tissue and rubbed it on the inside of one of the iron bars of Polecat's cell. The minute she walked away, he jumped up and howled like a mangy coyote in heat.

Gillespie ignored him. She sat at her desk and burned the tissue. She lit a second incense stick. She poured a cup of steamy coffee. It tasted great.

Then Jaybird began screaming like he'd been staked out naked over a fire ant mound in the hot Texas sun. "I want out! Why do I have to suffer just because my brother is a big fucking asshole? I'm allergic to skunks! I hate 'em! Please, please, Deputy, please have mercy on me!"

Polecat chimed in again. He ripped off another stink bomb. "You can't get away with this, you uppity bitch! It's a violation of my civil rights! I'm turnin' you into the judge! I'll sue! They'll fire your ass! I'll fuck you up if I get my hands on you!"

Gillespie didn't have nose plugs, but she did have earplugs and shooting muffs. She put them on. She opened her paperback book of puzzles and went to work. She would have filed and painted her fingernails but she decided that might be a little over the top.

Barlow arrived at work just about the time Gillespie went into the jail. He heard the ruckus. He didn't know what was going on, but Gillespie hadn't called for help so he gave her time to resolve the problem on her own. The noise finally abated. He waited until she had been in the dungeon for a couple of hours before he went to check on her. What he discovered both surprised and impressed him.

"Hey, Gillespie. How's it going?"

"All quiet here, Boss. We had a wee misunderstanding but it's all good now."

"I could hear it. Now I can see it for myself. Did you know your incense smells a little like a skunk?"

"Oh, it's not the incense. That smells like green apples. I rubbed a little skunk oil on Polecat's cell door in honor of his nickname. It's nearly worn off now. So long as he doesn't have a lapse in good manners, I won't use it again. By the way, I put the bottle in the top desk drawer so the other deputies can use it if they need to."

"Well, I swear. I bet in the entire history of this jail going back to the very beginning in 1910, no one ever thought about skunk oil being a behavior modifier. I'm sure back in the day they mostly gave the malcontents a "wood shampoo." In recent history, the jailers have just suffered through the ordeal of foul-smelling jailbirds. Leave it to our first female deputy to come up with a viable non-lethal solution. I'm impressed, and the rest of the deputies will be too. Kudos to you.

"What happened in court and the Grand Jury?"

"The Grand Jury indicted Polecat on outhouse burglary and Jaybird on accessory before the fact. Polecat's also charged with resisting arrest, making terroristic threats, and ownership of an unlicensed vehicle on a public street. Judge Sweeney set Polecat's bond at $5,000, and Jaybird's at $2,000. They both pleaded not guilty to all charges. Trial is set for Thursday at 10 o'clock. That's all I know."

"How did you feel about testifying?"

"I was scared stiff at first but everything was fine. Thanks to you we had "all our ducks in a row." The public defender didn't seem to have an agenda. In fact, Mr. Davis is a really nice guy. Ditto for the DA. Actually, I think Mr. DeWitt is a peach and Judge Sweeney is an old school patriarch - a true gentleman in the classical sense."

"Oh, jeez, Gillespie! Don't let the other fellows hear you call Able DeWitt a peach or you'll never hear the end of it. I agree with your assessment of Judge Sweeney and Sam Davis. We're fortunate to have all three of them in our local judicial system. They can be tough as nails, but they're all honest. A lot of venues aren't so blessed.

"By the way, I stopped by to relieve you. Take a break. Eat your supper. I got this for as long as you need. I brought the SRSU catalogue with me to figure out what classes Sarah and I will sign up for."

"Much appreciated. I'll take you up on your offer in just a moment. I'd like to catch up first. Did you all go out and buy a bug yesterday?"

"We did. Sarah picked out a Texas yellow one with black vinyl seats. She drove it home. She's driven cars with the shift on the column but not on the floor. She had a few rough starts, but I think she's got it mastered unless she has to stop on a hill and start from first gear without rolling backwards. When she gets home today, we'll drive over to the college and get enrolled for this semester. Sarah will drive both ways. That'll give her another couple hundred miles to learn the stick."

"What're you all studying?"

"History. We're starting our junior year. We're planning to take the same classes so if one of us is absent, the other can catch him up."

"How many hours?"

"12. We're hoping to get classes Monday through Thursday but we'll take what we can get. Night school doesn't have a big selection. If it did, she'd enroll in agriculture and I'd enroll in criminal justice."

"That's a load. What courses do you plan to take this semester?"

"We're hoping for American History from 1600 to 1770, Western Political Philosophy, Survey of Western European History, and Federalism in the United States. The other option is to substitute one of those for the Sociology of American Indian Tribes."

"Well good luck. I worked part-time in college and that was tough enough. It'll be worth it in the end. Having a degree will open a lot of doors if you all are looking for change."

"We're not, but Sheriff Sol, Kirk, Randy, and you all came on board with a bachelors degree. Sarah and I just have an associates. Wouldn't surprise me in the future if all the newbies applying for law enforcement positions will have to have a bachelors degree. You can never tell what the Texas POST committee will demand now that they have all this power."

"Heck. A Ph.D. in criminal justice could never make up for the experience of my Uncle Leland or Slick or you, even though you've not got that many years on. How do you teach common sense or the art of reading people or how to avoid panic in a gunfight? You don't."

"Agreed, but we cops don't make the rules.

"Hey, bring me back a cuppa joe, would you? Take your time. I'm not in a rush, especially now that you've solved the air quality problem."

The rest of the night was quiet.

CHAPTER 6

The Saga of Emil and Oscar Cadigan is Over

Thursday, January 6, 1972

It had been a long, but gratifying week for Gillespie. She arrived early at the jail because she wanted to surprise Barlow. She pushed off Deputy Ernie Atwater at 11 o'clock. He did not "look a gift horse in the mouth." He thanked her and hit the "dusty trail like the (proverbial) cow turd."

Gillespie made coffee, and then she checked the jail cells to insure everything was in shipshape order. It was. She returned to the office and began tidying up there. Made sure the trash baskets had been emptied. All the chairs were pushed in their proper places. No condensation rings on desks or countertops left to be wiped up. Checked the clipboards hanging on the wall with the incident reports to confirm all the reports were there and in reverse chronological order (not a big deal because it was so early in the year.) Picked up a pencil that had rolled off Miss Loretta's desk. Gillespie hunted for any type of housecleaning job that had been left undone but there really weren't any. With nothing left to do, she poured herself a cup of java and took a seat at the desk reserved for the junior deputy and waited for Barlow.

He arrived at 11:40. He hung up his hat, put his lunch on the desk reserved for the senior deputy, poured himself a cup of joe, and sat down next to her. He said, "You look like a woman who just recovered her wedding ring from the trap in the sink drainpipe. Tell me all about it before you explode."

She gushed like Old Faithful in Yellowstone Park. "Barlow, I can't remember being this gratified. Keep your mind out of the gutter. I know what you're thinking. Not that type of gratification.

It was like I actually did something noteworthy, something that has an impact on the universe, our little universe here in Quayle County, and it feels so good.

"Judge Sweeney did not disappoint. It was almost exactly like you said it would be. We made the arrest Monday morning in the wee hours. I testified before the Grand Jury that afternoon. They were arraigned on Tuesday. They decided to cop a plea on Wednesday. They both pleaded guilty and were convicted this morning, and the Department of Corrections whisked Emil away this afternoon. I was involved in it all "from soup to nuts." Polecat looked like a "lost ball in the high weeds." Like a kid being lead to the woodshed to get his licks. I feel like I made a real difference here in Mosby, and you are the one most responsible for teaching me how to do it. I can't thank you enough. I mean it."

"You're welcome. Glad to do it. I pointed the way and you took it from there. You did a great job. You assimilated a lot in a short period of time. You suffered with the rest of us performing jail duty. Enjoy your victory. They won't all be this tidy or gratifying, but this one certainly was. What did they get?"

"From what Chief Alex told me, Judge Sweeney was as lenient as he's ever seen him. He sentenced Emil first. He got three years to serve for the outhouse burglary instead of five, and six months each for resisting arrest and making terroristic threats. The sentences are to run consecutively. He also got a $20 fine for no vehicle registration, plus court costs were $60.

"Chief said with good behavior Emil could get out in three years, but he doesn't think Emil is capable of good behavior. He also told me that though Emil may be stupid, that doesn't make him harmless. He said if I'm still living here in Quayle County after Emil gets released from prison, I better grow some eyes in the back of my head, because he's the kind of guy who would sneak up on me from behind and clobber me with a board to get revenge. He said Emil is incapable of thinking about what would happen to him after that, assuming he got caught. He's impulsive.

He will probably spend the greater part of his adult life going back and forth to prison until the judge finally gets sick of him and sends him away forever on "the high bitch".

"Gave me a cold chill what he said. I'm going to save up my money and buy a little Smith & Wesson Chief .38 to carry off-duty like you have. My Ruger is too big to carry in my purse, and I usually don't have it with me on my person when I'm off duty.

"Judge Sweeney sentenced Oscar Cadigan to two years in prison for accessory before the fact to outhouse burglary, plus $15 court costs. He suspended the sentence for five years. Then he put him on probation for two. Chief said if Jaybird stubs his toe in the next five years he'll be sent to prison to serve the full two years.

"Chief also said since the state doesn't have any probation or parole officers here in Quayle County - the nearest ones are in Alpine it Del Rio - we are responsible to monitor him. Essentially, Chief will be his probation officer, but the uniformed deputies will be tasked to perform spot checks on his residence, job, and so forth. Jaybird has to report to us the first Tuesday of each month at 10 o'clock without fail, or Judge Sweeney will revoke him and he will be sent to prison to serve his time. What do you think of that?"

"I think both were fair sentences. I'm happy Jaybird got probation. He's still got a chance to become a decent citizen. Polecat is beyond being salvaged.

"Also, I think you do need to get an off-duty gun. Mine saved my life last summer at a rest stop in Sonora. I know you heard about that. If I hadn't had it, both Sarah and I and maybe even Archie would be pushing up daisies now. Quayle may be a quiet little town, and we don't make the headlines here like they do in the big cities like Chicago or El Paso, but that doesn't mean our job is not dangerous. This isn't Mayberry. Sheriff Sol isn't Andy Griffith, and the rest of us aren't Barney Fife or Aunt Bea or Gomer. You might want to stop by Jake's Pawn shop sometime today and see if he can line you up. Don't put this off. Savvy?"

"Savvy. Thanks."

Chapter 7

A Call for Assistance

Tuesday, January 25, 2021

The previous three weeks passed without notice. Then just before the stroke of midnight, before Barlow and Gillespie even got settled in good, the phone rang. Barlow answered it. "Quayle County Sheriff's Office, Deputy Sheriff Adams speaking. How may I help you?"

"Deputy, this is Arnold S. Wrigley. I own the Circle A, just like the U.S Third Army patch. Red Circle around a white A on a field of blue. I'm 42-1/2 miles miles east of town just before you get to Big Canyon Creek. You know where that's at?"

"Yes, Sir. I think I do. Don't you fly an American flag and the Texas flag on either side of the gate?"

"That's me. How long it take you to get here?"

"Oh, 45 minutes or so, unless you need us faster. What's the problem?"

"You'll see. The flags ain't flying since it's night and I ain't got no lights out there. It's darker than Hades, too. Me and my hand will be waiting for you out by the gate in my Jeep. It's Army surplus. Not one of them civilian jobs. Make sure you bring a rifle or a shotgun. You can't never tell what's liable to happen around here no more."

"We'll be right out."

Gillespie asked, "What's up?"

"Not sure. Anyone showed you where the Circle A Ranch is?"

"Nope."

"The rancher who owns it, this retired Army sergeant major named Arnold Wrigley, has some kind of problem he didn't want to discuss on the phone. His ranch is 42-1/2 miles east of here on the south side of Highway 90. He's right on the border. He'll meet us at the front gate. He recommended we bring long guns. You take a Remington shotgun and I'll take one of the Winchester .30-30's. Load up and chamber a round. Put it on safe. Take some extra ammo. Check out the new Plymouth. You drive. I'll switch the phones, and don't forget that lethal flashlight of yours. I'll get my spanking new one. Also, you take the notes and write the incident report. The call came in at 11:59. That's 2359 hours to us military types."

"This sounds mysterious. I'm ready for a little excitement."

"Be careful what you wish for. This is the first time a caller recommended I bring a long gun. I'm taking it serious too, because Sergeant Major Wrigley is as "hard as forged steel." He's an old school infantry ground pounder with service in World Wars I and II, plus Korea. Combat Infantryman Badge, Distinguished Service Cross, Silver Star, three Purple Hearts you name it. He's got it. Even Archie's in awe of this guy and that's saying something."

"Say no more. You got my undivided attention. Are we running code two or three?"

"Nope. That might indicate to retired Sergeant Major Wrigley that we're too green, too eager, and that he's in charge. He's not in the Army anymore. We respect him, but we call the shots. Savvy?"

"Savvy. Have you met him before?"

"Nope, but I've seen him around town. He's the real deal. You'll see. Just make sure you look him straight in the eye and for gosh sakes, don't tiptoe around him. Act like he's just another citizen. I mean it. When I was in the Army, sergeant majors ate captains for lunch. You want him to respect you. Understand?"

"I do. I'll just follow your lead."

Gillespie watched the odometer. She slowed down to 30 miles an hour once she had driven 40 miles. It was pitch black and she didn't want to pass it up. Finally she saw his headlights. She stopped on the road while he turned around. She followed him south on a dirt path. You couldn't really call it a road. Maybe a toad trail. There were two men in the Jeep.

Barlow said, "Wrigley is the passenger. The driver must be his ranch hand. As I recall, he's a resident alien from a flyspeck across the river down here called Ciudad Lagarto. It means the City of Lizards, but I think it's meant as a joke. Lagarto is not a city. It probably only has 50 souls. No more than 100. I believe his name is Pedro Padilla . He's your typical vaquero. Good guy."

"How do you know all this?"

"I've lived here 2-1/2 years now. The population in Quayle County is only 3,000 souls. The other deputies, plus just doing the job, have introduced me to a lot of the residents. They've mentioned all the notable and the notorious ones. My goal is to know or at least recognize all the citizens in Quayle County. Besides, Pedro Padilla used to be on the local rodeo circuit. My wife knows him."

"Barlow, we've already driven eight miles on this goat path. How much farther do you think it is?"

"Can't be more than a mile or so or we'll be in the Rio Grande. Looks like they're fixing to stop. See the ranch house? Big barn off to the right with a security light on."

Once they stopped and everyone dismounted, Sergeant Major Wrigley and his hand walked over to Barlow and Gillespie. It was dark, but the light from the barn was bright enough to see that the complainant looked to be about 70 years of age, but he was probably older. He was roughly 5-feet, 10-inches tall, 180 pounds, and ramrod straight with gray hair cut in a burr haircut. He was dressed in a cowboy hat and jeans and a jean jacket. He had an M-1 Garand slung over his shoulder. He was wearing an OD canvas, World War II style web belt with ammo pouches around his waist.

His ranch hand was clearly Mexican. He was about 50 years

of age. He was shorter, maybe 5-feet, 8-inches, 170 pounds, muscular with a slight paunch, thick black hair, and a Pancho Villa mustache. He was dressed just like his boss, except he was wearing a full bandolier across his chest. He was carrying a Winchester .30-30.

They shook hands all around. Barlow said, "Sergeant Major Wrigley, I'm Deputy Barlow Adams. You can call me Barlow. This is my partner, Deputy Ella Mae Gillespie but she prefers to be called by her surname."

"Glad to finally meet you both. A woman without pretense. As a retired soldier, I can appreciate that. You all can dispense with the title. I retired in 1952 after 35 years in this man's Army. Call me Arn. This here is my hand, but in reality, my dearest friend, Pedro Padilla. He's been with me since I retired and bought this place.

"I called you all because illegal aliens have been crossing the border on my land now for more than a month. The first I knew of it was when I saw some trash on my land. Milk jugs, tin cans, dirty diapers, tissue paper, stuff like that. I don't tolerate a cigarette butt on my land unless its been field stripped. We picked it all up and then we began watching."

Barlow asked, "Do you own all this land from the river to Highway 90?"

"Oh, heavens no! I've got 2,400 acres, but my property ends about four miles north of here. The road to the highway crosses two other ranches. Hardly any of the land is fenced. Couldn't afford it. Sort of open range amongst the three of us. We all get along just fine. Besides that, none of us run much of a herd here anymore. You can't make any money at it. Me and my neighbors are mostly what you call cowboy hobbyists. I only run 40 head of cattle. Leonard Perkins and Elmer Jackson both run about the same as me. We're all retired from other ventures. We help each other out. You understand? We're not cattle barons like Judge Sweeney is with sheep."

"Thanks for the clarification. It helps. Mr. Perkins and Mr. Jackson have the same concerns as you?"

"I doubt it. They're not on the river like me. Nobody's been rustled so far as I know. That reminds me. Son, are you one of the deputies worked that big rustling case a year or so ago? The one that started on Judge Sweeney's Triple S?"

"Yes, Sir. I thought most folks forgot about that."

"Hardly. Me and Leonard Perkins would have loved to have been part of your posse. Slick and the Texas Rangers was in on that too, wasn't they?"

"Yes, Sir. You know Slick?"

"Oh, Hell yes! We bump into each other now and again at the American Legion. You belong?"

"I do, but I don't get by there very often. Working the midnight shift kind of hampers my social life.

"Getting back to the illegal aliens, do you know how many times they've crossed your land, or what nights, or how many there were, where they went, that sort of thing?"

"Three times for sure. It's always been on a Tuesday night so far as I can tell, but not every Tuesday night. That's why I told you to bring a long gun. There's a chance we could see 'em tonight. Let's pull your car into my barn and we'll turn out the light, if you don't mind."

Pedro pulled the Jeep up to the farmhouse. Gillespie pulled the police cruiser into the barn. Arn extinguished the light. They all stepped outside the barn and stood still waiting for their eyes to adjust to the darkness. It was deathly quiet. Nothing but crickets.

Finally Arn whispered, "Follow me down to the river. I'll take you to the shallowest part. The river can get as much as six feet deep in this area at times, but normally it's no more than two or three. Sometimes only six inches. The bank on the Mexican side is much steeper than on our side. There's one spot where the water is normally only about a foot deep. That's where we cross when we go over, except we're normally on horseback. Lagarto is only three miles south of us. That's where Pedro's extended family lives. He goes across more than I do. I've never had any trouble over there."

Barlow and Gillespie picked up their long guns and got in line. Arn lead, followed by Barlow, then Gillespie, and finally Pedro. They walked quietly single file on the west side of the corral about 200 yards to the river. Arn pointed to a cottonwood tree on the other bank. He said, "The shallow part is here to the right of this boulder. You make a beeline for that cottonwood tree on the other side. There's a half-ass (excuse my French) path from the tree to Lagarto. This is where we think they crossed. Can't say for sure but that's how we'd a done it."

Barlow asked, "Do you have a path from here to your house?"

"Nope, but they wouldn't walk anywheres near the house or the barn. We think once they crossed, they followed the river west about a 150 yards where they turned north. That's where we found the first bit of litter. It's also out of sight from me or either of my neighbors. It's an easy walk but you do gotta watch out for rattlesnakes. We definitely got a few rattlesnakes here and they can be a mite testy. They can turn a healthy human into a dead duck with just one bite. Anyway, we followed footprints and trash north all the way to 90, which is about 10 miles. Didn't see no vehicle tracks, but it's probably where a van picked them up. We didn't look that hard, but we didn't see no trash in that area north of 90 for as far as we looked and that was about a mile. Also, we're close to the Val Verde County line and Pumpville ain't but four miles north and a little east from 90 and the county line. I doubt they'd go there since less than 100 folks live there, plus it's off the beaten path, but you never know. A single stranger would stick out and a passel of illegal Mexicans would surely be noticed. If I was a coyote, I'd pick 'em up in a van just east of our driveway and go west to Dryden and then take Highway 343 north to Sheffield or someplace like that which is more'n 50 miles from the border, and thus where the Border Patrol ain't allowed to conduct warrantless searches."

"Speaking of Border Patrol, did you call them?"

"That's who I spoke to first. Wound up talking to a Captain Earnest Warfield in El Paso. He sent me an Agent Rafael Gómez who's stationed Del Rio. Nice guy. He spent half a day here checking things out. He said the coyote probably has a way station somewheres near here where he can stash a load of aliens for a few days so's they can rest up before being dropped off somewheres else. They usually have young kids with 'em and that's why."

"Are they going stake out your property?"

"Agent Gómez said they'd like to but this is a small operation, probably less than 50 aliens altogether if they've only made three or four trips, but they don't have the manpower to devote to an operation this small unless we could nail the crossings down to a specific day, like every Tuesday night. Even then, they would have to prioritize doing it because they've got operations with 100 or more crossing at the same time. He apologized and suggested calling the sheriff's office, so I did and now you're here."

"You said earlier that you think you've had three crossings. Is that right?"

"Yep. We first noticed the trash on Wednesday, December 15th. I'm positive it wasn't there the day before because we were out separating the herds. I'd a seen it. Pissed me off ('scuse me again) and we cleaned it all up. Then we saw more trash on Wednesday, December 29th. Me and Pedro staked the river out the next three nights, but nothing, so we blew it off. Then Wednesday, January 12th, more trash again, only this time it was worser. That's when I talked with my neighbors and called the Border Patrol. I was told very politely by everyone that sorry, this is my problem. If it's gonna get fixed, it'll get fixed by me. Me and Pedro was planning to sit up tonight, but then I decided to give you all a try. Can you help me out? I don't wanna kill nobody, but I will if that's my only option. I ain't ceding my property to a bunch of Mexican bandits. You understand me? I served my country and I served it well, and now I need my country's help and they say they're too dern busy! Can you believe it?"

"Arn, we're here to help tonight at least until 7 o'clock or it gets daylight, whichever comes first, or for however long it takes if we do bag somebody. I'll hafta get Sheriff Sol's permission if it becomes necessary to stake things out more than just one night. Gillespie and I are the only deputies on night shift to cover the entire county. No one's at the jail. The phone's been switched to an answering service, but they have no way to get in touch with us if someone does call. If something serious does pop up, the answering service will call and wake up the sheriff or Chief Alex. That's our situation.

"We staked out Judge Sweeney's for about two weeks, but Sheriff Sol doubled up some of the other guys so Slick and I could do it. I know Sheriff Sol will help you in any way we possibly can. Believe me, we don't want Quayle County to get the reputation that illegal aliens can cross over and stay as long as they want and do whatever they want. This is a law and order county. Sheriff Sol is a law and order kind of guy. Ditto for Judge Sweeney. I'll run all this by Sheriff Sol when we get back this morning. So let's get down to tonight's business. Where's the best place to set up?"

"Since there's four of us, I suggest me and Pedro set up where we think they're turning north. We know where there's a dead tree we can hide behind. Why don't you and Gillespie hunker down the best place you can find about 20 yards north of the crossing site? Wait until they're all on our side, if you can. We'll come a running if we hear you all talking or shots is fired. That work for you all?"

"Yep. Talk to you later."

Barlow and Gillespie decided to set up about 40 yards north

and east of the crossing site behind a roll of new wire fencing that was in front of a dip in the ground. It wasn't ideal, but it would do for tonight. He wished they'd seen this coming so they could have brought their sack lunches and a thermos full of coffee. At least he had a tin of Copenhagen in his pocket to help him stay awake. Gillespie didn't even have that, let alone a roll of toilet paper. She never uttered a disparaging remark. This girl was gonna be all right.

CHAPTER 8

The First Stakeout

Wednesday, January 26, 1972

It was 7 o'clock. Dawn was breaking. Tonight had been a bust. "Not a creature was stirring. Not even a mouse." Barlow had "been there and done that" but this was a first for Gillespie. It wasn't wasted time, though. They made two new friends tonight for themselves as well as for the sheriff's office. Arn had a serious crime problem and no one had been willing to help until tonight. Gillespie and Barlow were both happy to oblige.

Barlow thought that Sheriff Sol would go along with further stakeouts for a few days anyway, but there were bound to be trade-offs, as in only one of them participating or maybe a different team altogether. Barlow was pretty sure Gillespie would not be allowed to do it by herself. Too inexperienced. Sol might team her up with Slick like he had done with Barlow, or not at all. They'd know in a few hours.

Arn and Pedro we're walking towards them so they got up and met them. Arn said, "Sorry, you all. They didn't repeat their pattern."

Barlow replied, "Don't worry about it. Criminals have their own timetables. I'm pretty certain they'll be back. The question is when.

"We'll speak to Sheriff Sol when we get back. Someone will reach out to you today and let you know. We plan to recommend more surveillance for at least a few more days. Maybe even a week. Don't know who he will pick to do it, assuming he agrees. This wasn't wasted time for us. Don't think it was. Things didn't go that easy for us with Judge Sweeney's rustling problem.

"Nice to finally meet you all. We'll make an official report. Maybe even call the Border Patrol ourselves to see if they can break anyone loose as a favor to us. If we get our way, Gillespie and I will be back tonight. Hope to see you all then. Adiós."

"Nice meeting you all, too. Hope to see you both soon. Thanks a lot. We're much obliged. Adiós."

Barlow had Gillespie push the return trip up to code two (minus the siren) until they got to the outskirts of town where they slowed back down to just below the sound barrier. Barlow was hoping they'd arrive before Sheriff Sol or Chief Alex or Kirk arrived for day shift. He was also praying that nobody had called for assistance while they were out all night. He was pretty sure he'd be dressed down if they had missed a call.

As it turned out, they did not. Kirk strolled in five minutes after they arrived. They had already poured out the burnt pot of coffee and put on a new one. Gillespie got busy writing the incident report. They checked in the long guns and the cruiser. It was low on gas. Barlow mentioned that to Kirk so it would not become an issue.

Chief Alex arrived at 8 sharp. He was surprised Barlow and Gillespie were still there since they'd been pushed off by Kirk. Loretta Youngblood, the department's only "civilian" (who was titled as an administrative assistant) followed on his heels. Barlow was fixing to tell Chief that Gillespie and he needed to speak with Sheriff Sol when he walked in.

"Good morning, fellas and misses. Everyone have a good night?"

Barlow replied, "Hey, Sheriff. It was a very good night. Gillespie and I need to run something by you, and we think Chief Alex and everyone else should hear this, too."

"All right. Let me get a cuppa joe and I'm all ears. Anyone else want one?"

Chief Alex responded, "We're all taken care of but thanks for asking."

"Okay then, what's up?"

Barlow said, "Last night we got a call from retired Sergeant Major Arnold Wrigley. (He told us to call him Arn.) He asked us to stop by at our earliest convenience. He wouldn't say why. He said we needed to see it for ourselves.

"We got to his ranch about 1 o'clock. I'd never been there before but I knew where it was. Turns out he's about eight miles south of Highway 90 on the river.

"He told us illegal aliens had crossed his property at least three times. He knew it had happened because they always left debris on his property. Apparently he's a real stickler for any kind of trash, to include field stripping cigarette butts.

"He said he called the Border Patrol. An agent named Rafael Gómez from Del Rio stopped by. Bottom line is, the Border Patrol is stretched too thin to set up a surveillance at the Circle A unless Arn can pinpoint a specific night the aliens are supposed to cross. Even then, they might not be able to come because they're dealing with multiple bigger crossings, sometimes as many as a 100 at a time, instead of just a dozen or so. He recommended that Arn call us.

"Arn said they crossed his property the nights of December 14th, 28th, and January 11th. These are all Tuesdays. He and his ranch hand, Pedro Padilla, staked out his ranch for three nights after the first time, but nobody crossed. They figured that the crossing was a one-time deal but it wasn't. Finally after the third time, he noticed that they seemed to be crossing every other Tuesday. We staked it out with them last night but no one showed up.

"There's a chance we were spotted, because we didn't set up until 1:30 or so, plus Arn's outside light was on until after we arrived and I don't think that is normal. He seems to be a very spartan type of man. No muss. No fuss, and certainly no waste.

"Arn told the Border Patrol he thinks the three crossings collectively had about 50 aliens. Apparently the trash they left behind got worse as time passed. He and Pedro checked the trail of trash they left behind all the way north past Highway 90 for a mile before they turned around. He was surprised that they used that pedestrian route. He said if he were a coyote, he would have had a van standing by where they crossed the highway, and drive them north up Highway 343 to Sheffield or thereabouts to get past the 50-mile limit where the Border Patrol can no longer conduct searches without probable cause.

"Mr. Wrigley's problem hasn't gone away just because no one crossed last night. He wants to know if we will help him conduct additional surveillances."

Sheriff Sol asked, "Barlow, do you know if Arn spoke to anyone in the Border Patrol besides Agent Gómez?"

"Yes, Sir. He spoke with a Captain Earnest Warfield at the El Paso District Station."

"I've met him. He's this sector's administrative officer. I'll give him a call and see if he will shake anyone loose. Then Chief and I will stop by the Circle A and talk to Arn personally. He's not the kind of guy to "cry wolf".

"We will do all we can to see if we can catch the coyotes and the aliens crossing his land. If they're crossing at the Circle A, they're probably coming from Ciudad Lagarto. Doubt that's where the illegals are from, but that's probably home to the coyotes. I'll check with Slick and Arch and Chunk to see if they have any sources there."

"Sir, Arn said his ranch hand is from Lagarto. He might know someone."

"He probably does but if he gets caught sniffing around, his family will pay a steep price and there would be nothing we could do about it. However, he might be willing to direct us to someone not in his family who would talk to Slick or Chunk. We'll find out.

"Barlow, you got school tonight?"

"No, Sir. We have Wednesdays off, but anytime you need me

to work, I will. Sarah can go and take notes for both of us. Work comes first. It always has."

"I know.

"Gillespie, you have a private life, too. What are you doing?"

"Sheriff, I want to do anything I can to get more experience. I don't have a boyfriend right now and watching TV with Mrs. Beanblossom "takes second fiddle" to work. I want to be a part of this if you'll let me."

"Well, I won't parse words. Chief and I both think you're doing a great job. You're very pleasant and easy to work with, besides being a fast learner. Nobody has any complaints at all about you, but alien smuggling is a deadly serious business. Coyotes are usually armed, and they'll shoot first if it'll help them escape. I'm reluctant to put you on this surveillance simply due to your lack of experience. You've hardly even been out of POST a month yet. When I assigned Barlow to work with Slick on Judge Sweeney's rustling case, he'd been on almost a year, plus he had been in combat in Vietnam, not to mention the incident in his own neighborhood. I just don't know."

"Sir, you said it yourself. I'm a fast learner. I'll do everything I'm told to do by an experienced deputy. How can I get experience if I don't participate? Please, Sir, don't bench me. I promise to do a good job and make you proud."

"Gillespie, I'm already proud. All of us are. Your Uncle Leland calls me all the time to check on you. Bet you didn't know that. He wants you to succeed as much as you do. He's relenting some about the female deputy issue. The thing is, if you have a train wreck, there will never be a female deputy in Brewster County until after he's dead. In fact, there may not be another female deputy at all in West Texas if you "crash and burn." I'm afraid this may be too advanced for someone who's only got a month on the job."

"Sheriff, I know I can do this. I want you to believe in me."

Barlow piped in, "Excuse me, Sir. I was there when she

clocked Polecat. She did him more damage than I did with the butt stroke. What she did was instinctive. I'm sure the POST training helped, but she hadn't been on long enough for the training to be second nature. That was all Gillespie. I think she can do this if you'll let her."

"Hmmm. Let me think about this."

Sheriff Sol paused for a long, pregnant minute. Then he said, "Okay. Very well. Barlow you tipped the scales. Gillespie, you and Barlow will work the surveillance each night, including weekends if need be until this is resolved. Do not get yourself killed. Both of you. Is that clear?"

Gillespie was almost in tears she was so happy. She replied, "Yes, Sir. Thank you for giving me this opportunity."

Sheriff Sol looked Barlow, but primarily Gillespie in the eye. He said, "Listen to me. Different from the rustling case, everyone involved will continue to wear his uniform. No civvies. I'll have more information for you all when you come back to work tonight. Also, until further notice, you all are on 10 to 6. I want you set up by 11. Keep track of your overtime in your diaries and sometime down the road I'll let you cash it in. See if you can catch those sneaky bastards. Questions?"

"No, Sir."

"Good. Go home. We got work to do around here and you're making me burn daylight. And one more thing. If either of you two jaspers get yourself killed, it will seriously irk me. Understand? I swear I won't come to your funeral. I'll stay home and watch cartoons with my kids. Savvy?"

Barlow responded for both of them. He smiled and said, "Savvy." When he turned around to go, he noticed that Gillespie was almost dancing down the hallway to the backdoor.

CHAPTER 9

"It's Deja Vu All Over Again." - Yogi Berra

Wednesday, January 26, 1972

Sarah had already gone to work by the time Barlow got home. He wasn't sure how this was going to work out with her or with the school so long as he was assigned to this surveillance shift. He couldn't possibly go to school because it didn't let out until 10. They'd have to leave by 8:30 for him to get to work on time. What would be the point of going since class began at 6? Sarah would have to go by herself. No way around it. Maybe he could go with her if they had an exam, but they'd still have to leave early.

He hoped the instructors would work with him. He didn't think the surveillance would go on for very long. WTJC had been very understanding, but he was in a law enforcement program then. Maybe night school instructors were more merciful than day school instructors because everyone in night school has a full-time day job. Heck, the night school instructors probably have full-time day jobs, too! This would work out. It had to.

Barlow woke up about 5 o'clock when he felt Sarah's naked body slide between the sheets and tenderly caress him. He could smell her scent. Yummy! He planned to feign sleep to tease her but she had his number. She checked the tensile strength of his joy stick and he was busted.

"You can't fool me, Buster! You're harder than marble, hotter than molten lava, and throbbing like a migraine headache. Nobody could sleep with that much action going on. If I stuck you in your manhood with a straight pin right now you'd bleed out in less than a minute. You have 10 seconds to mount up and ride me to tomorrow and back before I expire with neglect. This better not be an 8-second rodeo ride, either, Cowboy. "Come on baby. Light my fire"."

He rolled over. "I thought you'd never ask."

The rodeo lasted until the participants were breathless and drenched in sweat. There were multiple events, each lasting well over eight seconds, the least of which was a 100 times eight seconds. They languished in the sodden sheets, too spent to get up. Finally, nearly breathless, Sarah said, "Oh my gosh. You "done good" Cowboy. Just what the doctor ordered. Now I suppose you're hoping I'll feed you if I can ever catch my breath."

"Nope."

"What?"

"I'm going to feed you. It's all planned out. I thawed out a couple of ribeyes before I went to bed. I boiled some potatoes in the skins and put them in the fridge. I'm going to cut them up and turn them into country fries. There's also a bottle of red wine in there. Your favorite - burgundy. Besides that, we'll have a wedge salad with blue cheese dressing. I'm going to grill the steaks medium rare. We've even got cherry pie left over for desert. You don't have to do a thing except get cleaned up - unless you'd rather not and continue to tease me au naturel."

"Oh my goodness! What have you done with my husband? Besides being Doctor Feelgood, you're also a cowboy chef and it's not even my birthday, although I am in my birthday suit!"

"Oh, it's me all right. This is me wishing we had more times like this together. Anymore it seems like I get less nookie than I did before we got married. What's wrong with that picture?"

"What's wrong is we're both burning the candle at both ends. Working full-time and going to night school full-time is consuming nearly all of our time and energy. In case you failed to notice, I just expended all of my left-over energy putting a smile on your face you couldn't rub off with Ajax. As soon as Gillespie sees you tonight she'll know exactly what you've been up to."

"Probably so. You've given me the perfect segue. We have an ongoing special operation similar to Judge Sweeney's rustling case. I'm gonna need your help."

"Oh really? I'm all ears. Barlow, I bet you're putting yourself in harm's way again. I know you too well. Don't sugarcoat it. Tell me straight."

"I will, but I'd prefer to tell you over dinner."

"Hmmm. Well in that case, why don't you go set the fire and get cleaned up? You cook the steaks and I'll do the rest. Otherwise, it'll be 10 o'clock before I know what's going on. Also, if you please, pop the cork on that bottle of wine and bring me a glass before you do anything else. And don't use up all the hot water! I need to clean up, too."

They had a fabulous meal on a white tablecloth with a lit taper in a cut crystal candleholder (wedding gift from Chief Alex and his wife, April) as the centerpiece. It was as romantic as anything they had ever done at home. Barlow told her everything he knew about the case. Sarah was grateful to be informed from the very beginning, rather than being kept in the dark like she had been until late into the rustling investigation. She was also pleased to hear that Barlow had finally met her rodeo friend, Pedro.

"How dangerous is this?"

"It's hard to say. I don't think as dangerous as it was at Judge Sweeney's. Sheriff Sol would never let Gillespie in on it if he thought it was."

"Barlow, Gillespie is a great deputy, but she's not on a par with Slick. I wish Slick were doing this with you."

"She's got great instincts, Sweetie. I told Sheriff Sol that I thought she was up to it. Also, Sergeant Major Wrigley will be there. He's probably got more combat time than anyone else in the entire county. Pedro Padilla seems solid enough too, although I haven't been around him long enough to say for sure. We'll be fine. Besides, the aliens wanting to live here are not fighters, though they all are probably runners. It's the coyotes who pose the greatest threat and I doubt there will be more than two. Three at the outside. Besides, we have the element of surprise. Also, it wouldn't surprise me none to find out that Sheriff Sol or Slick are "waiting in the wings" just like last time. We'll be just fine. Not my first rodeo. You know that."

"What about school?"

"That's where you come in. I don't think this will go on more than a week or two. I'll need you to talk to the professors for me. Take good notes. I can keep up with your help. One thing I've noticed so far. None of our classes have anything but a mid-term and a final, except for the two which also have a paper. This is a lot easier than classes with pop quizzes, although your grade's riding on just two exams. Not much of a chance to make up your grade if you blow the mid-term or the paper. That being said, if this assignment extends longer than two weeks, I'll ask Sheriff Sol to replace me."

"Be careful, You. Don't let anything happen to Gillespie, either."

"Always. Thanks for your support. I know this isn't easy."

"Hush. I knew what I was getting into when I married you, Mr. Adams. I knew there would be times like this. What's not easy is going to sleep knowing that your husband is out there "slaying dragons." Get on out of here! You're running late! You better hurry if you're going to get to work by 10. Don't forget your lunch. I slipped in a little treat. Don't peek, either. It's a surprise."

"You figured out a way to package pussy?"

"You're shameless. Be on your way, Mr. Adams."

"Sweet dreams, Mrs. Adams."

"Slay your dragons and come back to me in one piece - that is, if you want a piece."

"I knew it! You just can't get enough of me."

"Out! Get out! I have things to do."

Barlow arrived at the jail at 9:30. Gillespie was already there.

Tonight she had checked out Unit 81, the oldest car in their fleet, that being the 1966 Chevrolet Bel Air, four-door sedan. It had 277,000 miles on it and needed to be replaced (otherwise known as DXed). That probably would not happen until after the election for the 3-year position on the Quayle County Board of Supervisors (scheduled for June 27th), assuming Deputy Sheriff Archie Willis, retired, beat the skinflint (and current President of the Board), Mr. LaRue Dinkins.

Most folks considered that a foregone conclusion and Mr. Dinkins knew it, so he was more disagreeable than a rattlesnake with an abscessed tooth. Getting any purchase approved by the board these days was about as difficult as trying to pull said rattlesnake's abscessed tooth. Not only that, but Archie had already told Sheriff Sol that if he got elected, they would replace the Chevy and the 1968 Ford Custom sedan, and from this year forward, all the automobiles would have air conditioning. The other thing Archie promised to do was to give each Quayle County employee a five percent raise. (The last raise they had received was on July 1st, 1969, and it was only two percent.) The county was sitting on a huge ($30,000) rainy day fund in the form of three one-year certificates of deposit at Mr. Dinkins' Pecos Bank & Trust, not to mention that the property taxes were more than sufficient to cover the county's needs, leaving a modest surplus each year, so it was high time to upgrade the sheriff's fleet of vehicles and to give all the employees a well-deserved raise. Barlow was all for that. It meant Sarah would get a raise, too, since she was the event coordinator for the county rodeo grounds.

Gillespie had also checked out a Winchester .30-30 for him and a Remington 12-gauge for herself. She had a thermos full of coffee and another one full of cold water, a lunch, and toilet paper, all in her ditty bag. To say she was an "eager beaver" was an understatement. The only thing remaining for Barlow to do before getting down to business, was to jot down a few notes at

Sheriff Sol's briefing. Barlow decided he could get spoiled having a rookie this efficient.

Sheriff Sol said, "I spoke with Captain Warfield at Border Patrol. He apologized, but said they're short-handed and their budget is lean. They can't staff a surveillance at the Circle A unless the trafficking there starts bringing in a 100 aliens or more each month; however, his guys will pick up any aliens apprehended within 24 hours.

"He promised to provide me with any intelligence they pick up which might identify specific traffickers operating in the Quayle County area. Right now he has no information, but he's putting feelers out.

"He said it would be beneficial if we checked ranches and businesses for new Latino faces, especially Latinos who barely comprehend English. Check for papers. If they don't have any or if they look suspicious, apprehend them and call his office. He will send someone to verify their status, and if they're illegal the Border Patrol will take custody. We will start doing this beginning tomorrow on the regular shifts.

"Recently, in the El Paso sector, they have had an uptick of armed coyotes who will shoot if they get cornered. To date, none of them have been armed with automatic weapons, and no border patrolmen have been shot, but be alert just the same.

"If you encounter a group crossing, don't assume that any young male acting passive is a traveler. He may be a coyote trying to fool you to avoid criminal charges. If he doesn't have a gun, he most likely has a knife. If it's not on him, look around. He probably ditched it. If it has any value, he will probably come back for it.

"Understand that the travelers are afraid of the coyotes. The coyotes have already relieved them of nearly all the money they could muster to get across the border. The coyotes do not care about them. They are considered chattel. If they die, they die. There are always others willing to pay to get across. Think about that. If they don't care whether those in their charge die, they certainly don't care about you. They will kill you if it's necessary to avoid capture.

"The next thing he said was chilling. He said and I paraphrase: Perhaps the only thing worse than trafficking in drugs is trafficking in humans. These coyotes are not Greyhound bus drivers. Do bus drivers dehumanize their passengers? Of course not.

"They're not like cowboys or sheep herders, either. Cowboys and sheep herders care about their herds. Coyotes are not that benevolent to their charges.

"Coyotes are more like slave traders, except a slave has value until he's sold or dies. It doesn't work that way with a coyote. For a coyote, once the people pay him, those people no longer have value. At that point, those people become liabilities. People want to eliminate liabilities. So, if a coyote has to leave a group of illegals locked in the back of a truck in the hot sun without food or water or fresh air or toilet facilities until they perish so he can avoid capture, but not them, too bad. Sorry about that. It sucks to be someone who trusted him. Maybe he'll have better luck with the next group of travelers and they will survive.

"Finally, he said, If you forget everything else, remember this. It may save your life. Just because a person is being smuggled into the country does not mean he is an innocent. He may be a serial killer or a former Nazi concentration camp commandant trying to avoid capture by Mossad. He might be infected with small pox. He might be a Soviet spy. You just don't know. All you know is he's trying to enter our country illegally. It's not always about pursuing the Great American Dream.

"That's your crash course tonight on alien smuggling.

"Chief and I met with Mr. Wrigley. He appreciates our help. Most nights, at least initially, it will be just you two good will ambassadors out there with him and Pedro. I don't have to tell you all how to do your jobs. You already know that.

"Don't take any crazy chances. If you're forced to decide between pursuing an illegal migrant or a coyote, choose the coyote. Always. The migrant will be easier to catch later on. The coyote will try to get back across the river. Do not let that happen if you can avoid it. Remember, the coyote is an illegal alien also, but he's a higher value illegal than a fruit picker. Think a jack or a queen instead of a deuce or tres.

"If anything out of the ordinary happens, call me at home and wake me up. Otherwise, leave me a note when you get off shift. I will leave instructions for you all tomorrow night if I'm not here. I'll also pass along any intelligence that we pick up.

"That reminds me. Pedro was supposed to have gone across the river today to see if he could pick up anything helpful. Let me know what he says. I'm probably going to send Chunk or Slick or even Archie over there to see what they can find out. We seriously need to gather some intelligence. That's not for dissemination. "Loose lips sink ships." We'd have an international problem if the Mexican authorities ever snapped to that. Savvy?"

"Yes, Sir."

"Any questions?"

"No, Sir."

"Get to work. Adiós."

"Adiós."

Gillespie blew the carbon out of the carburetor as soon as they were out of town. The Chevy could still run like a scalded dog - 130 miles per hour on a straightaway. Tonight nobody was waiting at the front gate for them. She slowed down to a crawl once they entered the driveway. There were no lights on in the curtilage, but they could see Pedro waving them on into the barn. Once they collected their gear and stepped outside, Pedro pulled the barn door shut. It was deathly quiet. They noticed a saddled horse hitched to a post.

Pedro said, "Buenas noches. Mr. Wrigley said to tell you that he and I will set up on the other side of the river. We're on horseback. He's waiting for me now. We know you all are not supposed to cross, but we can. We do it all the time. It is not a problem once you know the way. There are never any policía along this section of the river. If, however, we do happen to see some, we will "beat feet" back to the Circle A. Do not worry. That has never happened.

"If the smugglers do come, once they cross the river we'll flush them north to you. We put out a couple of lawn chairs for you all where you set up last night. It should be more comfortable for you. How ever many we catch, we will hold them in the barn until you are ready to transport them to jail. Is there anything you need me to tell Mr. Wrigley before I mount up and join him?"

Barlow asked, "Did you go to Lagarto today?"

"Sí sí. I forgot to mention. There are two bad hombres who live on the south side of the village in a piece of shit house trailer. It's situated on five acres. There is a barn falling down there. The roof is caved in. Also a rusty orange tractor parked out by the road. Lots of trash in the yard. They also have five or six chihuahuas barking their asses off if anyone comes around. They are thieves. People stay away from them. They drive a black '60 Chevy pickup truck with a blue bed and a beat up white '63 Plymouth Valiant. Some say these hombres work for La Serpiente.

"Who is La Serpiente?"

"He is a killer who smuggles drugs and steals children, especially pretty girls. He has many men working for him. He is protected by la policía y los federales because he pays them off. No one can touch him."

"Where does he live?"

"He is from Ciudad Acuña but much of the time he lives in San Miguel in a big house with a wall all the way around it. Lots of guards with guns."

"Where is that?"

"It is about 15 miles south and east of Lagarto. It's a bigger town. That is where most of the people from Lagarto go when they need to shop for things they cannot buy in Lagarto."

"Are you afraid of La Serpiente?"

"Not him by himself. I am afraid of his gang. One cannot go against so many thugs and killers. He would die."

"Thanks Pedro. We'll pass this along to Sheriff Sol. Oh yeah. I forgot to ask. What are the names of the men who live in the house trailer? What do they look like?"

"The leader is Ernesto Robles. He's about my height, but mucho skinny. Maybe 35. Has a thin mustache. Wears a worn out cowboy hat, blanco, cowboy boots. Wears a long knife on his belt. Carries a revolver stolen from a man he killed. Lots of tattoos. Él es un demonio. (He is pure evil.)

"The other is called El Gordo because he is chubby. I do not know his real name. He's much taller than me and probably weighs 220 pounds. Young. Strong. Maybe 20. Baby face - no whiskers. Long curly hair like a hippy. One of his front teeth is missing. He always wears jeans and a tee shirt. Usually dirty. I don't think he has a gun but he nearly killed an old man he hit with a monkey wrench. They say he screws old women who have no husband. The younger women do not like him. He is a pig."

"Thanks again. See you when it gets light unless we catch someone tonight."

"Adiós."

After Gillespie and Barlow were ensconced in their lawn chairs, all set up and ready to catch some aliens, Gillespie whispered, "What do you think about them setting up across the river?"

"It doesn't bother me at all, although I never expected it. They know better than we do when it comes to this "neck of the woods." Not sure that Sheriff Sol would be pleased about it. They're big boys and we didn't ask them to do it. Tactically, it makes sense. No one would expect them to be there and they might keep the coyotes from escaping back into Mexico. Tell you the truth, I wish we were mounted. I thought about bringing my horse and borrowing one for you. You do ride, don't you?"

"Yeah, right, like on a merry go round at a carnival. I look like Dale Evans or Annie Oakley to you? You know what we have in Bakersfield? We have lots of cars and trucks and motorcycles. No horses. Not even one. You won't hold that against me will you?"

"No, of course not. I didn't learn to ride until I moved here, and I grew up in the Texas panhandle less than a half-mile from a working cattle ranch with real cowboys. I almost got bucked off my horse when we confronted the rustlers on Judge Sweeney's ranch. For a while after that they called me Bronco Barlow. What I think, is that learning to ride will more than likely come in handy for you sometime in the future. Sarah and I will even teach you if you're interested."

"Thanks. I'll consider it. Maybe I will. Not sure yet. I heard about that incident. I also heard you had no trouble shooting off that same horse the next time you confronted them."

"True, but I worked hard to train the horse to do that. Actually, Sarah's family did "the lion's share" of the training, but I was on Boyo's back shooting my gun when he graduated from saddle horse to being a lawman's horse."

"What do we do if they do cross tonight?"

"First, try to count how many there are. That'll come in handy later. Some could be children. We might have women carrying babies. They'll probably scatter to the four winds once Arn and Pedro jump 'em. Try to identify the coyotes. They'll probably be barking orders. Go for the adult males. You'll probably have to pick just one. I'll be doing the same thing, so don't go after the same one I'm after. Flashlight in your left hand. Shotgun in both. Make sure a round is chambered but leave your safety on until you need to shoot. Get him on his knees, fingers laced behind his head. Cuff him as soon as you can. You know the drill. Call me if you have trouble. I'll be doing the same as you. Try to remember where you see the migrants running. Arn and Pedro can run 'em down after we catch the coyotes. Be careful. They will probably be armed. Do not let anyone shoot or cut you. They get either of your guns we'll both probably wind up dead. Any questions?"

"I think that pretty well covers it. We could probably use some more help."

"No doubt about it, but don't forget, Arn and Pedro are here also, and being on a horse gives them a great tactical advantage. However, they are not trained to think as a lawman. Just pray they don't shoot someone who isn't trying to shoot or stab them. Now I wish we would have brought some additional handcuffs and leg irons. We'll bring some every night from here on out.

"One more thing. Gillespie, I know you are up for this. I'm glad Sheriff Sol put you on this assignment with me. I have faith in your judgment and ability."

"Thanks, Barlow. You have no idea just how much that means to me. Thanks for "throwing me a vouch" to Sheriff Sol. That changed his mind. If I was working for Uncle Leland and had 10 years on the job, I don't think he'd ever let me work an assignment like this."

"You know him better than I, but I think he might surprise you, especially if you had a few years experience. Nevertheless, that's why you're on Quayle SO instead of Brewster SO."

Time passed slowly and quietly. No action tonight.

They got back to the jail at 8. This time they gassed up the car. They briefed Sheriff Sol, Chief Alex, and Slick, all in person. Gillespie wrote the intelligence report. They both signed it.

Sheriff Sol thanked them. He did not oppose letting Arn and Pedro set up across the river. He said everyone was free to operate on "Big Boy Rules," meaning use your best judgment and be prepared to stand by your own decisions. The landowner and his ranch hand do not work for the sheriff's office. So long as this was their own idea and they were willing to take the risk, who was he to countermand them? He actually thought this was a pretty good idea. He said he would have more information for them tonight.

Based upon Barlow's previous experiences on surveillance, he considered this a pretty good night. You don't catch a fish every time you drop a line in the water. There were no snafus or fubars (Army acronyms for Situation Normal - All Fucked Up, or Fucked Up Beyond All Recognition). Ergo: "All's well that ends well."

CHAPTER 10

Probing for Intelligence

Thursday, January 27, 1972

Sheriff Sol needed some intelligence and he needed it sooner rather than later. He considered using Deputy Noble "Chunk" Bustamante, his only deputy of Mexican descent, to nose around Lagarto, but Chunk's personality was ill-suited for subterfuge. Chunk was an outgoing, gregarious, helpful soul. Everyone who knew him thought the world of him, but that was the problem. Chunk was a Boy Scout. He couldn't deceive a 3-year-old. Sol decided to call in a favor and bring in the heavy artillery.

Archie had only been retired for three months. He would turn 72 in a few more. He was born and reared here on the border. The only time he had been away from Quayle County for more than a week or two was during his hitch in the Army during the Great War. He spoke Mex better than a Mexican. He was an accomplished horse trainer, tougher than rhinoceros rawhide, and had been a lawman for over 46 years. His first gunfight occurred when he was only 15 years old, and that was with Mexican rustlers! Now that he was a "civilian" (although he had been sworn in as an unpaid special deputy of the sheriff's posse) he could come and go across the border without any angst. Besides that, Archie was bored and more than ready to "unofficially" lend a helping hand.

Sheriff Sol wasn't sending him alone. He was partnering him up with Deputy Clarence "Slick" Oldman, a 52-year-old native, whose daddy, Aloysius Oldman, and Archie had both graduated from Quayle School together back in the days when it was just a grammar school culminating with eight grades. They cowboyed on the same ranch until 1917, when they enlisted in the Army together during the Great War. Slick was a "chip off the old block" and enlisted in the Marine Corps during World War II. He was a veteran of the Pacific Theater. He was also a rancher, in addition to being a 25-year veteran of the sheriff's office. These were two, old school, deadly, no-nonsense, Texas ranchers and lawmen, whose bonds were stronger than twisted steel. They could take care of themselves.

Archie and Slick rendezvoused at Arnold Wrigley's Circle A. They all knew each other and spent a few minutes catching up. Arch and Slick brought their favorite mounts. Archie brought Leo, a tall sorrel stallion with a beige mane, and Slick brought Toby, a big bay stallion with three white stockings.

Since this was an undercover mission, Slick left his badge in his glovebox. However, he didn't leave his gun and neither did Archie. They both had carried a sidearm for so many years it was second nature. They would no more leave home without it than they would their boots or hat or wallet. The only difference today was that they concealed their firearms.

Both carried the same gun they had owned before they were sworn in as lawmen 20 years apart - a long-barreled Colt Peacemaker in .45 Long Colt. Slick was wearing a shoulder holster under his jean jacket, and Archie was wearing his on his hip in a cross-draw holster under a canvas farmer's coat. Both Texans were slim-built, so their firearms were adequately concealed without leaving a telltale bulge. That was important because it's illegal to possess any gun in Mexico and they both knew it. If they got rousted by any of the Mexican police, they'd have to figure it out. Bribe them if they could (since nearly all Mexican cops were corrupt), flee if they could get away clean, or have it out if they must, even if it meant leaving blood on the ground. No way they were going to a Mexican jail. That being said, neither of them expected to encounter a cop in Lagarto.

Why, you may ask? Because it was too small, too poor. There was nothing there for the cops to steal.

They had a pretty good ruse worked out. Archie brought a school photograph of his grandson, Leonard, who was in the 10th grade. They planned to ask if anyone had seen him. They would say Leonard ran away and that they heard he was hiding in Mexico. It wouldn't generate as much of an alarm as it would if they were looking for a 15-year-old female.

Before they left, Archie told Arn to send Pedro looking for them if they didn't return by sundown. That gave them plenty of time to scope out the probable coyote trailer and the two rat turds who lived there.

The weather was fair with blue skies and a slight breeze. It was a great day to mosey across the border mounted on your favorite steed, just like it had been in the days of yore. Use common sense. Rely on your wits and skill. Avoid the border checkpoints. Embrace the laid back ways of Mexico. Most of the natives were friendly. Wave at the hombres. Smile at the señoritas. Life was simpler in Old Mexico, if not more brutal. Keep an eye out for the predators, same as you would if you were in the poorer neighborhoods of the U.S. Carpe diem. "Seize the day." Channel and savor the excitement brought on by the mission.

They rode about three miles before they encountered the first dwellings. They were mostly small adobe houses with flat roofs. Most had wooden sheds. Some had carports, predominantly used for shade for cookouts or other family gatherings. The houses were close together, like an urban area would be, except it was rural. All the yards were bordered with dilapidated farm fencing. The fences didn't seem to help much in keeping the legions of barking chihuahuas penned in. It seemed like Mexico had more chihuahuas than people!

There were several adults in sight and more than a dozen children, maybe even two dozen, some riding bikes (most likely midnight acquisitions from Quayle and Val Verde Counties), while others less fortunate were scampering about on foot. Mounted gringos were a curiosity and maybe a source of charity. Young and old alike, male and female, everyone looked up to eyeball the gringos as if they were the circus rolling into town. Nearly everyone waved or uttered a greeting. It was pretty much the welcome they had expected.

Archie and Slick smiled, nodded, waved, returned greetings. They continued on into the center of the village and stopped at a corner cantina named Don Diego's. There they dismounted and tied their horses to a forlorn, withered, cottonwood tree. Slick looked around at the youth watching them and focused on a lanky one about 15 years of age who looked responsible and capable of handling himself. He motioned for the youth to come over. When he did, Slick asked, "Cómo te llamas?"

"I speak English. My name is Paco."

"Paco, my name is Slick and that's mi amigo, Archie. We want to get a bite to eat here at the cantina. I will pay you two dollars to watch our horses and make sure they're still here unmolested when we come back."

"Sí, Señor Slick, but it will cost you two dollars for each horse."

"Tell you what. I will give you three dollars to watch both horses, but I want you to water them both. I will also give you four quarters to hire some of the younger ones to fetch the water. Agreed?"

"Agreed, but you pay first."

"Paco, I don't pay for my meals up front nor I do I pay my whores up front. Payment is due when services are rendered. Tell you what. I will pay you one dollar now plus four quarters for the lads that help you. When we come back out, I will pay you two more dollars. Is that satisfactory."

"Sí. Why do you pick me señor?"

"Paco, I know an honest man when I see one. Send one of the

lads in to get me if you have any trouble. We won't be long."

"Sí, Mr. Slick."

Business complete, Archie and Slick stepped inside. The walls were thick and the ceiling was high. It was darker and cooler inside. There were six wooden tables with a variety of wooden chairs throughout the room, which also sported a bar with eight stools. A large velvet rug with a picture depicting a bullfight hung behind the bar. An attractive woman, no more than 40, stood behind it. A well-dressed man sat by himself reading the paper and nursing a cup of coffee. Probably the proprietor. Possibly named Don Diego. Maybe the husband of the barmaid. Maybe not, but he was definitely the hombre being serviced by her.

A table of four laborers were eating at another table. Arch and Slick selected a table near the entrance. Archie had his back to the wall facing the bar. Slick sat to his left so he could see the door.

The barmaid approached. She had black eyes and long, silky, raven hair. She also had a voluptuous figure and a disarming smile. Slick was in lust. Archie was satisfied just to be in the presence of such a beautiful woman once again. She said, "My name is Carlita. We don't get many cowboys here anymore. Hardly anyone rides horses today. Not enough cows I suppose. Probably all owned by the patróns. It's a puzzle because gas is so expensive. Who can afford it? Anyway, I am so happy to meet two handsome American cowboys from the past. Thank you for patronizing our humble establishment. What can I get for you?"

Slick flashed his best smile and replied, "Me and my dad here are both thirsty and hungry. My treat today. Bring us both a glass of your coldest draft beer. What's on the menu that is hot, tasty, and fast?"

"Were you referring to me, Señor? You sly devil, you! I'm getting wet. My shift ends at 6. Then I can get off. No pun intended. Will you still be around? A hard hombre is good to find."

"Señorita Carlita, you've got my undivided attention. It is unfortunate but I will not be here then. What if I came back another day? Would the offer still be good? How could it be you don't have a jealous boyfriend - a beautiful woman with all your charm? Are all the hombres blind here?"

"Señor, you have mucho charm yourself. Mi espouso is no longer living. Now I make my own decisions. I belong to no one. I think maybe you are stout like a bull with a large sack. You know? It saddens me that you will not be here tonight to show me. Is your business so urgent? I promise I will take your breath away."

"Sí, regrettably, but I pray you will give me another chance, very soon I hope. You make me hard like steel. Mi nombre es Slick. Mi amigo es Archie. We have urgent business today. Archie, would you show Carlita the picture?"

Archie pulled out the photograph and handed it to her. He said, "This is my grandson, Leonard. He's 15 years old. He disappeared yesterday. We live near Mosby. His best friend said Leonard went to Mexico, maybe to buy marijuana. I think he may have gotten involved with the wrong crowd. Have you seen him? Would you ask the others here if they have seen him?"

"Dios Santo! You must be out of your mind with worry. How big is he? Do you know what he was wearing?"

"He's about average size. I'd say 5-feet, 7-inches tall, and 130 pounds. Thin. Blond hair. Blue eyes. He dresses like everyone else his age. Blue jeans, big rodeo belt buckle, white tee shirt, jean jacket, cowboy boots, beige cowboy hat, maybe a school sweatshirt - brown with a yellow armadillo on the front. Says ARMADILLOS. You've probably seen them. Most of the kids who go to Quayle School have one."

"Sí sí. Let me go get your beers. Also, if you like we have beef tacos, frijoles, rice. I can bring you some. Also sopaipillas for desert. You want? When I come back I'll show the picture to the other hombres."

Archie smiled and replied, "Gracias. That would be great. Leave the check for my son. When he gets distracted, especially with a beautiful woman such as yourself, he gets forgetful."

The chow was great. The beers were frosty. Carlita showed Leonard's photograph to everyone present. Of course, no one had seen him. Slick paid the tab to include a hundred percent tip. They stepped outside, hoping Paco and their mounts were waiting. They were. Archie ponied up the two dollars. Before they mounted, he showed Paco Leonard's photograph and pitched the ruse. Paco said he had not seen him. He showed the picture to all the rest of the niños. It was obvious that each expected that a positive response would result in a tip. Sadly, no one had seen Leonard.

After the kids went back to their game of stickball, Archie pulled Paco aside and whispered, "Does anyone come to mind who might lead a young gringo astray? One who was in search of some weed or excitement or shelter? Someone who might take advantage of him? Someone you wouldn't want to get tangled up with?"

"You are asking a lot, Señor. A person could die by answering such a question."

Archie pulled a $10 bill which was folded into quarters discreetly out of his pocket and palmed it. He extended his hand for a shake. Paco shook hands and placed the sawbuck in his own pocket. Archie spoke up for wagging ears, hoping the pass was good enough to go by undetected. He said, "Thanks for watching our horses. If we stop by again and need a reliable person to watch after our horses, we will look you up. Gracias and adiós."

Paco replied, "Gracias." Then under his breath he said, "Go south through town. Look for an old orange tractor near a 100-year-old trailer. Be careful. The hombres who live there are killers. Maybe they grabbed him."

Slick was already mounted. Archie followed suit. They turned west to the edge of town and then south until they were well south of it. There wasn't much to see. This was barely a subsistence level community - a few scraggly cows, more goats, several burros, a couple of swayback horses, the odd cat stalking a rodent, an assortment of dilapidated 25-year-old vehicles, clucking chickens scratching for grub, dozens of ancient houses being held together with baling wire, weathered boards, duct tape, spit, and "a lick and a promise", and oh yeah, hordes of yapping chihuahuas in the yards of the occupied dwellings. The residents were slow-moving, hospitable for the most part, and curious as to why two gringo vaqueros were riding through town.

The gringos continued a mile south of town before turning east and circling around to the north. They picked up a dirt road leading back into town. Even though the description of the location of the trailer was from a northern viewpoint, it took them no time to identify it.

The lot was just like Pedro described. It was just a quarter-mile or so south of the last street in Lagarto. It probably truly was five square acres of junk, circumscribed by a rusty farm fence. The trailer was a really old one, maybe an early-'50s model, dingy white with a faded turquoise lateral stripe and patches of rust. It looked to be about 10-feet by 50-feet with rounded corners. No tires on the wheels, seated on concrete blocks. It had a small "rattler" (so called because the vibration causes it to rattle) window air conditioner. Both the black pickup with the blue bed and the white Valiant sedan were parked between the trailer and the barn, which, though the roof was beginning to cave in, was in better condition than they had expected. The barn doors were fastened wide open. It could easily hold a dozen or more pilgrims waiting for transport to The Promised Land. The orange tractor was just where Pedro and Paco had said it would be and, of course, a half-dozen junkyard chihuahuas were already fussing up a storm.

They rode around the fence and through the opening in it

where once upon a time a farm gate enclosed all the valuable belongings of this desert Shangri-la. The chihuahuas were nipping at the heels of both horses until Toby kicked one through the fence posts, scoring three points. It never got up. Probably already residing in dog heaven in the area reserved for low-wattage, pesky dogs. The type which chases cars and tries to buffalo rattlesnakes. Bottom end of the gene pool. The others gave a wide berth after that, but they never shut up.

Suddenly, the door to the trailer slammed wide open. Scowling at them, stood a 5-feet, 7-inch, 130-pound, 35-year-old Mexican with long hair, a pitiful, thin, Fu Manchu mustache, bare-chested, covered with jailhouse tattoos and what appeared to be a bullethole scar under his right nipple, barefoot, wearing greasy jeans, and a worn out, beige cowboy hat. He was holding a hunting knife with a 7-inch blade in his left hand. He yelled, "What are you two pendejos doing here on my property? Get out of here before I carve you up into dog food! Gordo, get your ass out here!"

By Pedro's description, this was most definitely Ernesto Robles.

Five seconds later, a 6-feet, 2-inch, 240-pound, 20-year-old Mexican, round face with peach fuzz, missing an upper front tooth, wearing baggy jeans, a filthy white tee-shirt, and worn out sneakers, edged around the charming, engaging homeowner, bounded down the steps, folded his arms across his chest, and faced off the gringos with a dull, but menacing look. He looked like he had gas pains.

This was obviously El Gordo.

Archie spoke softly, "Afternoon, gents. Sorry to bother you. My friend and I are looking for my grandson who's gone missing. We heard he ran off to Mexico. We're asking everyone if they've seen him. Would you all mind taking a look at his picture? His name is Leonard."

Archie held up the photograph.

El Gordo looked at it. His facial expression changed to one of sympathy. He replied, "No, Señor."

Ernesto shouted, "Shut up, Gordo! We ain't seen no gringo muchachos! Now get outta here! Gordo, Get your ass back in here!" With that, both residents ducked inside and the door slammed shut. A small, unfortunate lizard had chosen the wrong time to perch along the edge of the door. His head and front legs were facing outward, but his torso was smashed flat. Guess this is why they call this village Ciudad Lagarto. Even the lizards lead a perilous life.

Slick, who was closer to the barn than Archie, rode over and inside. He saw three wooden plank benches nailed up against the walls. He also saw an empty milk jug and a little girl's pink sweater. He turned around and joined Archie. They were back at the Circle A by 4 o'clock and the jail by 5. They reported their findings to Sheriff Sol, who thanked them profusely. Now they were pretty darn certain where the coyotes had "jumped off".

CHAPTER 11

A Busted Flush

Tuesday, February 8, 1972

They'd been hard at it for two weeks. Nada. Sheriff Sol said this would be the last night of surveillance absent some specific intelligence of a pending crossing at the Circle A, or for that matter, anywhere else in Quayle County. Barlow hoped the coyotes would cross with a group of aliens whose feet hurt too bad to run very far tonight.

Gillespie was beside herself with frustration. She wanted to make a bust in the worst way. She was fully prepared to sit out here in the dark for another month all by herself in her birthday suit if that's what it took. Normally, Barlow would have been right there with her, pleading for just a few more days. He was simpatico, except he was falling behind in school. Working seven days a week didn't leave him much time to get caught up in his studies. He was behind in the reading assignments, nor had he done the first bit of research for either of the two term papers he was assigned. All four of his instructors were cutting him some slack, but one of them voiced grave concerns to Sarah about his absence. Sarah wasn't all that happy about it herself, but as important as school was to both of them, work had to come first. She took copious notes and Barlow had copied all of them word for word in an effort to cement them in his mind. Be that as it may, Barlow was concerned, too. Ergo, he hoped tonight would be a resounding success, perhaps even more so than Gillespie, but for a different reason.

The drill was same-o, same-o. Arn and Pedro had set up on horseback across the river as soon as it got dark. They had been there for hours. Gillespie drove up the Circle A goat path sans headlights and parked in the barn. They took up their posts. Barlow filled his bottom lip with a dip of Copenhagen smokeless tobacco. He was primed and ready to go. Gillespie sipped on some hot coffee from a plastic cup with a sealed lid, praying the aroma stayed inside the cup. She didn't want to be responsible for blowing a stakeout. Neither one of them had much to say tonight. Both knew the coyotes were long overdue, but if they followed their past pattern, tonight would be the night.

About 2:45, they heard a noise from across the river which initially they could not identify. They both tensed up and stopped breathing so they could concentrate on listening. In the light of a half-moon and 10,000 stars on a crystal clear night, they saw the shadows of two motor vehicles without lights creeping from the south in single file towards the river. The second vehicle appeared to be larger than the first - possibly a Jeep or a small truck leading a van. The closer they approached, the easier it was to discern the sounds of running internal combustion engines.

The vehicles came to a halt. They were still in single file, roughly 200 yards short of the tree which marked the most shallow portion of the river. By listening as hard as they could, Barlow and Gillespie could hear the sounds of people disembarking. Hot diggity dog! Pay dirt at last! They both wondered where Arn and Pedro were hiding. Barlow hoped the horses would not begin neighing or snorting and give away their location.

The moonlight allowed them to make out a mass of bodies on foot headed towards the river. It was impossible to determine how many were coming or which ones were the coyotes, but they supposed that Arn and Pedro being closer, had figured it out.

The figures in the front of the group had just started to cross. Gillespie and Barlow were concentrating as hard as they could, trying to identify the coyotes. When the group was halfway across, Barlow whispered, "The one in the lead is a male. He's bigger than those closest to him. He's probably a coyote. You take him. I'll look for another."

"You got it."

A few minutes later, the first half-dozen intruders stepped upon dry soil in The Land of the Free and The Home of the Brave. The ones behind were hurrying just as fast as they could to catch up. No one wanted to be left behind. Then in the blink of an eye, it all turned into a soup sandwich. The tranquility of the peaceful night was shattered. Even a deaf person could hear men shouting - at least two, maybe more. Multiple shots rang out. Gillespie and Barlow could see the muzzle flashes but they couldn't pick out specific shooters. Barlow said, "Come on! Let's go, but we gotta stay on this side of the river! If you get a clear shot on someone shooting at one of us, light him up. Just make sure you're not shooting at Arn or Pedro!"

Barlow counted about a dozen shots. From the reports, he could tell that most were pistol shots. Also, the preponderance of muzzle flashes were coming from the west. He was relieved that none of the shots were fired from a fully automatic weapon. The louder reports were coming from the east. Those were fired by big bore rifles. The last time he had seen Arn, he was carrying a .30-06 caliber rifle. Pedro was carrying a .30-30. Therefore, Barlow deduced that the good guys were to his east and the bad guys were straight ahead or to the west.

By now, the illegals were screaming in terror, running hither and thither in every direction except north! Definitely not north! They were hoofing it back into Mexico like a gang of spooked turkeys, even though that's were the gunfight was ongoing! The illogic was primeval, not to mention suicidal, just like moths flying too close to a flame.

Barlow lost track of Gillespie once they arrived at the river until after the last shot was fired. He was feverishly seeking a hostile shooter in an effort to take pressure off Arn and Pedro. Because Gillespie had a shotgun instead of a rifle, she was unfortunately rendered beyond the range to swap lead with the coyotes so long as they remained in Mexico. Barlow had the .30-30, but even so, he was at maximum effective range, especially in the dark. Hard to see his sights.

The gunfight lasted for one mad minute, perhaps a little more. During the fury, Barlow clearly heard a single yelp from his southwest, so he figured the good guys probably scored a hit. The only safe thing Barlow could think of to do to help out Arn and Pedro was to send some rounds down range into the nearest vehicle. He shot five times. Besides hearing the impact of his bullets against steel, he heard a loud, steamy hissing sound, like that of an overheated radiator. Hopefully, he had disabled the lead vehicle.

Too bad for the bad guys. Assuming he did disable the vehicle, someone would have to walk. In the heat of that moment, Barlow was elated.

Suddenly the coyotes realized they were taking incoming from three different shooters. The result was they abruptly shifted gears, deciding to disengage and flee back to their safe havens, as far away as they could get from the pissed off gringos. At the same time, the pilgrims were beginning to arrive back onto the south bank, but no matter. "Tough titty said the kitty when the milk ran dry." The bigger vehicle backed up, turned around, and lit out as if the driver had an urgent case of diarrhea, and thus, skedaddled in search of a commode. Adiós pendejos!

Barlow and Gillespie waited in frustrated silence, each absorbed in his own thoughts, willing Arn and Pedro to beat feet back to the Circle A. Now that the bust was blown and concealment no longer mattered, Barlow fired up a maduro Punch robusto and savored its flavor.

It took the better part of an hour for Arn and Pedro to tidy up. They were disgusted and in no hurry.

Barlow was concerned that the smugglers might return with reinforcements. His worries were for naught. He wondered what would become of the pilgrims. Were they just screwed? Paid their money and left swinging in the breeze? Not his problem, but it was still a concern to him. They should be entitled to a full refund.

Gillespie wondered, "What now?" She wondered if the coyotes would take their charges across elsewhere. Would they come back looking for revenge? What would Sheriff Sol decide? She never saw the face of even a single coyote! One could walk right past her at the grocery store and she would never even know it. She had stood by like an astonished gawker, watching a gunfight unfold, helpless to assist, let alone to vanquish a villain. How long would it be before she got another chance to "play ball with the big boys?" This was like having sex which never culminated in a climax! To call tonight a disappointment would be a gross understatement!

It seemed like a week had passed, but finally they could see and hear Arn and Pedro crossing the river. They met at the river bank. Arn said, "Let's go to the barn. We can talk there while we groom the horses."

Barlow asked, "Are you all okay?"

Arn replied, "We're fucking peachy."

Gillespie was on pins and needles, but she willed herself to "button her lip" until it was her turn to talk.

Finally, Arn said, "I'm a little embarrassed. We know how to use cover and concealment. We crossed over around 8:30. We hobbled our mounts about 100 yards east of the tree marking the shallow water crossing, behind some scrub thicket. Then we walked back about 50 yards south of the crossing and 50 yards west of the horses. We've got on dark clothing with no shiny buckles or rings. No aftershave. In other words, we are in-fucking-visible. We spread our bedrolls in a little dip behind some creosote bushes after we checked the area real good for creatures that slither and go bite in the night. Then we waited. No coffee. No smokes. No chitchat.

"You all done good, by the way. We never heard nor saw you

all set up. Finally, we heard the two trucks. The first one was Ernesto Robles' raggedy-ass truck with the blue bed. The second one was about the size of a deuce-and-a-half, but with a box bed like an old, double-axle U-Haul truck. We watched them stop and unload. If I'm not mistaken, we counted 21 people. Pretty sure Robles was driving his truck. I think El Gordo was driving the U-Haul. Besides them, there were two other fellas we think was coyotes.

"El Gordo, if it was him, same Pillsbury doughboy profile anyway, was herding the wetbacks. We're pretty sure he was the first one in the river. Everything was going just as "slick as snot on a doorknob." Then it wasn't. One of the coyotes lit up a smoke. It wasn't the one I think was Robles. Robles was talking to the fourth coyote. No idea what they was saying. They was standing on the east side of Robles' truck. Then Robles and the fucker he was talking to pulled sidearms and started slingin' lead in our general direction. "As sure as God made little green apples" I got no idea what brought that on. I think Robles emptied a revolver at us. The other turd fired three or four rounds. Sounded like an Army Colt to me - a semi-automatic. I know what it sounds like. I got one back at the house.

"Took us completely by surprise. We was prone. Nothin' for 'em to see. Don't have a clue how the fuck they made us. None of those shots even come close. Pissed us off, so we returned fire. I shot four rounds and Pedro fired two. I heard the first shooter scream, and I know I hit him. Of course, now our muzzle flashes gave 'em a better target to return fire. Robles either reloaded or he had a second gun, because we traded shots again. These shots was much closer. Barlow, was that you who fired five rounds from over here?"

"It was. I had the .30-30. Gillespie had the shotgun. She was out of range and I was at my range limits, especially in the dark. I couldn't see a shooter clearly, so I decided to poke holes where I thought the engine of the first vehicle would be. I'm guessing it was at least 120 yards from where we were."

"Righto. It was every bit of 120 yards. Probably more like 130. Heck, the river's about 85 yards across from here. Then they were up at least 40 yards from that. Add in your distance to the bank. Me and Pedro appreciate the assist. The wets was scattering like chickens fleeing from the chickenhawks. We lost track of the fourth coyote. El Gordo was probably armed. What you done was to scare 'em off. Since the gig was blown anyway, it was the best thing you coulda done for us.

"By the way, you had a group like this (holding his thumbs and forefingers in a circle with a half-inch gap, indicating a five-inch grouping.) You done mortally wounded his truck. I decided to give it the coup de grâce, so I punctured all four tires and cut his spark plug wires, plus I took the cap off his alternator and give it a throw back towards Ciudad Acuña. He'll hafta tow his truck and it'll cost him at least 50 bucks to buy some used tires, spark plug wires, and a used alternator cap from a junkyard."

"What about the dude you shot?"

"We found a fair amount of blood. Robles and the other coyote helped him to the cargo truck. He was alive when they skedaddled. Not sure where I hit him, but that M-1 fires a powerful cartridge. Anything more'n a flesh wound without medical attention would probably be fatal."

"You worried about the Mexican authorities?"

"Are you?"

"Not unless Sheriff Sol says I should be."

"Barlow, think about it. You really think the coyotes will go to the Federales and say, "Capitán, we was smuggling some wets across the border. Then we saw some men hiding in the weeds on our side. We thought they meant us harm so we started blasting away at 'em. One of 'em shot back and hit mi amigo. Would you go arrest whoever shot him"?"

Gillespie finally piped in. "Arn, aren't you afraid they will retaliate?"

He replied, "Sweetie, they got no idea who they was shooting at. The firefight was initiated by them on their side of the river at unknown persons. They got no reason to think I was involved. Heck, it could have been a rival gang!"

Barlow replied, "That's true, except they broke it off after I fired from your ranch. That ties you in."

Pedro responded, "Jefe, the coyotes work for La Serpiente. He has no rival gangs. Those who opposed him are all dead, including some Mexican officials. You can be sure they will come here. Who else would shoot from your land? He will certainly come here for answers or revenge. You do not want to be interrogated by his men. If he finds out who I am, mi familia will be in peril. We must be prepared."

"Dern. You're right. Does Robles know you work here?"

"No. We do not know each other. We know of each other by passing by one another in town one time. We were on foot. He is not from Lagarto. He's only been there a year or maybe a little less, but El Gordo is a local. He knows mi familia by sight. I do not think he knows our relationship, but he might. He does not know I work here. All he knows is that I'm a rodeo man, or at least I used to be. Plus he es estúpido. Right now I think they are safe, but when I go back to visit, I will have to be very careful not to be seen by him or Ernesto in the presence of them."

Barlow asked, "Arn, how do you want to handle this? I doubt Sheriff Sol will allow us to continue the surveillance absent some new intelligence. If you think La Serpiente will retaliate, he might give us a few more days. Problem is, if the retaliation doesn't happen soon, I know he will call us off. After what happened tonight, I'd be surprised if they used this route anytime soon, to smuggle aliens anyway. Do you?"

"Probably not. What do you think, Pedro?"

"Well, I don't think they'll use this route for a month or so. They'll want to let it cool off. You can bet when they do decide to return, it won't be on a Tuesday, either. I doubt they'd give up on it altogether though, if for no other reason than the Border Patrol isn't active here. Also, if they do decide to retaliate, it could burn this route for good."

Arn replied, "Tell Sheriff Sol everything that happened tonight. Right now, we feel pretty secure, but we'll get our chores done by noon everyday so we can set up on watch for the next couple of weeks, anyway. I got a Remington Government Model 1911, .45 caliber pistol and two spare magazines that I liberated off of a dead Army captain on a battlefield in France during the Great War. The Army wasn't looking for it, so I kept it. I carried it in Korea, too. They issued me a different one during World War II, which they took back. I've seldom carried it except during the wars, but from here on out, where I go, it goes. If you all get any intel, please let me know. I will do the same for you. Thanks for everything. You all were here for me when the United States Government was not. Shame on them. I will not forget your assistance. I'm only sorry that they spooked before we could round 'em up. C'est la vie. Good day."

Gillespie spoke up. "Hey, you all. Is it okay if I check on you once in awhile?"

Arn replied, "Of course it is, Sweetie, but the mornings would be better for us than the afternoons. That's when we'll most likely be sleeping."

"You got it. See ya around."

Gillespie and Barlow refueled the cruiser on the way back to the office. Barlow cleaned the .30-30. Gillespie wrote the intelligence report. They briefed Sheriff Sol. He was extremely concerned. He said, "Good work both of you, and kudos for staying on our side of the river. I know how hard it was for each of you. It was all I could do, not to cross the river during our shootout at Judge Sweeney's, and it's my responsibility as sheriff to set the example.

"Barlow, I understand why you shot the truck, and how it may have saved Arn and Pedro from a disaster. At the same time, you may have inadvertently put them in harm's way vis-á-vis revenge from La Serpiente or his thugs. I'll stop by and see him this morning. We don't want anything to happen to them. I'll see if there's anything we can do. In the meantime, you both revert back to your regular work schedule.

"Oh, yeah. I'm giving you both Friday and Saturday off this week. (Nobody worked on Sunday except during unusual circumstances.) Unless we have a crisis before then, you all get a three-day weekend. You've earned it. Now get out of here so the rest of us can get some work done. We're burning daylight."

CHAPTER 12

Time Passes Slowly for a While

Wednesday, March 15, 1972

It had been more than a month, in fact, nearly two months since the first stakeout at the Circle A. The coyotes had not been back since the shootout. Life had returned to a slow, dull normal for Barlow and Gillespie on the midnight shift. They were both bored stiff, but in Barlow's case, he needed the hiatus to get up to speed on his school work. The semester was half over. The last day was May 12th. For a change, he was all caught up. Both term papers were written but not submitted, and right now he had two As and two Bs. Sarah was three and one. They were considering taking a class or two during the summer term, but maybe not. This term had been a hard push. Fortunately, they still had plenty of time to decide.

Gillespie had her mind on other matters. She wanted more time on the street. Permanent midnight shift in Quayle County was painfully slow. They didn't get enough calls. She was craving action. At the same time, she would slit her wrists and bleed out in the bathtub before complaining. Suppress all negativity. She was well aware that there wasn't another county in Texas with a female deputy on the road. She was blessed to be here. She prayed for patience.

Gillespie was doing something a little on the sly that neither Sheriff Sol nor Barlow were fully aware of. Two or three days a week she made a beeline to the Circle A in civilian attire in her own car just as soon as she was relieved from her shift. Sheriff Sol and Barlow both knew Arn said he would welcome anyone from the SO, especially if they dropped by before noon, but no one knew Gillespie was checking this frequently. The extent to which she did could have been construed as unpaid overtime. Gillespie documented the visits in her work diary as per SO policy, but neither the chief nor the sheriff had spot checked hers as often as they had checked Barlow's when he was the rookie. This was a potentially serious oversight.

Initially, all she did was stop by to make sure everything was okay. It was. Neither threats nor illegal crossings had occurred at the Circle A since February 9th. Arn had not called the SO to report a negative, so "out of sight, out of mind" was the logical result. Everyone "on the job" except for Gillespie had moved on to other issues.

That being said, Arn and Pedro enjoyed Gillespie's company. She was always upbeat and they both lacked female companionship. Gillespie was "a breath of fresh air." It was a real treat for them to spend time with her. It wasn't long before she coaxed Arn into driving her in his Jeep (instead of his preference of going by horseback) all over the thousands of acres on those three hobby ranches, searching for trash left behind by the illegals. They even searched the north side of Highway 90, slipping across the county line into Pumpville. Gillespie enjoyed the reconnaissance, but there had been nothing to find. It was as if the alien smuggling and the shootout had never occurred.

Tonight, Barlow and Gillespie were both immersed in their own endeavors. Barlow was reading ahead on his American Federalism course, and Gillespie was reading a funny, but somewhat distressing novel by John Nichols titled, *The Milagro Beanfield War*. The book was about water rights in Northern New Mexico, and how the corrupt state government was disenfranchising the working poor in order to provide an abundance of water to wealthy land developers. It had a similar ring to the true life situation in Nevada, where the ranchers had lost water rights in favor of the casinos in Las Vegas.

Ring! Ring! Ring! Barlow and Gillespie both jumped. It was

0406 hours.

"Quayle County Sheriff's Office. Deputy Adams speaking. How may I help you?"

"Deputy Adams. This is Pedro Padilla."

"Good morning, Pedro. Good to hear from you, but this must be really important if you're calling at this hour. What can I do for you?"

"Sir, about 30 minutes ago, we heard a loud boom and several shots fired. Señor Wrigley and I were watching the river from where you and Deputy Gillespie watched. It came from the highway. Señor Wrigley and I got in his Jeep and rode out there. Remember where we said we thought the coyotes were picking up aliens just east of our ranch?"

"I do."

"That's where the accident happened. It looks like a cargo truck was making a U-turn on the highway to go back west. A pickup truck was also going west. It must have been going very fast. It smashed into the back of cargo truck. We do not think the cargo truck was running with lights because the headlights switch was turned off. There are two dead people in the back of the cargo truck. One is a young woman and one is a child. There is a lot of sacks with belongings still in the truck and some scattered on the road.

"Señor, we are positive it was not the same cargo truck we saw that night a few weeks ago. This one is too big and it has three double-axles instead of two. The driver of the pickup was injured badly, but that is not what killed him. He was shot many times. Maybe four. There are no live people at the crash. Señor Wrigley is standing by at the highway waiting for you to come. Can you come muy rápido?"

"We're on our way!"

"Gracias."

"Gillespie, check us out a car. Grab a shotgun and a rifle. Get extra handcuffs and some leg irons and anything else you think we might need. We're headed out to the Circle A. Take your lunch and some water. We may be out there for a long time. I'll brief you in the car. Hurry! I gotta call the sheriff before we leave."

"On it!"

Barlow called the sheriff. He answered on the fifth ring. "Hello." It sounded like he was rubbing the sleep out of his eyes and trying to get his bearings.

"Sheriff, this is Barlow. Got a call from the Circle A. There's been a fatal accident on 90 just east of the ranch. Arnold Wrigley is standing by. One vehicle is a cargo truck, but not the same one that was bringing aliens to the river in February. This truck is much bigger with three rear double-axles. It was rear-ended by a pickup. Two dead illegals are in the back of the cargo truck. One was a child. The driver of the pickup was shot dead. No live participants at the scene. Gillespie and I are fixing to head out."

"Barlow, did it sound like the coyotes shot the pickup driver, and are you saying the coyotes and the surviving aliens are now in the wind?"

"Don't know for certain. I got the call from Pedro and he was all wigged out, but that's my read on it."

"Okay. Look at the schedule and see who's working the afternoon shift today."

"Let's see. Ernie Atwater and Dewey Carruthers."

"Okay. I'll call Chief to alert the others. The only ones I'm not sending are Chunk and Atwater. Since Chunk's on days, he'll replace you all on the desk. Atwater will relieve Chunk for the afternoon shift. Most of the guys will have to take their own cars to the scene. I'll be there as fast as I can. Help will trickle in. We're initiating a crime scene investigation, plus a search for the shooters as well as the illegals all at the same time. We may have to call out the posse. In fact, I think I will call out the more reliable ones. Roll up your sleeves. Everyone's going to be working some long hours today. Right now you and Gillespie are on crime scene duty. Do not go off searching for anybody. Savvy?"

"Savvy."

"See you soon."

Barlow switched the phones, grabbed his gear, locked up, and bounded out the door. Gillespie was waiting for him in their newest cruiser, a '71 Plymouth Fury with the 375 horsepower engine. She was primed to go. She had overheard enough of Barlow's call from Pedro to have a pretty good idea as to what was going on. She took off like a "bolt of lightning." Barlow nearly suffered a whiplash. Before the four-lane hardtop diminished down to two, she was running 138 miles per hour. It was every bit as much as she could eke out of this Detroit muscle car. It was more than enough. This girl could drive! Barlow never uttered a word until they got close to the Circle A, where she slowed down to a sedate 90. He didn't want to interfere with Gillespie's concentration while they were trying to set a new land speed record.

Arn had parked on the westbound shoulder of the road with his lights on. He was standing in front of the cargo truck waving a flashlight. It was stopped in the middle of the highway, front end facing southwest. Most of the eastbound lane was blocked. Gillespie parked in the middle of the highway with her flashers and the overhead oscillating "bubblegum machine" lighting up the darkness.

Barlow and Gillespie disembarked and walked over to speak to Arn. When they did, they noticed Pedro, who was standing with a flashlight on the east side of the wreck. Barlow whispered to Gillespie to take careful notes of everything she saw at the accident scene. It might be important. They would compare notes later. She nodded her head.

So far, so good. In Quayle County during this time of day, about the only living things out and about were deer, opossums, and predatory cats; however, dawn was fast approaching. The gawkers and news media hadn't heard about this yet but they would, soon after the first passerby arrived and had to wait until he was directed around the carnage and gore.

The accident was a bad one. The front end of the white, 1970, three-quarter ton, Chevrolet pickup truck was smashed about 3-1/2 feet up into the firewall and the cab. The front half of the engine compartment was buried underneath the bed of the cargo truck.

The pickup driver was a white male, approximately 35 years of age, lanky build, shaggy brown hair, lamb chop whiskers, wearing jeans, a red, western cut dress shirt with mother of pearl buttons, and from what they could see, well-polished Tony Lamas. His cream-colored Stetson looked like it had hardly been worn. It was upside down on the passenger side floorboard next to a cracked pint bottle of Heaven Hill which had leaked all over everything, including the crown of his hat. Actually, the aroma of bourbon was a blessing. It helped mask the odor caused by his bladder and bowels releasing their contents. He was wearing his seatbelt, but his forehead had hit the steering wheel anyway. His head was resting against the seat back. His chest was a bloody mess. It certainly looked like he had four bullet holes in the vicinity of his heart. What a way to die!

It was difficult for Barlow and Gillespie to climb into the bed of the cargo truck the way the pickup was wedged underneath it. The adult victim, a Latino female, approximately 20 years of age, wearing a print cotton dress and a light sweater, was piled up in a heap in the front of the box. The angle of her neck made it obvious that she suffered from a broken neck. The child, a little girl about four, was lying next to her. They couldn't see any external injuries on the child, so they had no idea what caused her death. They counted 12 pieces of luggage, to include bags, pillowcases, and cheap suitcases still inside the truck. When they climbed out of the truck, they counted three more bags on the blacktop.

Barlow whispered to Gillespie, "You take the rear with Pedro. I'll take the front with Arn. Sheriff Sol should be here any minute.

We could begin taking photographs, but I'm sure he'll want Chief to handle all the forensics. You can bet he'll initiate a manhunt. I hope he'll put us on that. Talk to you later."

Gillespie whispered back, "Barlow, this is embarrassing. Promise me you won't tell."

"What?"

"I was in such a big hurry, I forgot to go pee. I'm about to wet myself."

"Okay. Walk about 50 feet east and pick one side or the other. It doesn't matter which. In exigent circumstances, distance counts as modesty. Go about 10 feet off the road, but watch out for snakes. Don't get next to any bushes. That's where they sleep. I'll keep Pedro occupied until you get back so it won't be so obvious."

"Thanks. I owe you."

When she returned, Barlow said, "Before we go on traffic duty, let's take a peek inside the cab of the cargo truck."

They did. Apparently neither the driver nor the passenger had been wearing seatbelts. In fact, this truck didn't have any that they could see. It was too old. Also, sure enough, the headlights switch was not pulled out. There were two starbursts in the glass where the occupants did a face plant. The one on the passenger side was worse. There appeared to be blood on the dashboard and the floor on that side. Now they knew at least one coyote was substantially injured. The other thing they noticed was that there was nary a license plate anywhere in or on this circa 1950s Diamond T truck. Have to check the ownership by the VIN, which they both recorded in their pocket notebooks from a metal plate riveted on the driver's side door post.

Barlow whispered to her, "I'd really like to start searching for the path they took from here, but Sheriff Sol told me that we have to stay put. When you go back to your post, shine your light along both sides of the roadway to see if you can find it. I'll do the same on my side. For goodness sakes, do not get off the roadway or step on a blood splatter. You can bet the sheriff will get Slick and Archie and maybe some other guys on the posse who are well-known trackers out here to do that. If we mess up the trail, neither one of us will ever get off the midnight shift or jail duty. Savvy?"

"Savvy."

Now they waited impatiently for Sheriff Sol. This was the biggest law enforcement event Gillespie had ever been on, and the first for Barlow in the better part of a year.

CHAPTER 13

Crisis Management & Manhunt for a Killer

Wednesday, March 15, 1972

Dawn was breaking when Sheriff Sol made his appearance. He was a marvel - shaved, neatly attired in a crisp uniform, looking well-rested. One could say as cool as an autumn breeze in Chicago. He greeted the four of them warmly like this was a church social. He didn't appear to be rushed or frazzled at all. He started with Arn and had each of them walk through the crime scene with him one at a time and point out their own observations. When they were done, he relieved Arn and Pedro so they could do what they needed to do to join the posse. Barlow and Gillespie remained on traffic duty pending further instructions.

The second one to show was Slick. He was towing a horse trailer. Barlow prayed that Slick brought a second mount for him. Archie was third. He was the first special deputy in the posse to arrive. He, too, was towing a horse trailer. One by one all the deputies except for Chunk and Atwater, who had other assignments, made their appearances.

At least a dozen members of the posse, all towing horse trailers trickled in. Barlow cracked a smile a mile wide when Arthur and Cordell both showed up towing trailers. Surely one of them brought Boyo for him! All the mounted deputies were directed to go to the Circle A and await further instructions. They were gathered near the corral, "smoking and joking," standing by for the sheriff's briefing before setting out to catch a killer. It was a tight-knit group of well-armed, determined, patriotic neighbors and citizens.

Barlow was more than happy when Chief Alex finally arrived. He was the last one to make an appearance. Heck! Pete Ricketts even beat him here. Pete was waiting in the ambulance for permission to remove the bodies and take them to the mortuary. Ditto for Buck Boyd with the wrecker. Both wrecked vehicles were obstructing the roadway and needed to be towed. So far, nary a passerby had pulled up, so this had not become a problem yet.

Chief was in charge of the accident/crime scene, something which was of less interest to Barlow than hunting killers or illegal aliens. Chief was an old hand at this and extremely methodical, so both Pete and Buck had learned to be patient. They were sitting in their vehicles, sipping coffee out of their thermoses and listening to country and western music on their "good times radios." Nevertheless, Sheriff Sol was always concerned about gawkers and the untrustworthy press, not to mention that the roadway needed to be cleared for motorists, all of which meant that Chief Alex wouldn't be "dragging his heels."

Sheriff Sol had thought of everything. He considered the accident/crime scene a learning experience for the new rookie, so Gillespie was assigned to assist Chief Alex. She seemed both pleased and excited. Barlow could tell because she was beaming so much she put the moon to shame.

Finally, Sheriff Sol passed out assignments when every regular deputy who was supposed to be there had arrived. Of course, Gillespie already had hers.

He said, "Listen up. I'll try to make this brief. You all know we're looking for two coyotes, perhaps more, at least one of which is a murderer. Without a doubt, that one has a gun. One probably has cuts on his face from slamming into the windshield. Another one might, too. We don't have any descriptions, but I'm sure you all will identify them as not being Quayle County residents if you see them. It goes without saying, but I'll say it anyway. Consider them armed and dangerous. In addition, we probably have 15 or more aliens on the loose. They should be easier to locate. All of these folks are on foot, including the coyotes, unless they stole a vehicle since the accident, which occurred at approximately 4 this morning.

"These are the assignments. Some of you will need to swap cars. Just make sure that all the POVs wind up parked in the jail lot so you'll all have a ride home when you get off work.

"Chief and Gillespie are working the crime scene. Gillespie, if you all aren't done by 4 o'clock, knock off anyway so you can get some sleep before your shift tonight.

"Dewey, you're on patrol on the west side of the county. That means you stay centrally located so you can respond to the east side if needed, but you will be responsible for all calls on the west side.

"Kirk, you have the east side. Both you and Dewey will work traffic at the accident scene until Chief has finished. Then you all can get on patrol.

"Randy, you're on patrol, too, but I want you near the river. When we break up, drive down to the Circle A and ask Arn or Pedro where they think the group crossed last night. I'm pretty sure it was somewhere east of the Circle A. That's the general area where I want you just in case the coyotes or even some of the others try to sneak back across.

"Barlow, you hitch a ride with me. You're on the mounted posse. If they're not done by 4, I want you to break off just like Gillespie.

"Chunk's on the desk now. Ernie's got the desk on afternoons.

"All prisoners captured by the mounted posse will be transported to the Circle A for transport to the jail by one of our motorized units.

"All overtime for today has been authorized. Hopefully, we will be successful and it won't be necessary to repeat this exercise tomorrow. Any questions?"

No one spoke up.

"All right. Let's get to it. Be careful, fellas. Everyone goes home unharmed tonight."

It was almost 6:30. The deputies took up their assigned tasks. Barlow grabbed his gear and rode with the sheriff down to the Circle A. On the way, he said, "Barlow, I'm assigning you with the group that includes Slick, Arthur, Cordell, and Lane Barnes, commander of the American Legion Post. I'm sure you and Lane have met. Slick will be in charge. I've divided the southeast section of the county into four sectors. You will be in the sector which is the farthest east. I want you all to cross over into Val Verde County and check the area around Pumpville. Soon as I can, I'll call Sheriff Ambrose over there and let him know what's going on. I don't expect any heartburn from Alfred, but if he "gets his panties in a wad" and sends some deputies to run interference, let Slick handle it. Savvy?"

"Savvy."

"Also, unless you all are slinging lead, I want you headed home by 4 at the latest. Arthur said he would take you even if the others need to stay behind. Copy?"

"Copy. Sheriff, thanks for putting me on this assignment. I'll do you proud."

"I know you will. You always do."

The posse was already mounted when they arrived. Barlow counted 18. Arthur was holding the reins to Boyo. Barlow noticed that he had remembered to include a rifle scabbard, along with saddlebags, a lariat, and a two-quart canteen. After Barlow mounted, Cordell handed him a small paper bag containing three sticks of beef jerky and two Tootsie Rolls. Boy, his in-laws really looked out for him!

Sheriff Sol and Arn finished their confabulation. Then the sheriff walked over and greeted each rider by name and shook everyone's hand. He asked about their wives and kids. Then he addressed the posse.

"Thanks, fellas, for coming out so early this morning. We

really appreciate it. I truly consider this an emergency.

"I know you all were briefed by Archie as to who we're looking for and why. We can't ignore what these outlaws have done, and we sure as Hell can't let them shit in our sandbox and go home unmolested; however, we prefer prisoners over corpses. "If you shoot 'em, you clean 'em"."

Everyone got a chuckle ever that, especially the hunters.

"Just kidding. Don't kill 'em if you don't have to, but don't let 'em kill any of you, either. You all know if we arrest 'em, Judge Sweeney will max 'em out for the rest of their miserable lives at hard labor, busting big rocks into little rocks with all the other incorrigibles serving time at Huntsville. If you must shoot, shoot to kill.

"So far as we know, all the illegals, probably fifteen or so pilgrims plus two or three coyotes, are on foot. That's why we assigned a skilled tracker with each group. FYI - our office is on high alert for calls regarding stolen motor vehicles. We have three marked units available to respond, but unfortunately we have no way to communicate any of that to the posses.

"All four sectors begin at the Rio Grande and go north roughly 10 to 12 miles, ending at County Road 14. The sectors are four to six miles wide. We don't see how they could have walked farther than this area covers, even by the time you all get to your farthest boundaries. Remember, some of the pilgrims are women and children. Some are probably old. That will slow some of them down.

"The eastern limit is Val Verde County, with one minor exception. Slick's team knows what to do there. That sector goes west to the Old McCreary Ranch Road.

"The eastern middle sector begins at McCreary and goes west to the dry arroyo we used to call Devil's Gulch. Smitty, that's your responsibility.

"The western middle sector begins at Devil's Gulch and goes west to the road sign shows "Mosby 25 miles." Gabe, that's yours.

"The western sector goes from the road sign and goes west to about a half-mile west of Dryden at Highway 349. Morris, you have that sector. I say about a half-mile west, because you all need to check every single building anywhere near 349. Plus, that's the most populated sector of the four.

"Obviously, we don't have commo, so use your own judgment as to when it's time to turn around and come back in. I'll be right here next to the phone so I can coordinate with my office. If you're someplace where you can get to a phone, try calling here first. If you don't know Arn's number already, it's 921-5419. If I don't answer, call the SO. I'll have my car radio on speaker, so they'll try that if I don't answer the phone or the line's busy. Bring any prisoners here, unless you get lucky and a marked unit is nearby. All three of our marked units are on patrol on this side of the county today. Their job is to assist you all in any way they can.

"That's it. Hang back if you have any questions. Otherwise, good luck."

Before they headed out, Slick told his group, "Arn doesn't know where the wets crossed, but he knows they didn't cross here where the river's the shallowest. We'll begin here and go east looking for tracks or debris. Spread out so we can cover more ground. We'll turn north when we think we've crossed the county line by a couple hundred yards or so. Remember, criminals ain't got no boundaries. If we get caught trespassing in Val Verde, it's easier "to ask for forgiveness than for permission"."

They rode along slowly, searching for any signs of recent pedestrian traffic until they were certain they were in Val Verde County. The landmark which helped them most was Big Canyon Creek, which was shallow and studded with boulders. It ran north from the Rio Grande about two miles west of the Val Verde County line. Eventually the creek veered west before petering out somewhere in Pecos County. Today the current was unusually swift due to recent rains, but by May this creek would be down to a trickle or even bone dry. They continued east from the creek about three miles, not stopping until the terrain and the elevation changed. The land transitioned from flat and sandy to rocky with steep bluffs on each side of the river. Anyone crossing here would need to climb the cliffs. They turned north, veering a little west, still maintaining about a 100 yards between each rider.

They saw no signs of foot traffic all the way north to Highway 90. They were surprised. A couple of miles north of Highway 90, they crossed back into Val Verde County to check out the settlement at Pumpville. They still hadn't seen any recent tracks or debris. They received several curious glances in Pumpville, but nothing out of the ordinary. Slick spoke in Mexican with a Mexican male about 60 years of age who was tending to his garden. He was friendly. He did not appear alarmed. Slick said they were looking for two strangers, young Mexican males, men who shot and killed a motorist driving on Highway 90 last night. Also for a group of women and children fleeing from Mexico. The man responded that he had not seen nor heard about any such men, nor female border crossers last night or this morning. He would know if they came through here unless they came while he was drinking coffee and listening to the news from Del Rio on the radio. If they came by then he might not have seen them. Slick thanked him and stuffed a dollar in the old guy's pocket. They turned northwest back into Quayle County.

They crossed Big Canyon Creek, continuing north on the west side of it. They came upon an old one-lane road, a dirt path really, running east and west. It was almost indiscernible from disuse.

Slick stepped down off his horse and studied it closely. Finally he spoke, "I thought I knew every dog trot in Quayle County, but this here is one I didn't know about.

"Fellas, we're standing on land which was part of the old Whitaker spread. It was over a 100,000 acres at the turn of the century. My pappy and Archie was both cowboys on this ranch afore the Great War. Old Man Whitaker died afore I was born. He never married and didn't have no legitimate heirs. Mighta had some unclaimed bastards. Anyway, his land got seized or sold off in small portions for back taxes after he died, or so the story goes. An entire empire disappeared like a wisp of smoke on a windy day and so far as I know, nobody even raised an eyebrow. Course there wasn't many folks living here at that time and a passel of 'em was outlaws and rustlers.

"When my pappy and Archie come back after the war, the Whitaker spread was gone. Only the crooked bankers and lawyers got rich. There was a time, though, when Old Man Whitaker was as big and powerful as Ripsnort Sweeney. Now Judge Sweeney and his big shot brother, Senator Darnell Sweeney, are the onliest big dogs in all of Quayle County. Today, there ain't many who's ever heared of Old Man Cornelius R. Whitaker. "Ashes to ashes and dust to dust"."

Slick stopped reminiscing and returned to tracking. He studied the trail east and west. He saw everything he needed to see and remounted.

"From the looks of it, this trail ain't been used since Hernando Cortés and the conquistadors conquered Mexico, but today it has. Looky here. What we got is two pilgrims walking west in single file. One's small, most likely a child, so the other'n is probably his momma. Awful small feet if it's an hombre. We just come from Pumpville, and that's where this trail is coming from. It's hard for me to believe that old rascal lied to me, but maybe he did."

Arthur replied, "Maybe this woman came through before he got up or when he was listening to the news."

Slick replied, "Maybe so, but how did she get to Pumpville? Hell, we ain't even found where they come across the Rio Grande, unless it was west of the Circle A and that don't make much sense based upon where the accident occurred! Not only that, how did she find this path west?"

Lane Barnes said, "Maybe these tracks aren't made by an

illegal alien. Maybe it's just someone from Pumpville taking a shortcut "to Grandmother's house"."

Slick responded, "Lane, the one thing I do know is, this path ain't been used in a very long time until today. It goes west towards Dryden, which is more'n 20 miles as the crow flies from Pumpville. How many folks walk that far in the desert these days? It's gotta be two of the illegals from this morning. But this leads to another question. Why is she walking to Dryden? What's there?"

Cordell spoke up. "Come on, guys, Let's go. If we don't locate this woman, we still got a lot of miles to cover."

Slick said, "Oh, she's found already. She just don't know it yet. Unless someone's done picked her up, we got her. She can't get too far with a child. She's gotta find shelter. I expect she will wait until nighttime to do most of her traveling."

Once again, the five of them spread out, with Slick in the center following the trail. They didn't have to go far - maybe a mile. They all saw the remnants of a line shack and an outbuilding, such as a small stable. Slick pointed to the buildings and waved his hat, signaling that this was the destination. The riders tightened up the line.

When they arrived, Lane took the south flank and Cordell took the north flank. The roof was gone from the adobe line shack, but the one over the three-sided, six-horse stable was intact. Inside, a young woman, maybe 25 years of age, and a boy about five were seated on the floor next to each other along the back wall of the stable. The woman was holding a female toddler in her lap. The woman was lovely in spite of her wind-blown hair, worn dress, scuffed sneakers, and sweat and dirt smudged face. Her eyes reflected fear and exhaustion. The five riders remained on their mounts in a line about three feet apart, hands resting on their pommels.

Slick said, "Hola señora. Cómo estás?"

She replied, "I speak English. We are fine. What are you going to do with us?"

Slick said, "We are not going to harm you. That's for sure. Would you or your children like some food or water?"

"Some water, por favor."

Barlow dismounted. He brought his canteen. He handed it to the woman. She let her son drink first. When he was done, she gave some to her daughter. Then the woman drank. She handed the canteen back. Barlow took it. Then he extended his hand with a Tootsie Roll. He nodded his head towards the boy. The woman extended her hand and took it. She unwrapped it and handed three sections to her son. She gave two sections to the girl. Then she broke off one of the remaining sections and slowly ate it.

Slick asked, "What are your names?"

She replied, "Mi nombre es Marisa López. El nombre de mis hijo es Guillermo. El nombre de mi hija es Angela."

"Where are you from, Marisa?"

"Agua Dulce. It is a small village about 60 miles south of here."

"How did you get to the U.S.?"

"My uncle paid a smuggler in Lagarto. It cost $1,000 for the three of us. My uncle drove us to Lagarto. He paid the man. My uncle stayed with us until we boarded the truck yesterday evening. He wanted to make sure I didn't get raped or killed."

"Where is your husband?"

"He was murdered nine months ago. The killer is a man named Jorge Esposito. They call him El Lobo. He smuggles marihuana for La Serpiente. My husband was a shepherd. He worked for a wealthy sheep rancher. He worked three weeks in a row and then he had one week off.

"One day El Lobo saw us together. He was rude. He disrespected me and Carlos. He asked Carlos if he would sell me to him for $100. Carlos said no. Then he asked if Carlos would rent me out for just one night. Carlos lost his temper. He charged El Lobo. El Lobo had a gun but Carlos is very fast and strong. He took the gun away from El Lobo. Then he beat him badly. Carlos took the gun and poured out all the bullets onto the ground. Then he threw the gun into the hole of an outhouse. Carlos said he would kill El Lobo if he ever bothered me again. El Lobo said Carlos wouldn't live long enough to kill him.

"Carlos had to return to work three days later. I begged him not to go but he said he had to. He said he was not afraid. I said I was afraid El Lobo would steal me. Carlos took me and the kids to stay at la casa de mi padre while he was gone. Carlos was gone five days. Then his empleador sent a man to find me. He said someone had shot Carlos in the back six times. He said it happened while Carlos was tending to the sheep by himself. No one knew who did it, but I knew. This was the worst day of my life.

"My kids and I moved in with y papá y mamá. Now that my husband couldn't protect me anymore, I was afraid El Lobo would steal me. Family and friends gave me some money at el funeral. I sold everything we owned except for our clothes. My family are weavers. I went back to work weaving rugs and serapes which we sell in the market. I saved my money. I wanted to go to America and start a new life with my kids.

"My older brother Victor is a licensed able body seaman in the American merchant marine. He has a green card. He works on a vessel which ports in Colombia and Gulfport in Mississippi. The ship he sails on brings bananas to Gulfport and takes machinery and parts back to Colombia. The company has two houses in Gulfport where the sailors can sleep when the ship is in port. They hire women to cook and clean the houses. Victor said he can get me a job. He sent me $500 to help pay my way.

"For nine months me and my family have been saving money for me to go to Gulfport. All the time I was afraid El Lobo would find me and steal me. We saved $1,300 American so we could go. Now we are found and you will send us back. My life is over. Creo que Dios no me salvará ahora."

She burst into uncontrollable sobs. Her kids began crying too. Lane asked, "What did she just say?"

Slick replied, "I think she said something like God will not save me now."

Slick went over to Marisa. He hugged her and Guillermo and Angela all at the same time. All three were sobbing. He whispered soothing words to Marisa in Mexican. Eventually she calmed down. Arthur pulled some ham sandwiches out of his saddlebags and gave them to Marisa and Guillermo. Cordell brought out an apple and an orange. Lane brought out some Fritos and chocolate chip cookies. Everyone ate something. At least for the time being, all were friends.

CHAPTER 14

Finding a Solution to a Sticky Wicket

Wednesday, March 15, 1972

Now that a degree of safety and trust had been established and they had broken bread together, albeit, in a rather spartan fashion, it was time for more answers to several unasked questions.

Slick queried, "Marisa, do you know the names of the coyotes? How many they were and how many folks they brought across?"

"Señor, I know of four coyotes. El Jefe was a man named Ernesto. He is a very harsh man. Dangerous. Threatening. There was also a younger man, El Gordo. He is as big as a bull, but he was nice. Then they had a boy about 15 or 16. His name was Geraldo. His job was to help those of us traveling. When we arrived in the U.S., there was another man who drove the truck but I did not see his face or hear his name."

"Where did you cross?"

"I do not know for sure. It was dark. We left from Lagarto. We rode in the back of a big truck with hard sides and a roll up back door. Once we all got in, they rolled down the door. It was dark and stuffy and we could not see out. There were 22 of us altogether including children. Geraldo rode in the back with us. El Gordo drove and Ernesto rode up front.

"I heard Ernesto say the crossing was a different place than they used before. I remember when we got to the river, the water was up to my knees. I had to tuck my dress up inside my waistband. I put my shoes and socks in a bag. I carried Angela and our belongings. Geraldo carried Guillermo and another boy on his shoulders.

"Ernesto made us stand in the river until he found a creek. He was angry. He said we had to walk in the creek instead of the land, and if anyone disobeyed his orders he would kill them. He said nobody better leave no trash. He said we had to sneak to the highway without leaving no footprints.

"El Gordo lead the way. Geraldo was in the middle. Ernesto was in the back. We walked one behind the other in the creek for many miles. Everyone was tired and our feet were cold. Ernesto said he would kill anyone who dropped out of line. He had a gun. He pointed it at a man named Jesús who was complaining. We were all very afraid. We stood and rested for awhile and then we began walking again, but this time we went much slower.

"We walked maybe three hours. Finally we got to a blacktop road. It went east and west. Geraldo said this was 90. A very big truck with braces and a canvas tarp was waiting for us. It was very crowded. We had a hard time getting everyone inside because it was so tall. Geraldo was the last one to get in before they tied the tarp down. We could not see out. Then we started moving."

Slick asked, "Which direction?"

"We were pointing east. We didn't go very far when the truck stopped. It tossed us all around. We didn't have enough room to sit down so we stood. Our bags were all around us. We didn't know why it stopped so suddenly. We were very afraid. Geraldo said everything was all right and to be still. Then the truck began to go front and back, front and back, several times. I could tell we were turning around. Then there was a big crash. We were all knocked down. People were screaming and crying. Some were hurt, but it was dark and we could not see. We didn't know what was happening. Everyone was frightened. Then we heard a coyote shouting. I could tell by his voice. It was Ernesto. He called someone a pendejo. Then we heard four shots. Bang! Bang! Bang! Bang! Everyone shut up. Even the babies.

"El Gordo opened the tarp. Then he and Geraldo helped us to

climb out. The crash was caused by a new pickup truck wrecked under the truck we were in. Ernesto was shouting at El Gordo. He told him to hurry up. It was very dark and hard to see. Some of the passengers began running east. The others went west. It took me awhile to find my valise. It contains all our papers and everything we own. By the time I found it, the rest had run away.

"I didn't know which way to go. I was afraid of getting picked up by La Patrulla Fronteriza. I knew El Gordo and Geraldo went east so I decided to go east, too. I walked on the pavement until I got back to the creek. I decided to go north. I did not want to return to Mexico, and I did not want to run into Ernesto again. I'm pretty sure he and the other coyotes went back home, but not me. We paid a $1,000 to get across! Mi papá would be very angry if I wasted all that money. Besides, we might never get the chance to get away again.

"I did like before. I pulled up my skirt and tucked it into my waistband. I took off Guillermo's shoes and mine. This time Guillermo had to walk. We walked for a long time. Dawn would break soon. I saw some lights in the east. I decided to go there to seek shelter. We came to a small village.

"I saw an old woman milking a cow. I told her we were lost. She gave us some fresh milk and some tortillas and honey. She told us we should leave soon before someone saw and reported us. She said there was a trail going north from her house which would run into another trail, very old and hard to find, which goes east and west. She told me to take the west route. She said if we continued west we would come to a paved road called 349, but it was very far away - more than a day's walk. She said if we went north on 349 for many miles, 50 or a 100, she wasn't for sure, we would come to a small town on a wide highway called Interstate 10. They have a Trailways bus terminal there. We could take a bus west to El Paso or Los Angeles if we had enough money, or east to New Orleans or even all the way to the Atlantic Ocean, but she warned us that if la policía found us they would make us go back to Mexico. This place was as far as we could come today. Señor, are you going to make us go back to Mexico?"

Slick replied, "Well, I don't know. Maybe. We need to talk to the sheriff first."

Arthur chimed in. He said, "Slick, we all need to talk about this in private."

Slick said, "Okay. Back in a few minutes, Marisa. You all wait right there."

The five posse men huddled up out of earshot.

Slick asked, "What's on your mind? You know we can't just ride away from here and pretend we didn't see 'em. Sheriff Sol would skin us all like we was a herd of stolen sheep."

Arthur responded, "Hear me out. That's not what I have in mind. I agree we have to take them back to Sheriff Sol. What I'm wondering is, if he would have any objection to me taking them to my house. I can get her a green card. Heck, I got all three of my Mexican workers green cards. She can be a domestic, cleaning my house or the house my workers live in. Once she gets a green card, she can stay or go on to Gulfport to live with her brother. Fellas, you all know what will happen to her if we turn them over to the Border Patrol. They'll get sent back to Mexico, no questions asked, and that El Lobo, Jorge Esposito, will get his hands on her and that'll be "all she wrote." She might as well be dead if he doesn't kill her anyway. What do you all say?"

Lane asked, "What do you think the sheriff will say?"

Slick said, "I think he'll agree that this is a great idea so long as nobody has heartburn with it and stirs up a ruckus. Tell you the truth, I can't see sending her back, either. What do the rest of you say?"

Cordell said, "I'm in."

Barlow said, "Absolutely."

Lane summed it up. "I reckon we're all a bunch of softies. I'm in, too."

They broke up and walked back to the stable. Slick said,

"Marisa, Arthur has something he wants to run by you."

Arthur said, "Marisa, if you would like to work for me and my wife on our ranch as a domestic, cleaning my house and maybe Cordell's, and the house my three workers share - they all have green cards, but no wives - we'll ask the sheriff to let you and your younguns stay.

"If he says it's okay, I'll initiate the paperwork to get green cards for the three of you. After you're legal, you can continue on your journey to Gulfport or you can remain with us. I'll pay you of course, but it's possible you could make more money in Gulfport. I'm not saying for certain the sheriff will agree to this, but I suspect he will."

Marisa broke out in tears. It frightened her children and they both began to weep, but she told them in Mexican that these were tears of joy. She said it was possible that they had found a new home here in Texas. Then she ran over to each of the men and hugged them, repeating over and over again, "Gracias, señores. Gracias."

The men collected their belongings. Barlow took Angela; Cordell took Guillermo; and Marisa rode double with Slick. It was a slow ride back. Everyone was woolgathering except for Guillermo, who was thrilled to be riding a horse with Cordell. Guillermo's joy was infectious. Everyone seemed happy.

It was getting nigh onto 4 o'clock by the time they arrived at the Circle A. They returned "during a lull in the storm" between two other groups who had caught a total of eight aliens. Slick told Marisa and the kids to wait in the cab of his truck. He told Cordell to remain with them. He told Barlow to unsaddle their three horses and put them in the trailers. Lane said he would stand by to see what the sheriff wanted him to do. Slick and Arthur went in the house to see Sheriff Sol.

Sheriff Sol was pleased to see them. He said it might be a little while before Dewey or Kirk returned from the jail from transporting the last batch of illegals the posses had intercepted so far. He said nobody had seen hide nor hair of the coyotes. He imagined that they were already back in Lagarto, drinking tequila and trying to get laid.

He said the murdered motorist was a man named Casper T. Brooks, a 35-year-old former bronc buster and rodeo clown, current western singer and guitar player of some repute in the saloons in Del Rio. He was known to be somewhat of a rounder. He was divorced, had two children, with several arrests under his belt for drunk and disorderly. They were running a toxicology screen on him to see if he was drunk at the time of his death. He also said they had not identified the deceased woman or the child who were found in the back of the cargo truck.

Slick reported on what the partial search of their sector had turned up, to include the information Marisa López provided. Then Arthur ran his proposal by the sheriff.

Sheriff Sol said, "Arthur you all get on outta here before we get another load of illegals. Do what you gotta do, but don't make a big splash. Get that paperwork turned in to INS this week. Since you've already sponsored three other aliens and everything worked out just fine, I doubt you'll run into much red tape. Just keep the noise level down. Savvy? And Slick, make sure Lane's on board, too."

Arthur thanked the sheriff and left.

Slick asked, "Want me and Lane to go back out and finish checking the rest of our sector?"

"Nope. When the others show up I'm shutting this operation down. We'll double up on patrol this week and continue looking, but unless something breaks bad, this is now a Border Patrol problem except for the murder. We'll keep working that. What was your take on this Marisa López?"

"Sheriff, ain't a one of us who wanted to turn her in. I think she's a good person who can't help which side of the border she was borned in. Art knows what he's doing. I think he got hisself a first class maid."

"That's what I was hoping to hear. Get outta here. Go have a beer. Service one of your widow friends."

"Sheriff, you don't need to tell me twice. Adiós."

CHAPTER 15

Life Marches On

Wednesday/Thursday, March 15/16, 1972

It was past 6 o'clock by the time Barlow pulled into his driveway. Sarah had left a note on the table that there was chili in the fridge and an apple pie under the towel on the counter. She would be back from school before he left for work. She also said not to get dressed if he wanted some desert. She signed the note with XOXO. He smiled to himself. He would eat now, and when he woke up he would start off his new day with a bang. When he went to bed he didn't bother to set the alarm. He knew Sarah had a far better way to wake him up than the annoying ring of the alarm clock.

Barlow was in a coma when he felt Sarah insert his granite loveometer into her self-lubricating, magical heaven and earth mover, and start a slow canter. He awoke with a start and began to say something, but before he could formulate the words, she said, "Hush up, Cowboy. Get in the rhythm. I'm headed to ecstasy and I need your undivided attention right now. Give me everything you've got. Naughty boy, you haven't been keeping up with your homework, and I don't mean school, either. That's it! Don't stop! Keep doing exactly what you're doing. Oh my God!"

Sarah transported him to The Promised Land and even beyond, not once but twice. When they were sated, she was purring like a kitten lapping up milk. In fact, that's exactly what she did do.

Barlow glanced at his watch. It was only 10 o'clock! School should be letting out about now. He asked, "How did you get here so fast? You're more than an hour early, not that I'm complaining."

"Well, Cowboy, after the two-hour break, I raised my hand and told Professor Cotton that you'd been working long hours. I said I hadn't seen much of you, and I missed you, and I was wet and had an itch which needed to be scratched, and I needed to hurry home. He said there were probably other students in the classroom who were in the same situation, so being that we were in the Ides of March he was letting the whole class leave early in memoriam to Julius Caesar."

"You did not! I know you better than that."

"Okay, I said I was so horny I couldn't concentrate and he said I was excused."

"Nope. I know better."

"Professor Cotton said something important came up, and he asked if anyone would be upset if he let class out early tonight."

"That sounds more like the truth."

"Yeah, so I said thank you for letting us get off early (if you know what I mean) and that I intended to take full advantage of that. Then I said Peter Man was asleep at home and he's always harder than Chinese arithmetic when he wakes up, and it was my responsibility and pleasure to tenderize that swollen love muscle for him. I said that I have the magic touch. Then Professor Cotton said, "Be off with you and come in peace.""

"And did you attain your pleasure and come in peace?"

"Oh, I did. I surely did.

"By the way, I heard through the Mosby grapevine that there was a murder and two fatalities involving illegal aliens last night out near the Circle A."

"Yep. What I know is the coyotes we were after in the past smuggled 22 illegals last night. Then a pickup truck ran into their truck on 90, and the driver got shot dead for his misfortune by one of the coyotes. Sheriff Sol called out some of the posse, including your dad and Cordell and Archie. We searched the far southeast end of the county looking for the coyotes and the pilgrims. When I knocked off at 6 this evening, the coyotes were still "in the wind" and about half of the pilgrims were apprehended. You can repeat that to part anyone.

"What you can't repeat is your dad took in a young woman named Marisa López and her two small children. Marisa is going to work for your dad as a maid while he works on getting her and the kids green cards. Then she can decide to continue working for your dad, or she can take the bus to Gulfport to be with her brother, who's a legal U.S. merchant seaman and is home-based there."

"Is Marisa López nice?"

"Very nice. Slick and I were in the same group with your dad and Cordell, along with Lane Barnes. We all thought this was the right thing to do under the circumstances. Her husband was murdered by a drug smuggler because he wanted Marisa. To send her back would have been consigning her to a kidnapping or a death sentence, but your dad ran it by Sheriff Sol first. It's kinda humorous. From what I understand, Sheriff Sol sounded just like Sergeant Shultz in the TV show Hogan's Heroes. He said for us to get outta there, stay below the radar, and something akin to, "I know nothink!" Savvy?"

"Umm. Hmm. Good for Daddy. Good for all of you. I can't wait to meet her and her children. Basically, that's how we got Pedro, Angel, and Pancho. They were all illegals and Daddy sponsored them so they could get their green cards. You know that and so does Sheriff Sol. Nobody is more loyal to our family than them."

"Yep, and I think Marisa and her kids will be, too. Her son's name is Guillermo. He's five and he's already enamored with Cordell. Her daughter is Angela. She's two.

"I don't know much about the crime scene. Chief and Gillespie worked that. I'll get the rest of the scoop when I go back to work tonight. I do know we're working the murder, and we'll have the patrol units looking for the other illegals, but we're not going to do a grid search on horseback like we did today."

"That means you can go to class tomorrow night."

"Correctamundo."

Barlow only got about three hours sleep, so he was a whipped puppy when he returned to work at 11:45. Gillespie hadn't fared much better. They had two men, four women, and two children in the jail waiting for the Border Patrol to pick them up sometime in the morning. They were all asleep, or nearly so, when Barlow and Gillespie relieved Ernie Atwater. He offered to stay an extra couple of hours, but they both told him no. Ernie reminded them to get caught up in their diaries and then he bugged out. Barlow told Gillespie they'd do two-hour rotating shifts in the jail. He stood the first watch because he wanted to see the sheriff or Chief first thing in the morning for an update from a management perspective.

Gillespie said, "Well, this is the skinny. The cargo truck was an Army surplus Diamond T five-ton truck. It was stolen from a junkyard in Del Rio two weeks ago. The owner wants it back, wrecked or otherwise. The Val Verde SO has a theft report on file. The owner is going to bring a flatbed truck to haul it home.

"Also, they identified the deceased woman as María Sánchez from a small town named Luces Del Desierto. The deceased child, named Gloria, was hers. One of the men in jail is María's brother. He identified the bodies from a photograph. It appears that they both died from injuries received in the accident.

"The man driving pickup truck, Casper T. Brooks, was identified by his mother. She wanted Pete Ricketts to take him to Simms Mortuary in Del Rio, but Chief said since he was shot, they had to do an autopsy first. Chief said he would see if the coroner in Del Rio would perform it since he is also a medical examiner."

That was everything Gillespie knew, besides the fact that she was thrilled to have had the opportunity to work the crime scene with Chief.

It was a very long, but quiet night. They had no issues regarding the prisoners. Sheriff Sol thanked them both for all their hard work. He didn't elaborate on any future plans to conduct surveillances at the Circle A. He kicked them out and told them to go home. He didn't have to repeat it.

CHAPTER 16

On the Other Side of the Border

Thursday, March 16, 1972

It was late in the afternoon when Ernesto was awakened by the sounds of three, rapid-fire gunshots fired right outside of his trailer. He grabbed his pride and joy, which was a stolen, blue steel, Colt Diamondback, .38 Special revolver with a four-inch barrel, and leapt like a lion out of bed. He carefully pushed open the curtains just a crack, but he couldn't see anyone from this vantage point. He hurried to the living room.

Gordo was already there because his bed was the living room couch. He was standing, more accurately described as filling up the entire front doorway, which was wide-the-fuck open, holding his machete down by his side like he was fixing to go out to cut sugar cane or maybe lop the head off a two-legged snake that was shooting a gun.

Stupid fucker! One day he would die due to the limited abilities of his tiny pea brain. Even an ostrich has a bigger brain! A pistol trumps a machete always, unless you are within three feet. When will he ever learn? Size don't matter one whit when it comes to bullets. In fact, Gordo was a big fat target. That's why everyone called him El Gordo instead of his real name, Rafael Larosa. Easy to hit and hard to miss.

"What's out there, Stupid?"

"A turquoise and white '57 Chevy all tricked out with with four dudes in it. I think the right front seat passenger is La Serpiente, but he has on dark glasses and a straw hat with a large brim and I can't tell for sure. Whoever it is, he's holding a gold .45 in his hand which is hanging out the window."

"Get outta the way, Shithead. You know anyone besides La Serpiente with a car like that? Huh? He ever let a moron like you ride that fucking car? Of course not! Ever see a gold gun beside the two he has? No? Who else could it possibly be? Gordo, you're as sharp as a marble. You know that?"

"I know. You tell me all the time."

Ernesto put his gun inside his waistband and pulled his tee shirt down over it. He told Gordo to get out of his way. Then he stepped outside barefoot because he knew La Serpiente didn't like to be kept waiting. Gordo stood next to the steps picking his nose and scratching his balls, looking like the low wattage light bulb he was. Galloping Jesus! What a lout!

"Señor Afilado. What can I do for you?"

"What's this I hear about José's truck getting wrecked and you not delivering the paying customers where we promised we would take them?"

"Sir, things were beyond my control." Ernesto pulled his hair up over his forehead to show where his forehead been lacerated in the accident. He pointed to his left eye that was swollen with bruising all around it. He shoved his nose left and right, wincing with pain to show that it was probably broken. "I was injured in the accident. Some drunk gringo wrecked his truck into us. I shot that fucker for causing us so much trouble. We couldn't drive the truck. It was all fucked up. The customers all ran away. We did the best we could."

"This is the second time in what, two months? Your mistakes are costing me money, Pinhead. Nobody will trust us to deliver anymore. If you had been hauling marihuana instead of people, I would have already shot you dead."

"Señor, we had to find a new route across the border because of that rancher who shot up my truck the last time. I still ain't got it fixed. Can't find the right alternator cap. Now we think the gringo is watching the river all the time. Señor, please understand. I had no control over the accident. I regret José's truck was wrecked, but he was the one driving it. He shouldn't try to put that on me. The bonehead tried to turn around in the middle of the blacktop highway without any lights. Can you believe that? How stupid can you be? We are fortunate the accident wasn't worse."

"Is that right? You're fortunate? I'm fortunate? Two paying customers are dead! Are they fortunate? Only eight of them returned home, and that was without any help from you! I returned all their money! The rest were either caught or killed! You were in charge! You were responsible! You panicked! You made us all look very bad! I will give you one last chance. If you fail, I promise I will shoot you myself. Understood?"

"Sí, Señor. Gracias. What is it you want me to do? I won't fail! Promise."

"What you should have done two months ago! Go back and kill that gringo rancher who shot your truck. Shoot everyone in his whole fucking family! Fuck his wife in front of him while he watches, even if she is ugly! I don't care! We need that crossing route! If he's not dead by the end of the month, you and that pendejo picking his nose and rubbing his balls over there will both be feeding the buzzards! No more screw ups! I mean it! Are we crystal-fucking-clear, Señor Robles?"

"Sí, Señor. Gracias."

With that, La Serpiente fired one last parting shot as a wake up call, an inch to the right of El Gordo's head. Gordo fouled his trousers, his very best pair, and collapsed on a small fire ant hill, getting the shit bit out of him (assuming there was any left), causing some true pain, but not even a single hair on his vacuous head was molested. The bullet went through and through the thin aluminum walls of the trailer. Then while El Gordo was laboriously processing what had just occurred and trying to brush off fire ants and stomp on them all at the same time, the fabulous, painstakingly restored, classic motorcar roared off, enveloping Ernesto and Gordo in a tremendous cloud of pebbles and dust.

For the first time in many months, Ernesto was scared shitless, himself. He wondered if he should run off to the U.S. If he did, what would he do over there? How would he make money? If he got caught by Patrulla Fronteriza and brought back to Mexico, La Serpiente would torture him slowly as a warning to others, and he would suffer an agonizing death. He shuddered when the thought crossed his mind. A cold chill ran down his spine. He even dribbled a little pee down his leg.

He had to plan carefully. He figured the rancher must have at least two compañeros on his property. He knew they were not afraid to shoot, and that they nearly pulled off the perfect ambush. The thing which gave them away was the crickets stopped chirping all at once. He didn't know where the ambushers were hidden, but he knew they were out there somewhere.

Now the hunter will become the hunted, except now he, Ernesto, would have numbers and surprise on his side. Those gringos would pay with their lives! But God forbid, if he fucked this up, he would have to flee - steal somebody's car, and go north as fast and as far as he could go. He would have no other choice. He decided to take all his money and his bullets with him just in case. And someday either way, stay or flee, once things settled down, he would fuck up José for ratting him out and making it sound like it was all his fault. If it hadn't been for the accident, the delivery would have been made just as promised. José, and only José, was responsible for the accident. He didn't pull the trigger, but the dead gringo was on him, too.

CHAPTER 17

Slick Mixes Undercover With Pleasure

Wednesday, March 22, 1972

The murder investigation was at a standstill. Chief Alex knew damn well who the doer was, but he had no eyewitnesses and no murder weapon. He had the ballistics report (moved to the forefront of the state lab's workload because Senator Sweeney demanded it) which stated that the four bullets recovered from Casper Brooks' body (and the seat cushion) had lands and grooves on them consistent with bullets fired by a Colt .38 Special or .357 Magnum revolver. Chief Alex was 99.9% certain the shooter was Ernesto Robles - way beyond a reasonable doubt. He also knew where Ernesto lay his head, which was most likely the same location where the murder weapon could be found. The problem was, he could not ask the Mexican authorities for assistance because of the ingrained corruption over there.

Chief had done some asking around with American lawmen from El Paso to Del Rio, to include the Feds, specifically the Bureau of Narcotics & Dangerous Drugs, U.S. Customs Service, Immigration & Naturalization Service, Border Patrol, and the FBI regarding a suspected drug smuggler who goes by the monicker La Serpiente, and any of his known associates to include one Ernesto Robles and one El Gordo.

Del Rio PD, Val Verde SO, the Texas Rangers, and all the Feds had at least some information on La Serpiente. His real name was Augusto Afilado-Rojo. He was 42 years of age, a known trafficker of humans and marijuana with arrests in Mexico for possession of marijuana in 1954 and possession of a firearm in 1955, but none since. He paid a 100 peso fine for the pot, probably just a joint, and the gun charge was dismissed. It was apparent that he had purchased political protection sometime between 1954 and 1955. Also, the Border Patrol had picked him up in 1962 for illegal entry into El Paso, but they tossed him back across the border. BNDD suspected him of numerous murders in Mexico, some of which involved victims who had been gruesomely tortured. The deceased were all alleged to have been competing drug smugglers. BNDD also reported that Afilado allegedly resides in a walled compound with armed guards somewhere around San Miguel.

That was the sum of all official intelligence on Afilado by U.S. law enforcement agencies, other than the 1962 Border Patrol mugshot and fingerprint card. La Serpiento was a pretty boy back in those days. Chief wondered if he still were.

Val Verde and Del Rio both knew of Ernesto Robles. He was 35 years of age. He had been arrested for simple assault in a bodega near the river in 1957. He got in an altercation with the owner over the price of a six-pack of beer, which he wasn't old enough to purchase anyway. He got 30 days in jail and paid a $50 fine. The Border Patrol escorted him back across the bridge to Mexico and told him to beat it. That was it.

No one had ever heard of El Gordo. He must be a new recruit - a fat one too, since that is what his nickname means.

Chief needed more information, and a way to get Mr. Robles back into Quayle County, preferably with the murder weapon. He went to Sheriff Sol. Sheriff Sol went to Slick.

Slick said, "Sheriff, you remember when you sent me and Archie over to Lagarto to collect intelligence?"

"Yep."

"I know I mentioned a waitress we met at Don Diego's Cafe named Carlita Pasquale. She's a single woman who took a fancy to me. I guess she likes my smile. I go over there every now and then to enjoy some carnal pleasures with her. I take Toby over to the Circle A, and ride across the river just like me and Archie done the first time we went over. I park Toby in a little shed she has in her backyard, and we eat and drink and smoke cigarettes and relieve each other from all our worldly tensions. After dark, I ride back to the Circle A, load up Toby, and drive home.

"Carlita knows I'm a bachelor rancher who enjoys occasional female companionship. That's all. She doesn't know anything about my part-time occupation. As the opportunity presents itself, I express some casual interest about her likes, dislikes, relatives nearby, and her background. I want her to know that I consider her more than just a roll in the hay."

"Of course."

"She's lived in Lagarto since she was 16. She's 41 now. It's a poor village. She has a daughter who's married and lives in Ciudad Acuña and a son in jail in Júarez for stealing a car. She knows Ernesto Robles, but she stays as far away from him as she can. Besides, he likes to fuck younger women.

"She also knows La Serpiente. She calls him Señor Afilado whenever she mentions him. She is very wary of him, so whenever he does drop by the cafe, she is polite, but not overly friendly. Everyone in Lagarto knows about Mr. Afilado. From what she told me, even her boss, Don Diego, gives Mr. Afilado and his hired henchmen a very wide berth. They all carry guns and knives and they do not fear the law, which is non-existent in Lagarto anyway. Like I said. It's a poor village. The people have nothing but their thoughts for the police to steal.

"Ernesto Robles is Mr. Afilado's right-hand man in Lagarto. Those who wish to buy pot or want to settle in America go to him to seek passage. Robles is a fucking asshole, no doubt about it. No charisma, no charm, no class, just a thug who lives like a pauper, but allegedly has a fat stash from his employment with La Serpiente. He uses El Gordo to do all his heavy lifting as well as his dirty work. Carlita's never said what his real name is, so I don't know if she knows, but I'll try to find out. Also, she said he's so dumb he makes a cue ball look like an IBM computer. He comes to the cafe more frequently than Robles, and for the most part he leaves folks alone.

"Rumor has it, El Gordo is hung like John Dillinger, and he has more stamina than a Kentucky thoroughbred. Also, supposedly he has a penchant for blue-hair old ladies and he services at least one wore out old widow woman nearly everyday."

"Sounds a little like you."

"The hung part is right, but I prefer seasoned, good-looking, single women, just a little past their prime. I ain't into toothless geriatrics.

"Anyway, if someone got close to El Gordo, they might learn all they need to know about Ernesto Robles. Not sure how we could do that, though."

"Me neither, but it's a good idea. Let me think on that. Okay. Listen Slick, not because you have to, but would you let me know whenever you go over there? Just in case you have a problem. You understand."

"You bet."

Sheriff Sol and Chief Alex both pondered the question over and over. They thought and thought about it. They could not come up with any viable solution which would keep Carlita Pasquale out of harm's way or lure Ernesto Robles into the U.S. They knew he would continue to breech the border with illegals, but they had no idea when or where, and they didn't have the manpower to sit on the border every night. That was the problem.

They considered having Slick make a "chance" encounter with El Gordo. Establish some rapport. Get him drunk. Let him win at cards or come up with some other ruse just to give him some money. Make him feel important. See if he would start bragging and unwittingly give up something useful about his boss; but how could Slick do that without taking Carlita into his confidence? Also, the possibility always exists that Ernesto might show up. If Ernesto ever figured out that Slick and Carlita were consorting together, he would surely kill her.

They considered baiting a trap at the Circle A, letting information leak out to Ernesto or El Gordo that one of the illegals from the busted flush was staying there and was planning to identify Ernesto to the Border Patrol in two days in exchange for a green card. (This would shorten the time spent on the stakeout.) Of course, even if they were successful in catching Ernesto, the Circle A could expect fierce retribution by La Serpiente. It could make things a 100 times worse for Arn.

Another issue was, if the Mexican authorities ever learned Quayle County SO had been conducting a reconnaissance mission on their soil without permission, there would be Hell to pay. After several days of intense rumination with no viable resolution, Sol tabled the mission. He needed a low risk, high gain solution. He didn't have one. He decided, "Better safe than sorry."

That was a mistake. Sometimes a preemptive strike is the only way to beat a tougher opponent. "No guts. No glory." In the end Sol was terribly sorry he took no action.

CHAPTER 18

A Deed So Vile

Friday, March 24, 1972

Ernesto had been planning the most monumental event of his entire, worthless life for the better part of a week. The Mexican folk hero (depending upon your political perspective) and former President, Pancho Villa, and his army of bandits had attacked the U.S. City of Columbus, New Mexico, this very same month 56 years ago. They murdered and maimed Americans, created mayhem, and wreaked havoc before galloping away deep into Mexico. Americano General John "Black Jack" Pershing and his army of clueless Yankees searched all over northern and central Mexico for months trying to catch him but they never did. Pancho Villa was way too smart for them. This is why Pancho Villa was Ernesto's hero.

Now, in just a few minutes, Ernesto and Gordo and his crew of eight additional foot soldiers on loan to him from La Serpiente were going to repeat Mexican history. The Mexican chihuahuas were going to bite the American mastiffs on their balls, rip 'em out by the roots, and watch 'em slowly bleed out, all in their own backyard. Actually, as it turned out, there was just one Americano mastiff and one broke dick old Mexicano rooster. Where had he seen that rooster before? No matter. Both would die a violent death tonight.

Afterwards, the chihuahuas would slip back into Mexico as conquering heroes, just like David who slew Goliath, never to be captured by the Americano authorities. The Mexican people would revere all of them, especially Ernesto, who had planned and lead this breathtaking mission with military precision, and executed it with derring do. When the deed was accomplished, they would celebrate with abandon at the cantina. He would personally fuck the three best looking putas in the whole joint. Gordo could fuck his ugly old grannies. Undoubtedly, La Serpiente would promote Ernesto by giving him more money, more men under his command, and greater assignments to perform.

Ernesto and Gordo had diligently performed their reconnaissance for three days and three nights in a row. Ernesto had watched the ranch by day, and Gordo had watched it by night. They had concealed themselves near the river, using a pair of stolen military binoculars borrowed from La Serpiente.

Gordo reported that the assholes never went outside after it got dark. He thought they went to bed right after sundown because they never had any lights on. Gordo wanted to sneak up on the house to make sure, but Ernesto told him to stay put in Mexico. If there was one thing Ernesto knew for certain, it was that Gordo could "fuck up a wet dream." He'd be caught for sure and the gig would be up. Then La Serpiente would certainly kill them both. By demanding that Gordo watch from Mexico, Ernesto was saving both of their lives. The raid absolutely had to have the element of surprise to be successful. That was the key.

Ernesto divided his troops into two groups. José would drive a van across the river from Acuña with four men, one of which would be Gordo. They would drive right up to the ranch house without any lights. Ernesto and the other four men would cross where they crossed with the last group of customers - the unlucky ones. They would sneak up from the east. They would meet outside the ranch house at precisely 3 o'clock. Ernesto told José not to arrive one minute sooner nor one minute later. Timing had to be perfect so as not to wake up the targets until it was too late for them to put up a fight. Stealth was the key. It had to be a complete ambush!

José arrogantly told Ernesto this wasn't his first rodeo. He knew what he was doing, and that Ernesto needed to concern himself about his own group. José and his men would arrive exactly on time as planned. He closed sarcastically with, "Quit being such a nervous Nellie."

The drive from Acuña was a cakewalk. The Mexican guards had all been greased by José. The Border Patrol only had two agents at the bridge from midnight until 6 a.m. The only thing in the van other than the crew were farm implements. Everyone knew the Border Patrol would let farm workers cross so long as they returned to Mexico on the same day.

The Border Patrol agents checked their identification cards and then searched the van. Everything was in order. No guns and no contraband. They were cleared to cross. They drove to B.R. Armando's Scrap Metal, Incorporated, in Del Rio, where José's brother-in-law worked, and stopped to pick up their firearms. The guns were in the back of the wrecked Diamond T cargo truck in a gunny sack. They picked up two sawed-off, 12-gauge pump shotguns, a Colt .45 pistol, an old .38 Smith & Wesson revolver, and a raggedy Winchester .32-20 lever action rifle which had seen better days. All the guns except for one shotgun were stolen. The only guns with spare ammo were the shotguns. No matter. This was more than enough firepower to kill two old men. They had plenty of time to get to the ranch, so José drove slowly. Once they got out of town they didn't pass another vehicle or see another living soul.

Ernesto and his crew walked cross the river without incident. They were silent like scorpions, ready to sting. They followed the river westbound as silently as an army of ghost crabs scampering along the beach. They were a little early, so they stopped about a half-mile from the ranch house to take a smoke. Everything was going exactly like clockwork.

Arn and Pedro were sitting in the lawn chairs they had set up for Gillespie and Barlow, directly across from the crossing tree. There was a well used Farmall tractor parked right behind them, partially blocking their view of the barn and the house, which was to their north and west. They were both wide awake, and their eyes were fully adjusted to the darkness. Arn was working a mouthful of Mail Pouch loose leaf chewing tobacco. He was wearing his holstered Army Colt .45. His .30-06, M-1 rifle was resting in his lap. He was thinking about his wife, Eileen, who had died eight years ago. Pedro was nursing a 12-ounce bottle of Pepsi Cola. His Winchester .30-30 was leaning up against his chair. He was thinking he should have brought some peanuts to munch on. It was a beautiful starlit night with a waxing moon. All was well in their little slice of the universe.

José's "borrowed" '60 Ford Econoline van with 425,000 miles on it started to overheat about the time they approached the Diamond T accident site. He had to pull over and check under the hood. The radiator was belching steam and scalding water like a wrecked locomotive. It swallowed every last drop they had in their only gallon jug of drinking water. Unfortunately, that was not nearly enough, but it had to do. Then José couldn't get the van to start. He began to panic. Finally, the engine fired, but it was shaking and rattling like the worn out relic that it was. It sounded and vibrated like it was going to shake itself completely apart. He hoped the targets were heavy sleepers. He was afraid of being late. He willed the van to keep on running so they could continue on their mission. He knew he would be the one blamed if anything went wrong. They must arrive on time, no matter what the circumstances!

Surprisingly, José had no trouble locating the entrance to the ranch; however, the single lane, dirt driveway was rutted and winding with narrow and sharp turns, full of small boulders, and he had a very hard time seeing where he was going, not to mention keeping the engine of the worn-out beast running. They had much better roads in Mexico (but of course they were highways and not ranch driveways!) He was told he had about eight miles to the ranch house, so he used his headlights intermittently just to keep from running off the road into a ditch, or worse. When they had traveled about seven miles, he extinguished the lights until he ran completely off the road and nearly got stuck on a jagged boulder. He was lucky he didn't break an axle or rupture a tire. Of course the spare in the back was bald and flat. From then on, he kept the lights on until he could see the house. Between the engine noise and his headlights, he may as well have brought a marching band and set off some Fourth of July fireworks to announce their malevolent presence.

Arn and Pedro heard the engine racket long before they saw the lights. What now? Their rifles were already chambered with a round. They were not expecting any welcome guests at 2:50 a.m. They both were pretty sure they knew what this was - a Mexican mob hit. Who else would drive a clunker to an ambush? They had expected as much sooner or later, and they were prepared. The adrenaline was flowing. They crept near the back of the house and stood in the shadows. Arn went left and Pedro went right. They waited silently to see who came calling.

The derelict van pulled up just to the rear of the house and stopped. José had switched the ignition to off, but the engine continued to shake and sputter and cough until it completely expired. Arn and Pedro watched five men disembark. Four men were on the passenger side of the van, which was nearest to them. The fifth, probably El Jefe, was on the driver's side. Three had long guns. That was everything they needed to see. Arn exclaimed, "Murderers! Shoot to kill."

They fired almost simultaneously at the nearest two men, both of whom were facing them, but probably unable to see them because their eyes hadn't had time to adjust to the dim light. Both men fell to the ground like the earth had just opened up underneath their feet.

A third assassin fired back at Arn's muzzle flash with three hasty shots from a handgun, but Arn had already sidestepped to his left. The shooter was big and fat, plus he was wearing a white tee shirt, presenting a target nearly impossible to miss. Arn shot him twice in the belly. Arn and Pedro both heard him cry out in pain. He crumpled like a soggy potato chip.

A fourth assassin fired a hurried, unaimed shotgun blast between Arn and Pedro while running to the rear of the truck. Essentially, he was laying down covering fire to buy himself enough time to find some concealment before the ranchers shot him too, but he didn't react soon enough. Pedro shot him in the side. He collapsed like a flat tire.

At the same time, the last hitman fired three shots at Pedro from behind the driver's side of the van. He must have been shaking like a leaf because all three shots missed their mark. Either that, or the gun was too much for him to handle. Surprised, Pedro jerked around and returned one shot in response, also missing.

Arn came to his rescue. He ran around the rear of the van and shot this fifth man in the back. He dropped to his knees, seriously wounded. Arn gave him the coup de grâce in the back of his head. The impact of the bullet sent him sprawling face down in the dirt. This was a blessing for those who later saw his body, because half of his face was missing. Pedro followed Arn's example by shooting an "insurance round" into three of the would-be assassins on his side of the van. Arn double tapped the last one with his Colt.

Arn stood back. He removed his Stetson and wiped his brow. Though he had anticipated something like this, it was still a shock. Combat always is. Because these were Mexican invaders, he considered this an assault on American sovereignty, not just an assault on him, personally. He didn't start this fight. They did! He was simply protecting his home!

Pedro turned on his flashlight and kneeled down to see who these invaders were. Just then, Ernesto and his men came creeping up behind them. Arn sensed someone before he saw anyone. He began to turn around, but he was too late. Three paid assassins opened up on him simultaneously and shot him altogether 11 times. The other two murderers emptied their guns into Pedro, who had just stood up from examining one of the bodies. In 10 seconds or less, it was "lights out" for both of them.

The cessation of gunfire, and the immediate, eerie silence rendered Ernesto and the other hired killers momentarily dumbstruck. Their ears were still ringing. They had accomplished their mission, but it wasn't gratifying. None of them had been in danger. This was nothing to brag about. It left them empty. They didn't "cheat death." It was like having sex with a woman who was passed out drunk. What's the thrill?

Ernesto froze in place. He was completely discombobulated. Ernesto was the commander, but he couldn't channel his thoughts. He didn't know what to do next. He was absolutely certain from just a glance that the men with José were all dead, to include his pet "go-for", Gordo. Ernesto didn't even bother to walk over close enough to any of the bodies to examine the devastation they meted out to the ranchers, or to check his brothers-in-arms for signs of life. Instead, when he finally did regain his wits, all he did was yell, "Berto, see if you can start the van."

Berto did try, several times, but it was of no use. The engine of the van was just as dead as the seven bodies lying on the ground.

Ernesto's panic intensified. He screamed, "Fuck it! Leave it! Come on! Back to the river! We gotta get outta here! Someone's bound to have heard all this racket!"

The victorious, bloodthirsty chihuahuas, lead by their shaky El Jefe, fled back across the river as fast as their legs would carry them. They were too wound up to celebrate. Losing five of their colleagues was an unexpected blow to their collective psyche. It was a long, silent five mile walk back to Ernesto's trailer where they were parked, except for the squishing of water from their trousers and shoes. As soon as they arrived and without a word, the four foot soldiers from La Serpiente's casa piled into their tricked out, candy apple red, '66 Chevy Impala and scooted off back to their refuge. La Serpiente would probably be pissed when they told him what had occurred. Each killer was thankful that this had been Ernesto's responsibility and not his own.

Meanwhile, Ernesto trudged inside his tin can castle, and guzzled a nearly full bottle of rotgut tequila in a rapid-fire series of panicked gulps. Then he shed his wet garments and left them in a heap on the floor. He stood naked, absentmindedly scratching his balls, pondering what he should do next. He lit a cigarette and inhaled.

Should he try to make a run for it? Maybe set out for El Paso?

Would La Serpiente be pleased or would he be furious? He didn't know for sure. They had killed the ranchers. They did what they set out to do. Nevertheless, because of their disproportionate losses, La Serpiente probably would not have a warm, fuzzy feeling when he heard the news.

Shit! Once again, this was not his fault. José fucked everything up like he always does, but nevertheless, Ernesto knew he would bear all the blame. (What would be the satisfaction for La Serpiente in blaming a dead man who was no longer around to debase and abuse?) Ernesto had promised La Serpiente that he would successfully carry out this mission under a threat of death if he failed, but he didn't fail!

Fuck it! He cleaned and reloaded his gun. He opened his full bottle of tequila and slugged down nearly all of it. He would learn his fate tomorrow. His mind was pinging. It wasn't supposed to have gone down this way! He was supposed to be the hero! Fate was working against him! He could not win!

Ernesto had ardently tried to avoid this line of thinking, but he finally accepted the fact that La Serpiente would vent all his anger on him. The Boss, by definition, was the person who defined success and failure. How would he rule? Ernesto finally snapped to the conclusion that he was a dead man, and all because José was a monumental fuck up. Basically, he was doomed.

Ernesto was thinking about survival, about staying drunk for the rest of his life - anything except celebratory fucking, and then he wasn't. He passed out cold and fell prostrate on the couch.

CHAPTER 19

A Very Sad, Long Day

Friday, March 24, 1972

Ring! Ring! Ring!

Barlow looked at his watch. It was 3:15. He thought to himself, someone's in trouble. He picked up the receiver. "Quayle County Sheriff's Office. Deputy Adams speaking. How may I help you?"

"Hello, Deputy. This is Mr. Elmer A. Jackson. I own the Rocking J. I'm just north and east of the Circle A. In fact, I'm adjacent to it. You know where that's at?"

"I do. You're neighbors with Sergeant Major Wrigley."

"As a matter of fact, that's why I'm calling. About fifteen minutes ago, in fact it was exactly 2:55, I heard dozens of shots coming from over at the Circle A. I phoned Arn's house but got no answer. I haven't gone over there. I'm not really all that gun savvy but I do own a shotgun. It was my father's. It' a single shot, 16-gauge. I've got at least a dozen shells for it. All number sixes. He hunted but I never cared about it. I keep it mostly for snakes. You understand. Could you go see if Arn's in any trouble?"

"Sure I can. Thanks for calling, Mr. Jackson. I'll be right out. I'll let you know after while if everything's okay at the Circle A."

"Oh, thank you. I hate to be a pest."

"No problem. Goodbye."

Gillespie was returning from the restroom. She was rubbing lotion on her hands. "What's up? Someone invite us to go out and play?"

"I got a bad feeling about this one, Gillespie. I'll write the incident report. You check us out a car. Take both .30-30's this time, and plenty of extra ammo. A neighbor heard shots coming from the Circle A. I gotta call Sheriff Sol before we roll."

"Oh, goodness sakes! I hope they're both all right! At least I went pee first this time."

Barlow made the call. Sheriff Sol picked up after only two rings. "Pratt residence."

"Sheriff, it's Barlow. Just got a call from Elmer Jackson at the Rocking J. He said at 2:55, he heard dozens of shots at the Circle A. He called but got no answer. He's afraid to go look. We're headed that way just as soon as I hang up."

"Okay. I'm headed there, too. I'm also rolling Chief Alex. Hit me up on the radio if you arrive before me."

"Roger that. See ya there."

Barlow switched the phones and locked the door. Gillespie was already on full tilt, "sitting on G and looking at O" in the new Plymouth. As soon as Barlow buckled up she was "off and running to the races."

"What did he say?"

"Both he and Chief Alex are rolling on this one."

"Oh, please Lord. Let them be okay." Her eyes teared up. They were already flying at 138 miles per hour, but she eked out another two mph. Barlow didn't think that was even possible. They made it to the Circle A in record time. It was 3:55 when they turned off onto Arn's gnarly, axle-breaking driveway.

They saw the Econoline van in the backyard before they even stopped. Barlow told Gillespie to park way back so they wouldn't trample a crime scene. He'd already seen a body lying on the ground. He picked up the mike and said, "Quayle 1 or Quayle 2, this is Quayle 67. We've arrived. It looks bad. Copy?"

"Quayle 67, this is Quayle 1. Do not go in. I repeat, do not go in. I'm almost there. Wait for me. Copy?"

"Copy."

Gillespie said, "Barlow, we can't just sit here! I saw someone lying on the ground. Arn or Pedro should have already come out to see us if they're okay. We gotta check. What if they're hurt?"

"Agreed, but stay with me. Leave the rifle in the car. Ruger in right hand. Flashlight in the left. Do not track up the place. We won't touch anyone we see who's obviously dead. Also, keep an eye out for shooters who might be wounded, maybe playing possum, or haven't run off yet. We don't want to be ambushed ourselves. Understood?"

"Yes."

They both had already seen the dead Mexican near the driver's door of the van when they drove up, so they started at the right rear. They scanned the area from a distance with their flashlights. Arn was the nearest of six inert bodies. Pedro was the farthest from them. They'd both been shot dead, along with five unknown assailants. Gillespie burst into tears. Her worst fears had come true. Barlow held her tight because she began to rush towards Arn, but there was no point. They both could see Arn was shot to pieces. His lifeless eyes were open, staring into space.

Barlow lead her back to the cruiser and parked her in the right front seat. He stood outside the open car door. He said, "I'm so very sorry. I know you cared greatly for them both. You gotta get yourself collected before the sheriff gets here. If he sees you like this, he'll send you home. You don't want that, do you?"

"Oh Hell no! Barlow, these are my friends! I love them both! I want to kill whoever did this! Erase them from the face of the Earth! Make it real hurt bad! How on Earth could anyone do such a vile deed? These are two wonderful men!"

"I know. Me, too. Wipe your face. Your eye makeup is running. Check yourself in the mirror. I can hear the sheriff's car coming. Let me speak to him first."

"Okay. Thank you. I'll be fine."

It took more time for Sol to get there than Barlow had thought it would. By then, Gillespie had done what she could do to fix her makeup, and she was composed. "Stiff upper lip." They both leaned up against the left side of the cruiser, arms crossed, and waited for the sheriff to come to them. "Pete and Repeat," except Repeat was a female.

Sheriff Sol was not as crisp as he had been the last time they called him out. He was wearing yesterday's crumpled uniform. He hadn't shaved. Even though he was wearing his Stetson, they could see that his hair was unbrushed. His face was grim. Imagine a 6-foot, 4-inch Apache minus the war paint, with a face contorted which silently screamed, "on the warpath," but then he surprised them. His demeanor softened. He walked over slowly and gently asked, "Arn and Pedro are dead, aren't they?"

Barlow nodded his head.

Sheriff Sol moved closer to Gillespie. He gently placed a hand on each of her shoulders and gave her a soft squeeze. His gaze delved tenderly into her eyes. He said, "Ella Mae, I know these are two very special friends of yours. They were my friends, too, though probably not as much as they were to you. Ella Mae, I need you with me today more than ever. I really need your help. I need your professionalism.

"Are you up to it? Can you cowgirl up? We have a very difficult job before us today. When it's all done, we can take time to weep and mourn our losses, but not now. We gotta soldier on. Are you with me? You don't have to. You've worked your shift already. You can call it a day if you like."

Gillespie gave the sheriff a bear hug. When she stepped back, she said, "Thank you for being aware of my deep affection for Arn and Pedro. I didn't know it showed so much. I never had a friend murdered before. Now I have two. I'm okay now. I want to do whatever I can to help bring these killers to justice. At least Arn and Pedro got in some licks before they were suddenly called home."

"Good. You're a credit to the SO. We're fortunate to have you. After Chief shows up, you'll be his number one assistant. Both of you, same as before. If we're not done with the crime scene by 4 this afternoon, I want you all to knock off anyway. Understood?"

"Understood."

Sheriff Sol walked back to his car. He keyed the mike and said, "Quayle Base this is Quayle 1."

Barlow and Gillespie were both surprised to hear Ernie Atwater answer. "This is Quayle Base. Come in Quayle 1."

"Quayle Base, tell Quayle 4 to check out a car and report to duty. Ditto for Quayle 5. Also call Quayle 10 and Quayle 11 [Archie's new call sign as a special deputy] and ask if they could take on another special mission for me. They'll know what I mean. Send all of them to my current location. Call me back and let me know if each of them can make it. Copy?"

"Copy."

"Also, call Pete Ricketts and Buck Boyd. Tell Pete and Buck to meet me here at 8 o'clock. Roger?"

"Wilco."

"Quayle Base, one more thing."

"Go ahead, Quayle 1."

"Run a license plate for me, stolen and vehicle registration. Write the results down and send it to me via Quayle 4 or Quayle 5, whoever arrives first. Do not put this information out over the air. The number is Texas 377-451. Copy?"

"Copy. 377-451."

Chief Alex was pulling up as Sheriff Sol completed his radio traffic. The sun was just about to break the horizon. They all gathered around the sheriff's car. Sol said, "Chief, you made good time."

The chief responded with his typical dry wit. "This is very true. We've been getting called out so much by the midnight shift I started sleeping in my clothes. Didn't even remove my boots last night. I almost slept in my hat."

Barlow replied, "Chief, that's the only way Gillespie or I ever get to see your smiling face anymore. Good morning, Sir. Maybe I can rustle us up some coffee."

Sheriff Sol said, "First things first. Chief, you and Gillespie got the crime scene. Pete and Buck are supposed to report here at 8 o'clock to tow the van and transport bodies. Of course, Arn and Pedro go first.

"Barlow, I'm holding you back to assist me. First thing we'll do before conducting a thorough search of the house and barn, is to make a pot of coffee. Barlow, you also get to feed the horses and muck the stalls. See if you can find Arn's dog. His name is Grunt. He's a rat terrier. No telling where he's got off to. Also, you and I will go talk to Elmer Jackson and Arn's other neighbor - what's his name?"

Gillespie responded, "Leonard and Nicole Perkins. They own the Flying P."

"Right. Thanks. Also, I'm sending Chunk and Kirk to Del Rio in separate cruisers. They'll hook up with counterparts from the Val Verde SO. Chunk will track down the owner of this van and Kirk will meet with the Border Patrol to see if they have any information on these five deceased villains. We all know who they probably work for.

"Assuming Archie and Slick are available on short notice, I'm sending them on a little intelligence recon in Lagarto. That's all on the hush hush, so Barlow, you and Gillespie keep that between yourselves. No gossiping. Savvy? Anything I missed?"

Chief said, "I think that about covers it."

"Good. Barlow, let's go do a precursory check of the barn first and then the house, Then you can make some coffee. Make sure to bring your notebook and the camera from the car."

A quick look-see of the barn left them with the impression that everything was just as it had been the last time Arn walked out of it. Arn was a neatnik, so if anything were out-of-place, it would stand out like a wart on your nose. With the exception of being extra clean and tidy, the barn looked like any other barn - four stabled horses, Army surplus Jeep parked in its stall, hay bales stacked in the loft, sacks of oats in the bin, ranching implements and other tools neatly stowed away. Hardly any cobwebs and definitely no murderers lying-in-wait.

Barlow walked all the way around the barn to double-check. He was surprised to see a tidy, one-hole outhouse situated behind it that he had never noticed before. (Too bad Gillespie didn't know about this privy when they were on surveillance.)

The ranch house was not much bigger than Barlow's house. It was a single story, beige stucco, asphalt shingle, hip roof, three bedroom, one bath house. No garage, perhaps by design, since Arn parked in the barn. It's most endearing feature was a verandah which extended all across the back of the house.

Arn's house was furnished with rustic wooden, frontier-style western furniture with a wide, checked tan, avocado, and pale orange design on Mexican blanket-covered, padded cushions. It had a black and white RCA Victor television set in the living room older than the one in Barlow's house, and a desk model Philco AM radio in the kitchen. The kitchen table was a sturdy, white oak oval with six matching chairs. An empty gun rack hung over the fireplace in the family room. The house was as spartan and spic and span as an Army barracks under the control of a no-nonsense, infantry sergeant major. There was a double bed in the master bedroom and a single bed in the bigger of the other two bedrooms. That was obviously Pedro's room. The third bedroom was set up as an office.

There were family photographs hanging throughout the house, but the office was filled with artifacts and photographs of Arn's career in the Army. He had a shadow box with all his medals.

Barlow was in awe. It displayed:

1. Combat Infantryman's Badge with two stars, signifying combat infantry service in three separate wars.
2. Distinguished Service Cross, a valor award second only to the Medal of Honor.
3. Silver Star, the third highest award for valor.

4. Soldier's Medal, the fourth highest award for valor, but not during combat. (It was generally awarded for saving a life, such as in a fire or a near drowning in icy or rushing waters, stepping in to vanquish a civil assault, capturing an armed robber, or any other heroic deed which put the soldier's life in peril, etc.)
5. Bronze Star with a V device (for valor) and one bronze oak leaf cluster (signifying two awards), the fifth highest award for valor.
6. Army Commendation Medal with three bronze oak leaf clusters (four awards).
7. Purple Heart with two bronze oak leaf clusters (three awards) for wounds received in combat.
8. Good Conduct Medal with two silver knots on a rope (ten awards).
9. World War I Victory Medal with one Silver Citation Star, and four Army Battle Clasps with the following campaigns articulated: Aisne, Aisne-Marne, St. Mihiel, and Somme-Offensive.
10. American Defense Service Medal (for being on active duty during any period of time from the beginning of World War II in Europe, September 8, 1939, through Pearl Harbor Day, December 7, 1941).
11. American Theater Campaign Medal.
12. Europe-Africa-Middle East Theater Campaign Medal with four bronze stars (four distinct campaigns).
13. World War II Victory Medal.
14. National Defense Service Medal.
15. Korean Service Medal.
16. United Nations Service Medal (Korea).
17. U.S. Presidential Unit Citation.

Think this man didn't love his country? He defended it against foreign enemies with his blood, and today he defended his ranch against assassins with his life.

The house appeared to be unmolested. It didn't look as if anything had been tossed or stolen. Nevertheless, they photographed everything just the way they found it.

Next they returned to the barn for an exhaustive search. Everything was still in place. They didn't find any hidden gold coins or murder weapons or blood splatters. Barlow fed all four horses, put them in the coral, and mucked the stalls. Sheriff Sol asked Archie if he would take the horses back to his ranch until they knew what to do with them. He said he would.

Grunt finally showed up for his breakfast. He got a can of Alpo. It was consumed in less than a minute, with lots tail wagging and slobber and slurping and licking of chops. Sol asked if Archie or Slick would take Grunt home. Slick said he would. Then he and Archie mounted their horses and rode to Lagarto just to nose around a little bit.

In the meantime, Chief and Gillespie processed the crime scene. They recovered the identifications of all the deceased villains, including El Gordo, who's real name was Rafael Larosa. When Kirk showed up, he took all their ID's to show to the Border Patrol.

Chunk brought the information on the van. It was not reported as stolen. It was registered to B.R. Armando's Scrap Metal, LLC, in Del Rio. Now he knew where he needed to go once he joined forces with a deputy from Val Verde. Buck Boyd towed it to his storage lot, with its final destination probably being a salvage yard with a car crusher.

Chief and Gillespie finished the crime scene by 11 o'clock. Chief went back to the office to get a start on the mountains of investigative reports. Gillespie didn't leave until after Pete Ricketts had transported all the bodies to the mortuary. It was 1 o'clock before she left to drive back to the office to go home.

Sheriff Sol and Barlow drove over to the Jackson ranch first. Elmer Jackson was expecting the worst and he got it. It took almost an hour to peel him off the ceiling. He was concerned about his safety. He had lived here alone in peace for nine years after he retired as a mid-level supervisor from the Wranglers manufacturing plant in El Paso. He sought solitude here. Too much crime in the big city. Now his home was in the epicenter of a hostile Mexican crime family takeover. Look what they did to Sergeant Wrigley, and he was an experienced, brave man who had fought in three wars! He even had Pedro to help him out! What's become of our nation? How could Governor Smith allow this to happen? President Wilson sent the Army into Mexico to punish the Villistas who raided that little town in New Mexico. Of course, that was before World War I, when American sovereignty actually meant something. He railed on and on and everything he said was absolutely true.

Sadly, Sheriff Sol couldn't offer him anything other than to promise the swiftest response they could make if he called. Sol suggested buying a guard dog and putting up some lights around the back of his house. Sol said the sheriff's office was in the early stages of the investigation, and that he was every bit as concerned about this as Elmer was. In the end, Elmer said he was uncertain as to what he would do. He had 40 head of yearling steers to feed, and they were not ready yet for market. What about Sergeant Wrigley's steers? He has 45, if he wasn't mistaken. What will become of them?

All this handwringing reminded Barlow of something his grandmother used to say when folks got "tied up in their underwear" over fears which might never come to pass. She'd ask, "What if you had two children and one of them died?" Usually that sufficed, and folks quit moaning about the bogeyman who might be hiding under the bed or in the closet. Barlow was relieved when Sheriff Sol finally wished Mr. Jackson well and said they had to get back to the investigation. How do you spell "wimp?"

Lastly, Sheriff Sol and Barlow stopped by the Matthew and Nicole Perkins' Flying P Ranch. The Perkins had already spoken with Elmer Jackson. To put a fine point on it, no one was shoving them off their property!

Mr. Perkins was wearing a gun belt with a Smith & Wesson Model 29, .44 Magnum revolver. Nicole was wearing a similar rig with an S&W Model 28, .357 Magnum. They had at least six long guns in plain sight leaning in various corners of the house, to include two pump shotguns, two .30-30s, and two scoped rifles, likely .30-06s or .270s. They also had two well-trained German shepherds. (Mr. Perkins said he had learned the value of guard dogs when he was a K-9 handler in the Air Force.) To put it bluntly, they were much better prepared than Command Sergeant Major Wrigley had been, minus his combat experience. They were putting up additional pole lights around their property. They even had a state-of-the-art alarm system for the house.

Mr. Perkins said he would take care of Arn's cattle and Elmer's, too, if he asked. They had a grown son whose three years were almost up in the Army paratroopers, and he would be coming home to stay with them. If they heard or saw anything which might assist in catching the murderers, they would call. Mr. Perkins concluded with, "Sheriff Pratt, we appreciate everything you all do down there at the sheriff's office. If you all ever need anything from us, don't hesitate to call, and we'll keep an eye out for poor old Mr. Jackson. He's kind of like Casper Milquetoast and Chicken Little all rolled into one, but bless his soul, he means well. Good day."

That was the state of affairs when Barlow headed home at 3:30. He had a class at 6 o'clock, but he was off the next two days. He decided to stay up and drink more coffee and wait for Sarah to get home from work. They would eat. Then he would gut it out and go to class with Sarah. This day helped him make up his mind. He would not take any summer classes. He needed a break.

CHAPTER 20

Running Out Leads in Del Rio

Friday, March 24, 1972

Kirk was pleased to receive the assignment to check the identities of the deceased Mexican thugs with the Val Verde County SO and the Border Patrol. Of course he brought their identification cards, but they might be stolen or fraudulent. He also had Polaroid mugshot photographs of them taken at the crime scene on the off chance some of the detectives at the SO or agents at the Border Patrol might recognize them.

Both Chunk and he stopped at the Val Verde County Sheriff's Office, first to grease the skids, and second to get some local help. Captain Jay Ortman assigned Detective Miguel Valenzuela to assist Kirk, and Detective Sergeant Roy Rayburn to assist Chunk. The first stop for both of them was the Bureau of Identification (B of I) to check if any of the deceased bandits had been arrested in Val Verde County.

Rafael Larosa (El Gordo), José Salazar, and Roberto Peña were not on file. Jesús Alvarado, also known as El Pene Grande (The Big Prick) had an arrest for possession of marijuana (no disposition, meaning most likely case dismissed) and auto theft, amended to petty larceny for which he served one month in jail and paid a $500 fine. Ignacio Pastor had an arrest for armed robbery and aggravated assault, for which he received two 10-year sentences to run concurrently, after which he was shuttled off to the Texas State Penitentiary in Huntsville to serve his time before deportation.

The next stop was the Gang Unit. Nothing on file there.

The last stop at the sheriff's office was the Narcotics Unit. José

Salazar, Roberto Peña, and Jesús Alvarado were all listed as suspected marijuana dealers connected to Augusto Afilado-Rojo (La Serpiente). That being said, this information was gleaned by questioning informants, narcotics suspects, and arrestees. Narcotics had no hard proof. This was simply unverified intelligence. Nevertheless, this was the type of connection Chief Alex was looking for.

Kirk and Detective Valenzuela went to the Border Patrol station next. They met with a Lieutenant Bernard Willoughby, who confirmed that all five thugs had passed through the bridge checkpoint at 12:54 that morning. He called the home of one of the agents who worked the checkpoint last night, Carlos Benítez, and woke him up. Agent Benítez recalled their passage. There was nothing noteworthy about it. They claimed they were agricultural workers hired for one day to shear sheep at a ranch near Sheffield. They had to be there by 5 o'clock and hoped to be back by late afternoon. Benítez and his partner, Agent Chester Bryant, searched the men and the van. The men had no weapons or contraband. The van was empty except for farm implements. Kirk asked if there were any way possible that they had guns hidden somewhere in the van. Agent Benítez was adamant that the men and the van were clean. Kirk thanked him and Lieutenant Willoughby for their assistance. Detective Valenzuela drove Kirk back to his car. Kirk went straight to the Quayle County Jail and reported his findings to Chief.

Noble "Chunk" Bustamante and Detective Sergeant Rayburn drove over to B.R. Armando's Scrap Metal, LLC, where they met with the owner, Ramón Armando. Sergeant Rayburn asked if Ramón had had any problems with customers lately. He said he had not. Then Sergeant Rayburn asked how many full-time employees he had. Ramón said six, plus two part-time. Then he wanted to know what this was all about.

Sergeant Rayburn asked if he or the business owned a white, 1960 Econoline van. Ramón replied, "Yes, so what? I have eight vehicles here, including two flatbeds, a wrecker, two tractor trailers, two pickups and that piece of shit van. If you haven't noticed, we have 16 acres of junk cars and worn out heavy equipment on the lot, which is fenced in with barbed wire all the way around. I have two junkyard dogs on the premises roaming free at night. For the last time, what is this about? I've got a lot on my plate today."

Sergeant Rayburn asked, "Sir, could we see the van?"

Armando replied, "Sure. Follow me."

They walked around to the back of the enormous corrugated steel building where more than a dozen vehicles of all sizes, shapes, and colors were parked. Ramón stopped short, took off his greasy baseball hat, and scratched his bald head behind his ear where he still had some fringe. Then he exclaimed, "What the fuck?" He looked around and saw a worker and yelled, "Juan, where's the van?"

Juan ran over and said, "I don't know, Boss. It wasn't here when I got to work. I just figured Pinky or Doodlebug may have borrowed it since they wasn't here."

"What do you mean they're not here?"

"They ain't here. I thought you done give 'em the day off. I been busy crushing cars and never paid it no mind."

"Go check the office and get me the keys. Something ain't right here."

"Yes, Sir. Be right back." He took off on a fast jog.

Armando said, "These fucking guys! I swear, I'm gonna fire every last one of 'em. I know they're stealing me blind, taking car parts home, selling 'em on the side. Fuckers!"

About 10 minutes later Juan came running back, huffing and puffing. He said, "They ain't there, Boss. I checked everywhere."

"Okay. You can get back to work." He turned back around. "I don't know what to say. Maybe them guys borrowed it without my knowledge or maybe it's stole, but I don't think so since the keys is gone."

Sergeant Rayburn asked, "What's the real names of Pinky and Doodlebug?"

"Ah, they're a couple of Mexicans who work part-time here. They don't have no papers. Don't turn me in, okay? They call José Salazar "Pinky" on account of him being prone to catching pink eye. They call Roberto Peña "Doodlebug" because he's always drawing pictures when he's on break. You know, doodling."

Sergeant Rayburn asked, "You ever loan Pinky or Doodlebug your van?"

"Oh, Hell no! They live in Acuña. If I loaned them my van I'd never see it or them again. That's why I pay those assholes day by day. They're good workers when they wanta be, but they're flaky. Bastards probably spend all their wages on weed. Fuckers are probably stoned right now and that's why they didn't show up."

Chunk said, "Mr. Armando. They're not stoned. They're dead and your van's been wrecked in Quayle County, where I work. They got in a shootout with a rancher and his hand last night and came out the worse for it. This is the second time in just a couple of months your vehicles have been used in crimes in Quayle County. Remember the Diamond T cargo truck that was wrecked while hauling illegals? Now this. Makes me wonder what's going on over here in your shop."

Ramón's demeanor morphed from gruff to conciliatory. He said, "Guys, I ain't had nothing to do with none of that. Honest! I break my balls trying to run a legit business here. It ain't easy. This is a tough racket and a lot of my customers are a little shady. You know. I gotta be careful so's not to buy a stolen vehicle by accident. You gotta believe me!"

Chunk asked, "How did these guys get the van keys? You give them permission to take it back and forth across the river, because that's what happened last night?"

"Hell no! They must've stole the truck yesterday sometime when I was all tied up. Wouldn't surprise me none to learn that one or more of my other workers helped 'em do it."

Sergeant Rayburn asked, "Like who?"

"Any of 'em, especially the Mexicans. Juan is my right-hand man, but he's the reason I hired Pinky and Doodlebug to begin with. Sometimes we need a little extra help. He recommended 'em and besides, he's Pinky's uncle, or maybe his brother-in-law. I forget. Oh, Lordy! I've been had! I trusted him! No telling what all he's got me into!"

Sergeant Rayburn asked, "What's Juan's last name?"

"Juan Manuel Santos. He's got a green card. All my full-time workers have a green card if they wasn't born here. Let's go back to my office. I'll pull my file."

Sergeant Rayburn said, "Good deal. You can file a police report while we're at it."

Armando preceded them into the dim, cluttered, smelly, building with greasy, slippery concrete floors filled with various types of heavy equipment and machinery. They walked from the rear of the building to the front and and entered Armando's small office. It was unlocked. A pegboard filled with keys was hanging by the door.

Besides furniture, the office was overstuffed with thick catalogues, papers, invoices, empty soft drink bottles, full ashtrays, used paper coffee cups, an overflowing waste basket, and too many dead flies and cockroaches to count.

The furniture consisted of a very used, green metal Army surplus desk obscured with a scattering of documents, pens and pencils, an adding machine, a small metal knickknack shaped like a chihuahua pissing on a fire hydrant, two full ashtrays, a ceramic coffee cup, two crumpled packs of Camels and one nearly full one, and untold other items. The office also had three matching Army surplus filing cabinets with files and documents piled a foot high on top. The remainder of the furniture consisted of a rolling chair behind the desk and two wooden kitchen chairs in front of it, one of which had a broken leg and was out of commission as a seat. Maybe it was there for sentimental reasons.

By way of decoration and junkyard ambiance, the office had a half-dozen framed photographs of vintage automobiles hanging on the wall, plus an 18-inch, fly-specked wall calendar from Chico's Cantina, located in Ciudad Acuña, with a picture of a voluptuous, naked Hispanic woman bent over a table and looking back over her shoulder. She had long black hair, beautiful melons, a perfect derrière, and luscious pink lips. It was dated 1963, not that anyone probably ever noticed.

As soon as they jammed into his cramped office, Armando began to search for a file in the cabinet nearest to his desk. He finally found it and stood up. He saw the officers looking at the calendar. He smiled and said, "I keep that calendar because that chiquita looks just like my old lady did when I met her. That was in 1963 also. It was a good year." He paused, smiled, and handed the thin manila file to Sergeant Rayburn.

Sergeant Rayburn flipped through all six pages. He copied some information from the file and handed it to Chunk. Chunk followed suit. Then he handed the file back to Armando.

Chunk said, "Mr. Armando, if everything you say is true and you want our good will, you will do two things. First, you will not fire Juan until we can take a better look at him. Second, you keep your mouth shut about everything we've talked about today. Not a word to anyone. In return, I'll get Sheriff Pratt to release your van, but you'll have to haul it back on your flatbed. The engine's all seized up."

Sergeant Rayburn concurred. He said, "Ditto if you want our good will. Otherwise, besides us, the Border Patrol, INS, IRS, DOT, the county business inspectors, and anyone else I can think of will be crawling up your ass with a microscope. I'm positive you are hiding something you don't want the regulators to look at. Comprende?"

"Sí."

Last thing was, Ramón completed a police report provided by Sergeant Rayburn.

Chunk and Sergeant Rayburn returned to his unmarked unit and drove back to the SO where Chunk was parked. Chunk thanked Sergeant Rayburn. They agreed to keep in touch.

Then Chunk drove back to Mosby and reported his findings to Chief. All in all, Chunk had a pretty fruitful day. The big ticket item he was bringing back with him was that B.R. "Ramón" Armando's foreman, Juan Manuel Santos, was the uncle or brother-in-law of decedent José "Pinky" Salazar, and both vans which were used in smuggling or hauling killers originated at B.R. Armando's Scrap Metal, LLC. How was that for a coincidence?

CHAPTER 21

Archie and Slick Bend the Law

Friday, March 24, 1972

Archie and Slick were the only two men in the Quayle County Sheriff's Office who could break this case wide open and they knew it. Sometimes you have to "color outside the lines" just a wee bit to obtain justice for the people you were sworn to "serve and protect." Officer Dudley Do Right just isn't capable - too bound up in "doing things by the book."

Sheriff Sol knew this, and so does every law enforcement officer who's "worth his salt," i.e., competent enough, bold enough, and tenured enough to have learned when it's "time to fish or cut bait." It should only be done as a last resort, and then only in a very few select situations.

It must be done right. It can never be mentioned, especially if the statute of limitations hasn't expired. The officer(s) deploying such an option must be willing to live with his decision without remorse. Simply stated, in order to achieve true justice, sometimes this is the only way because the criminal justice system doesn't always work for the victims, who are real flesh and blood and not theoretical constructs. When a victim is told it's not personal, that's a baldfaced lie. Think about it. Anytime a person is the victim of any crime, it's very personal to him. Both Archie and Slick knew that Sheriff Sol needed them to go "dark ops" but they also knew he would never ask. It's extremely risky, and the sheriff needed plausible deniability if something did go wrong. Think CIA missions during the ongoing Cold War. Same-o, same-o. "The Government will disavow all knowledge if . . . ."

Archie and Slick had discussed this two days earlier after

Slick's meeting with Sheriff Sol. They formulated a plan which they put on hold. When they received the notification about this morning's vile deed, coupled with Sheriff Sol's request for them to do a quiet recon in Lagarto via horseback, they knew the time had finally come. Slick called Archie as soon as he received the call from Sheriff Sol to confirm. Archie agreed. They came fully prepared when they showed up for duty at the Circle A.

They crossed the river same as always at the back of Arn's ranch in the shallow area to check it's depth. Today the water was less than six inches deep in the most shallow spots. This was perfect.

Instead of going south along the trail straight to Lagarto, they followed the river west for a couple of miles. Then they turned south. It was broad daylight, but this was an area of barren desert which was unpopulated. They needed to arrive at their destination unobserved if at all possible. So far, so good.

They rode approximately five miles, well south of Lagarto, before turning east. In essence, they were circling Lagarto from west to south and back east before turning north to their target location, all to avoid being seen. Now it was only a mile or so to their destination. Things were still looking good. They hadn't seen a solitary soul.

They paused long enough to scan their surroundings one final time. The very last thing they needed was a chance encounter with someone who might remember them. All remained clear. Then they rode onto Ernesto Robles' five acres of shitbird heaven and tethered their horses inside his barn. Today there were four pesky chihuahuas, but remembering their fallen brother slain by a kick from one of these gringo horses, they barely yapped and they didn't come too close. These mutts were obviously in the upper end of the gene pool compared with their recently departed pack member.

Arch and Slick walked back to Ernesto's front door and tried the doorknob. It was locked.

Archie pounded on the door like he was driving nails with his fist for a full minute before Ernesto finally opened up. He was still pie-eyed from consuming too much tequila. He was also still naked. This was way better than what they had hoped for.

Ernesto was staggering and waving around a brand-new-looking, blue steel, Colt Diamondback, .38 Special caliber revolver with a four-inch barrel in his right hand. His eyes were glassy. They also appeared to be unfocused. He asked, "Qué quieren cabrones? Salgan de aquí antes de que mate a un par de viejos gringos más," in which it was understood by both Archie and Slick to mean "What do you two fuckers want? Get outta here before I kill me a couple more old gringos."

Archie replied, "I thought you habla Inglés, Ernesto." Then Archie reached up and twisted the Diamondback out of Ernesto's limp hand and passed it back to Slick, who was standing on the step behind him. Slick slipped it into his waistband. At the same time, Archie shoved Ernesto back into the trailer and bulled his way in. Slick followed Archie and closed the door. Ernesto exclaimed, "What the fuck?"

Archie pushed Ernesto down on the couch and said, "Looky here. Ernesto does speak English. Hey, amigo. We heard you was having a party. Look what we brung ya." Then he reached into his jacket pocket and brought out a quart of the cheapest tequila on the planet. "Ya like tequila, don't ya?"

Ernesto grabbed the bottle, twisted off the cap, and began imbibing as if he were in the desert (he was!) extremely parched (he must be), and the liquid he was lapping up wouldn't "peel the paint off your car" (except that it would). At the same time, Slick pointed at a half-full bottle of tequila and two more empties on the kitchen counter. He was dangling a set of car keys and a sack of dry dog food. He said, "Looks like you made a friend. I'll step outside and put this (pointing at the revolver in his waistband) away, and feed the dogs. Might be awhile before they get another meal. Be back in a few." Then he stepped outside and closed the door.

Ernesto paused his drinking, ripped a loud fart, and asked, "Do I know you, amigo?"

Archie replied, "We're your guardian angels, amigo. Have another taste. It will clear up your mind."

Ernesto surprised Archie. Even though he was small, he made up for it by pure, cutthroat meanness. He was a bonafide badass the last time they saw him. Now he was drinking out of the bottle just like a toddler. How much could a 130-pounder like Ernesto hold, anyway? It wasn't even noon yet. He must've done the dirty deed and come straight home and started drinking. Ernesto consumed more than half the bottle. Then he slid face down on the couch on a pile of El Gordo's dirty clothes, including a pair of foul-smelling, shit-streaked underwear, and began snoring.

Archie started tossing the trailer. Not much here. He checked the bedroom first. A veritable pigsty. He found a medium-size, plastic, grey and green zippered gym bag big enough to hold more than one set of clothes. He stuffed it full of Ernesto's finest attire, to include his toothpaste, toothbrush, and safety razor from the bathroom. He checked all the dresser drawers and under the mattress as well as under the bed. He threw everything out of the closet. He didn't turn up anything that looked like something Ernesto truly cared about. Nevertheless, he did pick up a Saint Christopher medal on a silver chain, some personal documents, a half-box of Winchester Western .38 Special bullets, and a small, framed photograph of a woman he presumed to be Ernesto's mother. He put all this in the bag too, and zipped it up.

In the meantime, Slick returned and searched the rest of the trailer, which only included the bathroom, already searched by Archie, the living room, and the kitchen. He found a small closet for the propane water heater. He opened it up, and saw a loose piece of wooden veneer on the back wall. He pulled it back and found a crumpled, brown paper lunch sack. He pulled it out, unfolded the top, and looked inside. It had two stacks of paper currency. The one-inch stack had Mexican pesos - probably worth no more than $100. The bigger stack had American currency. The bills were mostly $10s and $20s with some $5s and a few $1s. Slick estimated $2,000. He brought it out, closed the door, and placed it on the kitchen countertop.

Ernesto began snoring even louder. He sounded like a Bengal tiger purring. Slick said, "I found his stash, pointing at the paper sack."

"What about his truck? I didn't see it."

"That's because it ain't there."

"Dern!"

"But El Gordo's raggedy Plymouth is, and it runs good enough to get to Quayle County! I got the keys."

"Very good. Put the stash in this gym bag. Help me dress him. We gotta remember to put his wallet and watch on him, and anything else he has up there on the countertop, including his smokes and matches. I couldn't find any other shoes, so he'll have to wear these wet boots. Then we'll cuff him and stuff him in the trunk. You still wanna drive?"

"Yep. You take the horses. We'll retrace our steps. Hurry up. I wanna be out of here before someone comes looking for him."

"You bet. Don't forget these two bottles that are partially full and the two empties. We need to put them in the car, too. Make sure you don't leave any of your fingerprints on them in case Chief decides to print all the stuff in the car."

"Good point."

Ernesto was out cold like a dead mackerel. They got him dressed, cuffed, and stuffed into the back seat of the Valiant. (They decided he was too drunk to put up much resistance even if he did wake up.) Slick drove away slowly the same way as they came in. Archie was mounted on Leo and leading Toby. They made a clean getaway.

It took nearly all afternoon to get back. Slick had to keep stopping and wait for Archie to catch up. The Circle A was deserted when they returned. Slick drove the car right across the river. Their badass killer never woke up. They loaded up their own horses, plus one each of Arn's in both trailers so they could make a hasty exit, hasty being a relative term in this situation. Slick lead off in the Valiant and Archie followed in his truck (without a trailer.) They went about three miles west of the Circle A on Highway 90. There was no one in sight.

They uncuffed Ernesto and placed him in the driver's seat and propped him up against the driver's door. They turned the engine off but left the set of keys in the ignition. They hid the pristine Colt Diamondback under the driver's seat. They put three of the tequila bottles on the front passenger floorboard, and the fuller one in his right hand, dropping the bottle cap on the seat next to him in plain sight. They put his gym bag on the back seat. Ernesto never stirred. He was still unconscious like a cold-cocked, strong-arm robbery victim.

Archie did a U-turn and headed back to the Circle A. They hooked up both trailers and departed for home. When they drove up next to the Plymouth, they stopped to look. Ernesto was still zonked out.

Archie said, "I'll wait here. I live closer than you. When you get home, as soon as you unload, call the jail and tell them there's a car on the side of the road here and it looks like the driver's asleep at the wheel. Then circle back to the Circle A and pick up the other two of Arn's horses. Don't forget Grunt. When I see you coming back, I'll take these horses to my house and wait for you. I think Dewey Carruthers is on afternoons today. Hopefully he won't pass by me before I get home. If he does, I'll just say I saw the Plymouth but didn't stop since I got two more horses to bring home. If Dewey sees you, stop to make sure he's okay. Then try to get out of there before Ernesto wakes up and remembers seeing you at his trailer. Agreed, compadre?"

"That's a big 10-4, good buddy. See you on the flip-flop."

Slick arrived at his ranch and put Toby and one of Arn's

horses in the corral. He called the jail. Dewey answered. Slick said, "Dewey, I just got back home from the Circle A. I was toting horses, and I gotta go back and get two more plus Arn's dog. I saw a car headed westbound stopped on the highway about four or so miles west of the Circle A. It was an old, white Plymouth. Probably an early '60s model. I could see a guy who looked like he was asleep. Not sure though. It's possible he's dead but I don't think so. Could you check on it?"

"Sure thing. Let me finish my sandwich and I'll be on my way.

"That was a sorry thing those bastards done, wasn't it? Poor old Arn and Pedro. They was some good fellers. At least they took out five of 'em before they was kilt."

"You got that right. Look, I gotta get back. If ya have any problems or need me for anything, give me a shout."

"Will do. Take care."

Slick headed back to the Circle A. When Archie saw him approaching, he waved and headed home. He did not pass Dewey.

Slick put the last two horses in his trailer. Then he called and Grunt came running. Slick got the rest of the dog food and Grunt's bowls and opened the door of his truck for him to jump in. Grunt almost knocked him down with his wagging tail. Slick decided that Grunt was a keeper. Then he turned around and headed for home. When he arrived at the Valiant, Dewey was trying to wake up Ernesto, who he had already cuffed.

Dewey said, "Thanks for stopping by. Can you help me get him into the cruiser? He's passed out drunk and I can't seem to wake him up. What an idiot!"

"No problem." Between the two of them they carried Ernesto to the cruiser and placed him face down (in case he aspirated) in the back seat behind the cage.

Slick said, "Did you search his car?"

"Looky here." He pointed to the right front seat of the cruiser. He had Ernesto's Colt revolver, the gym bag opened up where he could see his stash, and four tequila bottles.

Slick asked, "Who is he, anyway?"

"Mexican drivers license says he's Ernesto Robles! I think he's one of the shooters. I believe he was making a run for it. Thing is, the car ain't registered to him. Registration says it belongs to some dude named Rafael Larosa. Ain't he one of the killers, too?"

"Sure is. Larosa's one of the dead guys. You got you a trophy catch, Dewey! Good job! Want me to wait for the wrecker while you run him in?"

"No. I got it. Thanks for giving me a hand, though. Sheriff and Chief are still at the jail, so I'll have some help when I get there. I called it in and they're both waiting."

"I bet they're salivating and licking their chops. Especially Chief. He wanted this asshole bad. Well, okay then. Probably see you tomorrow. When I get home, I'll call the jail and let Sheriff Sol know what Archie and I discovered today, but it ain't nothing nearly as big as what you got. Congratulations."

"Thanks. Yep, this is my biggest bust ever. I owe it all to you!"

Slick smiled and left for Archie's to let him know that "all's well that ends well." It was time for an adult libation in silent, deliberative celebration.

CHAPTER 22

Talk of the Town

Sunday/Monday, March 26/27, 1972

It was 11:30 Sunday eve. Barlow arrived a little early to relieve Randy Meacham, who was just leaving the cellblock to put on a fresh pot of coffee. When Randy saw Barlow, he said, "Well, I guess you heard about Dewey bagging that little sidewinder we got back there in Cell #1."

"Yep. A person would have to be deaf or dead not to have heard about it. What a great bust! I heard Slick called it in and then gave Dewey an assist. The whole town is buzzing. I bet even the dead bodies in the cemetery heard about it. What can you tell me about Ernesto? Does he whine or does he keep his trap shut?"

"Well, it's kinda funny. Chunk said the asshole came to Saturday about 4 in the morning. He had a splitting headache. He also didn't have the foggiest notion as to where he was. When Chunk told him he was in the Quayle County Jail in Mosby, he started howling like a hyena in heat, screaming he wanted out and the like. When he finally calmed down, Chunk told him in Mex that he was going to be tried for murder of an American military hero and his ranch hand, plus a guitar player shot in a car wreck with a truck hauling illegals. Then he really came unhinged. He claimed he didn't do it and so forth and so on.

"Chunk told him it didn't "make no never mind." We got your gun and we took it to the lab to check it for ballistics. If it's a match, we're gonna try you and hang you from that big oak tree out back. He said the whole town would show up to see it because we haven't had a hanging here in over 40 years. Then the punk pooped his pants. I kid you not! Chunk said Ernesto was too drunk to clean himself up, so he left him alone to stew in his own mess for about two more hours until he could."

"What could he possibly have been thinking? I understand trying to escape if he thought we were hot on his heels, but why run to the U.S., especially in the very same county where he committed the murders. Who would even attempt such a thing as drunk as he was?"

"Well, I'm wondering if someone who knew he did it, his boss maybe, told him he was a dead duck for fucking up the hit so bad. He left five of his own crew dead on the ground! That would definitely get you waxed by the Mafia here, even if you were a made man."

"You could be right. I guess you could say he's "scared shitless." How's he doing tonight?"

"Ha! A comic. Well, I think his headache is mostly gone. When I stepped out just now, he was lying in the fetal position and staring off into space. The only infantile thing he wasn't doing was suck his thumb."

"He know he has court in the morning?"

"Oh, yeah. Chief laid it all out for him earlier this afternoon. By the way, Atwater probably already left to go to the state lab with the gun and the spent bullets to see if he can get a rush analysis this morning. Sheriff told him to stay put until he got the results and to phone it in as soon as he got 'em."

"That's a tall order."

"Yep, but it's all taken care of. Our own favorite state senator, the Honorable Mr. Darnell Sweeney, himself, who's chair of the Texas State Senate Justice Committee already made the call. Look, I hate to run, but we're shorthanded and I'm making your push in about eight hours."

"Oh, sorry. I didn't know. Don't sweat it if you're a little late. We got you covered."

"Thanks. See you all in a few."

Gillespie was just walking in the door as Randy was making

his exit. She was effervescent as always. She said, "Did you hear about Dewey arresting Ernesto Robles? Can you believe it? Passed out in his car on Highway 90! I wish I could've been there.

"Do they have firing squads in this state? If so, I'd like to volunteer. I want to inflict pain on him so bad, but then I think. It won't bring my two friends back to me." She teared up and had to use a tissue to blot her eyes so as to not mess up her makeup.

Barlow replied, "I know your pain. Look, why don't I take the first shift? Randy said Ernesto's basically in a catatonic state now, lying in the fetal position. If he keeps that up we should have a peaceful night. Not that it affects you or me, but Ernesto's got court this morning. He's charged with DPP [drunk in a public place] and CCDW [carrying a concealed deadly weapon]. I expect whether he pleads guilty or asks for a trial, either way, Judge Sweeney will keep him in the slammer. Oh yeah, the Border Patrol put a hold on him for illegal entry into the U.S., so he isn't going anywhere no matter what. Also, with any luck, we'll have the lab results on the ballistics and fingerprints on the gun sometime this afternoon.

"By the way, Arn's funeral is Tuesday morning. From what I understand, he's a widower. He didn't have any kids, or any that're alive, anyway. Nobody knows of any living relatives. They did find a will but it's handwritten. The witness is an old Army buddy, a retired master sergeant named Norbert Ellison from Killeen. Chief tracked him down but he's dead. The will stated Arn was leaving his livestock, tack, guns, Jeep, and all other personal belongings to Pedro Padilla. The real property is to be sold by auction, the proceeds of which are to be donated to a children's home in Amarillo called Hope for the Future. Chief said it's a cattle ranch, school, and home for orphans, both boys and girls. Supposed to be a righteous organization."

"So what happens? Pedro's wife inherits all his stuff since Pedro's dead?"

"Looks like it, but I'm sure everything has to be adjudicated by Judge Sweeney."

"What about Pedro?"

"His wife is making arrangements to have the body transported back to his hometown in Mexico. Not sure where that is, but I don't think it's Lagarto. Not sure, though. Pete Ricketts said he would transport the body for free once they get him the paperwork. Probably a bureaucratic nightmare."

"What about the five other stiffs?"

"Supposedly all seven bodies have been transported to Val Verde County for autopsies. Pretty sure they're done with Arn and Pedro. I got no idea what happens to the bodies of the Mexican killers after that."

"Chief will probably be working on all the paperwork for a month."

"Yep. How would you like to have his job?"

"I like processing crime scenes. I plan to take a correspondence course on it from Michigan State University. I wouldn't like all the stuff related to matching bodies with relatives, but I guess that's all part of it."

"Sounds like you've found your niche."

"You never know. Okay. I'll push you off at 2."

"Good deal."

The shift was "easy peasy." Ernesto never stirred. Gillespie thought he looked so small and pitiful. How could that scrawny weasel have been the murderer of three men in less than two weeks? How many others had he murdered? How many lives had he shattered? It was incomprehensible. If a jury saw him looking like this, they'd probably have mercy and find a reason to find him not guilty. She was freaking out!

Then she pulled herself together. Best case scenario for Ernesto, he gets life without parole and dies in prison. Worst case is they fry him and all his worldly troubles are over. But what if his defense attorney, Sam Davis, convinces him to squeal on the person who hired him to do the hits - something like murder for hire? How could they prove it, especially if the contractor is a Mexican still in Mexico? How would they ever get him extradited back to the U.S.? Who would she rather see executed, the shooter or the contractor? What if Ernesto lied about a contractor just to get a reduced sentence? What happens then?

She had to stop! She was getting ahead of herself again. Chief Alex and Sheriff Sol were both smart cops. They'd get to the bottom of it. She needed to concentrate on doing her own job and let them do theirs. Consider her minor role in this investigation as part of learning the job.

What's that old saying, "It ain't over 'til the fat lady sings"? Tomorrow would be another day.

CHAPTER 23

Back in Old Mexico . . .

Monday, March 27, 1972

La Serpiente was beside himself with rage. Five of his men were dead! That punk Ernesto Robles was nowhere to be found. All his shit was gone. His truck was at a garage pending repair, but Gordo's car was missing. He had men searching high and low for Ernesto, but so far no one had seen him.

Then today, he saw the headlines in Ciudad Acuña's daily rag, *La Paz del Pueblo,* about a shootout in Quayle County, Texas, between two American ranchers and five Mexican citizens. All were dead. Names of the deceased were being withheld pending notifications to the next of kin. La Serpiente had known who they were since the morning it happened. What he didn't know was that a suspect named Ernesto Robles from Lagarto was arrested by American authorities near the site of the gunfight in a car belonging to one of the deceased Mexican citizens. He was currently being detained in the Quayle County Jail without bail pending a hearing scheduled for today. The sheriff's office was not releasing any further details. Mierda!

He needed more details. Lots more details. Ernesto needed to die for his incompetence and to shut his big fucking mouth, but how? It was doubtful they could rub him out in the archaic dungeon in that one-horse town without a full-fledged frontal assault. He was probably the only asshole in jail. There would be lots of guards. It would be a bloodbath of epic proportions. It would make international news. Even La Serpiente's corrupt politicos would not be able to protect him. He needed to find another way.

He decided to send a semi-trustworthy Mexican lawyer licensed to practice law in the U.S. to pay Ernesto a visit. Try to get himself appointed to represent Ernesto. Carry a message to him. He knew just who to send, too. He'd been on retainer for two years in the event something like this ever occurred.

He contacted Señor Eduardo Castillo and paid him $1,000 in cash up front. Now all he could do was wait.

CHAPTER 24

And the Phones Kept Ringing

Monday, March 27, 1972

It had been a busy weekend and Monday was even busier. Sheriff Sol and Chief Alex had both worked Saturday and Sunday until their heads were ready to explode. Today was no different. Randy Meacham was in the jail babysitting Ernesto. Noble "Chunk" Bustamante was working the desk. Dewey was on patrol and running out leads and loose ends as assigned.

The phones kept on ringing. It was difficult to get an open line and they had four! This is what happens when you have a shootout with seven dead participants.

Sheriff Sol took all the calls from news organizations. Chief Alex handled the lion's share of the investigative calls that Chunk couldn't resolve. Most of the callers wanted information. The FBI, BNDD, ATF, and the Texas Rangers all called to see if they could assist, and each did in its own individual way.

The FBI and BNDD squeezed snitches for information. The FBI didn't glean any new information on Augusto Afilado-Rojo. They did warn that he was well-connected with political and law enforcement officials on his side of the border, and anything provided to the Mexican authorities would make it back to him muy pronto.

BNDD called back and said, for what it's worth, a reliable informant came forward and reported that La Serpiente was furious about the loss of five of his henchmen. He found it highly improbable that two old men could inflict such losses on his soldiers absent a tip off. He was searching in all the dusty corners looking for the rat. He was also looking for Ernesto Robles, an up-and-comer in his organization who had been in charge of the hit, and now was missing. He was offering $500 to whomever located and brought Ernesto to him. If nothing else good comes of these murders, at least Mr. Wrigley and his hand really "rattled Afilado's cage."Maybe now he will do something rash and set himself up for arrest and prosecution in the U.S.

ATF ran traces on the recovered firearms. It was a long shot. Nothing helpful turned up. Not even a theft report.

The Rangers flexed some muscle and persuaded DPS to run complete histories back to the origin on the Diamond T truck, the disabled Econoline van, and the Valiant. There was always a slim chance the vehicles had been owned by La Serpiente or someone in his organization, or used in a previous crime, but nothing popped. The Rangers also whispered to Sheriff Sol that if it became necessary to run a clandestine operation in Mexico, to call them first. They would assist. Keep it in mind.

Even the Federales stationed in Ciudad Acuña called to express (most likely) insincere sorrow and to extend whatever assistance might be required in Mexico (probably really an intelligence-gathering mission). Chief expressed appreciation for their thoughtfulness and asked if they could help locate the next of kin of the only decedent, Jesús Alvarado, for whom he had been unsuccessful. They eagerly agreed. They were successful in locating a sister and putting her into contact with Chief Alex.

Governor Smith called to ask if Sheriff Sol thought Quayle County was under siege. If the answer were affirmative, he would send a contingent of national guardsmen to cover the most probable routes of illegal ingress into Quayle County from Mexico. They would stay for at least a month, longer if needed. Sol thanked him profusely, but said they had everything under control. The governor gave Sol the telephone number of his private line and told him to call if the situation changed.

At 9:50, Sheriff Sol, Chief Alex, and Deputy Randy Meacham took Ernesto upstairs to the courtroom for his initial appearance for the charges of DPP and CCDW. (The lab report had not come in yet.) They had Ernesto trussed up like a Thanksgiving turkey. He looked just like a typical gangbanger from the barrio. He was wiry. His hair was mussed. You could see the homemade tats on both his hands and the left side of his neck. The only thing different was, instead of swaggering and affecting bravado, you could also see the fear in his eyes. His hands were shaking.

There were newspaper reporters present in the courtroom from Mosby, Del Rio, Ciudad Acuña, Alpine, El Paso, and Austin, and more than just a few curious local citizens and others who weren't local. The small courtroom had seating for 96, not including the jury, court officers, or defendants. It was nearly full.

Judge Sweeney was imposing, ramrod straight, stern, white hair in a crew cut, sky blue eyes, with a nose that was slightly hooked and resembled a hawk's beak. His stare was piercing just like a bird of prey. His black robes shone like glistening raven feathers. He was aloof, a stickler for proper decorum, as well as for the constitutional administration of criminal law in the pursuit of justice. He emanated raw power. He "ran a tight ship" and nobody doubted for "a New York second" that he would come down hard "like the wrath of God" if someone violated the sanctity of his court.

Court was called to order. District Attorney Able DeWitt read the charges. Samuel W. Davis, Esquire, representing Mr. Robles, tugged his client up to his feet, and stated that Mr. Robles wished to plead not guilty to both counts.

All the correspondents craned their necks to get a better look at one of at least six alleged Mexican murderers (five others were killed and perhaps others fled with the accused) of two Texas ranchers who had the misfortune of owning and operating a working ranch directly on the Mexican border where the water was shallow, and in which the law enforcement presence was less than 12 officers to cover an area of more than 2,200 square miles. It was nearly an impossible job if faced with organized criminals, especially if they could flee back into political safety in Mexico. The reporters came to exploit their xenophobia in an area where it barely existed. (How else could one explain a half-breed Apache getting elected sheriff twice?)

Judge Sweeney scheduled a trial date for Thursday, March 30th, at 10 o'clock absent any new developments. He stated that were the Grand Jury to return an indictment on additional charges before then, the trial would be postponed and Mr. Robles would have an arraignment. Furthermore, he stated that due to the nature of the pending investigation, plus the fact that he considered Mr. Robles a flight risk and a threat to society, he was holding the defendant without bond pending trial. He also noted that the Border Patrol had issued a detainer against Mr. Robles for illegal entry into the U.S., and that case would be heard by the U.S. District Court in El Paso upon resolution of the charges in this court. Business complete, the judge adjourned court, banged his gavel, and departed through the door behind his bench into his private chambers. Chief and Randy escorted Ernesto back to the jail. He was shivering with fright. Sheriff Sol stayed behind because he was besieged by all the reporters.

While the sheriff and the chief were still tied up in court, Deputy Atwater called the jail to provide verbal results on the laboratory examinations. He passed the message to Chunk.

First, four latent fingerprints were recovered from the Colt Diamondback, .38 Special caliber revolver in the possession of one Ernesto Robles. Three prints were determined to belong to Ernesto Robles. The other latent print belongs to an unknown party at this time.

Second, three .38 caliber projectiles recovered from the person of one Casper T. Brooks and one recovered from the seat back of his truck were fired from the same Colt revolver found in the possession of Ernesto Robles. Five .38 caliber projectiles recovered from the person of one Arnold Wrigley were also fired by that same Colt revolver.

Third, none of the other projectiles recovered from the bodies of Arnold Wrigley or one Pedro Padilla were fired from any of the weapons recovered at the crime scene. Arnold Wrigley's body had a total of 11 projectiles fired by handguns - five from Robles' .38 caliber Colt, and six from a Beretta 9 millimeter semi-automatic pistol, plus 26 BBs fired by a shotgun(s) of unknown origin. Pedro Padilla's body had two projectiles fired from a Smith & Wesson .38 caliber revolver, five by a Harrington & Richardson .32 caliber revolver, and 18 BBs from a shotgun(s) of unknown origin.

Fourth, two projectiles recovered from the body of one José Salazar, two projectiles recovered from the body of one Rafael Larosa, and one projectile recovered from the body of one Roberto Peña were fired by the same .30-06 caliber M-1 Garand which was recovered next to the body of Arnold Wrigley. In addition, two additional projectiles recovered from the body of Roberto Peña were fired by the .45 caliber Colt pistol which was also found next to the body of Arnold Wrigley.

Fifth, two projectiles recovered from the body of one Jesús Alvarado and two projectiles recovered from the body of one Ignacio Pastor were fired by the same .30-30 caliber Winchester rifle which was recovered next to the body of Pedro Padilla.

Bottom line - Robles shot Brooks and Wrigley. He did not shoot Padilla. Also, as many as five other unknown shooters shot Wrigley and Padilla. Neither Sheriff Sol nor Chief Alex were surprised. Arn had been shot in the back. Pedro had been shot in his back, left side, and front. It looked as if Arn and Pedro killed the first group of assailants before being ambushed by a second group. They were looking for five or more additional shooters.

Would La Serpiente have been there in person? Doubtful. He had minions to do his bidding. Chief was waiting for the Feds and the Rangers to get back with him after talking with their informants. So far Ernesto hadn't squealed on anyone.

Chief called Able DeWitt to tell him of the lab results. Chief wanted to use these results to squeeze Ernesto. Chief wondered if this would be enough to induce him to talk. Probably not. Chief knew he wouldn't if he were the defendant "in the trick bag" unless the death penalty were taken off the table. Dern! He needed the identities of the other shooters.

Able told him, "Call Sam Davis and give him the results. Let Sam speak to Ernesto. See what Sam comes up with. I'm sure I already know, but I'm not willing to "give up the farm" unless Ernesto provides enough information to assure a capital murder conviction on everyone else involved, which presumably includes Señor Augusto Afilado-Rojo.

"As soon as I get a copy of the lab report, I'll begin drafting a proposed indictment on Robles. I'll load it up with everything we've got. We'll present it to the Grand Jury Wednesday morning.

"Better get Dewey prepared to testify. Remind him to look spiffy. If he isn't up to it, you'll have to do his portion for him. Belay that. Upon further reflection, it might be better for you to present Dewey's portion. That way the defense, who gets a copy of Grand Jury testimony, won't have a statement from Dewey to pick apart once he takes the stand to testify. Let me think about that. I'll let you know.

"You or Gillespie need to testify regarding the crime scene investigation, too. We'll only present a bare bones scenario. Enough to secure the indictment, but not so much we give away everything. Full discovery isn't required just yet.

"Get that lab report to me as soon as you can. Bring it yourself so we can talk about the Grand Jury. Bye."

Chief called Sam Davis. Sam said, "Soon as you get the report, call me and I'll come right over, even if it's midnight. I need to talk to Mr. Robles today, not tomorrow. Things will be in full disarray with Mr. Wrigley's funeral in the morning."

"No rest for the weary and the wicked don't need none."

CHAPTER 25

Command Sergeant Major Arnold Wrigley is Laid to Rest

Tuesday, March 28, 1972

The entire town of Mosby was closed for the day in honor of the funeral for Command Sergeant Major Arnold Wrigley, the county's most decorated war veteran. The school was closed. The courthouse was closed. None of the merchants were open. Just about everyone in town turned out for the services at the Mosby Baptist Church, the biggest building in town, and it was beyond overflowing. The only soul that Deputy Kirk Shoemaker knew for certain who was working today was himself. He drew the assignment because he was the third junior deputy; otherwise, he would have attended the funeral. Barlow and Gillespie were junior to him, but they were on the midnight shift. Kirk split his time between manning the silent telephones and checking on Ernesto, who was lying quietly in his rack, pondering who knows what.

The Army brought in a 10-man honor guard commanded by a major, including a seven-man rifle team for the 21-gun salute, from Fort Bliss in El Paso, 300 miles away. Dozens of active duty, retired, and former Army veterans from all across the state and elsewhere, many of whom were previous colleagues of the decedent, were there to pay their last respects.

Most of the veterans who could still fit into their uniforms wore them with all their ribbons. This included Barlow, Slick, and Dewey. (Kirk was on desk duty.) The moths had consumed too much of Archie's doughboy uniform, but he still had it. Sheriff Sol, Chief Alex, Ernie, and Chunk had expanded waistlines from their youthful prime, so they wore their SO uniforms with all their ribbons. Archie wore his, too. Chief's Purple Heart received a lot of attention from those who did not know he had been wounded in WWII, while serving as a coxswain in the Coast Guard at Anzio and during D-Day. Officers from the American Legion wore their blue, full dress American Legion uniforms. Boy Scouts, Girl Scouts, Cub Scouts, and Brownie Scouts all wore their uniforms.

Lieutenant Governor Ben Barnes came to represent Governor Preston Smith. Texas State Senator Darnell Sweeney and other lesser state elected officials were there. Each business and home which owned a flag was flying it at half mast. Barlow had never seen anything like it. Neither had Sarah.

The service was conducted by Reverend Conrad G. Stokes. Being a member of the Methodist Church, Barlow had never heard him preach. Barlow and hundreds of others quickly learned that Reverend Stokes was a profound orator. By the time he finished, there wasn't a "dry eye in the house."

The funeral procession, lead by Sheriff Sol in a marked unit and concluded with Chief Alex in another, extended for a mile or more. They took Command Sergeant Major Wrigley's remains to the Quayle County Cemetery just north of town. The interment was deathly quiet, except for the 21-gun salute. Judge Sweeney accepted the folded flag which had draped the casket. Eventually the flag was placed on display at the Lieutenant Colonel Robert G. Cole American Legion Post 79 in Mosby where Command Sergeant Major Wrigley had been a cherished member.

It was over by noon and everyone drifted away, most of whom were too sorrowful to speak, while others were too angry about Arn's murder to trust themselves to speak. Those who had to work went to work. The rest took the remainder of the day off.

About 11 o'clock, when Kirk was returning to the office from checking on Ernesto in the jail, he heard a maniac pounding furiously on the back door of the courthouse. This was the door folks used when they wanted to go directly to the sheriff's office. The main door at the front of the courthouse was locked. Kirk turned around and walked to the door to see who was causing all the commotion. He opened the door and asked, "May I help you, Sir?"

He was handed a business card from a well-dressed man in a grey sharkskin suit with a bolo tie, 12-karat gold and turquoise clasp, spit-polished Tony Lama, lizard skin boots, and a beige 25X Stetson. A spotless, white, 1972 Cadillac Sedan de Ville was parked in Judge Sweeney's marked, private parking space. Kirk could guess to whom the car belonged. The card read, Eduardo K. Castillo, attorney-at-law, 306 Main Street, Suite 201, Del Rio, Texas, telephone # 905-574-1111. Licensed in Texas & Mexico.

Kirk examined the card and asked once again, "How may I help you, Sir?"

He responded, "I'm here to speak with my client, Ernesto Robles. I understand he is incarcerated here."

"Sir, Mr. Robles already has an attorney of record, Mr. Samuel W. Davis, Esquire. Maybe you should speak with him first."

"If I am correct, Mr. Davis is an appointed attorney. I am Mr. Robles' hired attorney."

"Hired by whom? Mr. Robles has no money to hire an attorney. He's made no calls. Not one. He has not asked to speak with you."

"I am afraid I cannot divulge that information. Just take me to Mr. Robles and I will straighten everything out."

"Mr. Castillo, I don't know if you've noticed, but the whole town and the courthouse are closed today. They're holding funeral services for Command Sergeant Major Arnold Wrigley, who was brutally murdered just a few days ago. I'm sure you can guess by whom. Everyone but yours truly are at the services. I expect it will be over in an hour or two, and some people will most likely return to work, possibly including Mr. Davis and Judge Sweeney, not to mention Sheriff Pratt. I suggest you come back about 1 o'clock. I'm not permitted to allow you to speak with Mr. Robles until one of the three of those folks I just mentioned tells me it's okay. I will give one of them your card, whomever I see first."

"Perhaps I could wait in your office or you could direct me to a diner."

"Sir, normally this door and the front door to the courthouse would be open during business hours. Unfortunately, right now I'm the only person other than your potential client who is in the building, and I cannot do that. There are two diners in town. One is called Betty's. It's at the west end of U.S. 90 on the south side. The other one, called Crabtree's, is on the main north-south drag, Texas Street, right here at the traffic light, about a block north on the east side. They both might be closed right now due to the funeral. I'm not sure."

"Very well. I shall return. Adiós."

"Adiós. One last thing. You're parked in the space reserved for Judge Sweeney. It's even marked. If you're still parked there when he returns, I can guarantee he will have your car towed. "A word to the wise is sufficient if the wise is sufficiently wise"."

Mr. Castillo smiled and gave Kirk a facsimile of a proper military salute as he walked back to his car.

The first person to return to the jail was Chief Alex. Kirk handed him the card.

Chief said, "Well, well, well. Isn't this interesting? Thanks. Glad I wasn't here. I'll give Sam and Able both a call. Able should be here in just a few minutes, anyway. The attorneys and the judge will have to slug this one out. But I wonder. Will Ernesto want this attorney to represent him? You know Mr. Castillo really represents La Serpiente, not Ernesto. How better for "the big kahuna" to line up a hit on Ernesto than through his attorney? I also wonder if Judge Sweeney will allow Mr. Castillo to represent Ernesto without divulging the name of the person who's paying him. We should know soon."

Sheriff Sol, Able, and Sam all arrived together about 12:45. They had a powwow with the chief behind a closed door in the sheriff's office.

A few minutes later, Sam came out. He asked if Kirk could take him to see Ernesto. Kirk was happy to comply. He was anxious to see how Ernesto responded to Sam. He locked Sam in with Ernesto and walked to the rear jailer's office to respect their privacy. It took about 10 minutes. Sam shouted, "All done here."

When Kirk unlocked the cell door, he tried to get a look at Ernesto's face, but he couldn't. Ernesto was lying in his rack with his face against the wall. Kirk walked Sam to the front of the jail, past the metal mesh door leading to the arched door with iron bars, to the wooden office door. Once they got there, Sam whispered, "He's scared. I don't know what he will decide. Mr. Castillo will probably be here soon. Once they meet, Ernesto will make up his mind."

Kirk replied, "Thanks for the info. Guess now that both the sheriff and Chief are back, I'll just stay in the cellblock. Are you going to wait up front with the sheriff?"

"No place else I need to be. Besides, I want to talk to Mr. Castillo before he talks to Ernesto. Will you search him for a weapon before he gets back here?"

"Oh yeah, unless Chief Alex or Sheriff Sol search him and his valise first. I don't think he would do a hit himself, but he might smuggle in a weapon or a handcuff key. Maybe even some poison. The entire Quayle County Sheriff's Office would be in deep kimchi if Ernesto died or somehow managed to escape. That ain't happening on my watch."

"Good."

When Sam returned to the office, he saw Mr. Castillo talking with Sheriff Sol, Chief Alex, and Able DeWitt. Able was saying, "Of course you can speak with Mr. Robles, and if he says he wants you to represent him instead of Mr. Davis, we'll need to schedule an appearance with Judge Sweeney. Assuming your credentials are in order and Mr. Robles makes this declaration to the judge in court, he will probably sign off.

"You do need to know that Judge Sweeney doesn't tolerate theatrics in his court, and he doesn't let "any moss grow under his feet." This case will be tried and recorded in the clerk's office before you can blink your eye, so if you become the defendant's counsel, you better hang on. In the meantime, let me introduce you to Mr. Davis. Then Chief can take you to the cellblock and you can speak with Mr. Robles."

"Thank you."

Introductions were made, hands were shaken, and Chief unlocked the wooden office door into the jail. He motioned for Mr. Castillo to follow him inside. It was 85 degrees outside the courthouse, so it felt similar to a sauna inside once Chief shut the wooden door. Kirk came out of the cellblock and conducted a thorough search of Mr. Castillo and his briefcase. All was in order. Kirk unlocked the arched door with the thick metal bars, letting them in, and locking the door behind him. He unlocked the wire mesh door, locking it behind them, and lead Mr. Castillo and Chief to Cell #1. He unlocked the cell door so Mr. Castillo could enter. Then he locked it behind him. Chief Alex and Kirk went back to the rear jailer's office to give Mr. Castillo and Ernesto some privacy.

Kirk asked, "What do you think?"

"I think you took some of the starch out of Mr. Castiilo. I'm sure he thought the jail was air conditioned. He's already melting and he just got here. Now, if Castillo is approved to represent Ernesto, I doubt he will fare any better than Elton Stonebreaker did when he represented Joe Schitt. Castillo is a peacock and he'll wind up pissing off the judge. Able warned him, too.

"Everyone here knows Castillo doesn't have Ernesto's best interests at heart. His purpose is to silence Ernesto. Either way, Ernesto is a dead man. His only hope for life without parole is to hand up La Serpiente and the other shooters, but I doubt he's capable of pulling that off. So, if we don't arrest La Serpiente, or if he winds up dead at the hands of his enemies or even law enforcement, nothing Ernesto says will get him a reprieve from Old Sparky. At least that's the way I see it."

"That's pretty much what I think, too. How was the funeral?"

"It was about what you would expect. The town's really upset about Arn's murder. In another era, Ernesto would be swinging in the breeze out behind the courthouse on a limb on that big oak tree before the end of the day. Are we doing him a favor by dragging this out? I wonder. Back then, La Serpiente and his entire nest of vipers would have already been exterminated by a posse unless he got wind it was coming and fled all the way to Mexico City. Ask Archie if you think I'm exaggerating."

"I don't have to. I know what you're saying is true."

They continued chatting for about 20 minutes. Then they heard Ernesto shrieking like a mad man. He was yelling, "Vete a la mierda! Vete a la mierda!" When Kirk and Chief got to the cell, Ernesto was whaling away on the frightened lawyer who was trying to get away from him. Kirk unlocked the cell and peeled Ernesto off the lawyer. Chief Alex shoved the lawyer out of the cell and followed him out. Kirk pushed Ernesto onto his rack, followed the chief out, and slammed the cell door shut.

Mr. Castillo didn't even wait to straighten his clothes or wash his face. He wanted out now! Once he set foot in the office, he uttered, "That man is a psychopath! I'm through with him! Good day!"

Kirk asked, "Does vete a la mierda mean what I think it does?"

Chief replied, "It means get the fuck out! I wonder what Castillo will charge La Serpiente for getting his fancy clothes crumpled and almost getting his crooked ass kicked."

Able said, "Good question. Well, I reckon we know who's representing Ernesto. Sam, I guess you've already figured out we'll being going to the Grand Jury tomorrow to present an indictment for two capital murder counts among other things. You've got an easy day on Thursday. All we'll have is the arraignment. After that you've got your work cut out for you."

Sam replied, "Works for me. Just "another day in paradise." Any idea what Castillo said to Ernesto?"

Chief said, "We haven't got a clue. Whatever he said, it turned Ernesto into a homicidal lunatic instead of the wilting flower we've seen since he sobered up. Kirk and I saved Castillo from a serious, old fashioned, ass whipping, if not something worse."

Sam said, "He probably needed it. Good day, gentlemen. See you all on the flip flop."

CHAPTER 26

Deputy Gillespie Has an Opportunity to Shine

Wednesday, March 29, 1972

When Gillespie showed up for her midnight shift, she was beaming like a lighthouse on a dark, foggy night. She was flickering like a lightning bug on a hot summer night. She sparkled like a diamond in a bright sunshiny day. Take your pick. She put her thick pile of stuff down on the junior deputy's desk, and rushed over to the coffee counter to pour a fresh cuppa joe. She sat down beside Barlow and said, "Guess what." She was nearly breathless.

Barlow said, "You bought a new car - a bright red Camaro. Can I take it for a spin?"

"Don't I wish! Chief Alex called me this afternoon - actually yesterday now that it's past midnight. He woke me up from a sound sleep. I was so tired after the funeral. It was so somber. I miss those guys so much."

"Me, too."

"Chief wants me to make the entire presentation at the Grand Jury today! I get to do it all - the car accident where Casper T. Brooks was murdered, the arrest of eight illegal aliens, both crime scenes, the murders of Arn and Pedro, the leads in Del Rio, the lab reports, medical examiner reports, and Ernesto's arrest - the whole enchilada!"

"That's great. How come Chief and Dewey aren't doing this?"

"That was my question. Hearsay is admissible at the Grand Jury. You know that. Other than the stakeouts, my role in this entire case was being Chief's assistant at the crime scenes. Unless something goes haywire, I won't be called to testify at the trial.

"The defense gets a copy of the Grand Jury testimony. Everyone knows Sam Davis is a straight shooter, but this is a double capital murder trial. Suppose someone like Elton Stonebreaker becomes the defense counsel. An attorney like him would do everything in his power to twist the meaning of statements made during Grand Jury testimony, looking for any wedge he could drive in to make the case all about mistakes or misstatements made by the cops. You know, "make mountains out of molehills"."

"If Dewey or Chief were to say something that isn't 100 percent correct, like where a gun or shell casings were found, but the crime scene photos show it was actually six inches away in another location than where they said it was during the Grand Jury, that could be all it takes to convince a jury that the witness isn't credible, even if it was an honest mistake.

"I won't have to testify in the trial. Dewey or Chief could say I was mistaken and that's that. This is why "in an abundance of caution" Able suggested that I do all the Grand Jury testimony. It's been years and years since they've had a capital murder trial here. They want to do everything they can legally do to prevent any mistakes."

"That's pretty smart. Are you prepared?"

"You bet. Chief brought a copy of the proposed indictment and a copy of the case file over to Mrs. Beanblossom's house yesterday about 5 o'clock. I've been studying it, and I've got 'til 10 this morning to get it down pat. Plus, I can look at the file or rough notes if it becomes necessary but I don't think it will be. I'm so excited! Lots of officers never have an opportunity to do something like this in such a big case."

"True enough. I know you'll slay 'em. Uncle Leland will be proud of you.

"I'll go babysit the man of the hour. Give me a push about 2. Gillespie, if you need to conk out, it's fine by me. You got another very long day ahead of you."

"You got it. Thanks. I might take you up on that except right now I'm so wired."

"Do what's best for you."

The shift ended without a hitch. Barlow went home and straight to bed. No class tonight. Hallelujah! Gillespie went to Crabtree's for a pancake breakfast. She continued to cram like this was a final exam in her hardest college science course.

The Grand Jury lasted for almost two hours. The jurors were hungry for some red meat after yesterday's heart-wrenching funeral. The Mosby grapevine was humming. Gillespie nailed it. Chief, Able, and Sheriff Sol took her for a celebratory, meatloaf and mashed potatoes lunch at Betty's. She capped it off with peach pie à la mode. Then she went home and crashed. It was a great day for them all.

CHAPTER 27

La Serpiente Receives Some Bad News

Wednesday, March 29, 1972

E duardo Castillo was no fool. He told Señor Afilado to come to his law office in Del Rio at 10 o'clock. No way Eduardo was going to La Serpiente's fortress in Mexico. If he didn't like the news and flipped out, Eduardo could well wind up "one of the disappeared," his body being deconstructed with all his body parts scattered throughout the desert for the carrion-eaters to consume every last morsel of him.

La Serpiente did not like crossing the border. He knew BNDD wanted him in the worst way. He didn't fully trust ese hijo de la chingada Castillo (that motherfucking son of a bitch Castillo) not to sell him out. Mr. Afilado sent his two most trusted men, Fernando Reyes and Julio "El Toro" Valdez, to scope out the situation first to see if it was a trap. After waiting for an hour to give them time to call if it were, Enrique Calderon drove him to the lawyer's office in the yellow, '64 Ford Galaxie 500 XL with the 390 cubic-inch, 300 horsepower engine, in the event they had to outrun the cops. Before they entered the parking lot, El Toro flashed Enrique the "thumbs up."

It goes without saying that all the men were armed. La Serpiente was wearing twin, engraved, gold-plated Colt .45 caliber, Government Model pistols under his beige, linen suit coat, not to mention his signature, gold-plated, switchblade with mother-of-pearl grips which was in his right trouser pocket. He wore his snake ring which was coiled around his left pinky. It had two ruby eyes. He wore glossy black, alligator skin Tony Lamas. The band on his beige Stetson was made of rattlesnake skin. The head was in the front, mouth wide open, bearing its fangs. When La Serpiente smiled, you could see that his two front teeth were gold-capped. Though he was not a big man, maybe 5-feet, 10-inches tall, with a medium frame, and thick, glossy black, slicked-back hair, he made an indelible impression wherever he went. He was truly unforgettable, especially so if one incurred his wrath.

Enrique stood post outside the suite door. Mr. Castillo lead La Serpiente into his well-appointed office and closed the door. He sat behind his mahogany desk, not quite as large as an aircraft carrier, and offered him coffee. La Serpiente sat before him in one of four, matching, caramel-colored, leather wingback chairs with brass studs all along its outline. He said he would prefer tequila.

Mr. Castillo picked up the phone and buzzed his stunning, long raven-haired, Latino secretary, who was wearing a short, cobalt blue, silk dress which accentuated her long, smooth, shapely legs and magnificent bosoms which were nearly popping out of a low-cut top. She entered a minute later with a sterling silver tray laden with crystal cut glasses, a bucket of ice, some sliced limes, and an unopened bottle of Clase Azul Reposado tequila. She set the tray down on an end table and poured each of them a generous portion. She bent over at the waist and let La Serpiente feast his eyes when she handed him a glass. She did the same for her employer. Both times she served one, the other got a commanding view of her perfect derrière. Then she sashayed out of the office in her blue, spike heels. She was so smoking hot, she could give a Pope with a glass eye a "diamond cutter" "in a New York second" in front of the entire College of Cardinals.

Mr. Castillo staged this exhibition so Señor Afilado would be thinking pleasant, amorous thoughts when he received the bad news.

They both savored their drinks. Mr. Castillo opened a humidor and offered Señor Afilado a premium cigar. He selected a maduro Monte Cristo panatela. Mr. Castillo selected a Punch robusto with a Connecticut wrapper. They clipped their cigars and enjoyed ten minutes of smooth, satisfying smoking while they sipped on their drinks. They finished those drinks and poured another.

Señor Afilado appeared relaxed. He asked, "What news do you have for me?"

"It is neither good nor bad. I visited with Mr. Robles in his cell in that miserable, 1910, unimproved dungeon for about 20 minutes. (I do admit it was sanitary). I told him you sent me to be his counsel. I told him things looked muy malo - that the gringos planned to try him for capital murder. Think of it! They had just laid Mr. Wrigley to rest about the time I arrived! The mood in that tiny, somnolent, one-horse town was ominous. Much different than the other times I've passed through there. It seemed peaceful then. Not now, though. Ernesto's lucky they haven't already strung him up! Mr. Wrigley must have meant a great deal to those people.

"Ernesto said they captured him when he was passed out drunk. He doesn't remember the arrest. He did remember the raid, and how the ranchers had killed all the men in Josés' group before he arrived. That's because José "jumped the gun" and arrived early. The ranchers must have been waiting for them. He didn't know how they knew, unless Josés' group made too much noise. He said maybe you had a rat in your employ. Ernesto and the guys with him mowed both the ranchers down. The van would not start, so they had to walk back to his trailer. He swore he was not fleeing. He swore he had not told the authorities a thing. He said he was afraid you were going to kill him.

"I asked why he was driving El Gordo's car in Texas if he wasn't fleeing.

"Then he went completely berserk and almost killed me. He choked me by my tie. I thought I was going to die at that very moment by a maniac I had been hired to help. Suddenly, he let up and began beating me savagely with his fists about my face. He bloodied my nose and cut my lip. My left ear is still ringing. Thankfully, two deputies ran in and pulled him off of me. I departed the jail and Quayle County in haste, driving just as fast as I could go.

"I am sorry, Mr. Afilado, but I cannot represent that worthless dog. He is pure evil."

"Do you think he was telling the truth?"

"It is hard to say. I do not believe he was just taking a scenic drive through South Texas. That's absurd under the circumstances; however, I am persuaded that he has not informed on anyone yet; however, you can bet he will "sing like a canary" once he knows for certain he's facing the electric chair. What would he have to lose at that juncture? Does he know enough information to put you in jeopardy?"

"He knows he works for me. Isn't that enough?"

"It could be if BNDD wants you bad enough, assuming they are building a historical case against you. However, that is far from certain. Do you think you have an informant in your midst? Ernesto seemed to think so."

"That's the $64,000 question, isn't it? It's always possible, but it's more likely José fucked up and arrived too soon just like Ernesto said, or he made too much fucking noise. Oh well, I'll figure it out. Thank you. I appreciate your efforts and insight."

"That's why you keep me on retainer, Señor Afilado. Adiós."

"Adiós.

CHAPTER 28

The Hangman Measures Ernesto for a Noose

Thursday, March 30, 1972

It was 10 o'clock. The man of the hour was standing in court before Judge Maxwell B. Sweeney, otherwise known as "Maximum Max" but Ernesto did not know that. What he did know was that Judge Sweeney looked like a very hungry bird of prey, such as a hawk or an eagle. Ernesto felt like un conejo asustado (a scared rabbit). He knew his fate was sealed. Mr. Castillo had already said so. Ernesto wondered how much time he had before they exacted justice on him. He prayed that it would be quick and painless. Now the best he could hope for was that he wouldn't shit his pants. That would be the ultimate humiliation.

Court was called to order. Judge Sweeney announced that the trial was postponed. New charges had been levied against the defendant by way of an indictment. He asked the district attorney to elucidate those charges.

District Attorney Able DeWitt responded, "The Grand Jury finds that there is sufficient cause to believe that the defendant, one Ernesto Robles, should be tried for the capital murders of one Casper T. Brooks on or about March 15, 1972, and one Arnold S. Wrigley, on or about March 24, 1972. In addition, sufficient cause was found to believe that the defendant should be tried for accessory to capital murder of one Pedro Padilla on or about March 24, 1972, all such events having taken place in Quayle County, Texas. Furthermore, the misdemeanor charges against the defendant for being drunk in a public place and for carrying a concealed deadly weapon on or about March 24, 1972, will be tried the same time as the charges listed in the indictment."

Judge Sweeney asked, "Mr. Davis, would your client like a formal and complete reading of the indictment before the court?"

"No, Your Honor. The clerk of court has already provided a copy to Mr. Robles and another to me. I read and explained the indictment to my client."

"What plea does your client wish to make?"

"Not guilty on all charges, Your Honor."

"Mr. Robles, do you understand that two of those charges bring about the possibility of your execution if you are found guilty?"

"Sí."

"Very well. Normally, I would schedule trial for Monday, April 3, 1972, but since this is a capital murder trial, I will set it for Thursday, April 6, 1972, at 10 o'clock. Mr. Davis, this seems like a straightforward case. I can't imagine it will take two days at the very most to try it, unless you need additional time to round up witnesses. What say you on this matter?"

"Truthfully, Your Honor, my client has not provided me with any information whatsoever to help me to prepare his defense. I have zero background information on him. I cannot assess his mental state.

"I request that the court order a psychiatric examination of my client and provide you and me and District Attorney DeWitt with his findings.

"I'd also like to hire a private investigator to go to Mexico to conduct a background investigation on my client. I know what the prosecution has, and at this time, it looks straightforward to me, too. I just don't know what I have as rebuttal, and I need some time to determine that. Also, quite frankly, I would be surprised if the state laboratory experts and the medical examiner would all be available on such short notice.

"Your Honor, I'm asking for at least another week."

"Very well presented, Mr. Davis. What say you, Mr. DeWitt?"

"I agree with counsel, Your Honor. Another week would benefit me as well."

"So be it. The clerk of court will contact Dr. Wiroslaw J. Snihirowicz of Corpus Christi and see if he can come tomorrow or Monday to examine Mr. Robles. Mr. Davis, do you have a competent private investigator in mind?"

"I do, Your Honor. Mr. Oswaldo Nighthawk from Alpine. He speaks excellent Spanish. I've used him in the past for some civil matters. He's retired from the Bureau of Indian Affairs in Arizona."

"Very well. Submit his voucher to the court for reimbursement."

"Thank you, Your Honor."

"Very well, gentlemen. Trial is scheduled for Thursday, April 13, 1972 at 10 o'clock. If there are no other matters before the court, court is adjourned. Good day, gentlemen."

CHAPTER 29

Mr. Nighthawk Earns His Money

Friday, March 31, 1972

Oswaldo Nighthawk was happy to receive the call from Sam Davis. The contract called for a minimum of two days - maximum of three - at $65 per day plus expenses. Oswaldo owned two vehicles, a raggedy-looking, faded, baby blue, '63 Dodge 100 pickup truck which ran a whole lot better than it looked, and a white '71 Dodge Dart which was way too nice to drive into Mexico. Might as well beg to be carjacked.

He drove the truck. He had to remove his trusty Marlin .30-30 lever action carbine and a full bandolier of cartridges from behind the seat. No firearms allowed in Mexico. Damn Mexicans! He'd be the only one without a gun over there if you discount women and children less than 15. Normally he kept a Harrington & Richardson .32 caliber revolver in the glovebox, but that stayed behind, too. He kept his folding Buck hunter in the sheath on his waist. That would only cost $15 to replace if it got confiscated but he didn't think it would. Every Mexican, including women, had numerous knives in his personal defense arsenal.

Oswaldo drove to Del Rio, about 200 miles east of Alpine, and gassed up before he crossed the border. His first stop was at the Ciudad Acuña police station. He asked for El Jefe. He thought it would probably be a lost cause, but he needed to know for sure.

He was ushered into the office of Capitán Donaldo Luna. He handed the capitán a business card which read "Oswaldo Nighthawk, Private Investigator, Alpine, Texas, telephone 905-561-1811". He said, "I've been hired by the defense attorney representing Ernesto Robles, who's been charged in Mosby with murdering three people. One is a Mexican citizen, I believe. I'm looking for anyone who knows anything about Mr. Robles, in an effort to help mount a defense for him."

"Why would anyone try to help that piece of shit? I for one, am glad he's facing the gallows. I would shoot him myself for free if you brought him before me. Just about everyone else who knows him is happy about his misfortune, as well."

"Capitán, I suspected as much, but it is my job. All I seek is the truth. If it is all bad, it's all bad."

"Mr. Nighthawk, you seem like a pleasant man. We are everyone of us very busy here today. I would have to call someone away from an important assignment to assist you. I'm sure you understand."

Oswaldo reached into his shirt pocket and retrieved two $10 bills. He offered them to el capitán saying, "Maybe this could help defray expenses."

"Gracias. This will defray mine. Sargento Gómez will require $10, and Oficial Nuñez will require $5."

"Of course." Oswaldo handed him another $10 and a $5 bill.

Capitán Luna stepped into the doorway of his office and looked out to see how many men were sitting around in the squad room "cooling their heels." There were six. They all looked up. He motioned to Sargento Gómez, who scrambled over to him. Capitán Luna handed him the $10 bill and said, "This is for you." Then he handed him the $5 and said, "This is for Nuñez. Take Mr. Nighthawk to all the regular locations where Ernesto Robles is known to frequent. Ask as many people as you can find what they know about him. Everything. Squeeze hard if necessary. Make sure Mr. Nighthawk remains unmolested. When you are done, bring him back here. Understood?"

"Si, mi capitán."

The cops drove him in their broke-dick-dog, marked, '60 Ford Falcon sedan, coughing and belching exhaust fumes all through the tenderloin district. They stopped at every single dive and seedy whorehouse. Altogether there were 11. They helped him to interview 27 denizens who knew Ernesto. Only one needed coercing. A sharp tap on his testicles by the sargento's nightstick turned the key to his memory (probably because his testicles nestled so close to his rear end where his brains were located.) Suddenly he remembered a lot. Amazing!

Only one person, a big-breasted soiled dove of indeterminant age with unkempt hair and a killer body, dressed in a short see-through dress with nothing on underneath, had something good to say. She said Ernesto knew how to please a woman with both his mouth and his cock. Then she licked her lips, smiled, and winked.

No one knew if Ernesto had any living family members. Oswaldo wrote down the names of everyone he interviewed and what they said. The cops drove him back to his truck, and he headed muy pronto southwest to Lagarto before it became necessary to fight his way out of the bowels of Acuña.

Lagarto was a much smaller, sleepier town. More like a village. No cops there. Oswaldo dropped into Don Diego's cantina, which was the only establishment big enough for folks to gather except for the pequeña Iglesia Católica. He zeroed in on the person who exuded the aura of having the most power, speaking with Señor Don Diego first. Señor Diego looked down and spat on the floor when Oswaldo mentioned Ernesto's name. He said, "Es una mala semilla. Buenos días." The meaning was crystal clear. Ernesto was a bad seed. Mr. Diego held him in absolute contempt.

The breathtaking waitress Carlita said everyone was happy when Ernesto left town. Ditto for his sidekick, El Gordo. Three diners said they barely knew Ernesto, but he did not have a good reputation. He was suspected of being a coyote, a drug dealer, and a murderer. A fourth diner directed Oswaldo to Ernesto's lodging on the outskirts of the village. Oswaldo wrote everything down.

Business completed, Oswaldo ate a scrumptious Mexican meal of tamales, enchiladas, tortillas, refried beans, and rice, which he washed down with two Dos Equis. Then he drove over to Ernesto's trailer. He looked inside the window of the door. It was a hovel. Nothing much to see. There were piles of dried dog shit in the yard everywhere he stepped, but no dogs to be seen. He guessed the dogs had died or found a new home. The open stable was empty.

Finally, mission nearly complete, Oswaldo drove southeast to San Miguel. Even though it was a decent-size town, he had no problem locating La Serpiente's compound. Just like the ancient saying, "All roads lead to Rome," all roads in San Miguel lead to La Serpiente's fortress. Oswaldo had been dreading this portion of his assignment. He recalled the time King Darius cast Daniel into the lions' den. This is exactly how he felt - cast into the lions' den. He prayed he would fare as well as Daniel. (Daniel 6).

The manor was large and impressive with numerous guards that he could see from the street. It was constructed of tan stucco. The walls surrounding it were even crenellated. The roof was made with red barrel tiles. It was constructed like a huge, modern day Alamo.

Oswaldo walked up to the iron gate in front, and was immediately accosted by two hostile armed guards. He gave one his card and asked if it were possible for him to speak to Señor Afilado about a man named Ernesto Robles. The guard passed the card to another inside the gate and whispered something. Then he turned back to Oswaldo and told him to wait in his truck. He said if Mr. Afilado were not busy, they would motion for him to come back.

Oswaldo returned to his truck and lit a cigarette. He was prepared for a long wait. Less than 20 minutes later he was motioned to return. He uttered a silent prayer to St. Christopher and walked back to the house.

The guards opened the iron gate for pedestrians and ushered

him in. Another guard had him "assume the position" up against the wall. He searched Oswaldo thoroughly and unsheathed his Buck knife. He laid it on a table and said Oswaldo could have it back when he was ready to leave. Another guard lead Oswaldo across the manicured courtyard, through the sallyport, past the main, two-story dwelling, to a fabulous, sparkling, turquoise swimming pool with a shaded portico and a dozen or more chaise lounges. Four luscious females in the skimpiest bikinis that Oswaldo had ever seen in the flesh were cavorting in the pool with a beach ball. This place was filled with "eye candy."

La Serpiente was sitting in the shade, nibbling on some pineapple chunks and almonds, smoking a big fat Havana cigar, and drinking from a crystal tumbler filled with ice and presumably tequila, since a fancy bottle of same was occupying space on the table next to him. He offered Oswaldo a drink. Oswaldo accepted. An armed servant poured him a very generous portion over ice in a crystal tumbler and handed it to him. He took a sip. It was as smooth as a kiss from the nude Lady Godiva herself.

Mr. Afilado held up Oswaldo's card and asked, "What can I do for you, Mr. Nighthawk?"

"Sir, Mr. Samuel Davis, court-appointed counsel for Ernesto Robles, hired me to do a background check on his client, in an effort to bolster his defense in trial, which begins on April 13th. He directed me to come see you, to learn if you might have any information which would be beneficial to his client."

"Did he tell you that I hired a very good defense attorney for Mr. Robles, but he treated him rudely and told him to go away?"

"No. He did not."

"Did he tell you that on occasion I employed Mr. Robles to perform certain deeds for me?"

"Yes. He said you were alleged to be the biggest crime lord in all of north central Mexico, and that Mr. Robles was believed to be a smuggler of drugs and illegal aliens for you."

"You are bold, Mr. Nighthawk, to say such a thing to my face, although I understand that you are repeating what you were told, and not making an allegation of your own. Is that not true?"

"Yes. That is true. I make no such allegation. I have no direct knowledge of such activities by you or by your employees. What I see is a man of great wealth surrounded by bodyguards, and I wonder why such a man as yourself would have any dealings with a person such as Mr. Robles, although I tell you that I, myself, have never laid eyes upon him. It's just that the charges against him are so vile, so reprehensible, that if they are true, he deserves the punishment which is likely coming his way muy pronto."

"Of course. Mr. Robles was a poor street urchin, hustling for a living when I first met him. He had no familia. He never knew his father. His mother was a prostituta. He has no siblings, at least none that he knew of.

"He lived by his wits in Ciudad Acuña when I first encountered him several years ago. I hired him as a "step-and-fetch-it." You understand? Someone to run minor errands for me. I bought him some clothes. I fed him, helped him find a place to stay. I felt sorry for him. That was all. Eventually, I saw that he showed some potential, even though he was "rough around the edges." He cannot read, but he can add and subtract sums in his head very quickly.

"I sent him to Lagarto to see if there were any business opportunities, even though it is very small and poor. He hired that retarded oaf, El Gordo, to assist him. Ernesto found very little in the way of economic opportunities, nothing truly profitable, but I left him there and continued to send him a few pesos each month because he was my eyes and ears over there. I have many enemies, as do all powerful men of means.

"That's all I will say about me and my business. It's a private matter. I know what the American Bureau of Narcotics and Dangerous Drugs says about me. It's all false with a lot of innuendo, but that was why I continued to keep Ernesto on the payroll. He was useful to me. I had no idea he would shoot anyone, let alone kill someone. I still like Ernesto. That's why I sent the lawyer over there whom he rebuffed. So be it. It was his decision. If what I heard is true, Texas will execute him one day. It's all too sad a tale of woe.

"Is there anything else? If not, you'll need to excuse me. I have other matters which require my attention."

"No, Sir. Thank you for taking time to talk with me. You have been extremely helpful in my efforts to provide information to Mr. Davis, who is making a great effort to understand Ernesto. Adiós."

"Adiós. Good luck in your quest."

The guard returned Oswaldo's knife as he was on his way out the gate. It took him six hours, another tank of gas and a chicken fried steak dinner at the Sinclair Truck Stop in Del Rio, plus a final top-off in Alpine before he walked in his front door. It was way past midnight. Fortunately, old Mrs. Simpson next door had already fed and walked his pooch, Geronimo, like he had asked her to do. Geronimo was thrilled to see his master after such a very long, lonesome day. Oswaldo had a belt of bourbon and went straight to bed.

Saturday he typed his report. Then he called Sam Davis, who wanted the report right away. He confirmed that payment for three days of wages, plus all expenses, including bribes, would be tendered after Oswaldo delivered the report, plus an invoice with receipts, to him at his office Sunday afternoon.

Sam read the full report before listening to a comprehensive debriefing from Oswaldo. It was much worse than Sam thought it would be. Great Scott! The only socially redeeming virtues Ernesto possessed were that he gave good cunnilingus, and he could do sums quickly in his head? Seriously? How was he supposed to use that to curry sympathy from the judge and jury? Sam needed the report to show to Dr. Snihirowicz before he interviewed Ernesto on Monday. Hopefully it would provide the psychiatrist enough ammunition to pursue an insanity defense. He doubted it, though. Ernesto was just a bad egg. "Born to lose" from the moment he came out of his mother's womb. Ernesto was doomed. He was a "dead man walking."

CHAPTER 30

Life Is Not All Work

Saturday, April Fools Day, 1972

It was 8 o'clock. It was also a beautiful Saturday morning. Barlow and Gillespie had just been relieved by Slick. They were both off duty until 11:45 Sunday night.

Barlow and Sarah had plans that evening to go to the Bijou with Cordell and his wife, Darla, to see *The Godfather*, starring Marlon Brando and an all star cast. Happy wasn't invited. He had to stay at home, but on Sunday after church - they planned to skip Sunday School - they were going to the Casa de Baker for a horseback ride and an early barbeque before returning home so Barlow could nap before pulling his midnight shift. Happy was invited to go, too. Sunday's post-church activities would not have been possible had not both Sarah and Barlow been completely caught up in their school work. The last day of classes was May 12th, and both of them could hardly wait.

This was a short weekend, in that Barlow had already pulled a shift on Saturday, but they planned to take full advantage of the time they did have. Sarah ensured that they would begin with a bang by bathing, fixing her hair, dabbing on a touch of cologne, wearing her sexiest negligee, and posing artfully on the bed when Barlow entered the bedroom. Her irresistible charm worked just like she intended for it to. Barlow stripped off, gave his teeth a quick brushing, and rushed back to the bedroom to "knock the bottom out of it." He was possessed by the Greek god Eros. It was exactly what Sarah needed. It took Barlow thrice to quench her desire, but he took pride in his work, and when it was a mutual fait accompli, she nestled up close to him and listened to his heart beat as he drifted off into La La Land.

Gillespie planned to visit her family in Alpine over the weekend after she slept. She, her mother, and her grandmother had plans to go out with her aunt and uncle, Sheriff Leland Waters and Aunt Muriel, at the Texas Longhorn Emporium for a few beers and a Saturday night steak supper.

They had a lot of catching up to do. For one thing, Ella Mae wanted Uncle Leland's opinion on her new off-duty revolver, a Smith & Wesson .38 Special, Model 36, otherwise known as a Chief Special, which was highly favored by many officers as a back-up or off-duty weapon. She hoped he would fully approve of that selection.

What she really wanted to know though, was what he thought of her new leather purse with a shoulder strap, and a slot with a snap in the fore-end for easy access to a concealed holster which secured her new gun. She contracted for the purse from a shoe repairman/leather smith in Mosby named Eugenio Santobol, who made it custom just for her and the Model 36. He only charged her $11. She could think of no other way to carry her gun concealed, since she normally wore a dress or a skirt. The climate was generally too hot to wear a shoulder holster under a jacket.

Archie was in Robstown spending time with his new squeeze named Twyla that nobody in Mosby knew about except for Slick. Archie preferred to "run under the radar" until he knew exactly where this new relationship was headed. He couldn't believe he was so lucky. Surely she would come to her senses and fall in love with a man closer to her own age.

Twyla had come to visit Mosby one time on the Trailways bus, and Archie had introduced her to Slick. Twyla was a delicious peach. Slick understood why Archie was smitten. He also believed that Twyla was fully committed, and that Archie should get on with it and announce their engagement. In fact, he should have married her yesterday. Even today was too long of a delay.

Slick took care of Archie's horses whenever he was away, which in the past was almost never. Slick laughed to himself. Lately, it seemed like he should fix himself a bed in the barn, since Arch was running back and forth to Robstown nearly every other weekend. The saving grace for all this was that Slick only lived about eight miles away. It didn't interfere with his squiring of the single, good-looking cougars of Quayle County. Tonight he was seeing Ida Mae Chambers, a gorgeous widow woman whose husband had died two years ago due to a heart attack. Slick could easily understand why. Ida Mae was insatiable. She could go all night long. That's why Slick always ate beef liver for dinner the day before he went over to satisfy her nymphomania. He needed to keep his iron count up. Otherwise, he could wind up just like her husband, Harold, who must have been a tireless, iron horseman in bed before he died of sheer exhaustion.

Sheriff Sol and Joanna were taking the kids to Fort Stockton today to watch a rodeo. Sol had a nephew named Wolf Pratt, known professionally as The Apache Wolf of Texas, a top PRCA (Professional Rodeo Cowboys Association) rider in several events, including bronc riding, bareback bronc riding, calf roping, and steer wresting. There would be a number of other relatives in attendance. Not only that, Kirk Shoemaker was an ex-rodeo man and his wife was a former rodeo queen. They had been to many rodeos in Stockton. He mentioned to Sol that they might see them there.

Chief Alex was one of two coaches for the Mosby American Legion Post junior league baseball team, ages 13-17. His boy was the catcher. Chunk's boy was 10, too young to play, but he loved baseball. He was the batboy. The senior league was for ages 17-19. The Mosby teams called themselves the Hawks. Both wore beige flannel uniforms, just like the major leaguers. The junior team had red and white striped socks and red caps. The senior team wore blue striped socks and caps. Today both teams had a home game with the Bakersfield American Legion Post 110. They were called the Giants. After both games, the post sponsored an all-you-can-eat pork barbeque, open to everyone. The cost was one dollar for adults, and kids ate for free. It was an all day affair. The post generated a few bucks from the barbeque, but mostly they were trying to gin up community involvement in American Legion baseball.

Everyone on the SO had something going on over the weekend. Work hard. Play hard.

CHAPTER 31

Dr. Snihirowicz Evaluates Ernesto

Monday, April 3, 1972

D r. Wiroslaw J. (for Josef) Snihirowicz was 50 years old. He stood 5-feet, 6-inches tall, weighed about 170 pounds, perhaps best described as being pleasantly portly. He had bright blue eyes, was bald on the very top, with shaggy, curly white fringe around the sides, and a white, bushy walrus mustache.

He usually wore a dented brown fedora with the brim slightly turned upward all around, a white lab coat with his name stitched in red over the pocket, over a crumpled, brown, baggy three-piece suit, the trousers of which were pleated and cuffed and held up by thick red suspenders - no belt, and a white dress shirt. He always wore a tie that was at least 15 years out of style. Today's was a one-inch, skinny blue one which blended into silver at the bottom, circa 1958, which was held in place by a sterling silver tie clasp, artistically designed as a racing roadrunner replete with an exquisite piece of turquoise set into its body. He wore new, sturdy, but slightly scuffed brown, hightop brogans. His vest was usually unbuttoned, but held together by a thick, antique, gold-link chain through a buttonhole attached to a gold, antique, hunter style pocket watch, the face of which had Roman numerals instead of English numbers, which was tucked inside his left vest pocket, and on the other end attached to a 12-karat gold crest of the City of Lodz the size of a silver dollar, tucked into the right vest pocket to counterbalance the weight of the watch.

He was an inveterate smoker of regular, unfiltered Camel cigarettes, usually carrying two or three packs in his coat pockets.

Recently he had developed a taste for small brown, Mexican cheroots, which he carried in an old, sterling silver cigarette case bearing his initials, in his left inside upper coat pocket.

He was born in Lodz, Poland, where his father had been a professor of mathematics and his mother was a distinguished amateur pianist. His father foresaw the proverbial "handwriting on the wall" just like the prophet in the Old Testament Book of Daniel in Chapter 5, with the rise and power of Adolph Hitler and the German Nazi Party, long before most other Jews. In 1935, he secured a teaching position at Southern Methodist University and emigrated to Dallas with his parents, wife, two sisters, and four children. Though Wiroslaw was only three years old when he arrived in America, he still spoke a sort of ruptured, not just fractured, English.

Wiroslaw was a gifted individual. Besides making top marks throughout his school years, he had quick hands, great hand-and-eye coordination, and he was both quick and fast on his feet. He played football, basketball, and baseball in high school, lettering in all three.

His best sport was baseball, in which he was a second baseman, and in which he became a prolific bunter. He seldom hit a long ball into the outfield, but he collected many singles by hitting grounders and line drives in the holes. He also learned how to disguise his decisions as to when to lay down a bunt, to the extent that he kept the opposing teams confused, allowing him to be successful in beating out a bunt two-thirds of the time.

He was fast enough to steal bases, and he stole his fair share, but he always considered stealing bases as cheating. This was America! People were rewarded for hard work and perseverance, and there were plenty of opportunities for an industrious person. An honest man did not have to steal. He never understood why it was okay to steal a base in baseball. To steal bases or not to steal - it did not matter to the cosmos. Wiroslaw won a baseball scholarship to attend Texas A&M University, where he graduated summa cum laude with an A.B. degree in humanities in 1943.

He served until 1946 in a U.S. Army military intelligence unit which was headquartered in Great Britain. He was honorably discharged as a captain. He was awarded the Legion of Merit, the Army Commendation Medal with V Device for valor, the Europe-Africa-Middle East Theater Campaign Medal with three campaign stars, and the World War II Victory Medal.

Because many of the duties he performed in military intelligence, infiltration of Axis-controlled nations being his primary assignment, where he set up and conducted clandestine operations with the partisans, he learned very quickly about the value of carrying a concealed weapon on his person at all times.

The weapon issued to him, which he always carried regardless of any other weapons he might have been issued, was a Browning, .25 caliber, semi-automatic pocket pistol, referred to as the Baby Browning. The magazine holds six rounds plus a seventh can be safely chambered in the pipe. The Army issued it as a last resort pistol, to be used only in an emergency to shoot your adversary at close range in order to flee or to avoid capture. If the small caliber bullet succeeded in killing the enemy, so much the better. The point was that this gun was small enough to be concealed on the body of nearly everyone without fear of detection.

Wiroslaw surrendered that issued pistol back to the Army after the war, but he purchased a new one just like it at war's end, except his personal one was nickel-plated. He also purchased a spare magazine because it only came in the box with one. (The Army had taught him well with regards to not leaving a magazine filled all the time, in an effort to prevent malfunctions or jams.) He had carried a Baby Browning on his person nearly every day of his life since 1943, and he would continue to do so until he met his Maker. This was the same reason he also carried a well-made Italian switchblade knife in his left trouser pocket.

Wiroslaw used the brand new G.I. Bill to attend Medical School at the University of Texas. He earned an M.D. degree in 1950, and went on to become a board certified psychiatrist, working at the Veterans Administration Hospital in Dallas. He married late in life to a psychiatric nurse named Olga from Corpus Christi. They had twin boys named Ivan and Igor. They moved to Corpus Christi to be closer to her family. There they set up a private practice which became quite successful.

Dr. Snihirowicz was a well-known, engaging psychiatrist. He was charismatic, cheerful, upbeat, inquisitive, humble, honest, and filled with a sense of humor. Judge Sweeney and he were well-acquainted with one another, as a result of their common interest and fundraising activities for the Texas A&M Alumni Association. Both were distinguished grads. Their mutual interests developed into a long, cordial relationship. They attended Homecoming together each year. In fact, Dr. Snihirowicz lodged at Judge Sweeney's house at his express invitation the night before he interviewed Ernesto.

There was one unusual protocol between Judge Sweeney and Dr. Snihirowicz. They always called each other by their surnames with no title. They never called one another by their given names or nicknames. Judge Sweeney's intimates called him Max. Dr. Snihirowicz's intimates called him Wiro, which was pronounced WE-row (long E) by some and WEIR-row (short E, like weirdo) by others. The last time anyone probably dared call Judge Sweeney by his untitled surname was when he was a cadet at Texas A&M. On the other hand, virtually no one attempted to call Dr. Snihirowicz by his surname because they couldn't spell it, let alone pronounce it. Most patients referred to him as Dr. S at his suggestion. Neither of the wives understood this practice, which was never extended to anyone else.

Dr. Snihirowicz arrived at Sam's office at 9 o'clock in his well-maintained '62, white over turquoise, Plymouth Belvedere four-door sedan. After cordial greetings, coffee, and a Camel cigarette smoked by Dr. Snihirowicz, they got down to business. He pored over all the police investigative reports, Sam's personal notes, all the crime scene photographs, the laboratory reports, and finally Mr. Nighthawk's background investigation report. He looked up and said, "Mr. Nighthawk is a very thorough investigator. He interviewed nearly forty people who knew your client personally. What a sad, hopeless life your client has lived! Where will I conduct the interview?"

"Well, we don't have many choices. The sheriff's office has no privacy apart from Sheriff Sol's personal office. He probably wouldn't mind if we used that, but it might give Ernesto the willies. The jail is secure and you would have privacy, but I don't know to what degree it would have in terms of chilling free speech. He nearly choked a private defense attorney to death in there. You're welcome to use my office, but truthfully, I think the sheriff would be uncomfortable doing that with a murder suspect. He'd worry about escape or even a rescue attempt. The only other place I can think of is the witness waiting room outside the Grand Jury's chambers. It's vacant today, and it is just above the sheriff's office."

"Why don't we try the last one? I presume the sheriff would post a deputy or two outside the door."

"He would. Okay. Let me make a call. Do you want to take my file with you?"

"No. Thank you. I remember everything that I need to know. It works best if all I do is jot down a few cryptic notes. I always write in Polish to make it difficult for prying eyes to read. I do all I possibly can to develop a degree of intimacy without crossing that invisible line. If I do it right, the patient forgets he's even being interviewed. It simply becomes a stimulating conversation with a stranger he will probably never see again."

"Gotcha."

Sam called Able DeWitt first to ensure the Grand Jury room was available. Then he called Sheriff Sol, who said he would have two deputies escort Mr. Robles upstairs just as soon as Sam was ready to proceed. About 30 minutes later, Deputy Atwater and Deputy Bustamante escorted Ernesto upstairs. At Dr. Snihirowicz's request, they removed the handcuffs, but the leg irons attached to the bellyband remained on. Sam and the deputies stepped outside the room. They sat in hardback chairs they carried out of the room. Deputy Atwater brought along the *American Rifleman* and *Sports Illustrated* magazines, both of which he shared with Chunk. Then they waited. "Patience is a virtue."

At first Ernesto was wary of the old, pudgy, gringo doctor. Ernesto knew the inevitability of the fate which awaited him. This gringo could not save him. Ernesto knew he wasn't crazy. He knew where he was, what he had done, the day of the week if not the exact day of the month. He knew right from wrong. He knew God would punish him. He knew he could not escape. He wasn't happy about it, but there was nothing he could do. Even if he did manage to escape, La Serpiente would order his men to hunt him down and they would torture him beyond human endurance until at last, he expired. It was hard to swallow, but the electric chair was the easy way out.

This old, pudgy man, this doctor who spoke American with a worse accent than his own, wasn't so bad after all. He seemed to really give a shit when he asked after Ernesto's well-being. He generously shared his cigarettes with him. Between them both, they nearly smoked the entire pack. The doctor asked about his mama, his papá, brothers or sisters, what was the most fun thing he ever did, what was the most important, who he liked the most, who he didn't like, and if he could have changed his life five years ago, no matter how fantastical the dream, how would he have changed it, things such as that.

The pudgy doctor got Ernesto to thinking way beyond his pathetic little world, about things which made life worth living, about how joining the wrong crowd, or not excising oneself from the wrong crowd, shapes a person's future. Ernesto never really considered that before. He just did what he had to do, putting forth the least effort possible, just to get by, just to fall asleep in a drunken stupor and wake up the next day no better off than he had been before. Possibly even worse. He was dumbstruck just how many times he had had opportunities to "straighten up and fly right," to get his act together, but instead he chose not to. Now here he was, sitting in jail, facing the death penalty.

When they were nearly done, the kind doctor asked if he would like a Bible written in Spanish. Ernesto said he couldn't read either English or Spanish. He did say, however, if a Spanish-speaking priest were available, he would like to talk with him. The kind doctor gave him one last cigarette. They smoked in silence. Then he got up and opened the door and told the guards they were done. He even asked if they could get Ernesto some lunch since they had talked through the lunch hour. The deputy they call Chunk said they would bring him some food once he was back in his cell.

Ernesto thanked the kind doctor. He said he wished he could have met him a few years earlier before he fucked up his life. The doctor said that he would get a priest to come speak with him; that though Ernesto would surely die someday, he could still have eternal salvation if he prayed to God and repented of his sins. Then Ernesto began to understand. That kind old doctor was really an angel in human form sent from heaven to help him mend his ways. He began to weep softly.

After Ernesto was escorted back to his cell, Dr. S asked Sam if he thought Judge Sweeney and DA DeWitt would be available for a late lunch, or even just a cup of coffee at a diner. He said he would give them all a verbal report. His written report wouldn't be ready until Friday.

Sam knocked on Judge Sweeney's door to his chambers. He was free. He picked up the phone and called DeWitt and Sheriff Sol. Both were free. They gathered outside the rear courthouse door leading to the sheriff's office, and walked over to Crabtree's.

They had a delicious Southern fried chicken lunch with mashed potatoes and gravy, green beans, cole slaw, fresh biscuits, ice tea, and topped off with a delicious cherry pie.

Dr. Snihirowicz told them that Ernesto was of sound mind; that he knew right from wrong; that he expected to be punished; and further, he expected to be sentenced to death. He said he thought Ernesto was suffering from a neurotic form of depression, but not a psychotic one. Bottom line: Ernesto was sane and had been sane all along. He suggested two things. First, allow Ernesto to smoke. It would alleviate stress. Second, allow him to meet with a Spanish-speaking priest, particularly a priest of Mexican extraction if one were available.

This is not what Sam had hoped for, but it was what he had expected. DA DeWitt, Sheriff Sol, and Judge Sweeney uttered a silent prayer of relief.

CHAPTER 32

Gillespie's Obsession with the Circle A

Thursday, April 6, 1972

Gillespie had made discreet inquiries about the disposition of Mr. Wrigley's estate. The only thing she had learned so far was that everything was still "up in the air." Pedro Padilla's wife, Angelina, had not come to grips yet with Pedro's death. She had just laid Pedro to rest. She responded to Judge Sweeney's letter regarding the probate of Mr. Wrigley's will, in which he alluded that she likely had an inheritance as a result of her late husband's demise; further, that either she or her attorney needed to be present when the will was probated.

Mrs. Padilla requested at least 30 more days to give her a little more time to mourn. In that Mr. Wrigley had more than sufficient funds in both of his accounts at the Pecos Bank & Trust to pay for his utilities and taxes, and that his neighbor, Mr. Matthew Perkins was caring for Mr. Wrigley's herd of cattle pending the appropriate time to sell, and that Archie was caring for his horses, Judge Sweeney responded by granting her wish and tickling the matter for 60 days.

Gillespie had a key to Arn's house. He gave it to her once they became close friends. She never mentioned it to anyone. She wanted to know the status of the probate because she had taken to going over to the Circle A after work to sit in his house, to walk in his fields, to watch the river flow where they had set up their ambushes, and lately, to drive his Jeep along the property of all three connected ranches. She sorely missed Arn and Pedro, but mostly Arn.

Gillespie was friends with Mr. Jackson and Mr. and Mrs.

Perkins. They had grown accustomed to seeing her traversing their collective properties slowly, an apparition almost, like she was in her own little war zone, carefully searching for land mines. (Actually, she was searching for signs of illegal aliens who had sneaked across the property in the middle of the night, something Mr. Jackson, in particular, would never think to do.)

Once in awhile she would stop by to say hello. They were comforted by her presence, because all of them had been on edge since the coyotes had started running illegals across their land. She was an extra pair of eyes, who also happened to be law enforcement. They felt like she could get things done that they might not be able to do.

Anymore, Gillespie had quit changing out of her uniform into civvies to patrol the Circle A and the adjoining ranches. It saved time, but more importantly, she avoided quizzical looks or questions from her colleagues since her commute to work was only five minutes long. Why the hurry? She was afraid Sheriff Sol would tell her not to do this. For one thing, the Circle A was considered an unsafe place to be by every single one of her colleagues since all the troubles began with the Mexican criminals. For another, her visits could be considered trespassing. However, Gillespie did dress in civvies whenever she stopped by on one of her days off.

Ella Mae had come to love the Circle A, and she would be sad when it was sold. She had no idea what it would bring at auction. Once in awhile she would fantasize about what it would be like living way out here. It was nearly a 50-mile commute each way from the farmhouse to the courthouse. That was about seven gallons of gas in her '68 Ford Fairlane, just to get to and fro. Not only that, she was all by herself and it could get very lonely so far away from everyone she considered a friend.

What if Uncle Leland offered her a deputy job in Alpine? What if she decided to take it? She would be stuck trying to sell this ranch. Not only that, even if she could manage to purchase it, she didn't own a single horse let alone a saddle and tack, plus she didn't know how to ride! Not sure that she even wanted to. Furthermore, she didn't own a solitary calf or lamb. Not even a dog or a cat! What did she know about livestock?

This was a reverie for someone who dreamed of being Dale Evans, married to Roy freaking Rogers. Not her. Time to think about something else, like finding a boyfriend, what it would be like when she turned 30 later this year, whether she should let her hair grow out a little more, how long it would take to graduate from the midnight shift to days or afternoons, or whether she could ever make investigator once Chief Alex retired. In the end, she decided to go to the Baptist church with Mrs. Beanblossom this Sunday. Scope it out for eligible bachelors. Better to look there than the Dry Gulch Saloon.

She roamed around "like a lost ball in the high weeds" until lunchtime. She gassed up on her way home. She stopped off at the market to buy some lunchmeat and apples and Oreo cookies for her midnight meal. She called her mom. Then she set the alarm for 10 o'clock and went to bed. She was bushed. It had been a good day. She had a lot to be thankful for.

CHAPTER 33

Ernesto's Trial

Thursday, April 13, 1972

This was the big day. All 12 cabins at the Travelers Rest Motor Lodge, the only motel for 100 miles east or west, were occupied. The medical examiner from Del Rio, both of the state laboratory examiners from Austin, the ex-wife of decedent Casper T. Brooks, an incognito representative of the Free and Sovereign State of Coahuila de Zaragoza, Mexico, who was sent to determine both whether Mr. Robles was given a fair trial and whether justice was served in the murder of Pedro Padilla, Special Agent Enrico Baca of BNDD, laser-focused on La Serpiente and hoping for a few nuggets, newspaper journalists from Austin, El Paso, Del Rio, and Ciudad Acuña, plus several parties unknown had all checked in.

Both Crabtree's Family Style Restaurant and Betty's Diner were packed to capacity with folks waiting outside to squeeze in. There wasn't enough parking at the Quayle County Courthouse either, so some folks had to park three or four blocks away and walk.

This was the first murder trial in Mosby that anyone could recall, all other murderers having been killed before they were captured. The last exciting trial had been the State of Texas versus Joseph P. Schitt, an aggravated assault case, in the autumn of 1969. It was dramatic because of the dangerous and intimidating outlaw biker defendant, his flamboyant, big city defense attorney with his scandalously, luscious secretary, and the key witness being the spanking new, young Deputy Barlow Adams that few folks had had an opportunity to size up. (Many had thought he was too young and inexperienced for the job. A few weeks later these same skeptics were compelled to admit they were wrong.)

This murder trial was somewhat of a disappointment by comparison, at least in the beginning. The defendant was a scrawny, tattooed Mexican about 35 years old, 5'7" tall, 135 pounds, with a scraggly mustache. He looked more like an itinerate fruit picker or a busboy in a big city restaurant, than a vicious, cold blooded murderer. He did not instill fear by his very appearance. He looked more like someone you would just try to avoid, like a stray dog on the street. His stare was vacant. He seemed unafraid, maybe a little dazed, but certainly not scared.

Judge Sweeney called the court to order at 10 o'clock on the dot in his no nonsense manner as he was wont to do. The voir dire of the 24 jury pool candidates only lasted 35 minutes. The first 14 interviewed were selected, two being alternates. Lester MacDougal, a local plumber and deacon in the Baptist church, was chosen as jury foreman. Opening remarks by District Attorney Able DeWitt and defense counsel Samuel Davis, Esquire, were brief, but poignant.

Mr. DeWitt said the state had proof beyond a shadow of doubt that the defendant shot and killed Casper T. Brooks and Arthur S. Wrigley in cold blood with malice aforethought. In addition, he was one of five or six men, all the others of whom were still unknown, who murdered Pedro Padilla in cold blood, also with malice aforethought, although Mr. Robles was not the triggerman, himself. Once the jury had the opportunity to hear the testimony of all the witnesses and see the evidence for themselves, DA DeWitt was absolutely certain they would unanimously vote to convict Mr. Robles on two counts of capital murder, for which he could be sentenced to death, and one count of murder, for which the penalty was capped at life without parole, not to mention the two misdemeanor charges of being drunk in a public place and for carrying a concealed deadly weapon.

When it was Mr. Davis' turn, he said that Mr. Robles was not a wicked man, but he had done wicked things in his past for which he was filled with remorse. He implored the jury to keep an open mind. Then he said, "Sometimes things are not always what they seem. I am reminded of a quote attributed to the pious martyr, John Bradford, in a treatise published in 1822, in which he saw a criminal being led to the gallows. He said, "There but for the grace of God, go I". Keep that in mind when you listen to the evidence being presented to you today."

The first witness was Deputy Barlow Adams. His job was to set the stage. He testified to the call he received just before midnight from decedent Arnold Wrigley on Monday, January 25, 1972. Mr. Wrigley asked if he could respond to the Circle A right away. Mr. Wrigley told him to bring a long gun. Deputy Gillespie and he both responded as quickly as possible.

Upon arrival, Mr. Wrigley narrated three separate incidents of illegal alien smuggling, detected after the fact due to debris left behind, which had occurred on his property during the wee hours of the nights of December 14, 1971, December 28, 1971, and January 11, 1972. Those were all on Tuesdays, two weeks apart. Mr. Wrigley had called the Border Patrol, who didn't have the manpower to set up a surveillance of illegal alien smuggling unless the numbers coming across the border were larger than what had transpired on the Circle A to date. Mr. Wrigley said that if the smugglers held true to form, they would make another crossing that particular night.

The two deputies sat up all night with Mr. Wrigley and his ranch hand, decedent Pedro Padilla. The smugglers did not make an appearance. The deputies reported this to Sheriff Solomon Pratt, who decided to keep the deputies on midnight surveillance for at least a week.

They had no activity until Tuesday, February 8, 1972. That night, both Mr. Wrigley and Mr. Padilla set up across the river. The two deputies remained on Mr. Wrigley's ranch facing the river.

Finally, in the wee hours of the morning, two trucks approached the river from the south. An unknown number of people, estimated at 20, got out of the trucks. Most of them began fording the river on foot. Before they all crossed, at least two, maybe three individuals began shooting at Mr. Wrigley and Mr. Padilla. The decedents returned fire. Those persons who had managed to cross the river, and those who were only part way across, returned to the south side. None of the people involved in the illegal crossing nor the ones who shot at Mr. Wrigley and Mr. Padilla were ever identified.

Sheriff Pratt called off any further surveillance at the Circle A absent new, specific information regarding another attempt to cross there. It was Deputy Adams' belief that the surveillance was terminated because of the shooting incident, i.e., that the smugglers would look for another, safer route. Nevertheless, Mr. Wrigley said he and Mr. Padilla would continue to conduct a surveillance every night, because they still felt strongly that this wasn't over; however, they would watch from the Circle A, itself, and not from across the border.

The next incident occurred in the wee hours of Wednesday, March 15, 1972. Deputy Adams fielded a call from the decedent, Mr. Padilla. He reported that there had been a fatal motor vehicle accident on Highway 90 near the Circle A, between a cargo truck carrying aliens, and a pickup truck driven by decedent Casper T. Brooks. There were two deceased aliens in the back of the truck. Mr. Brooks was also dead. He had been shot several times.

Every sworn officer on the sheriff's office responded, except for two Sheriff Pratt held back. Deputy Adams personally saw a female, later identified as María Sánchez, and her daughter, Gloria, in the back of the cargo truck, both of whom appeared to have died from injuries sustained in the accident. He also saw Mr. Brooks sitting in the driver's seat of his pickup truck. He had four distinct bullet holes in his chest.

The accident/crime scene investigation was conducted by

Chief Deputy Alexander Snodgrass and Deputy Ella Mae Gillespie under the overall supervision of Sheriff Solomon Pratt. Sheriff Pratt called out more than a dozen members of the mounted posse to assist regular deputies in tracking the smugglers and the illegal aliens. Deputy Adams was one of the searchers. Eight illegal aliens were apprehended. The others got away. Two names cited by the apprehended illegal aliens as the smugglers - two others were unidentified - were Ernesto, later identified as the defendant, Ernesto Robles, and El Gordo, later identified as Rafael Larosa (who was subsequently shot and killed on March 24, 1972.)

Autopsies were performed on all three decedents by the Val Verde County Medical Examiner, Dr. Claiborne Cleveland.

The next incident occurred during the wee hours of Friday, March 24, 1972. Deputy Adams received a call from Mr. Elmer Jackson, owner of the Rocking J Ranch, which is adjacent to the Circle A. He reported hearing a series of shots fired in the vicinity of the Circle A. Sheriff Pratt, Chief Deputy Snodgrass, Deputy Gillespie, and Deputy Adams all responded to the scene. They discovered the bodies of Mr. Wrigley, Mr. Padilla, and five armed Mexican citizens subsequently identified as Rafael Larosa (El Gordo), José Salazar, Roberto Peña, Jesús Alvarado, and Ignacio Pastor. Chief Snodgrass and Deputy Gillespie conducted the crime scene investigation under the overall supervision of Sheriff Pratt. All seven autopsies were performed by Dr. Claiborne Cleveland.

Thus endeth Deputy Adams' testimony. Mr. Davis waived cross-examination.

Deputy Dewey Carruthers testified second. He described the arrest of Mr. Robles, who was passed out drunk in the driver's seat of Rafael Larosa's sedan on Highway 90 in the late afternoon of March 24, 1972. He identified the Colt Diamondback revolver, which he found under the driver's seat.

Mr. Davis waived cross-examination.

Chief Deputy Alexander Snodgrass was third. He testified that he recovered one bullet from the back of the front driver's seat which passed through Mr. Brooks. (There were three others recovered by the medical examiner from Mr. Brooks' body.) Chief Snodgrass also recovered the Colt Diamondback, .38 Special caliber revolver from the vehicle in which Mr. Robles was arrested by Deputy Dewey Carruthers.

Chief Snodgrass testified that he recovered nine firearms either adjacent to, or in the grasp of each of the seven bodies found at the Circle A crime scene, but none of them pertained to the defendant.

Chief Snodgrass also introduced 21 selected photographs of 66 taken at both the accident crime scene and the ranch crime scene. They were passed to the jury for examination. (The remaining photographs were not introduced because they were duplicates, or they didn't aid in understanding the crime scene, i.e., too blurry or accidentally snapped of the sky or someone's feet, etc., or because they were considered too gruesome.)

Thus endeth Chief Snodgrass's testimony.

Mr. Davis waived cross-examination.

Mr. Delbert R. Peabody, Fingerprint Examiner, Texas Department of Public Safety, Forensic Laboratory, testified that he recovered four latent fingerprints from the Colt Diamondback revolver recovered from the motor vehicle the defendant was in at the time of his arrest. Three latent fingerprints were those of the defendant. The fourth was from a person unknown.

Once again, Mr. Davis waived cross-examination.

Dr. Claiborne Cleveland, Val Verde County Medical Examiner, testified that he conducted autopsies on the three victims of the motor vehicle accident which occurred on Highway 90 just east of the Circle A Ranch during the early morning hours of Wednesday, March 15, 1972. These include:

(1) María Sánchez, age 20, died from a broken neck, consistent with whiplash from a motor vehicle accident.

(2) Gloria Sánchez, age 3, María's daughter, died from a head injury consistent with being severely thrown into something hard, such as the side of the cargo truck in which she was riding without restraints, which had been severely impacted during the motor vehicle accident.

(3) Casper Brooks, age 35, whose blood alcohol content was .014% at the time of his death. He had three broken ribs and an open gash on his forehead, all consistent with an impact against the steering wheel or the windshield during a motor vehicle collision. Those injuries were not fatal. He also had four bullet wounds in the torso: two in his heart, one in his spleen, and one through and through, the last of which did no serious damage. The other three were all fatal wounds. Dr. Cleveland recovered three .38 caliber projectiles from the decedent's body, which he surrendered to Miss Julian Danforth, Ballistics Examiner, Texas Department of Public Safety, Forensic Laboratory.

Dr. Cleveland also conducted the autopsy of seven individuals, all of whom were killed by multiple projectiles from firearms which were related to a shooting altercation at the Circle A Ranch on March 24, 1972. Only the deaths of two of the decedents, Arnold Wrigley and Pedro Padilla, are relevant to the charges filed against the defendant in this case.

Arnold Wrigley, age 75, died from 37 gunshot wounds - five of which were .38 caliber projectiles, two of which entered through the back of his head.

Pedro Padilla, age 43, died from 25 gunshot wounds. The relationship between his death and Mr. Wrigley's is proximity of location and time. Specifically, both decedents were shot at the same location, at or nearly at the same time by multiple shooters.

Mr. Davis waived cross-examination.

Miss Julian Danforth, Ballistics Examiner, Texas Department of Public Safety, Forensic Laboratory, was called to the stand. She testified that all four .38 caliber projectiles which entered into Casper Brooks' body, and all five of the .38 caliber projectiles recovered from Arnold Wrigley's body were fired from the same Colt Diamondback, .38 Special revolver, which was recovered from the motor vehicle the defendant was in at the time of his arrest.

She also examined 32 other projectiles recovered from Mr. Wrigley's body. Six were fired from an unidentified Beretta 9 millimeter, semi-automatic pistol, and 26 BBs were fired from an undetermined type of shotgun.

Furthermore, she examined 25 projectiles recovered from Mr. Padilla's body. Two were .38 caliber projectiles fired by a Smith & Wesson revolver; five .32 caliber projectiles were fired from a Harrington & Richardson revolver; and, eighteen BBs were fired from an undetermined type of shotgun.

Other ballistics examinations that she conducted included:

Two .30 caliber projectiles recovered from the body of José Salazar; one .30 caliber projectile recovered from the body of Ignacio Pastor; two .30 caliber projectiles recovered from the body of Rafael Larosa; and one .30 caliber projectile recovered from Jesús Alvarado. All six of these projectiles were 180-grain bullets fired by the Springfield M-1, .30-06 caliber rifle owned by Mr. Wrigley.

Two .30 caliber projectiles recovered from the body of Roberto Peña; one .30 caliber projectile recovered from the body of Ignacio Pastor; and one .30 caliber projectile recovered from the body of Rafael Larosa. All four of these projectiles were 150-grain bullets fired by the Winchester .30-30 caliber rifle owned by Mr. Padilla.

Two .45 caliber projectiles recovered from the body of Jesús Alvarado, which were fired by the Colt Government Model, semi-automatic pistol owned by Mr. Wrigley.

Mr. Davis asked one question during cross-examination of Miss Danforth. He wanted confirmation that the Colt Diamondback was not used to fire any projectiles into Mr. Padilla's body. She did confirm.

The final prosecution witness was Sheriff Solomon Pratt. He was the closer. His job was to reconstruct the shooting incident at the ranch as best he could from where the bodies fell, which weapons were recovered in their proximity, and the ballistics report.

Sheriff Pratt selected a dozen photographs of the crime scene at the ranch, depicting the seven bodies, their proximity to each other, and the weapons which were found either in their possession or next to their bodies.

He testified, "From the photographs, we believe that there were two separate shooting engagements at the Circle A. It appears that the gunfight erupted as soon as the van off-loaded the five dead bandits. Mr. Wrigley and Mr. Padilla must have been prepared for them. We believe this because not one of the rounds fired by the five dead bandits hit either Mr. Wrigley or Mr. Padilla.

"José Salazar was driving the van, because his body was found just outside the driver's door. We found a Colt .45 caliber pistol next to him. Three rounds had been expended from it. Ballistics confirm that he was shot by Mr. Wrigley with his M-1 rifle - once in the back and once in the head. We think he was the last bandit killed.

"Roberto Peña had an unfired .32-20 rifle by his side. He was twice shot by Mr. Padilla with his .30-30 rifle - once in the chest and once in the head. We believe he was one of the first bandits shot because he did not fire any rounds, himself.

"Ignacio Pastor had an unfired 12-gauge shotgun next to his body. He was shot in the chest by Mr. Wrigley with his M-1 rifle and once in the head by Mr. Padilla's .30-30 rifle. We believe he was also one of the first bandits shot, for the same reason. In addition, we think the head shots on all these bandits occurred after they were down - a double tap so to speak, to ensure that they didn't come back to life and shoot either of the ranchers. Remember, Command Sergeant Major Wrigley was a highly decorated combat infantryman of three separate wars. Old habits die hard.

"Rafael Larosa, a/k/a El Gordo, had a Smith & Wesson revolver in his hand. Three shots had been fired. He was shot twice in the stomach by Mr. Wrigley with his M-1 rifle and once in the head by Mr. Padilla with his .30-30 rifle.

"Jesús Alvarado had a 12-gauge shotgun next to his body. One shot had been fired. He was shot once in the stomach by Mr. Wrigley with his M-1 rifle and twice in the head by Mr. Wrigley with his .45 caliber Colt pistol.

"The second phase of the gunfight was just as one-sided. Mr. Wrigley and Mr. Padilla were the ones ambushed this time. We believe it occurred mere seconds after the first exchange of gunfire, because their bodies were found about five feet apart, facing the van. They were unprepared. Probably didn't see it coming. Thought it was all over. That would indicate they were killed at the same time. They may have been trying to determine the identities of the bandits they had just killed. We will never know. Both were shot from behind and/or the side. Other than the defendant's pistol, which was recovered when he was arrested, we only know the types of weapons used to kill them. We don't know who their killers were other than the defendant. There are four, or perhaps five other murderers still on the loose.

"Ladies and gentlemen, Mr. Wrigley and Mr. Padilla were outnumbered and murdered defending Mr. Wrigley's ranch from armed intruders in the middle of the night, who were only there to commit mayhem or murder. There's no other way you can interpret this crime scene."

Thus endeth Sheriff Pratt's testimony.

Mr. Davis waived cross-examination.

DA DeWitt stood and said, "Your Honor, the prosecution rests." It was 12:15.

Judge Sweeney pounded his gavel and exclaimed, "Court is adjourned until 2 o'clock."

When they returned, Judge Sweeney called the court to order. He said, "Your turn, Mr. Davis."

Mr. Davis stood and said, "Your Honor, I find myself in a very unusual situation. I have only one witness - Mr. Robles, himself. He is emphatic about testifying. I've done all I can to dissuade him. In an abundance of caution - I don't want to be labeled as incompetent counsel in an appeal we all know will be forthcoming, if he is found guilty - I request that you address this matter yourself with my client."

Judge Sweeney replied, "This is highly irregular, but not unheard of. However, I cannot recall ever hearing of something like this transpiring in a capital murder trial.

"Mr. Robles, stand and address the court. Is this true you want to testify on your own behalf?"

"Yes, Your Honor."

"I've known your attorney professionally for a very long time. I know he is an extremely honorable, trustworthy, competent, knowledgeable attorney. Is it true that he has informed you that testifying on your own behalf is both ill-advised and foolhardy."

"Yes, Your Honor. He told me not to do it many times."

"I advise against it as well. Do you still insist on testifying?"

"Yes, Your Honor."

"You do know that Dr. Snihirowicz, the psychiatrist who examined you, reported that you were sane and of sound mind at the time these crimes occurred for which you stand accused, and that you are sane and of sound mind now. In other words, down the road if you are convicted, it would be highly unlikely that you would be successful in claiming mental incapacity in an appeal. You understand that, and still want to testify?"

"Yes, Your Honor."

"So be it. The court finds that you fully understand the potential consequences, and that you are fully competent to testify.

"Bailiff, help Mr. Robles to take a seat at the stand and swear him in."

Once that was done, Mr. Davis stood from behind the defense table and said, "Mr. Robles, you are free to speak."

"Thank you. Judge, I did all these things I am accused of. I killed Mr. Brooks and Mr. Wrigley. The men who killed Mr. Padilla did so at my direction. I was there and I saw them do it. I will never identify them because the blame is all mine. I also smuggled people into your country several times. I was paid to do that.

"I was a lost soul then. I drank alcohol to excess, used illegal drugs, fornicated with loose women, hurt anyone who interfered with me. I regret all of those things. I wish I had never done any of those things, but I did.

"Now I have found Jesus. I repent of all my sins. I am prepared for whatever punishment you give me. I apologize to all those I hurt, and to the family members who suffer now because of my actions. I know when I die, after I suffer for all my sins in Purgatory, I will be set free, a spotless soul, in the House of Many Mansions prepared by my Savior, Jesus Christ. Amen."

The entire courtroom was stunned. The silence was so absolute it hurt your ears. Mr. Robles stood and waited for the bailiff to escort him back to his chair.

DA DeWitt waived cross-examination.

Mr. Davis said, "Your Honor, the defense rests."

Judge Sweeney replied, "Mr. Davis, you may make your closing remarks."

Mr. Davis walked over to the jury box. He looked each juror in the eye. He said, "When the Pharisees brought a woman who had been caught in the very act of adultery before Jesus, and asked what should be done to her, Jesus said, "He that is without sin among you, let him first cast a stone at her. (John 8:7)" Then Mr. Davis turned away and returned to his seat.

DA DeWitt stood, and he too, walked over to the jury box. He paused for a full minute, collecting his thoughts. The crescendo created by Mr. Robles' confession left him momentarily discombobulated. Everyone in the courtroom was craning his neck to hear what he would say.

"Wow! I'm stunned. Friends and neighbors, we just witnessed what I believe to be a first in Texas jurisprudence. I'm almost speechless. I promised to prove all the charges against Mr. Robles, and I did. I never expected he would make an unvarnished confession before the court.

"I applaud Mr. Robles' repentance and salvation. I really do. I believe he's sincere, but we still have a job to do. We need to close the books on the murders of Casper T. Brooks, Command Sergeant Major Arnold S. Wrigley, and Mr. Pedro Padilla. That's all up to you. You need to return a guilty verdict against Mr. Robles on all counts. Then all of us in Quayle County will rest easier, knowing that justice has been served, and Mr. Robles will be vindicated with respect to his repentance. Anything less than that would be an abdication of the duty we all swore to uphold before the court. May God bless everyone in this courtroom today. That includes Mr. Robles. Good day."

Judge Sweeney gave the jury its instructions, including all the elements that the state had to prove on each count. Then they filed out to deliberate in the jury room.

Nobody left the courtroom except for Judge Sweeney. He returned to his chambers.

It took 45 minutes. The jury returned to the box, followed by Judge Sweeney to the bench. The room was as silent as a mausoleum in the middle of a soft rainy night.

Judge Sweeney addressed the foreman, Mr. Lester MacDougal. "Has the jury returned a verdict on all counts?"

Mr. MacDougal stood. "Yes, Your Honor."

"How did the jury find on Count 1, being drunk in a public place?"

"Guilty."

"Count 2, illegal possession of a firearm?"

"Guilty."

"Count 3, capital murder of Casper Brooks?"

"Guilty."

"Count 4, capital murder of Arnold Wrigley?"

"Guilty."

"Count 5, murder of Pedro Padilla?"

"Guilty."

"Thank you, Mr. MacDougal. Please be seated.

"The court is ready to pronounce the sentence. Mr. Robles, please rise."

Mr. Davis and Mr. Robles both stood. Mr. Davis looked grim. Mr. Robles had an almost imperceptible smile.

Judge Sweeney said, "On Count 1, the court sentences you to 30 days in jail, with credit given for time already served.

"On Count 2, the court sentences you to 6 months in jail, to run concurrently.

"On Count 3, the court sentences you to death by electrocution.

"On count 4, the court sentences you to death by electrocution.

"On Count 5, the court sentences you to life without parole.

"Mr. Robles, very soon the Texas Department of Corrections will remove you to the Texas State Penitentiary for execution of your sentences. May God have mercy on your soul.

"Thank you to the jury, the officers of the law, the court officers, the witnesses, and to all who witnessed this trial. Court is adjourned!"

Judge Sweeney was the first to exit the courtroom, back to his chambers.

It was over...

Postscript:

On June 29, 1972, the U.S. Supreme Court, in *Furman versus Georgia,* by a 5-4 vote, struck down the death penalty, stating that it had been enforced in "arbitrary and capricious ways." All death penalty convictions were commuted to life without parole. By 1976, the federal government and most state legislatures had rewritten their laws according to Supreme Court guidelines. The Supreme Court lifted the ban. In 1977, Gary Mark Gilmore, a career criminal who murdered an elderly couple because they would not lend him their car, was executed by a firing squad in Utah. He was the first person executed after the ban was lifted.

CHAPTER 34

Gillespie Reveals Her Grief

Saturday, May 20, 1972

A month had passed since Ernesto was sentenced. As expected, the Texas Department of Corrections had picked up Ernesto the day after the trial and whisked him off to the Texas State Penitentiary in Huntsville to begin his sentence of life without parole, pending whatever appeals would be heard in the various appellate courts, to include the federal courts, before frying him like an egg on the sidewalk on a hot summer day in the desert. Folks had mostly forgotten about him in Mosby. Sometimes you wonder . . . .

Currently, the main topic in town was the upcoming local election on Tuesday, June 27th, for the Quayle County Board of Supervisors position currently held by Mr. Scrooge himself, Mr. LaRue Dinkins, sole owner of the Pecos Bank & Trust. Mr. Dinkins was running for his fourth 3-year term. The only other candidate was none other than Mr. Archibald X. Willis, himself.

The only get-out-the-vote sign Mr. Dinkins had erected was a billboard at his bank, which was located at the major intersection in Mosby, on U.S. Highway 90 (America Avenue) and Texas Highway 651 (Texas Street). Everyone saw it. It bore a picture of his scowling mug and read, "Vote for Experience," like his nine years of ruthless, iron-fisted control was something the citizens of Quayle County were begging for some more of.

On the other hand, dozens of 2-feet by 2-feet signs stapled to wooden posts were cropping up everywhere in yards, plus they were prominently displayed in the windows of local merchants who didn't owe the bank more money than they could afford to pay back. The only words printed on these signs were "Archie 1972."

Judge Sweeney had sponsored a fundraiser at his ranch for Archie in October, and nearly the entire population of Quayle County had turned out. Unless someone "bumped off" Archie ahead of time, this election was looking like it would be a tsunami of epic proportion. Mr. Dinkins would be swept away with the tide like a dog turd on the sandy beach - "a gone pecan."

Gillespie was still stopping by the Circle A every chance she got. She knew she didn't have the lettuce, scratch, dough, moola, shekels, Green Stamps, you name it, to buy it. She also knew Mrs. Padilla's 60 days before probate would expire soon, and that an auction would probably follow within another 60 days. She roamed all over the property like a wraith, getting her fill before she could do this no more. One thing she didn't do, was to go or remain there after darkness. That's when all the evil spirits and bad men lurk - in the darkness, waiting to spill blood. This ground was a testimony to that. Brave and honest men had not been killed here during the light of day, but in the darkness. Neither did evil men tarry here during daylight hours.

One night at work, thinking about how much she enjoyed roaming the Circle A in Arn's Jeep with him, and how much more he would have preferred that she do it with him on horseback, she decided to hit up Barlow - to "go balls to the wall, cowboy up." She said if the offer were still good, she'd like to take him up on learning how to ride. Barlow cracked a smile. He responded that he thought Sarah and he were available on Saturday, and that he would let her know tomorrow.

Sarah was thrilled. She was excited to teach another tenderfoot how to ride. This opportunity did not come along very often in a location where darn near everyone was a seasoned rider. Barlow had been her first tenderfoot. Now he was lovingly referred to as Bronco Barlow, courtesy of Slick Oldman, who witnessed Barlow almost get bucked off a horse which had not been trained to allow the rider to fire a gun over its shoulder. (Almost was the operative word here.) Yes, indeed, riding was Sarah's favorite pastime except for rodeoing with Barlow when she was naked and he rode her bareback. Nothing could match that.

Saturday morning, Sarah and Barlow introduced Ella Mae to the Bar B's gentlest horse, a 20-year-old paint mare named Splotch. (Sarah, like Mrs. Beanblossom, absolutely refused to call Gillespie by her surname, at least to her face.) Sarah gave Ella Mae a carrot to give to Splotch, which resulted in Splotch nuzzling up against Ella Mae, which resulted in the desired effect of love at first sight for Ella Mae with Splotch. Introductions had been made, and trust was beginning to be established by woman and beast alike. They had a pleasant ride. Different than with Barlow, Sarah capped the ride at two hours. She wanted Ella Mae to come back and do it again. Sarah had kept Barlow out all afternoon on his first ride because she was falling in love and she didn't want this mystical day to ever end. Besides, he never "cried uncle" - too proud or too much falling in love with her too, most likely. The concept that she was stoving him up for a couple of days never occurred to her while they were still riding. She realized her mistake once they finished and he could barely stand up - erect, as it were. Besides, at the time, she didn't understand just how important it would be for Barlow to stand erect whenever he was alone with her.

During the ride, Ella Mae mentioned all the times she and Arn had criss-crossed all over the three adjacent ranches in his Jeep, searching for signs that illegal aliens had crossed their properties. He would have preferred to have gone horseback, but she had been scared to try. Now, whenever she drives across his land, she wishes that she would have let him teach her. He had been like her grandpa, and she truly missed him.

She broke down in tears, and had a hard time recovering her composure. They dismounted and took a break. Barlow wondered, what did she mean by "now when I drive across his land?" Barlow didn't mention it. This was definitely not the time.

When they were done riding and had groomed the horses, giving each a carrot for good behavior, they gathered under the copse of trees where the wooden Adirondack chairs were strategically placed next to a cooler full of adult beverages, plus a few Orange Crushes, Bubble Ups, and Barq's root beer, for those who were too young or disinclined to imbibe, such as Marisa López's two children, Guillermo and Angela. Arthur Baker had obtained resident alien (green) cards for all three of them and they were thriving.

Marisa had decided to stay on at the Bar B as a domestic, rather than take a Trailways bus to Gullfport to be with her brother, Victor. For one thing, he was gone most of the time. Besides, she would probably have to fight off all the other merchant seaman when Victor was at sea. All young men are horn dogs. Sex is all they think about. It would be a bad situation. Here, she was safe. They treat her well. She and her kids live in the two upstairs bedrooms. They are very spacious and private. She was saving her wages.

Marisa would never say this out loud, but the three Mexican ranch hands were all muy simpáticos, (very nice), and they also made her feel welcome. They were from the same family in Ciudad Juárez, in Chihuahua, across the border from El Paso. It is a very poor city. They were also rescued by Señor Arthur, who got them green cards and gave them jobs as sheepherders and a small house to live in. The oldest one was Pedro Ramírez. He was 44. The middle one was his brother, Angel. He was 37. The youngest one was Pedro's son, Pancho, who was 26. He was muy dulce y guapo (very sweet and handsome.) He smiled at her every time he saw her. She liked him very much.

Today Señor Arthur and Señora Clarice decided to have a barbeque for all the family, including everyone who worked on the ranch, all of whom were just like family, which now included

Marisa and her kids. Señor Cordell, Señora Darla, Señor Barlow, Señora Sarah, and their friend, Señorita Ella Mae, who is una mujer policía (a police woman - Imagine that!) were all going to be there.

Guillermo was being a little rambunctious, running around playing fetch with Arthur's dog, Groucho Marx, and Happy, but none of the men seemed to notice. It seemed natural to them - a boy being a boy and dogs being dogs.

Arthur was busy roasting a small ewe, which had broken its leg and had to be "put out of its misery" on a spit over an open fire. He was nursing a glass of Henry McKenna bourbon on ice. Cordell, Pedro, Angel, and Pancho were savoring frosty cold bottles of Dos Equis beer, a special treat for the sheepherders. They seldom purchased premium beer because it was too expensive. Sarah poured Ella Mae and herself a glass of burgundy before they went to the kitchen to see what they could do to help the ladies. Barlow followed Arthur's lead and poured himself a tall glass of McKenna on the rocks. Then he lit up an H Upmann Churchill in a maduro wrapper and joined the men in their festivities. School was out for the summer. Sarah earned three As and one B, while Barlow was two and two. They were ready to party hearty, and they did.

A good time was had by all. They stayed way too late. Barlow and Sarah were both whipped dogs when they awoke at 7 o'clock to go to church.

CHAPTER 35

Impatience is the Province of Kings and Tyrants

Thursday, May 25, 1972

La Serpiente was still fuming over the incompetencies of Ernesto and José. Those pendejos had cost him a lot of money, not to mention soldiers. It had been a couple of months since Ernesto shot ese tonto (that fool), who ran into the back of the truck transporting paying customers.

The people-smuggling operation which they had just gotten off the ground was in a state of limbo. Ernesto had discovered the perfect route to foil the U.S. Border Patrol, showing a great deal of initiative, and then he fucked it all up by shooting ese tonto in a fit of rage! Better he should have capped José for being so stupid as to attempt a U-turn on a 2-lane highway with a 5-ton truck in the middle of the fucking night without lights!

The Americanos couldn't care less about un Mexicano muerto (a dead Mexican), but killing an unarmed Americano motorist? That created a shit storm within the population of heavily armed Neanderthals living in that desolate, worthless, American county that even the State of Texas had forgotten existed. Then José arrived too early for the hit at that pivotal ranch! Probably made so much fucking noise in that old, broken down van that La Serpiente probably could have heard them himself all the way to San Miguel! Call that the proper way to conduct an ambush? José got himself and four other soldiers waxed. Stupid, stupid, fatal mistakes!

The Americano authorities were nipping at La Serpiente's heels. He'd also lost two loads of herb in the last month! One he sent across at Eagle Pass, which got confiscated at a surprise road check by a pair of Texas DPS troopers, a half-dozen U.S. Border Patrol agents, and one BNDD agent. No one would take a bribe! That load was 16,000 kilos, plus the rig, and his men were being detained without bond. The abogado said they were facing at least 15 years in a federal penitentiary. They would be of no use to anyone by the time they were released, including to themselves!

The next load was smaller. It was only 10,000 kilos. Somehow the fuel tank got water in it. What the fuck? They had to pull over at a truck stop in Kerrville. Naturally, they parked right next to a DPS car which had a dope-sniffing dog. Idiots! Can you even imagine that? You can't make this shit up! What were they thinking? He was certain that BNDD had connected the true ownership of both rigs back to him, even though they were registered to shell corporations. He needed to make some cash fast to offset his losses.

Fortunately, he had 45 customers with cash in the palms of their hands waiting for transport to the U.S. He needed coyotes who were both loyal to him, and who could think on their feet. He decided to appoint two, highly trusted subordinates, Fernando Reyes, as El Jefe, and Julio "El Toro" Valdez, as Segundo. He picked two half-wits as helpers. Leonardo Trujillo was a good driver and Felipe Zapata followed directions to a fault.

La Serpiente would send 20 customers on the first trip, and if everything worked out, he would send the remaining 25 a week later. They would use two 15-passenger vans to transport them from San Miguel to the river. They would remain overnight at the dead man's ranch. El Toro had a stolen church bus which would come from Del Rio to transport them from the ranch to Sheffield the second night. The first group would leave Monday night, May 29th.

If this didn't pan out he was jodido (screwed).

CHAPTER 36

Drawing Water from the Well One Time Too Many

Tuesday, May 30, 1972

As soon as Gillespie got off work Tuesday morning, she headed back to the Circle A. En route, she stopped by Buck's Phillips 66 to top off her car and to fill two 5-gallon, metal jerry cans that she took from Arn's barn to top off his Jeep. She also bought a Bubble Up and a pack of peanut butter and cheese crackers to assuage her appetite, basically "the breakfast of champions" for those who were too busy to stop and eat, much less take time to fix his own breakfast.

It was a beautiful morning. Clear blue skies and 85 degrees. The slight breeze was refreshing. She thought she might stop by and see Mr. Jackson and Mr. and Mrs. Perkins. If she had time, she might even pop some caps at the half-dozen tin cans she brought along. She hadn't shot for a month or so and she knew could use the practice.

As soon as she pulled into the backyard, her female intuition began pinging. Something was not right. She was certain something was amiss. Then she saw. The barn doors were shut! Arn only closed them once as long as she had known him. As a result, she never closed them. She almost turned around to drive to the Perkins' ranch, but curiosity overtook caution. Maybe one of the neighbors had closed them, thinking they were doing the right thing.

She parked and shut off the motor, but she left her keys in the ignition. She was still in uniform. She drew her revolver and crept up to the barn. Before she reached to open the door, she glanced back at the house. She thought she had detected movement through the kitchen window, but visibility through the screen enclosure of the back veranda was difficult at best. Just as she was about to open the barn door, someone pushed it open from the inside.

The biggest, meanest-looking Mexican she had ever seen in her entire life stepped out of the barn. He was grinning like a jackass eating briars and pointing a Smith & Wesson revolver directly at her chest! Her heart almost exploded! Her lizard brain took over. Shocked, she jumped back a step or two, and shot him three times in the chest in rapid succession - all bullseye shots. He never uttered a sound. He fell thump, like a load of horse manure just outside the door. He smelled like it too, because his bowels let loose the second he died.

She bent over to pick up his revolver, but as soon as she did, two more Mexicans bolted out of the house and began shooting at her. One had a lever-action rifle. She fired two hasty rounds at the closest one who had a revolver, certain she had missed, and scurried into the barn. She took a huge chance pulling the door shut. Two more shots rang out, leaving bullet holes in the door just inches from where she had been standing. She ran back behind the Jeep and squatted down. She reloaded the five empties with cartridges from her gun belt. Thank God she was still in uniform and had twelve reloads secured in loops on her belt.

What was she gonna do now? No one knew she was here. She didn't have enough ammo to sustain an extended shootout. She needed to get back to her car where she had a full box of cartridges in the glovebox, but she was cut off. Not only that, she had left the keys in the ignition. Damn! She was in a pickle!

She could hear at least two, maybe three men speaking Spanish quietly in the barnyard. She only had two ways out - the double doors the same way she came in or a small window about four feet up on the back side of the building. It would be a tight fit and a long drop down. She hoped they hadn't noticed it yet.

She decided to climb the ladder up to the loft. She cracked the board window open a couple of inches and looked down. Two men were dragging the giant's body back towards the house. She couldn't see the dead man's revolver.

She pushed the window open a little wider, leaned out, aimed, and fired two rounds, hitting one man in the leg. He yelled in pain. In return for her trouble, she received another shot in her direction, whizzing past her head from the same man with the rifle. He was standing farther away, close to the verandah, all by himself. He looked young. This bandit certainly had the advantage in firepower, but he wasn't a very good marksman. Praise the Lord for miracles!

She dropped down out of sight, leaving the window open, and scrambled back down the ladder as quietly as she could. Her stomach was turning flip flops in her throat. Bile juice soured her mouth. She almost vomited.

She crept back to the door and unfastened the latch. Then she lay on her stomach and pushed it open about four inches. She could see that the dead man was still on the ground. There was a large puddle of blood where he had fallen and a trail of blood where they had dragged him. It was hot and the blow flies were already beginning to feast on him and the pool of blood.

She pushed the door open another four inches so she could get a better field of view. The two man-draggers were nowhere to be seen. The rifleman was standing near the house, looking inside. He finally woke up from his stupor and fired another round at her, kicking up dust near her face. His rifle, being a lever-action, was a little slow returning to battery compared to an automatic, which is why he only got off one shot. Gillespie was in a prone, resting position, the most stable shooting platform, and she sent three quick rounds center of mass right back at him. She must have scored at least one hit, because he screamed like a little girl who had her dolly ripped away by a vicious dog, just before he bounced up and scurried back inside the house. She heard the screen door slamming.

She thought about running back to her car, but the other two bandits scrambled back outside and opened up on her with everything they had. She saw that one was limping significantly. She rolled out of harm's way, leaving the door still open about eight inches, and retreated back behind the Jeep, once again to reload. She had fired ten rounds altogether, leaving only two cartridges in the loops after filling her cylinder to capacity. Damn! She prayed that these yahoos hadn't brought many extra rounds either, or she would be in big trouble.

She hated to do it, but she had no choice. Her bladder was about to burst. She was afraid they'd rush her while she had her pants down, but once again, the Good Lord was watching over her.

Business complete, she climbed back up the ladder to keep watch. It was a little past 10 o'clock. Now it was a waiting game. The next skirmish would probably be her last.

CHAPTER 37

Calling for Reinforcements

Tuesday, May 30, 1972

Fernando Reyes, El Jefe, was in a great deal of pain from the bullet wounds which shattered the fibula, or calf bone, on his left leg. It was throbbing like an abscessed molar. He had been unable to completely stop the bleeding, but at least it was not flowing like a river.

Further complicating matters, his Colt, .38 Special revolver was empty. Bone dry. No more fucking bullets. Nada. Piss poor planning on his part. However, since his segundo, El Toro, was no longer among the living, Fernando had appropriated his Smith & Wesson, .357 Magnum. It was fully loaded, but that was all. If he had brought any spare ammo, it was tucked away in his trouser pockets, directly in the female officer's field of fire. Who among them ever imagined he would need so many fucking bullets? This should have been a "milk run!"

As if that weren't bad enough, Leonardo Trujillo had been gut shot three times. They definitely had not been able to stop his bleeding. El Jefe did not know if Leonardo would make it or not, but probably not. Leonardo was whimpering quietly, sequestered out sight from the clients in a wicker chair placed behind a couple of tall potted plants on the back veranda. El Jefe had also appropriated his Winchester because Leonardo was no longer an effective soldier. He was done - "all she wrote." Unfortunately, Leonardo only had three rifle cartridges remaining.

Who was that policewoman anyway, Annie Fucking Oakley? Where did she come from? What was she doing here? Had a neighbor spotted them and called the law? Did they send her by herself? They must have. Look at all the damage she had already done! He did not want to expose his body to her again! He would kill that bitch slowly if he ever got the chance.

The dipshit, Felipe Zapata, with an IQ under 70, was the only one of the four coyotes fortunate enough to remain unharmed - at least so far. He was armed with a Smith & Wesson .22 caliber revolver, because who would trust him with anything more potent? Zapata still had a pocket full of bullets simply because it was a .22. Ammo was small and cheap, but a .22 was not the first choice of weapons in a gunfight. Yes, it could kill, but unless the shot went through the heart or the brain, it could take a week before the target succumbed to his wounds. Felipe, the bandito brain trust (not!) was now the soldier upon whom El Jefe was compelled to rely upon to fetch reinforcements and save the day. Sweet Mother of God!

The growing racket in the living room was becoming wearisome. The clients were in Panic City. They were moaning and crying and begging to flee back across the border. It was all Fernando could do, via slaps, threats, and intimidation, to keep them huddled where they were, in a house with only one bathroom. If they ever escaped, Fernando would be doomed. He'd have no hostages if the police did show up. Furthermore, if he didn't deliver the customers on time in Sheffield, La Serpiente would put a bullet in his head. It was as simple as that, so he did the only thing he could do. He had no other choice.

Fernando called Felipe to the kitchen. He watched while Felipe checked his 6-inch barrel, .22 caliber rodent-slayer to make sure it was fully loaded. It was. He asked if Felipe knew how to get back to La Serpiente's house. Yes, he could find it. He asked if he knew how to drive. Yes, but he didn't have a drivers license. Satisfied, El Jefe said, "These are your orders. It is muy importante. I want you to walk across the river without being seen by that policewoman in the barn. Can you do that?"

"Sí sí, Señor."

"Muy bueno, because if she sees you, she will most certainly shoot you dead! Take the newer van. The keys are under the driver's floor mat. Drive to La Serpiente's house. Tell him la policía showed up this morning and that we had a shootout. Tell him El Toro is dead and Leonardo is in bad shape. Tell him I have been shot in the leg and can barely walk. Tell him we have una mujer polícia trapped in the barn. Tell him we need more men and ammunition. Ask if he wants me to kill the policewoman. Can you remember all of that?"

"Sí, Señor."

"Bueno. Ahora date prisa! Hurry!"

Felipe scurried off, exiting through the front door, so as to avoid detection from the policewoman. He circled wide to the west away from the barn. He took off his sneakers and socks before crossing the river. He was thrilled to be on such an important mission. He did not know there was an adage, "Don't shoot the messenger." It was coined for a reason. Even King David of Jerusalem slew the messenger who claimed he killed King Saul out of mercy, as commanded by King Saul, himself. (2 Samuel 1.)

It took the better part of an hour for Felipe to return to the vans. It took him more than two hours to drive to San Miguel. He drove very slowly and carefully because he had never driven any motor vehicle more than 10 miles until this very moment. Upon arrival, he waited more than 30 minutes, standing in the hot sun, before Mr. Afilado had time to see him.

When finally Mr. Afilado called Felipe in, he recited El Jefe's message almost verbatim. When he was through, standing with his hat in hand, frightened to death, Mr. Afilado slammed his palm on the top of his desk and screamed, "Am I to understand that one, lone, female Americano officer shot and killed El Toro and wounded Fernando and Leonardo?"

"Sí, Señor. It is true."

"For crying out loud, why didn't someone shoot her?"

"We tried, Señor, but she was hard to hit. She must have a lucky charm. Fernando used all of his bullets. Leonardo only has three left. El Toro didn't shoot because she shot him dead first. I shot all six of my bullets twice, but I reloaded. I still have many bullets.

"You go back and tell Fernando I'm coming. I'll bring more men and ammunition. Tell him if that bitch escapes before I get there, he might as well go ahead and shoot himself in the head, because I will shoot him myself right between the eyes, and then I will "filet him like a fish" to allow the buzzards easier access to feast on his carcass. Entiendes?"

"Sí, Señor. I understand. Gracias. I will leave right away."

Felipe bowed, turned around, and dashed out of the office. He ran headfirst into Antonio Fuentes, Mr. Afilado's assistant, in the hallway, almost knocking him down. Felipe almost soiled his trousers. What else could go wrong? He apologized profusely. Then he said, "Señor Fuentes, Señor Afilado told me to return to the river right away, but I cannot. I'm out of gas and I have no diñero."

"I see. Have you eaten today?"

"No, Señor. Not since yesterday afternoon."

Mr. Fuentes handed Felipe a 50-peso note. Then he said, "Before you leave, stop down in the kitchen and tell Bonita I said to feed you well. Also she is to give you a large lunch to take back to Fernando and Leonardo. Fill up your truck with gas. Keep the change. Do not disappoint me. Okay?"

"Sí, Señor. Gracias."

Felipe only weighed 59 kilos, but he gobbled down two kilos of enchiladas, frijoles, and rice, washed down with two half-liters of a watermelon-flavored soft drink. He waited until he started up the van before he belched like a hippopotamus and ripped off an earth-shattering fart that he strung out for 10 seconds. It cost him 39 pesos for gasoline. He bought some smokes with the change. Then he headed out of town en route to the river across from the Circle A.

When he arrived, sometime around 4 o'clock (he didn't own a watch), the only thing which had transpired in his absence was the expiration of Leonardo Trujillo. Fernando didn't look very good, either. He was all bloody and pasty white. Felipe could see the pain in his face. Fernando told Felipe to take Leonardo out and lay him in the barnyard next to El Toro. He said for him to make damn sure the woman did not see him. He also told Felipe to strip the sheets off the bed in the small bedroom and to wrap each body. When he was done, he was to find a shady place to keep an eye on the barn. If he saw any movement at all, he was to fire a warning shot in that puta's direction.

CHAPTER 38

The Alarm Is Sounded

Tuesday, May 30, 1972

It was nearly 4:30. Sarah had just pulled into the driveway after a full, but satisfying day at work. She loved working at the rodeo grounds where she was the event planner. They were in the planning stages for four, smaller rodeos scheduled on alternating Saturdays before Quayle County's annual gala event, Cowboy Days Rodeo & Festival, which was scheduled for Saturday, July 29th. The first rodeo was scheduled for this Saturday, June 3rd. Sarah still had a lot to do to get ready, especially since she planned to compete as a barrel racer in two of the rodeos.

The phone was ringing like a drunk monkey pounding on a set of symbols with metal drumsticks in an empty Chicago synagogue on a Sunday morning, when Sarah breezed in the door. Barlow, who had been sound asleep after working the midnight shift, finally trudged to the kitchen and picked up the receiver (on the wall phone) on the umpteenth ring. He uttered, "Adams' residence. Barlow speaking."

Sarah waived hello and went on about her business, checking to see if the hamburgers had thawed out for supper. Barlow, standing at half mast in his nudies, smiled and blew her a kiss. She couldn't resist giving him a little yank on his semi-erect crank as she passed by. (It wouldn't take much to whip that bad boy into action.)

"Deputy Adams, this is Mrs. Beanblossom. Sorry to bother you Dearie, but I'm a little worried. Is Ella Mae over at your house? Did you all go riding today? The reason I'm calling is she hasn't come home yet."

The cobwebs in Barlow's lizard brain completely evaporated. "She hasn't been home all day?"

"No, Dearie. All she talks about any more is going riding with you and that sweet little wife of yours. I confess, Ella Mae's been gone so much recently that I've gotten a little jealous of you all."

"No, Ma'am, she's not here right now, but I have an idea where she might be. I'll go find her and let her know it's nearly time for supper. Don't you worry, you hear?"

"You don't suppose she's back over there at the Circle A, do you? After all the recent problems there, I would think she would avoid that accursed ranch belonging to the late Mr. Wrigley at all costs. It's awful what all they put that poor man through. What do you think?"

"Wouldn't surprise me at all if she did go there. She's still mourning for Sergeant Major Wrigley and Pedro Padilla." (Then Barlow lied with fingers crossed.) "Look. I'm dressed and ready to go. I'm leaving right now to go check on her. Thanks for calling. Give me an hour to find her. If Ella Mae hasn't returned by then, call Sarah here, okay?"

"Oh, thank you so much. I'm cooking a roast beef with all the fixings for supper tonight. That's Ella Mae's favorite. Plus, I baked a lemon meringue pie. I'll send you a slice with Ella Mae when she leaves for work."

"Well, aren't you sweet? Thank you so much. Bye, bye now."

"Bye."

Barlow tended to urgent business in the bathroom before pulling on his jeans. He asked Sarah to get his boots.

"What's up? Ella Mae gone missing? I'll go looking for her with you."

"Not this time, Sweetie. I think she's at the Circle A. Maybe she had an accident or possibly she ran into some trouble. I'm headed there first since she's been gone way too long. Dial Slick's number for me while I finish tucking in my shirt, would you?"

Sarah recognized possible disaster when she heard it. Her

heart began to sink. She went back to the kitchen and dialed. The phone was ringing. She handed the receiver to Barlow. Slick answered, "Hello."

"Slick, it's Barlow. I need your help. Gillespie's been missing since we got off work this morning. Biddy Beanblossom just called. She thinks Gillespie's at the Circle A. I'm headed out the door soon as I hang up. I'm taking my rifle. Could you meet me there in the driveway? We'll go up together."

"Sure thing. Did anyone call the office yet?"

"Nope, but I'm asking Sarah to, just as soon as I hang up. Slick, I got a real bad feeling about this. I think she might have run into some coyotes. We might be facing a little dust up. If so, I want it to be with you or Archie. No disrespect to the others, but you understand."

"'Nuff said. I'll call Archie before I leave. He lives closer than anybody. Tell Sarah to speak directly to Sheriff Sol or Chief Alex - no one else. Who's on the desk, anyway?"

"Ernie Atwater. He just pushed Chunk."

"Sheriff will probably roll everyone he can get aholt of. I know I would if I was an elected sheriff, but you know, sometimes a body can have too dang much help and it gets in his way. Savvy?"

"Savvy. See you there."

Sarah heard every word. She had tears in her eyes. She gave Barlow a bear hug and jumped up and wrapped her legs around his waist as he was picking up his rifle and bandolier. She whispered, "Barlow Adams, you come back to me in one piece. Find Ella Mae, but come back to me in one piece. Understand? I know what to do here. I'll take care of the rest."

"I will. Always do, don't I? Love you. See you soon." He ran out the door.

She whispered, "I love you more."

Barlow's '65 Dodge 100 wouldn't run as fast as one of the police cruisers. It topped out at about 100 miles per hour. Once he cleared the Mosby traffic, he was "balls to the wall" all the way to the Circle A. He arrived at 5:25, just inside the unimproved driveway off Highway 90, eight miles north of the farmhouse. Slick and Archie were already there. Both were loaded for bear. Besides their Colt Peacemakers, Archie had his lever action 10-gauge. Slick left his 10-gauge at home. Today he carried a pre-'64 Winchester .30-30, same as Barlow. In addition to wearing gun belts in which the loops were filled to capacity with handgun cartridges, each was wearing a bandolier cross-shoulder, Mexican-style, filled with long gun ammo.

Archie asked, "Sheriff Sol been notified?"

Barlow replied, "Sarah was calling him as I ran out the door."

Slick said, "Barlow, if Gillespie's disappearance has anything to do with the alien smugglers controlled by La Serpiente, you know what we have to do. We probably only have 10 or 15 minutes before well-meaning assistance will begin to arrive what's too squeamish to settle this frontier style. We ain't carrying no handcuffs and we ain't makin' no arrests. Savvy? Besides Atwater and us, there ain't a deputy in Quayle County what's drawn blood, and you remember how much that wracked up Ernie. I wasn't sure he would return back to work.

"I say we leave two trucks here and jump in the other one to get as close as we can before we ditch it and hike the rest of the way in. Archie's truck and mine make more engine noise than yours. You drive. Archie can ride shotgun, and I'll jump in the back. Soon as we lay eyes on them sons a bitches, open up. We ain't got time to pussyfoot around. We gotta take care of business pronto if they got Gillespie. Everyone agreed?"

Archie and Barlow both nodded.

They loaded up and began the long, tedious trek to the ranch house. Barlow had to take it slow to keep the dust down, as well as to keep from bouncing Slick over the side. After a little more than seven miles, he stopped as far to the right as he could on this one-lane goat path. They eased out of the truck and started walking. There was no need for any of them to check the loads in their long guns. Everyone was topped off and had a round chambered.

They could hear low, intermittent Mexican chatter before they even got within eyesight of the farmyard. They spread out about five feet apart, insofar as it was possible and remain substantially abreast. Archie was in the middle. Barlow was a little behind and to the right. Slick was to the left. They were getting very close, so they were taking flatfooted baby steps like hunters do when they stalk game, doing everything they possibly could to be quiet, and to avoid unwanted attention by not making a sudden motion which might be registered out of the corner of an enemy eye.

They came to the sharp left bend in the road which ran between a four-feet tall bluff to the left and a series of six-feet tall boulders to the right. They knew this was the last blind spot before they entered the ranch's backyard where they would be completely exposed. They stopped and listened. They heard a slamming screen door and some more garbled Mexican conversation.

Archie motioned for Slick and Barlow to hold tight. Then he crept forward a few steps and stopped again. He turned and pointed to his front left and motioned for them to come forward. What they saw when they crept up was the rear end of Gillespie's car about 10 feet in front of them, and a '57 turquoise and white Chevy parked all the way across the lot between the house and the barn. The barn doors were pushed to, not necessarily locked, but the loft window door was partially open. Since they had seen only one recent set of tire tracks in the driveway, they could only conclude that those tire tracks belonged to Gillespie's car, and that the Chevy had been driven through the river.

They still couldn't see anyone in the yard from their field of view, but they sensed at least two guards somewhere to the front of Gillespie's car, even though the Mexican chatter had ceased. In fact, they became certain of it because the smell of cigarette smoke suddenly wafted through the air.

Barlow slowly pointed to the barn up high. The loft door was open a few inches wider. Someone was watching. He was absolutely certain that someone was Gillespie.

CHAPTER 39

La Serpiente Assumes Operational Control

Tuesday, May 30, 1972

La Serpiente knew he was taking a huge risk when he elected to cross the border. The problem was, everything was turning into a shit sandwich. He no longer trusted any of his men who were alive and free from incarceration to make sound decisions or to implement a plan to a satisfactory conclusion. If you want something done right, you have to do it yourself.

He told Taco to round up Humberto, Ricardo, Xavier, and Espantapájaros (Scarecrow) to take a trip with him across the border. He told Taco to make sure they all had guns with plenty of ammo, and to throw in two spare guns with extra ammo just in case of emergency. Taco was also responsible for getting the '57 Chevy ready, making sure it was full of gas, that the spare had air in it, and that it was 100 percent operational. They should be ready to depart in one hour. Tell everyone to make sure they have eaten and voided their bowels and bladder because they weren't making any stops until they reached their destination.

The question was, how should he dress for such an occasion? Since this was a working trip, he did not want to be encumbered with a jacket. Too formal. He decided to wear one of his Hollywood cowboy outfits. He selected the amarillo one. He even had matching lizard skin, Tony Lama boots to go with. The trousers and shirt had complementary embroidery stitching with pictures of black coyotes howling at a blood red moon, green saguaro cacti, and Texas bluebonnet flowers. He wore his floral design, hand-tooled, El Paso Saddlery, double-holstered gun belt, with two double-magazine pouches to show off his engraved, gold-plated, Colt Government Model, .45 ACP caliber pistols.

Of course he had his gold-plated switchblade in his right trouser pocket, and his coiled snake ring with the ruby eyes on his left pinky. He topped off his entire ensemble by wearing his beige Stetson with the fanged rattlesnake hatband. He had decided he would kill the foolish policewoman after he raped and tortured her for all his men to see. He wanted to make an indelible impression in the minds of all his men. He wanted the whole world to hear about this. It would be good for his flagging business. Everyone would fear him and be in awe whenever they saw him.

It was absolutely necessary because what would his enemies think if they learned a solitary, Americano policewoman buffaloed and even killed one or more of his soldiers? It was humiliating! If he didn't do this, he was done. None of the bad boys would want to work for him, and he would be disrespected by friends and enemies alike. This is why he was exposing himself to capture by the Americano authorities. This "catch-me-if-you-can", "spit-in-your-eye" attitude would increase respect for him by tenfold. He would retain and even surpass his legendary stature among everyone within his purview. Such are the comforting thoughts of a megalomaniac.

They arrived at the Circle A about 5 o'clock. The bonehead, Taco, pulled into the barnyard and made a U-turn facing the river before stopping. Maybe he thought they would have to make a fast getaway. Nevertheless, he parked way too close to the barn, just to the right of two sheet-draped bodies. La Serpiente had ridden in the right front seat. Humberto, Ricardo, Xavier, and Espantapájaros were jammed into the back seat. Espantapájaros was as thin as a scarecrow, hence his nickname, so he and Xavier, who was only 16, were consigned to the middle. Espantapájaros was the last one to disembark, and the fool did so from the left side, which was closer to the front of the barn where the door and the loft window would give someone inside a clear line of sight.

That bitch was hiding in the loft and she shot Espantapájaros twice in the middle of his back just as he walked in front of the car. He was felled like a beetle-infested, slash pine tree. The retard almost got blood splatter on the spotless, painstakingly restored, classic Chevrolet! He drowned all alone in his own blood within two minutes.

La Serpiente had almost completed the walk to the verandah door when the shots rang out, so he didn't return fire. He couldn't see the bitch anyway, but the other four soldiers and Felipe apparently did, because they fired an entire salvo into the loft, but to what avail? All they did was waste precious ammo! La Serpiente "called off the dogs" except for Felipe, whom he commanded to reload and to stand poised in the event she exposed herself again. The others were ordered to come with him inside the house.

Shit on a stick! It was worse than he had imagined! Besides El Toro, Leonardo was dead! Now Espantapájaros was dead! Fernando was delirious. He might as well be dead. Four casualties by one female officer! Inside the house, there was fucking blood everywhere! The clients were cooped up like chickens in a slaughter house, moaning and weeping and begging God for deliverance. The commode was backed up, and the entire house smelled like an Indian reservation shithouse.

La Serpiente gathered his men back out into the verandah so he could breathe. He gulped a slug of tequila from his silver flask, which he retrieved from his left hip pocket. His grandiose plans had just gone up in two puffs of gun smoke.

He looked around, and realized that the only long gun they had with them was Leonardo's .30-30. He checked. It had only three, lousy rounds. Taco said they brought two shotguns, but they were in the trunk of the car. Of course! Why should he have expected anything different? He pulled another slug and thought. Four sets of eyeballs were riveted on him. He concentrated for several more minutes. He had to come up with a bold, lethal plan. They had to annihilate this bitch and move these clients before they all became hysterical.

Finally, he said, "Time is of the essence. We need to move fast. This is what we are going to do. Xavier, you take up a position in front of the white car out there with Felipe. Initially, your job is twofold. First, I want you to make sure that bitch doesn't manage to escape. Watch the barn, but be aware of your surroundings. Second, we don't know if the neighbors heard shots and called the police. If the police do come flying in with lights and sirens, it'll be up to you and Felipe to fight them off until the rest of us can assist. Can you do that? This is a very important job."

"Sí, Señor."

"Muy bien.

"Taco, Humberto, and Rico. We will breech the barn door. It's probably got a sliding board crossbar inside. Possibly a metal latch. Humberto, I want you to take Leonardo's rifle. Use it to keep the bitch pinned down until it's out of bullets and then switch to your revolver. Once we get inside, then you can come in. Until then, it's your responsibility to keep the bitch occupied so she can't shoot the rest of us while we're going in. If she shoots me, you die. Understand?"

"Do not worry, Señor. I will make sure she doesn't shoot you."

"Muy bien.

"Taco, you and Ricardo and I have the most dangerous job. We will go in and kill the bitch; however, in the event she drops her gun or is out of bullets, I want to take her alive. We will drag her outside and fuck the very life out of her. We will fuck her in every orifice. Teach her a lesson. Then we will torture and kill her. However, if she continues shooting, so be it. Shoot her dead.

"Before we try to breach, I will use both of my .45s to shoot the lock or brace, whatever is there keeping the door shut. It may take a dozen or more bullets. If so, give me time to reload before we enter. I don't want to get shot while I'm reloading. Got it?"

All three men answered affirmatively.

Very well. Make sure your guns are all fully loaded. Go take a leak or whatever you have to do. Then take up a position where you won't get shot before we launch. Any questions?"

There were none.

The men sauntered out. When they were gone, La Serpiente unzipped and pissed in a potted plant. It was extremely gratifying. He lit a cheroot and inhaled the nicotine. He saved the Monte Christo Churchills for his victory smokes.

CHAPTER 40

Good Versus Evil

Tuesday, May 30, 1972

Gillespie had been waiting for the end to come now for more than eight hours. She was thirsty, hungry, and hot, but foremost thirsty. She was down to her last six rounds. With the arrival of six more bandits, one of which was sprawled out like varmint roadkill on a country backroad, she knew her time was about up. She had whispered at least a hundred prayers asking God for deliverance. She had deliberately tried to avoid the passage in *The Lord's Prayer*, "Thy Kingdom come. Thy will be done," but she could do that no longer.

She really wasn't ready to to depart this world for the Kingdom of God. She had so many things she still wanted to do. Then she thought about Jesus praying in the Garden of Gethsemane, where he sweated blood before praying, "Father, if thou be willing, remove this cup from me; nevertheless, not my will but thine be done." (Luke 22)

She began praying for forgiveness. She accepted her fate - God's will. A tear escaped out of the corner of her left eye. Another sneaked out from the corner of her right. Then she shivered and more tears leaked out. Afterwards, she felt a sense of well-being and comfort. She was ready, fortified by His presence. She crawled back over to the window and inched it a little further out so she could get a broader view.

Oh my gosh! She saw Slick partially crouched down behind her car. There were two bandits in front of it leaning against the hood, having a smoke. They hadn't noticed her yet. She took off her Stetson and moved it slowly across her forehead like she was brushing away sweat. She hoped Slick saw it. She thought he nodded, or did she just imagine that?

Then a bandit with a rifle, the one who was hiding behind a roll of fence wire, fired a shot that clipped her on the outside of her right upper arm. Ouch! It burned, but it didn't really hurt that much - yet. It did bleed like the dickens, though. She ducked back down after the fact, and scooted about six feet further back from the window, lying on her back. She didn't have anything to wrap around the wound, so all she could do was apply pressure.

Three more bandits came scurrying out from the verandah. The one dressed like a yellow cowboy rodeo pimp was obviously the boss. He was wearing two, gold-plated .45s in a fancy gun belt around his waist. She had only gotten a quick glimpse of him when they first arrived. She wondered if he were La Serpiente. Wouldn't that be something if he came across the border just because of little ol' her?

Boss Man began shouting rapid fire instructions. He was pointing up at the loft. She rolled left to get out of sight. Suddenly a multitude of shots rang out, sending wooden splinters all around her in every direction. They all missed high. Praise the Lord!

She decided to get back down on the ground floor behind the Jeep, utilizing it for cover and as a stable firing platform. She cocked and aimed her revolver towards the door, using the hood as a stabilizer. She knew they would eventually break the crossbar which was holding the door shut. She planned to expend every last round she had to kill Boss Man even if another bandit killed her in the exchange of gunfire. She hoped Slick had some assistance with him, even though she knew he could handle this bunch all by his lonesome. Was Barlow here, too? She could only hope.

Slick saw Gillespie give him a modified hat wave. He pointed towards the loft and then gave both Archie and Barlow a thumbs up. Just then a rifleman they hadn't seen took a well-aimed shot at her. Then three more bandits came rushing out of the verandah. The fancy dandy had to be La Serpiente. All the bandits started firing up at Gillespie at the same time. At least a dozen shots were fired at her.

Archie and Slick both smoked the two assholes standing in front of Gillespie's car. The one Archie shot from less than 12 feet away was nearly severed in half. Slick's wasn't messed up nearly so bad, but he did sport an eighth hole in his head, spraying some missing brain matter into the air.

Barlow took careful aim and blew a big hole in the side of La Serpiente's head. He never saw it coming. Lucky dog. His Stetson went sailing into the air. He crumpled like a cheap suit. "Dressed to kill" became "dress to be killed." Then Barlow noticed that the "all hat and no cattle" GQ [Gentlemen's Quarterly] bandit boss had a gold-plated pistol in each hand. What a pretentious pimp!

The rifleman next to the roll of fence wire had turned and lined up his sights on Barlow, who hadn't seen him. Police refer to this as having tunnel vision in times of dire stress. Too bad for Humberto that he had tunnel vision, too, because he wasn't paying attention to his closest threat. Archie blew him halfway to Kingdom Come. Were this vanquished gangster still standing, one could have seen daylight all the way through his chest.

The other two yahoos, Taco and Ricardo, turned around and spotted all three of their adversaries at the same time, but it was too little, too late. Archie quickly dispatched Taco into the bloody baptismal fount of Hell. Barlow and Slick delivered simultaneous fatal rounds into Ricardo's previously healthy body, of which he had been incredibly vain. His dying thought was, "Where did these assholes come from?"

It was deathly quiet for about a minute. Archie said, "Slick, we gotta check inside. Barlow, you go look for Gillespie."

Archie and Slick cleared the house in seconds. The illegals were cowering. Fernando was the only bandit, and he was lying unconscious on the couch in the verandah. His leg was a bloody mess, perhaps with a fatal injury, and he, too, might have been knocking on the Gates of Hell. Hard to say for sure. Slick was already cocking his revolver to ensure his unencumbered passage, when he glimpsed Archie out of the corner of his eye, shaking his head no. Then Slick looked up and saw a couple of illegals staring at him with mouths agape. He picked up both of Fernando's revolvers and stuck them in his waistband.

Barlow double-checked the seven dead bandits on the ground. He didn't see the two sheeted bodies. They were on the far side of the '57 Chevy. Barlow checked to confirm that nobody in the recently departed crowd was "playing possum." Satisfied, he was just about to pull on the barn door when he heard a noise inside. He hoped it was Gillespie, but he was ready either way. He held his rifle at the ready and sidestepped to his right.

The door opened slowly. Whew! It was Gillespie! She looked a mess, with blood all over her upper right arm and the front of her shirt and her pants. She was holding her Ruger revolver in her bloody right hand. It was cocked. She said, "Oh, Barlow, I'm so glad to see you. I thought I was a goner. Do you have any water?" Then she fainted.

Barlow scooped her up off the ground and rubbed her face softly. He whispered, "Gillespie, you slipped and fell. Let me help stand you up before Archie or Slick see you. I don't want to hear any girl jokes about my partner."

She smiled and slowly stood up. She said, "I gotta go pee. Can you cover for me?"

He started to respond when she said, "Just kidding. I know you got my back. I know you'd never tell."

They both heard a motor running and looked towards the driveway. Sheriff Sol and Chunk rolled up in the sheriff's unmarked unit. Shoemaker and Meacham were right behind in a marked unit. Chief came up next in his Jeep Wagoneer. They all had grim countenances.

Sheriff Sol ran over and asked, "Gillespie, are you all right?"

"Yes, Sir. It's not as bad as it looks. What I really need is some water."

Kirk Shoemaker popped his trunk and brought her a two-gallon jug of water. She began slugging it, spilling at least a quart all over her bloody uniform. Randy Meacham brought the first aid kit and began hunting for salve and bandages.

Archie came out of the house and said, "Boy, are we glad to see you all."

Sheriff Sol asked, "Did you kill 'em all? Did any survive?"

Archie replied, "Maybe one. Slick's watching a bandit Gillespie shot early this morning from the looks of it. It's questionable if he's gonna make it. There's also 20 illegal aliens in there scared shitless. Not sure how many dead bandits we have, but the one you really care about is the joker in the yellow outfit. I'm pretty darn sure that's La Serpiente. Barlow gobbled his lunch for him."

Sheriff Sol said, "Randy, call the office. Have Atwater send an ambulance from Val Verde County for Gillespie. (Gillespie started to object but he waived her off.) Tell him to call Mrs. Beanblossom and Sarah to let them both know their loved ones are okay. Then have him call the Border Patrol over in Del Rio and tell them to come pick up these aliens. Lastly, have him call Pete Ricketts to get the meat wagon moving this way. Tell him he could have eight or more bodies. If the phone inside is disconnected, find the nearest pay phone. Do not put this out over the air. Then get back here as soon as you can. Bring us some cold drinks, too. I'll reimburse you from the imprest fund. Oh yeah, don't forget to have Buck Boyd bring his wrecker.

"Kirk, you get to help Chief with the photographs and the crime scene.

"Barlow, you and Archie join me inside with Slick and Gillespie and tell me word-for-word exactly what transpired. It's my primal inclination to commend everyone of you, except you jaspers didn't call me first, nor did you all wait for reinforcements to arrive. I understand there's a good chance you couldn't, but I also recognize a black flag operation when I see one. We'll have a little confabulation about that, too.

"And as for you Gillespie, I know you had a harrowing experience, but you never should've been here in the first place and you know it. You do realize you're the first deputy ever shot in Quayle County so far as I can recall? What is your Uncle Leland going to say? You think he will be happy with either one of us? I don't believe so.

"Come on. We've all got a mountain of work to do."

CHAPTER 41

The Aftermath

Tuesday, May 30 - Sunday, June 4, 1972

Tuesday was a long evening for everyone. Gillespie got an ambulance ride against her wishes to the emergency room in Del Rio where everyone fawned all over her. Nobody there had ever heard of a uniformed female deputy, let alone a uniformed female deputy who had been wounded in a dramatic shootout with members of a Mexican cartel. The ER staff cleaned her wound and gave her six sutures and called their family members and best friends to tell them all about this celebrity in their midst. (Think Wonder Woman from the DC Comics going back to 1941, and later the TV show starring Linda Carter.)

Naturally, the lone TV station in Del Rio got wind of it. They were already set up with cameras filming when Deputy Gillespie was rolled out into the lobby. Sheriff Sol had anticipated this, so when Randy Meacham returned with the cold drinks, he was turned right around to head to the hospital Code 3 with ironclad instructions to waive off any interviews of Gillespie by the press, until 10 o'clock Wednesday morning at the Quayle County Sheriff's Office. Sheriff Sol needed time to prep her just like he did Barlow three years earlier, before the press could package her into whatever image they wanted, and milk this image for all the publicity they could reap.

It took six hours for Chief and Kirk to wrap up the crime scene. Part of that time was spent waiting for the volunteer fire department to bring lights so they could continue to examine the crime scene well into the dark. Also, the Border Patrol needed to do a quick interview of all the illegals before they bused them to a detention facility in Del Rio. In addition, Pete Ricketts had to call in reinforcements from the ambulance service in Del Rio to help remove ten bodies to the morgue. (Fernando expired before the ambulance arrived to take Gillespie to the hospital.) Buck Boyd came to pick up the '57 Chevy. And finally, Chunk was posted all night at the entrance to the Circle A to keep curiosity seekers and the press out. It got so bad, Sheriff Sol rolled Dewey to stay at the ranch house overnight in the event the press attempted to sneak in through a back way.

Around 9 o'clock, Sheriff Sol sent Archie, Slick, and Barlow home. Slick had a shortchange to work the desk Wednesday morning. Barlow had even less of a reprieve. He had to relieve Atwater at midnight.

Barlow arrived home about 10 o'clock. Sarah was prepared to feed him as soon as he walked in. He said he needed a shower first. Before he was halfway done, Sarah had stripped off her dress and stepped in. She washed Barlow's entire body, looking for any signs of injury. Her soft, soapy ministrations awoke a sleeping trouser trout. She feigned surprise, but she didn't stop what she was doing. No indeed! Once the soap was rinsed off she decided to give it the taste test. After that, things really got heated up and she found herself up against the wall, being pile-driven into a state of blissful nirvana. The hot water was was all used up but it didn't matter. An itch must be scratched until it quits itching. What's a little room temperature water when compared with a series of explosive climaxes? That's what Sarah was thinking about. Barlow was thinking he caught a tiger by the tail. Fortunately Sarah melted into his arms before he collapsed from exhaustion.

They had to hurry in order to build up Barlow's strength. He wolfed down two cheeseburgers, a plateful of pork and beans, a side salad, and a slice of pineapple upside down cake, washed down by ice water and black coffee. He had 15 minutes to get to work. He put on his hat, grabbed his lunch, gave Sarah a peck on the cheek and turned to go. Sarah grabbed him by his love muscle and held on tight until he gave her a proper kiss. Then he raced out the door. He took his rifle so he could give it a thorough cleaning while the rest of Quayle County was busy "counting sheep."

Barlow got to work at midnight, technically 15 minutes late by local custom, but Ernie Atwater didn't mind. He was happy to stay a little late just to hear all the details of the day's supercharged hullabaloo by an actual participant. Ernie inherently knew why Barlow and Slick and Archie had handled this incident all by themselves. Everyone knew. They were everyone's all-star "go-to" crew in times of peril or disaster. Ernie wasn't the least bit surprised that there were no bandits left standing when the fight was over. (Sheriff Sol wasn't either. At least they didn't have a trial to contend with.)

Did Texas Ranger Captain Frank Hamer bring Bonnie and Clyde to jail, or just their bullet-riddled bodies? What about FBI Agent Melvin Purvis and John Dillinger? La Serpiente and his cartel had been the target of law enforcement for years, especially for BNDD, for all the lives he had ended or ruined, and now he was no more. Justice had been served frontier Texas style with whipped cream and a cherry on top. Amen and amen.

That night/early morning Barlow wrote the incident report and his formal statement. He was certain DA DeWitt would impanel the Grand Jury on Friday to determine if the 10 homicides were justified. Normally they would do it on Thursday but there were too many loose ends to tie up, plus the press would be like a pack of hungry wolves.

About 2 o'clock, Mrs. Beanblossom and Gillespie showed up unexpectedly. Barlow was cleaning his rifle. They didn't stay long - just long enough for Gillespie to thank Barlow for everything he did and to show him her stitches. Besides that, Mrs. Beanblossom owed Barlow a slice of lemon meringue pie.

Barlow told Gillespie that this incident was bound to have law enforcement agencies all over the state offering her better paying and more prestigious jobs. Maybe even the FBI or BNDD, not to mention Dallas or Houston PD.

She smiled and said, "I know. Uncle Leland has already offered me a deputy job in Brewster County with a $1,000 bump in pay. You know what, Barlow? You're from Texas. You know what they say. "You go home from the dance with the one what brung ya." Nobody but Sheriff Sol would take a chance on me. Not even Uncle Leland. Now most of my friends are here. Now this is my home. I don't want to go to Dallas or Houston. I could have gotten a job on one of those big city police departments a year ago, but I wanted to be a deputy, and now I am.

"Maybe someday I'll pursue a federal agent job. I have a college degree, but probably not. I love it here. Who else would have rescued me from six armed bandits like you and Slick and Archie? I'd be dead now if it weren't for you all. I was down to my last six bullets. (Don't tell anyone.) If Mrs. Beanblossom had called the office instead of you, by the time Ernie, and Sheriff Sol, and Chief had rallied the troops, I'd have been just a slab of meat, assuming they hadn't kidnapped me and taken me back to Mexico for fun and games. We all know that.

"Tell you what. One day if you decide to move on, let me know where you're going and maybe I'll apply. I don't believe you ever will. Your home is here. But I'm telling you right now. Down the road, if you ever get elected sheriff, I want to be the investigator. Keep that in mind.

"Gotta go. I have to be back at 9 o'clock so Sheriff Sol can brief me for the interview with the press. And between us girls, I don't want to be the poster girl for women in law enforcement. I want to be recognized as a fully competent deputy sheriff, not a fully competent female deputy sheriff. I wish folks would finally figure that out."

"They will in time. Sheriff Sol and I snapped to that by the time you'd completed the academy and busted Jaybird and

Polecat. You working tomorrow night with me?"

"Sheriff Sol said no, but I plan to work on him this morning. Ciao."

"Adiós. Goodnight, Mrs. Beanblossom. Thanks for the pie."

"Anytime, Deputy Adams. Goodbye."

Gillespie sailed through the interviews, including the two by talking heads from the TV stations, after she was coached by Sheriff Sol. Barlow and Sarah watched it on the 6 o'clock news. Over the next several weeks, Gillespie received a dozen or more job offers. She thanked them all, but politely turned each one of them down.

Chief Alex went to the Grand Jury on Friday. They deemed all the homicides justified. (Anything other that that would have been baffling.)

Gillespie ate supper with the Adams on Friday night. The three of them went to the rodeo on Saturday. Mrs. Beanblossom was also invited but she declined. They had a fabulous time.

On Sunday night at 11:45 pm, Barlow and Gillespie began a new week on the midnight shift. Life had pretty much returned to normal in Mosby, Quayle County, Texas, at least for now.

EPILOGUE

More Good Tidings

Tuesday, June 27, 1972

Even though the voting hours were from 8 o'clock to 6 o'clock, with the only polling place being on the third floor of the courthouse, the election was really over with by noon. There was only one race - County Supervisor for a 3-year term. There were only two candidates. No political affiliations were declared. The ballots were paper. Voting consisted of marking an X in the box situated next to the name of the voter's selected candidate, and placing the ballot into the solitary, locked, wooden box with a slot on the top.

Before voting, the citizen showed his proof of identification - usually a driver's license, maybe a military identification card, social security card, college identification card, selective service card, passport, whatever he had. Sometimes it was a birth certificate or a legal document. Then the clerk of court and one other witness watched while the voter signed his name in the register of voters and compared his signature with previous signatures.

In Quayle County, they only had 3,063 residents, of which only 1912 were registered voters. Everyone knew everyone and it was unthinkable that (a) someone would try to pass himself off as someone else to vote, or (b) someone would try to "stuff the ballot box." In this "neck of the woods" voting was almost a sacred duty. The adage around here was, "There are three types of boxes which keep America free: the jury box; the ballot box; and the cartridge box."

By lunchtime, 1632 ballots had already been cast. That's an 85 percent turnout rate. Historically, very few voters sign in after 2 o'clock. Nevertheless, the clerk waited until 6 o'clock sharp before closing the poll. Three trustworthy citizens-at-large tallied the votes in front of the clerk and his assistant. They checked the tally thrice. Once it was confirmed, they placed the ballots back into the locked box and secured it in the clerk's vault.

The clerk posted the results on the front door of the courthouse. Mr. Phineas Rumsfeldt, the sole proprietor and employee of the *The Trail's End*, Quayle County's weekly newspaper, was waiting patiently. He had been a journalist for the *Los Angeles Times* in his previous life. *The Trail's End* was both his hobby and his passion. It was established in 1921, by Mr. Cyrus R. Cobb, his maternal grandfather, and Mr. Rumsfeldt had at least one copy of every issue ever printed. He knew that by the time the citizenry read his scoop, it would be old news. It didn't matter. Mr. Rumsfeldt's news usually morphed into an op ed and he had plenty to say about the ousting of the meanest human being he had ever come into contact with.

The clerk also called Del Rio Radio Station KLUC, 960 on your AM dial, "Home of the Big Rooster" to report the election results for the local area-wide news which KLUC read with the weather report five minutes before the hour, each hour, ad nauseam. Then he went home and poured himself the first of several toddies, his personal preference being a gin and tonic.

Judge Sweeney sponsored a post election barbeque for Archie. Nobody would have been crass enough to refer to it as a victory celebration, even though that is exactly what it was. Hundreds showed up. They sold tee shirts with the American flag printed on the front for $3 apiece to help defray costs. Draft beer cost a quarter and soft drinks were a dime. The barbeque and other eats were free. Financially, the beer and tee shirts covered all the expenses.

Once the results had been announced on the radio, Archie made his victory speech. It was both short and sweet. Then he asked his new fiancée, Mrs. Twyla Jo (née Davis) Armstrong from Robstown in Nueces County, near Corpus Christi, to stand so he could introduce her to the crowd. Nearly everyone was stunned, even though Archie had been a widower for years. Twyla Jo had to be 15 years younger than Archie (actually it was 17) and she was still a head-turner! What else should one expect? Archie was still a handsome man in his own right. So what if his hair and mustache were alabaster white?

Archie said Twyla had two adult children - a son who was career Army and a married daughter with two children. He and Twyla were getting married in Corpus Christi at the Presbyterian church on July 8th, followed by a weeklong honeymoon in the historic Palmer House in Chicago. Then they were moving her to his ranch in Mosby, where they planned to have six more children. That made Twyla blush, but it brought a lot of raucous hoots from the crowd.

At the end of the evening, everyone went home sated, perhaps even a little buzzed, and ecstatic that Archie had beaten Mr. LaRue Dinkins. When they read Mr. Rumsfeldt's newspaper Friday morning, they were astonished. The vote was 1641 ballots for Archie and eight for Mr. Dinkins. Everyone knew Mr. Dinkins had quite a few more than just eight relatives in town, even if he didn't have any true friends. This meant even some members of his own family voted against him! Jeez Louise!

Thus endeth the Saga of Command Sergeant Major Arnold Wrigley and La Serpiente, with supporting appearances by Deputy Sheriff Barlow K. Adams and Deputy Sheriff Ella Mae (née Beaumont) Gillespie and all the others, in the Year of Our Lord, One Thousand, Nine Hundred, and Seventy-Two.

Making Mountains Out of Molehills

- Author: Earl Snort
- Publisher: TotalRecall Publications
- Paper Back: 9781590954324
- Ebook: 9781590956533
- Number of pages: 320
- Publication Date: 2019

It was 1969. Barlow Adams, age 20, was a recently discharged veteran. He was driving late at night on a lonely stretch of highway in the Trans-Pecos region of Texas. He stopped to render assistance to a motorist with a flat tire. What he stepped into was a vicious attempted rape. He rescued the victim, which catapulted him into an appointment as a deputy sheriff.

Along the way he encounters an enchanting woman who will change his life forever. In addition, he will be confronted by a gang of outlaw bikers who are obsessed with killing him while he is still learning the ropes of becoming a lawman. Will they succeed?

This is the story of a young man in the 1960's, an era which has long been forgotten except for those who lived it.

Barlow Adams Series Book I

When Dreams Come True ~ Sort Of

- Author: Earl Snort
- Publisher: TotalRecall Publications
- Paper Back: 9781648830006
- Ebook: 9781648830013
- Number of pages: 320
- Publication Date: 2020

The year is 1970. Barlow Adams is a young deputy sheriff in a rural county in the Trans-Pecos region of Texas. He's a rookie still learning the ropes. Up until now, his experience has been limited to working in the jail and performing routine patrol work that is anything but routine when bad men decide to exert themselves in furtherance of their wicked ways.

In recent months, a gang of rustlers had begun to prey on the livestock of unwitting ranchers. The sheriff has decided to stop them cold wherever he finds them. He employs all the limited resources at his disposal to achieve this goal. One of those resources is Deputy Adams, who learns new law enforcement skills in teamwork, criminal investigation, surveillance, and undercover operations.

Barlow also learns something else. The crime may be solved and plans may be hatched to catch the evildoers, but, in the end, there's usually a joker in the woodpile who upsets the applecart and then suddenly Life becomes a free for all.

Barlow Adams Series Book 11

A Lethal Odyssey of Cat and Mouse

- Author: Earl Snort
- Publisher: TotalRecall Publications
- Paper Back: 9781648830785
- Ebook: 9781648830792
- Number of pages: 320
- Publication Date: 2021

The year is 1971. Barlow Adams is a young deputy sheriff in a rural county in the Trans-Pecos region of Texas. After two years of instruction, he completed the Texas Police Officers Standard Training Course, and now he is fully certified as a law enforcement officer. As important as that is, something even more important is about to take place.

Barlow and Sarah, his fiancée, are about to be married.

They don't know it yet, but a depraved outlaw biker Barlow arrested two years ago has decided to stalk and murder Barlow and Sarah while they are on their honeymoon. The outlaw biker isn't operating on his own. He recruits criminals as savage as he is to pull off his barbarous scheme.

By the time law enforcement learns of the plot, the newlyweds have already departed. Until, and unless, they call home, there is no way to warn them.

Tick tock.

Barlow Adams Series Book III

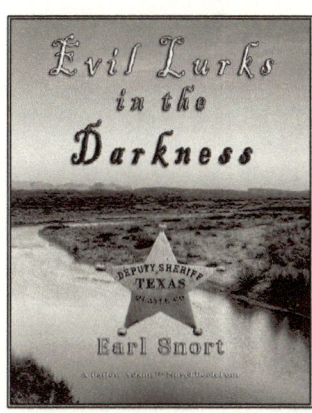

Evil Lurks in the Darkness
Even When Strong Men Stand Watch

- Author: Earl Snort
- Paper Back: 9781648831782
- eBook: 9781648831799
- Number of pages: 306
- Publication Date: 2022

The year is 1972. Quayle County, located in the Trans-Pecos region of Texas, has seen an uptick of illegal alien smuggling from across the Rio Grande. The alien smugglers are determined and violent. The Border Patrol is overwhelmed with greater numbers of human trafficking cases in other areas, and therefore is unable to assist. Illegal aliens and Americans are dying alike. The small sheriff's office and the local population are left to their own devices to resolve this crisis.

Once again, Sheriff Solomon Pratt, Deputy Barlow Adams, Deputy Slick Oldman, retired Deputy Archie Willis, plus the new rookie, Deputy E.M. Gillespie, and the rest of the staff on the Quayle County Sheriff's Office rise to the occasion to vanquish the threat.

Barlow Adams Series Book IV

The Lawrence County Moonshine War

- Author: Earl Snort
- Paper Back: 9781648831782
- eBook: 9781648831256
- Number of pages: 200
- Publication Date: 2022

This is a tale of a changeling shortly after these powers were bestowed upon him. Jack, who began life as a rabbit, fell asleep in arid West Texas shortly after wishing he had a home someplace else in a more temperate climate. When he awoke, he was a young man in a forest glen in such a place. He got exactly what he wished for! The problem was, he was wearing an Army uniform and he did not know his location. He didn't even know which century it was! Jack was suffering from a serious case of amnesia.

He soon learned that the year was 1920 and that he had been slumbering on his own property in Eastern Kentucky. He was re-introduced to his cousin, Gerard, whom he did not recognize, yet with whom he had maintained a best-friend relationship since childhood. Gerard also introduced Jack into his moonshine business during these, the early days of Prohibition. Before long, Jack found himself situated between big city gangsters and state investigators.

Lead was flying in the hills of Eastern Kentucky and Jack was in the thick of it.

A Jack Rabbit Novel

ABOUT THE AUTHOR

Earl Snort is the nom de plume of a retired law enforcement officer with more than 40 years experience toting a badge and a gun. Before that, he served in the armed forces.

He and his wife have been married more than 50 years. They have one son, also a career law enforcement officer, and two grandchildren.

This is the author's fifth foray into the world of writing fiction. After a lifetime of writing non-fiction to document investigations of true crimes, he decided to try his hand in make believe.

He hopes you enjoy this yarn and all the others.

June 2022